BELOVED KISS

The waves pounding on the shore made a tumult. Callie raised her head and looked at Mick. He smelled of saltwater, bracing and fresh. She dropped her eyes abruptly. If she looked at him a moment more, in his naked splendor, she would do something she was sure to regret.

"I . . . want you, Callie. As I have never wanted anything in this world. I want to take you. Now."

"No." Yet even to her own ears, the protest rang hollow. He leaned forward to kiss her. She bent against the unyielding rock, and then, as his mouth closed on hers, closed her eyes, surrendering.

His mouth was impossibly warm, sweetly salty. He kissed her hungrily, anxiously. "Callie. Oh, Callie." He covered her with kisses, her mouth, her eyes, her wild hair. "My sweet, sweet Callie." His fingers fumbled at her bodice, and she was deliriously glad that she had worn this gown, with its simple laces rather than intricate hooks, for in his fervor he would have ripped anything more complicated right away. As it was, he tangled up the knot until she had to push his hands aside.

"Let me," she whispered.

He knelt on the rock, watching, waiting, until she worked the laces free.

Then he fell on her with an intensity that would have been frightening had her own desire not matched it . . .

Books by Mallory Burgess

BELOVED KNIGHT

BELOVED HONOR

BELOVED LORD

BELOVED HEART

Published by Zebra Books

BELOVED HEART

Mallory Burgess

Zebra Books
Kensington Publishing Corp.

http://www.zebrabooks.com

ZEBRA BOOKS are published by

Kensington Publishing Corp.
850 Third Avenue
New York, NY 10022

Zebra and the Z logo Reg. U.S. Pat. & TM Off.

First Printing: June, 1997
10 9 8 7 6 5 4 3 2 1

Printed in the United States of America

For Barb and Michael

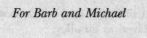

A little girl and a little boy
Lived in an alley.
Said the little boy to the girl,
"Shall I? Oh, shall I?"

—*Mother Goose*

Prologue

Ayrshire, Scotland. June, 1743

"Tell him just another minute more, Zeus," Callie Wingate
pleaded, frowning as she tried to capture the boy's lithe leg.

"That's what I've been attempting to convey for the past
half-hour," her brother Zeus declared as he thumbed through
the pages of the book he held. "But it's a bugger of a language."

"Mind your tongue, Zeus!" She had got the leg now, and
needed only the face and throat.

"It doesn't matter; he can't comprehend a word we say. Here,
boy!" Zeus snapped his fingers, and the youngster standing in
the shallows of the sea, wickerwork creel in one hand and crude
spear in the other, turned toward him. "How'd you like to marry
King George's daughter and go live at Windsor Castle?" The
boy's wide hazel eyes stared at him blankly. Zeus barked a laugh.
"There, you see? One might as soon converse with a stone."

The boy had flinched at his laughter. "You've frightened
him again," Callie chided, tongue between her teeth as she
struggled to master the planes of the face, gaunt with want,
stern with a dignity that seemed to belie the child's age. "Give
him another toffee."

Zeus obliged, rustling in his purse for one of the foil-wrapped sweets. The boy's unblinking eyes followed his movements; when Zeus held out the toffee, he waited for a heartbeat, then snatched it from his hand, popping it into his mouth. Callie paused, charcoal hovering above her sketchbook. "The poor thing looks half-starved," she said softly. "What's left of dinner, Zeus?"

"Nothing but that veal neither of us would touch, and a heel of Cheshire." Zeus rummaged in his horse's pack. "There's half a loaf here. Oh, and those wretched pickles."

"Still, 'twould seem a feast to him, I'll wager." She was sketching again, while the boy's head turned from her to Zeus and back, following their voices if not their words. "Give it to him, Zeus. Lay it on the rock there."

"And what if I get hungry?" her brother demanded.

"Save the cheese, then, if you must."

Zeus heard the scant disdain in her tone. "Oh, it's very well for you," he said shortly, "who can live on your charcoal and good westerly light. But we poor mortals must eat."

"I *said* you could keep the cheese."

Hand in the pack, he hesitated, then brought forth all of it, cheese included, and laid it on the broad stone by the water's edge. "Food," Callie told her model. "For you. What's the word for food, Zeus?"

"Damned if I know. But he can tell by the smell." Sure enough, the boy's nose had tipped skyward, sniffing like a fox's. Oh, God, Callie thought, turning over a page in the book and sketching furiously, if I could just get that look, so wonderfully *feral*—

"You're *not* starting another!" Zeus groaned.

"Just his face." But it wasn't to be; the boy glanced beyond them to the swath of forest lying just past the strand, yanked open his creel, stuffed the food in, and ran, his bare feet slapping the rocks. "Wait!" Callie cried. "Wait, I meant to pay you!" He glanced over his shoulder briefly and saw her reaching into her purse. He stopped, seeming to hover like one of the yellow butterflies dancing above the prickly purple sea-holly.

"The universal language of the purse," Zeus muttered. Callie ignored him, searching for a shilling-piece and tossing it underhand toward the boy. It spun, glinting in the fierce light. He caught it in mid-air, grinned for the first time since they'd encountered him fishing there an hour before, and vanished into the trees.

"Father was right," Zeus said, standing looking after him. "They're like wraiths, these Gaels, half of this world and half of the next. What do they do for food, anyway? We haven't seen a tilled field since we left Girvan this morning."

"Live off the land, I suppose. Fish and nuts and berries . . ."

Callie wasn't really paying attention. She had her eyes clenched shut, trying to recall the way the boy had looked with his thin nose probing the air. Like a young satyr on the trail of a nymph . . .

It wasn't any use, though; she'd lost the image. "Damn it all."

Zeus saw her slumped shoulders and came to pat them. "Never mind, then. You have two fine sketches, that old woman with the pile of sticks on her head and this." He turned back in the book to the portrait she'd made of the boy. "You truly are getting good, Callie. See here how you've got his expression, starved but defiant. Do you reckon he knew we were English?"

"I doubt he's ever heard of the English, living way out here." She studied the sketch. "Do you know what it reminds me of, Zeus? That story Father told us of the savages in Guinea, who won't let you make a picture of them lest you steal their spirit. He looked that wary, didn't he? As though we were taking something of his."

"We have, in a way, you know."

Her green-gold eyes slanted toward him. "What? What did we take?"

"Well, not from him, exactly. But from the Gaels. There aren't many pockets of Scotland left where England hasn't laid her fist."

"And what is wrong with that? Christ, Zeus, you saw how thin that poor boy was. And that old woman, without a tooth in her head, clad in those filthy rags. You cannot tell me they wouldn't be better off if more English came here, physicians and clerics and workers to look after the poor."

He was contemplating the sketch she'd made of the old hag. "I don't know. No one we've seen here looks unhappy, exactly."

"Only because they don't know what they're missing." Callie snapped her three-legged stool shut with a sharp click and hung it from her saddle. "Human beings were not meant to live in such misery."

"No," he agreed, "we were all meant to sit about in drawing rooms, sipping tea and nibbling biscuits while we earnestly discuss Aristotle's *Poetics.*"

She stared at him in frank astonishment. "And what is wrong with that? What's gotten into you, Zeus? It's marvelous, it's right, that man's intellect has advanced to the point where we have leisure enough to do just that. Perhaps you'd prefer to spend your days standing on a rock in the hot sun, trying to spear a fish to hold body and soul together."

Her brother's eyes, clear green, were oddly distant. "The water's nice and cool. It wouldn't be so bad."

"Lord, what romantic twaddle." She shoved the sketchbooks into her pack. "You wouldn't last a week in this wilderness before you came crawling home, your feet blanketed in blisters, begging for a glass of sherry and a good hot shave."

He laughed and rubbed his chin. "You're right—about the shave, anyway. I never have understood how men can abide having whiskers scratching up their faces." He gave her a hand onto her horse, then swung atop his. "And now that you mention it, that sherry has a certain allure. Shall we head back to civilization, then?"

Callie paused, surveying the surrounding countryside. "I don't know. The summer days here are so long, we must have another three hours of sunlight, at least."

"But no food," her brother pointed out.

She jammed her straw hat down atop her auburn curls and spurred her horse northward along the strand, away from Girvan. "You can always catch a fish!" she threw back over her shoulder, and Zeus laughed and followed, his mount's hooves firing off a small barrage of stones that skittered back into the sea.

The land through which they rode was beautiful but desolate, the scrubby forests of pine and larch reaching up the sides of cliffs that beetled over the water or gave onto short stretches of rock-and-shell-studded beach. The road they followed was, their father had determined, Roman, at least in part, which was why they went that way. Where there were Roman roads, those sturdy remnants of the land's first non-barbaric conquerors, there were, or ought to be, Roman dwellings, according to Professor Wingate—fortresses, temples, perhaps even villas built by officers to mimic their far-off homes. But if there were such vestiges of the eagle's glorious past along this thorough-fare, the well-trained eyes of Zeus and Callie had yet to find them. In this, their second day of riding out from the headquarters their father had established in the town of Girvan, they had not come upon a single site worth recording in Callie's sketchbook—at least, in her official sketchbook. The other, the one she kept hidden from her father, now had four fine drawings: the boy, the old woman, two young sisters they'd seen the day before drinking water from one of the tiny burns that criss-crossed the land, and a mother and her baby, captured by Callie's charcoal while they dozed unaware in the doorway of their daub hut.

Zeus had caught up to Callie by the time they reached the next headland. "The light's rather like Greece, don't you think?" he asked, gazing out over the sea.

She snorted. "It's not a bit alike. Greece is all clear and dry and thin. This is cooler. Denser."

"I defer to your superior eye. Nonetheless, it looks the same to me."

"Might as well call a Titian a Giorgione."

"Where did we see them? Florence?"

"Venice, you Philistine."

Zeus remained unruffled. "Each of us has his forte. I'd like to have seen you talk us out of that pickle Father got us into in Constantinople, when he had all those gold coins stashed in his luggage."

"If you're so good at languages, why can't you speak to the Gaels?"

"Be fair, Cal! Up until three weeks ago, I thought we were spending the summer in Turkey again."

"I wish we were. Those marketplaces, the mosques, the ruins—now *there's* a place worth sketching!" She wrinkled her fine nose as the hilltop gave onto another barren vista.

"It's the land of our mother."

She glanced at him sidelong. "Do you feel some deep-rooted pull in your soul?"

"Frankly? No. But we've only been here a few days."

Callie laughed. "Be honest, Persues Apollo Wingate. You know as well as I that any wild Gael in our blood has long since been winnowed out by a steady diet of proper English university life."

"Still." His voice was wistful, even above the pounding of the horses' hooves. "I wish I remembered her. Tell me again what you remember."

Callie masked a small sigh of exasperation with a quick yawn. Zeus had been three, she four, when their mother contracted pestilential fever in Cyprus and died, and her memories of Laurie MacCrimmon were scarcely more substantial than his. Yet time and again he begged her to repeat them, mist-covered and vague though they were. Ordinarily she did not begrudge the sharing; on the whole, she felt lucky to recall what she did. But since they'd come to Scotland, barely a week before, she'd been troubled by dreams of their mother—dreams in which the shadowy image of Laurie, red-haired, porcelain-skinned, her eyes clear green like Zeus's, called out to her from the opposite shore of a lake out of which fog spiraled up, thin and ghostly. Her practical nature revolted against the notion that this wild country held some mystical significance to her, to Zeus. But the dreams had unnerved her a bit. She found herself searching the faces of the few human inhabitants they'd come upon on their sorties, and wondering whether her own blood was somehow, through the long reach of centuries, mingled with theirs. Of course, the MacCrimmon clan was from the Isle of Skye, hundreds of miles away.

"I've told you, Zeus, so many times, what little I remember."

"But did she look like them, these folk we pass? Did she speak Gaelic?"

"I remember she sang me cradle songs I did not understand."

"Then they must have been Gaelic."

"I'm not certain. Ask Father."

"You know he doesn't like to speak about her."

Callie had known that for a long time. Only recently had she begun to have a glimmer of understanding why William Wingate was so reluctant to discuss his dead wife: he blamed himself for having brought her to the distant island where she'd met her death. But that was silly; fevers struck as often in civilized London as anyplace else. She looked at Zeus. His handsome face, poised between boyhood and manhood, was earnest and plaintive, quite unlike the cool, ironic mask he cultivated at Oxford. She tried to imagine how she'd feel if she, like he, had no memories at all of their mother. But all she conjured up was envy: better bleak nothingness than the occasional tantalizing glimpses that her mind retained. Still, "Their laughter sounds like hers," she admitted.

"Does it?" His linguistic curiosity was engaged. "How?"

"It's impolite," she said, surprising herself—and, she saw from his raised brows, her brother. "In comparison to an English titter, I mean. More free, somehow. More open."

"We haven't heard much laughter since we got here," he said thoughtfully.

"No. But in the inn at night—my window gives out on the front doorway of the taproom. They laugh as they are leaving." Callie remembered their farewells in the odd, gutteral language that had been their mother's native tongue. Sometimes the sound made her shiver, coming as it did on the heels of her dream.

Zeus, always sensitive, seemed to discern that the topic made her uncomfortable. "Well," he said, laughing himself, "you'd think the bloody language would be easier for me to learn if Mother spoke it!"

"Do you really think there's some sort of inherited lingual tendency?" Callie asked, glad to guide the discussion back into the safe, cerebral channels to which, as an academic's offspring, they were accustomed.

"Oh, absolutely! There's a German professor at Munich who compared the size of the *fraenum linguae*—that's the band of muscle beneath the tongue that connects it to the floor of the mouth—of various races, and determined that its elasticity was consistent within, say, speakers of Dutch versus speakers of Hindi. If his research proves correct, it would provide a biological basis for the diffuse development of human language.''

"You don't say."

Zeus frowned. ''You needn't poke fun at science, you know, just because your bent is otherwise. Not everyone can be an artist.''

"I wasn't poking fun. I'm interested. Truly I am. Tell me more.''

But the dark side to Zeus's sensitivity was his prickliness. ''Why don't you just tell me again how different Scotland's sunlight is from that of Greece?''

"Oh, Zeus, go hang." She spurred her horse forward along the ancient road.

''I really think we should start back,'' he called from behind her. ''It is going to be dark in just a few hours, and I for one shouldn't care to negotiate this stretch of road at night.''

"Just a little farther," she coaxed him. "We haven't found anything of interest yet to show Father. I hate to come back empty-handed.''

"It's too dangerous, Cal." She could tell from the tone of his voice that he meant it; he'd even reined in his horse. "We are the enemy here, in a manner of—dammit, Callie, come back!''

"I am only going to the top of the hill!" she cried, and let the rest of his argument be whirled away on the wind. Higher and higher she rode into that butter-thick sunlight, with the blue sea pounding far below her and a flock of bronze-glossed black cormorants rising up before her into the cloud-stippled—

"Zeus!"

He heard her cry and spurred after her in white terror. Christ, he'd warned her, hadn't he? What was it—a band of wild Gael warriors, woad-streaked, bent on havoc? What had he to defend her with? Only his knife and sword, and he was none too adept with either. Why didn't she turn and run? Why was she poised atop that headland, unmoving? *Callie, hide! Callie, flee!* But as he drew up beside her, he saw the brightness in her gold-flecked eyes came not from fear, but from wonder. ''Christ!''

he burst out angrily. "You scared me half to death, Cal! What the bloody devil . . ." His voice trailed away as he followed the line of her outstretched arm and saw where she was pointing. "Christ," he said again, in quite a different tone, this one hushed with awe.

There on the bleak stretch of rocky crest before them stood a ruin unlike any he had ever seen, a ruin worthy of Thebes or Thasos, an apparition so unlooked-for in this waste of heath and scrub pine that he blinked, thinking it might be a dream. The whole was built of pale yellow stone; the walls, a drawn-out octagon, enclosed a small pearl of a palace crowned by two thin turrets whose elongated spires would have looked apropos in Cairo or Spain. There was a Moorish cast, too, to the red tile roof, the lancet windows, and the graceful black arches that framed the doors.

"What *is* it?" Callie asked from his side. "A mosque? A monastery?"

Zeus answered truthfully: "I haven't any idea."

"Well, let's go see!"

Quickly he caught her bridle. "No. Wait." For some reason, this incongruous relic, fraught with heathen embellishments, unnerved him. "Let's go back and bring Father tomorrow."

"Oh, honestly, Zeus! How can you *bear* not to look inside?"

"It could be someone's home."

She laughed out loud at that. "Are you daft? It's a wreck, a shell. It doesn't look as though anyone has lived there for a thousand years!"

"Still . . ."

"Oh, come on!" She shook his hand from her reins and started toward the walls. "I'll just make a few sketches, very brief, very quick—though I daresay Father won't believe his eyes when he sees them. I know I couldn't as I topped the hill. Perhaps we've stumbled onto Fairyland. What was that song Mama used to sing to us about Tam O'Shanter?"

"I can't remember." He was coming after her, though he was still subdued. Half his mind was noting the flaking but promising frescoes adorning the gateposts, the fine, thick glass, barely green at all, in the casements that remained unbroken.

The other half was scanning those same casements for the ghosts of whatever outlandish souls might have built the place.

Callie did remember the song, and was singing softly:

> Where gotten ye that blud-red rose
> Y-holden in yer hand,
> And why come ye to Carterhaugh
> Withouten my command?

"Stop it," Zeus said, more sharply than the circumstances could warrant. His sister looked at him curiously.

To his shame, he lingered at the gatepost, pretending to examine the frescoes, while Callie dismounted and ventured into the overgrown thicket of greenery within the walls. "My Lord, Zeus," he heard her call, "there's a damascene rose here! And grapes, and figs—who would ever have believed they could survive so far north?"

"I once heard a professor of botany posit that the climate is more temperate in the northwest of Scotland than in much of England," Zeus said absently, watching her straw bonnet bob through the tangled leaves and vines. "Something about a sweep of warm current that runs across the Atlantic from the Ameri—" He stopped, hearing her squeal. "What now?"

"It's an apricot tree! Oh, Zeus, do you remember on that island—what was the name of it, the one where those poor knights that fought the Crusades had their castle?"

"Cyprus?"

"Aye, that's it. The apricot trees in bloom against those stark white ruins . . ." Her voice trailed away; he knew she was seeing it again in her mind, the beauty captured there forever by her artist's eye. But what she'd said intrigued him; he went so far as to step inside the rusted iron gates.

"It could have been Crusaders," he said, glad for a logical explanation of their barbarous surroundings. "That would certainly account for the Moorish influences. Some lucky soul who'd served in Palestine and managed to survive, and came back to build this place—"

"In a ship packed with apricot saplings and rose roots." Callie laughed, enjoying the image. "What an odd sort of warrior he must have been.'' She'd picked her way through the gardens to the threshold of the open front door. ''Coming in?''

''I thought you were going to make—'' She vanished. ''Sketches,'' he finished lamely. ''Callie, get back out here! You are trespassing!''

Her head, russet curls loosened beneath her bonnet, bobbed into the sunlight just long enough for her to call: ''You *must* come see this floor!'' Sighing, still glancing around in expectation of specters, he stomped through the undergrowth and entered the house, finding her on her hands and knees, brushing away dust in the vast front hall. A glimmer of azure, a speck of carnelian, mottled glints of gold and teal and emerald.

''My God. Is that—''

''A mosaic.'' She nodded, still scraping off debris. ''And an extremely fine one. Quite reminiscent of the floors Father uncovered in that sultan's palace in Tripoli.''

''But they were third century B.C.! There wasn't any civilization in Britain then to speak of.''

''I know. Perplexing, isn't it?'' she said happily, opening her sketchbook and rendering with a few deft strokes of charcoal the pattern of stylized flowers and arabesques.

Though there was no sound in the abandoned house but the distant pounding of the sea far below, Zeus felt the hairs along the nape of his neck grow tingly. ''Callie, let's go,'' he pleaded, backing toward the door.

''But there's so much we haven't seen yet!'' She straightened up to stand on tiptoe, twirling in a circle, surveying the long, curving twin staircases with their carved balusters and the newel posts in the shape of two clenched hands, the soot-blackened walls, the arched entrance to what might have been an armory to their left, and the ceiling high above them, decorated with what in the slanting sunlight looked to be another fresco, this one of a battle scene.

''No.'' He said it firmly, reining her in, too. ''It is one thing to come back tomorrow with Father and the surveyors, to make a proper study of the place. It is quite another to poke about by ourselves where we haven't been invited. What if someone should find us? We've no means of showing we've any reason for being here but rank curiosity.''

''And what is wrong with that?'' But he'd made the right appeal, to her sense of decency. She closed her charcoal case and picked up her sketchbook. ''Very well, then. You win.'' She trailed after him into the gardens, though she craned her neck about for a last glimpse of the floor.

Once outside, though, she ran and fetched the stool from her saddle. ''What?'' Zeus demanded. ''What now?''

She turned pleading green-gold eyes on him. ''Just let me make an outline of it, Zeus. I'll be ever so quick, I promise. Just in case it's a mirage and we can't find it tomorrow. In case it crumbles away.''

''We are losing the daylight!''

''What date is it?''

He blinked at the non sequitur. ''What date? I don't know. The last Friday in June. The twenty-third, I think. No, the twenty-fourth. What difference does that make?''

''It's the twenty-fourth. I thought so. Midsummer's Eve. The longest day of the year.'' She'd already sketched in the fluted outline of the tiled roof and was starting on one tower. ''Didn't the ancient Celts celebrate this as a holy day?''

''So they did. With human sacrifices.''

Callie laughed, eyes never leaving her drawing. ''Really, Zeus, you are too—'' She stopped abruptly, with a drawn-out gasp. Zeus whirled about and saw what her sharp eyes had caught sight of: a man, a huge one, a giant, black-haired with a wild black beard, clad only in leather breeches, standing with one bare foot atop a gap in the garden wall, a heavy axe in his hand.

The giant didn't move. For an instant, neither did Zeus. Then he edged protectively toward his sister, his hand on his sword. ''Say hello to him,'' Callie hissed beneath her breath. ''Give him some greeting.''

''Ah,'' said Zeus, his mind utterly blank at this sudden apparition of his worst imagining. ''Ah—''

''Where's your bloody book?''

The book! He groped for it in his breast pocket. ''Christ! I've left it in my saddlebag.''

"Well, run and fetch it!"

"And leave you here alone with him?" Zeus hissed back. "He looks a right ruddy savage!"

"That he does." Zeus saw with shock that her charcoal was moving; there was an odd undercurrent of gratification in her tone.

"Good God, you can't mean to sketch him!"

"Of course I mean to sketch him! Have you ever seen such a gloriously splendid creature in all your life?"

Filled with dread, Zeus let his gaze turn back to the giant. He was still standing as motionless as the rock beneath his feet. Whatever Callie glimpsed in this subject, Zeus saw only danger, danger as grave as any he had ever faced in what suddenly seemed his extremely brief life. He grabbed for his sister's arm. "We are *leaving*, Cal. *Now.*"

"Two minutes," she whispered, drawing furiously.

"Cal, no picture's worth your life!" *Not to mention mine* . . .

"This one is."

Despite his fear, Zeus found himself intrigued, as always, by his sister's very different sense of vision. He stole another glance at the fierce, scowling Gael. It made an arresting tableau, he had to admit: the wild-haired man, nearly naked, with the heathen spires of the house behind him, and beyond that the wide Scottish sky above the sea, already streaked with madder and ochre. Still . . . "Callie," he began, and stopped; she was scowling at the savage.

"That . . . that thing he is wearing is all wrong," she said crossly. "Ask him if he's got some other clothes."

"Callie, this isn't some artist's model in a studio!" he whispered, aghast.

"Don't you think I know that?" Her voice was suddenly brimming over with emotion; looking down at her, he saw with amazement that her eyes were awash in tears. She blinked them back angrily. "Zeus, don't you see? He is perfect! He *is* Scotland! He . . . he's the spirit of the Gael come to life. I have *got* to have him, Zeus. I *need* him." Her voice caught on a sob. She gathered her composure, charcoal hovering above the page. "So won't you please ask him to change his clothes?"

"I haven't got my grammar," he said, hating his own primness. But, God, it was madness to toy with the brute this way!

"Do it, Zeus."

"Callie, he could *kill* us!"

"He hasn't so far, has he?" she snapped, filling in the shading on the savage's shoulders and thighs.

Zeus swallowed. Christ, those muscles . . . "Callie—"

"Do it, or so help me God, I'll never speak to you again!"

She did not mean the threat, he knew, but he knew also, only too well, that she would make him suffer. And it was true the savage had done nothing untoward so far. Best to give her what she wanted; at least then when he came for them, she'd have only herself to blame. "Ah . . . *Dia's Muire dhuit,*" he stammered at the stranger.

"What does that mean?" his sister demanded.

" 'Jesus and Mary give you welcome.' "

"Well! I don't think you need feign we are deities!"

"It's the traditional Gael greeting," he muttered curtly. "And, let me add, the entire extent of the tongue I've committed to my memory."

"Then use pantomime," she told him, equally curt as she worked her sketch.

Zeus rolled his eyes toward heaven. "What exactly would you like him in, milady? Evening clothes, perhaps?"

She ignored his irony. "One of those plaids would be perfect. You know, those blankety things they throw around themselves and then over a shoulder."

"Shall I offer him your saddle-blanket?" He saw she was seriously considering it. "For Christ's sake, Callie! What about the poor creature's dignity?"

"He has enough and to spare, as wretched as he no doubt is. 'Plaid' is a Gaelic word, isn't it? Go on and ask him if he has a plaid."

"I don't know how they pronounce it."

"How many ways could there be?"

Zeus looked again at the man, who'd made no answer to the greeting. Probably my intonation is wrong, he thought ruefully, and fought back a sudden strong impulse to try Greek or French. Likely it would all sound the same to this fellow, who seemed scarcely sentient. How could anyone of normal resources remain still for so long? Beside him, Callie's expression was mutinous. "Ah," he said, clearing his throat, and spread out his hands, mimicking the action of wrapping a plaid around himself. "Plaid," he said, then tried "plee-ad," and "play-id" and "plah-eed," just for good measure. "Plait? Pleet? Plight?"

"Oh, Zeus, for Christ's sake!" Callie stood up, sketchbook clutched to her lap, and roared at the fellow:

"HAVE—YOU—A—PLAID?"

There was a moment of complete stillness. Then the savage took a step forward, and let his leather breeches drop to the ground.

He wore, of course, nothing beneath them. Flush with mingled outrage and horror, Zeus clapped his hands over his sister's eyes. "Hey, there!" he shouted angrily at the black-haired barbarian. "I say! You've a hell of a nerve! Put them back on this instant, before I—what is it?" he barked. Callie was clawing at his hands.

"Let me see, let me see!"

"Callie, the man's stark naked!"

"As if I've never seen a naked man before!"

"Not a living, breathing one, I dearly hope!"

"Oh, what's the difference, marble or flesh?" She'd freed herself from his palms and was staring at the savage in awe. "Oh, dear God. That's better than a plaid. Much, much better. Tell him not to move, tell him to stand just that way."

"Callie, you can't mean to draw him like that!" Zeus heard his voice crack in disbelief.

"Why the devil not?" she asked, frantically sketching away.

"Father would have your hide!"

Her green-gold eyes met his for an instant; he saw fire in them. "He'll never know unless you tell him."

Zeus felt utterly helpless. He tried to raise his gaze again toward the Gael, but found he did not dare. What was one to *do* with a sister such as his? Finally he threw up his hands in despair and stalked over to a small stone bench, sitting with his legs crossed. "Two minutes," he decreed, then added ominously, "if the brute doesn't come at you first."

She was paying no mind at all to him; her small face beneath the brimmed bonnet was taut with concentration. He'd seen her often enough in this sort of creative frenzy. He could have told her the earth was opening beneath her feet and she'd not have glanced down. "God, isn't he beautiful?" he heard her say beneath her breath.

"If you like the tall, dark, feeble-minded type. What in the world do you suppose his little pea-sized brain imagines you are doing?"

"Hush, Zeus!"

Zeus had pulled out his pipe and was stuffing it. "If he'd any notion at all what we're saying about him, he'd have come at me a long time before now." He sneaked a glance at her sketch and saw her painstakingly tracing in the man's genitalia. "Honestly, Cal! Must you?"

"You know women can't even sit in on the life-drawing classes at the university," she said calmly. "Who knows if I shall ever have such a chance again? And anyway, I don't think he's stupid."

Zeus sucked in smoke and exhaled it in a great cloud. "Don't you? Then looks are deceiving."

"I imagine he's simply rather puzzled," she went on charitably, "as you'd be, if two such creatures as us stumbled onto your little corner of paradise here."

"If this is paradise, give me the netherworld of civilization." He examined his pipe-bowl. "One minute more."

Callie squinted at her subject against a raised stick of charcoal, to judge the perspective. "It would be rather desolate, I suppose. Still, you would have fresh figs. And Adam was lonely in Eden, up until Eve came."

"Then he was simply henpecked and guilt-ridden. Thirty seconds."

"I'm not finished yet."

"Then I'd suggest you work fast."

She spun on her stool to face him. "I'd very much like to know who made you arbiter of my comings and goings! Why should I have to leave just because you say so?"

"Because I am right, and you know it."

Her eyes glinted pure gold in the sun. "That's what you

think. I intend to stay here until I am finished. And if you don't like it, you can hightail it back to Girvan with your coward's tail stuck between your legs!" She spun 'round again with a flap of her sketchbook. "So there." Then, "Oh. Damn," she said, in quite a different voice, rueful, regretful.

Zeus looked up from knocking his pipe against the bench. "What is it now?"

"He's gone."

Surprised and grateful, Zeus saw that the giant was gone indeed; the breach in the stone wall was vacant. "Splendid!" he declared, springing up from the bench. "Now let's us be, too, before he comes back here with a bunch of equally brutish brothers and cousins and uses that axe to chop us into small bits."

"I wanted to offer him something for having posed for me."

"Did you? Well, I'm fresh out of toffees." He grabbed her stool. "Come on, then. We'll have a hard enough time getting back to Girvan in daylight as is."

"I don't like to take something for nothing," Callie said stubbornly. Fishing in her purse, she came up with three English shillings, and ran to lay them on the stone wall where he'd been standing. "There. He'll find them, don't you think?"

"I am somewhat more concerned with him finding us . . . in the darkness, perhaps on that exceedingly narrow stretch of road along the cliffside." He started back toward the gate. Still Callie lingered, staring at the silver she'd laid on the wall.

"Rather like the offerings to the gods the peasants leave at Parnassus," she murmured.

"*Will* you please come on?"

Reluctantly she made her way back through the maze of overgrown garden. "You must admit," she told her brother as he lifted her into her saddle, "he made quite an imposing figure. How I'd love to assay him in oils!"

"To what bloody purpose? You'd never be able to show it to anyone. You can't even show the sketch. Speaking of which, I see you've managed to make it in the wrong book."

"Jesus, so I have." Quickly but carefully, she tore the sheet of parchment from the sketchbook she would show to her father and slipped it instead into the one she kept hidden. "Thanks for reminding me."

He shrugged, swinging onto his horse. "Even I wouldn't care to witness the tempest were it discovered that Professor Wingate's proper young daughter has been drawing nude men."

Her eyes in the slanting late-day light were wistful. "Still. It is a pity. It would make a magnificent painting, I know. I would call it *The Noble Savage*. That's what he was, you know. A noble savage, untainted by civilization."

"Aye. And if I *had* been able to strike a conversation with him, likely his end would have consisted of grunts and moans, interspersed with a few choice observations on how empty his belly was."

"He can't have been so hungry as that," Callie said thoughtfully. "You don't grow muscles such as his out of wild berries and nuts."

"No," her brother agreed. "You grow them out of swinging an axe, day after day, month after month, year after year, until you're too old to lift it. Savage, yes, I'll grant you. But noble? 'Idiotic' is more apt."

She smiled at him from beneath the straw bonnet. "And this from the romantic soul who thought spearing fish from a rock so alluring."

"That was before I got so bloody hungry," he growled at her. "Come on. I'll race you back."

Part I

Oxford, England
September, 1743

1.

"What wine with the oysters, then, mum?"

Callie, dipping a finger into the sauce for the lamb, paused to lick it. Damn. Too much dill. "The St. Emillion, I think. Might as well start with the best. It's wasted on them anyway, you know they'd all much sooner have a schooner of ale."

The cook, Dorcas, tittered. "Oh, mum. You mustn't say such things about your father's students."

"Why not? It's God's truth. They'd be far happier dining on fried fish and chips. Besides, it would mean a lot less trouble for you."

"Oh, I don't mind the work," Dorcas said shyly. "After all, it's only twice a year he gives the big parties. Gives me a chance to stretch my wings a bit, as they say."

"Mm." Callie tasted the lamb sauce again. "Well, stretch them with a bit more broth and cream in this, and boil it down; you've added too much dill again. What did I say we'd have with the oysters? St. Emillion. Then the Brauneberg Moselle with the artichokes, and the Château Margaux with the lamb—Christ, it's a pity to serve them that, but it's the only red we have enough of; that damned Monsieur de Renate's missed a shipment again. I must make a note to find a new wine merchant.'' She did so, on a pad she had hooked to her apron.

''Very good, mum. And for the salad?''

Callie had been distracted by the other notes she'd made on her list: to send for the chimney-sweep—Zeus said his room was smoking; to order in another dozen sketchbooks; to buy her father's tobacco; to complain to the butcher that last night's brisket had been tough. Lord, was it any wonder she had no time to work? Dorcas saw her scowling, and waited patiently until her mistress looked up again expectantly. ''What?''

''The wine for the salad . . .''

''Ah, yes. What dressing did we decide on?''

''The cream with capers, mum.''

''Capers. Good God, what goes with capers? Well, throw the Riessling at 'em; they won't know what to make of capers anyway. Then the amontillado with the sweet—*not* the fino, just the *oloroso*. No need to spoil them completely.''

''Ah, now, mum, you know 'tis a kind thing Professor Wingate does, to have them all in for supper when they're lonesome and lost, being so far from home—''

''Lonesome? Lost? Hah! Having the time of their lives is more like it, free of their families and all responsibility for years and years! What I wouldn't give to be so lonesome and lost!''

Dorcas clucked her tongue, plunging artichokes into a boiling bath. ''Now, mum, you don't mean that. University life may be fine for menfolk, but a woman's place is at her hearth and home.''

Callie opened her mouth to argue, saw the chaos in the kitchen, and decided this was not the time nor place to offend the cook by promulgating her ideas on that subject. She was deprived of the opportunity anyway by the butler, Bingham, coming in for another tray of glasses. ''They're all here now, mum,'' he said rather apologetically. ''All thirteen.''

''An auspicious number,'' Callie murmured, taking off the apron that covered her green damask gown dotted with semé stars. ''Will you be all right, Dorcas?''

''Oh, aye, mum. After so many years, I could do this with my eyes closed.''

As could I, Callie thought, but nonetheless stole a glance in the hallway looking-glass as she headed for the drawing room. Another year's worth of antiquities students; another dozen or so pimpled, obsequious boys at the table, eating oysters and sipping St. Emillion. Each September she argued with her father that these semiannual supper parties were superfluous, and each year he gave the same little speech about English universities being the last bastions of civilization. Might as well contend with a statue, she mused, and then tucked a loose red-brown curl back into her chignon. After all, Harry was here.

The first person she saw, though, upon coming through the wide oak doors was her brother, perched on the arm of a sofa and conversing with his usual intensity with a student she did not know. Professor Wingate, champagne glass in hand, caught his daughter's eye above the heads of the throng—the house really was too small for this sort of gathering, at least if more and more students kept choosing antiquities as their course of study—and smiled serenely, imparting his contentment. And why not? Callie thought with a rush of fury. It wasn't *he* who had to clean up after these adolescents who couldn't hold their wine! Her practiced eye noted that the hors d'oeuvres trays needed filling—not that a smidgen of caviar or shrimp mousse on toast was likely to counteract the effects of champagne— and she was about to turn again for the kitchens to inform Bingham when someone caught her arm. "Darling," whispered Harry Godshall. "Where on earth have you *been?*"

"Imbibing arsenic for my complexion," she muttered, and when he blinked, said impatiently, "In the kitchens; where the devil do you think?"

His grip on her sleeve was silken. "But why? Everything is going so swimmingly."

"Precisely because I have been in the kitchens." Bingham had come with the champagne in glasses, and Harry appropriated one for her. "Bingham, when you've made the rounds, do put out the last of the hors d'oeuvres."

"Very good, mum."

"Oh, I think you make too much of it," Harry told her, grinning. "Mama throws parties like this four and five times a week without lifting a finger."

"Your Mama has a staff of forty—or is it fifty?"

"Fifty-three, at last count. You ought to hire more help."

"What, on Father's salary?"

Harry's hand caressed her waist. "Well. Soon his problems won't be yours, will they?"

" 'A daughter's a daughter for all of her life,' " Callie quoted absently, eyeing a second-year student who was looking rather green. "What's the matter with Ormond there? Too much champagne?"

Harry barely glanced at his colleague. "Nay. His sweetheart's up and left him."

"What? Lady Alice?"

"Not her. His unofficial sweetheart. She's some sort of flower-seller in town."

Callie repressed a shudder. "Lord. The cream of the aristocracy, isn't that what Oxford attracts?"

His hand tightened. "You know I'd never dally when I have you."

"I should bloody well hope not." Callie saw her brother frowning in her direction, and almost instinctively disengaged herself from Harry's hand. "I'd best go cheer him up."

"Cheer me up instead."

She looked up into his gray eyes, saw the brightness of champagne gleaming there. "I rather think he needs me more."

"No one needs you more than I do, Callie."

She patted his cheek. "Run along, why don't you, and try and set some of the freshmen at ease."

"To hell with the freshmen." But Callie slipped out of his grasp, leaving him scowling and signaling to Bingham for more wine.

"Milord Ormond." He looked surprised at being addressed. "Harry—Lord Godshall—tells me you have suffered a loss."

"Harry's got a big mouth," the young nobleman snarled.

"So he has," Callie agreed readily. "Still, any student of my father's must be aware of how rocky the course of true love can be. Consider Andromeda and Persues, Helen and Paris—"

"She's a worthless slut," said Lord Ormond.

Callie shrugged slim shoulders within her green silk cocoon. "If that's so, you must not let her ruin your fun."

She watched as his small eyes narrowed. "You're quite right, you know. I daresay *she* isn't moping. I daresay she's out carousing with some baseborn knave."

Callie, baseborn herself, did not take offense. "Most likely she is," she said cheerily, while surreptitiously waving for Bingham and the champagne tray. "Anyway, the attachment cannot have been so great. Didn't Father tell me you spent the summer in Italy? Another glass for Lord Ormond, Bingham. Did you happen to visit the baths of Caracalla? Our guide there told us lovelorn Romans used to remain in the *calidarium* until their hearts were eased." Callie tried to catch her brother's eye to summon him to her aid, but he was still engrossed in conversation with the new student.

At least the champagne seemed to assuage Lord Ormond's misery; he downed it in a gulp, then focused again on Callie. "I saw the sketches you made of the Roman coins and bottles your father unearthed up in Scotland. Quite a nice little talent you have."

"How very kind of you to say so," Callie told him from between gritted teeth.

The young nobleman glanced across the room at Harry, who was munching an hors d'oeuvre. "Lord Godshall doesn't mind you traipsing about all over creation every summer?"

"I scarcely know. I haven't asked."

"Really. I understood that you and he—"

"He and I are very good friends," Callie said tersely, and sent a baldly pleading glance at Zeus. It was intercepted by the student he was speaking with, who nudged his arm and inclined his head Callie's way. Zeus turned, annoyed at the interruption until he saw his sister's expression. Then he sprang up, striding across the floor to take her arm.

"I say, Ormond, how very good to see you! Have a fine summer, did you? But your glass needs refilling. Bingham!" He signaled the butler. "Callie keeping you entertained? Good! Good! Have you two met Father's latest prodigy? He speaks, I much regret to report, more languages than I do, including Assyrian. Or so he says. I really don't know how we'd check up on him, do you? Come this way. Bingham, do bring the bottle!'' Still holding Callie's arm, steering Ormond by the elbow, Zeus led them to the sofa on whose edge he'd been perched. "Lord Ormond, this is Mick Harding. Mr. Harding, Lord Ormond. And, of course, my sister, Calliope Chloe Wingate.''

The young man on the sofa started up to his feet, but Callie waved him back down. "Delighted,'' he said shortly to Ormond, then looked up at Callie. "Calliope?''

"The Greek muse of epic poetry,'' she said in standard explanation, then laughed. "But if you are Father's student, you must know that.''

"Rather an unusual set of names,'' he observed, "Zeus and Calliope.''

"Oh, Zeus isn't his real name. It's Persues Apollo. But when he got to school, the boys began calling him Percy, so he chose another.''

"Can you blame me?'' Zeus demanded, wincing. "Anyway, I figured if I was going to be named for a Greek, then why not the best?''

"My father's name is Percy,'' Lord Ormond said somewhat stiffly.

"Is it? He has my gravest condolences, then.''

Callie, stifling a laugh, went on to explain to the newcomer, "We were born during Father's Greek phase.''

"I see.''

"It could have been worse,'' Zeus offered. "He might have had us when he was doing the Germans. Then I imagine we'd have been Sigfried and Brunhild.''

Mick Harding looked at him from behind tortoise spectacles. "And your mother would have acquiesced in that?''

"Oh, Mother acquiesced in everything Father did.'' Zeus grinned cheerfully.

"Is she here this evening?''

"Only in a manner of speaking. Those are her ashes in that urn there on the mantlepiece.''

"Oh, really,'' said Lord Ormond, shuddering. "How awfully macabre.''

"You think so?'' Zeus tilted back his blond head. "I find

it rather sweet. He could hardly have brought her body back, you know, since she died in the full flush of Mediterranean summer. And all the peoples Father admires most—Greeks, Vikings, Carthaginians—made pyres of their dead.''

Lord Ormond shuddered again. "If you'll excuse me, I find this conversation in most questionable taste.'' He wandered off across the room with his wine glass.

"As opposed to, say, prying into the affairs of the living,'' Callie murmured, and smiled at her brother. "Thanks, pet.''

Mick Harding had been sitting with his knees spread, his clasped hands between them. "There's some question, you know, about the Carthaginians,'' he told Zeus. "A recent French expedition has posited that those ovens at Douimes were for pottery, not corpses.

"You don't say. I hadn't read of it. Nor, I'm sure, has Father. You see, Cal, that's what we get for spending the summer in the wastelands of Scotland. Who led the party?''

"That little monk from Rouen, Frère Descoux. He gave a paper on it to the Académie. I have a copy, if you'd like to see it.'' The invitation included Callie. She warmed a bit to him; at least he didn't dismiss the possibility of intellectual endeavor on her part, as so many men did.

"Is Carthage your arena of specialty, Mr. Harding?'' she inquired.

"Only so far as it related to Greece.''

"Mr. Harding spent the summer in Athens,'' Zeus offered.

"Lucky you!'' Callie said with genuine envy. "Which did you like most, the Parthenon or the Temple of Apollo at Delos?''

"I should warn you,'' Zeus put in dryly, "this is the touch-stone question by which my sister judges all human beings.''

"Pity, then, I can't answer. I spent little time on the hill, and never made it to Delos. Most of the summer I was crouched in a trench on the ground, brushing away dust with a little whisk.''

"Still, you were better off than we,'' Zeus said with feeling. "Three months in the most backward corner of civilization you could ever imagine. Would you believe there are hundreds, nay, thousands, of English subjects up north that can't even speak the bloody damned language? And nothing to show for it but a few dozen urns, a handful of brooches—none of them fine—and a few eagle coins.''

Mick Harding smiled. ''So your father didn't find Boadicea.''

''Not so much as her sandal. Do us all a grand favor this semester, Harding, and try to distract him back to ancient Greece. Otherwise I greatly fear he'll drag us off to that hellhole again.''

Between keeping an eye on Lord Ormond's champagne consumption and monitoring the state of the stuffed shrimp platter, Callie had been studying her father's new student. He was sturdily built but not bulky. His black hair curled back from his forehead in crisp waves that reminded her of a second-century statuette her father had of Pan. His eyes behind the spectacles were either blue or gray; it was hard to tell in the lamplight. His dark serge breeches and waistcoat were standard Oxford fare; altogether, he seemed little different from any other young man in the room. The only qualities that marked him out were an odd habit of stillness—he did not seem to move much, especially in contrast to Zeus, who had the trait of gesticulating all the time he spoke—and a very slight lilt to his otherwise precise English that bespoke a birthplace well beyond the Home Counties, in Devon, perhaps, or even Cornwall. She and Father and Zeus had spent a lovely holiday in Cornwall once, searching for the landing place of Hengist and Horsa. ''Are you perchance Cornish, Mr. Harding?'' she asked.

Without moving his head, he turned his eyes toward her. ''Actually, Miss Wingate, Scottish.''

''Oh, well, shoot me in the mouth,'' Zeus groaned. ''Beg pardon, Harding. I didn't mean to insult your homeland.''

''Quite all right. Back in Edinburgh, we look upon our wild Western cousins in much the same manner you do.''

''Callie liked it there,'' Zeus offered in expiation. ''She liked the sunlight. She's an artist.''

''Are you? I should very much enjoy seeing your work someday.''

Callie laughed. ''If you are studying with Father, you will be sick to death of it by the end of the term.''

"Callie does all the sketches that accompany Father's lectures," Zeus explained.

"Then I've already had the privilege. Just yesterday Professor Wingate showed me the copies you'd made of the frescoes at Cnossus. Exceedingly fine likenesses."

"Thank you," Callie said.

"But what do you paint for pleasure?"

"Oh, Father keeps me too busy for much extraneous work. Speaking of busy, I must go see how Dorcas is coming along with that sauce. Will you excuse me, please?"

Again Mick Harding started to rise to his feet, and again Zeus thrust him down. "If you begin popping up and down each time that one comes and goes, you'll look like a bloody jack-in-the-box," Callie heard her brother say as she hurried away.

Passing through the dining room, she saw the placecards she'd written out in elegant script, and frowned, remembering that she'd set Lord Ormond on her right. Quickly she switched his card with that of the student opposite him, then rushed on.

The sauce had been corrected; the lamb on its spit was sizzling; and the two young maids, Bea and Mary, were getting a final going-over by Bingham, who was adjusting their aprons and caps. This was Mary's first major dinner at the Wingate house; Dorcas had hired her only three months before to take the post of a girl named Ginny, who, to the professor's horror, had been put in the family way by one of his students. Callie's father had fought an uphill battle to secure a pension for the poor thing from the young man's exceedingly blue-blooded family, but at length had prevailed. Bea was Dorcas's own daughter, and the cook had made sure that Mary, neat but quite heavy-set and plain, was not the type to attract any roving eyes.

"Ready when you are, mum," Bingham said crisply.

"Dorcas?"

"There's the oysters there, mum, and the wine set to pour."

"Very good. I'll call them in, then, before they all swim away on a sea of champagne." She flashed a smile at Mary. "Good luck, my dear. I'm sure you'll do just fine."

"Yes, mum," the girl said complacently, and Callie smiled again, this time inwardly. No, Mary wasn't the sort to turn any heads.

She went out again to the drawing room, caught her father's eye, raised a brow, and saw him nod. "Gentlemen," she announced, gesturing toward the doors, "won't you come this way, please? Dinner is served."

In groups of twos and threes, they drifted toward her over the Persian carpet. Some idiot had set his wine glass down atop the case of the harpsichord; she hurried across the room to move it before it left a ring. Then she took her father's arm at the rear of the procession. "Well? What do you think of the new crop?" he asked, much as a farmer would speak of his latest cull of oats.

"Very much of a piece with the last one, and the ones before that. I'm really not at all sure I see public school education progressing."

"Ah, but neither is it regressing," he whispered, and kissed her before pulling out her chair. She sat, and so did all the young men, and Bingham poured the wine while Bea and Mary handed the oysters 'round.

The student on her right had his hand out over his wine glass. She saw it was Mick Harding whose placecard she'd exchanged with Ormond's, just as the lord across the table smiled, none too pleasantly, and said, "What are you, Hardwick, some sort of Presbyterian?"

"I don't drink, if that's what you are referring to," Mick Harding said evenly.

Well! There's a first for a student at Oxford, Callie thought, and quickly told Bingham, "Please bring Mr. Harding an orangeade."

"Thank you," said Harding, "but water will be fine."

Ormond was rolling his wine on his tongue with relish. "You don't know what you're missing. Very nice, this. St. Emillion, isn't it?"

"You should have to ask my daughter," said Professor Wingate, "I've no nose for such stuff. I know white, and I know red, and that's the lot of it."

"He distinguishes those by the color," Zeus said, grinning. Harry was seated across the table and a few seats down from Callie; she saw him lift an oyster shell to his mouth, suck the contents down, and give her a wink.

A thin, intense young man with hair a good deal redder than Callie's, seated next to Zeus, was considering the huge array of utensils lined beside his plate with a bewildered air. Callie caught her brother's eye, nodded toward the unfortunate freshman, and hid a smile as Zeus first bumped the newcomer's elbow just hard enough for it to seem accidental, then very deliberately selected his two-tined oyster fork, spread a bivalve with it, and raised it to his mouth. Relieved, the redhead quickly followed suit. Callie watched his face; it had to be his first raw oyster, but he got it down without gagging, she was pleased to see. It was odd, she thought, that aristocrats like Harry and Ormond, who knew all the table rules, felt free to ignore them by virtue of *noblesse oblige,* while the less fortunate scholarship students struggled manfully to master their intricacies. Mick Harding, she noted, handled his oysters in a very nice way, using his fork with no wasted motions and without fanfare. Was he public school or private? she wondered. Public, probably, she decided, but a Scottish one, where the students wouldn't give themselves airs.

Christopher Wallace, one of Harry's cronies, was regaling the table with tales of his summer trip to Rome, where he'd made a harrowing descent into the catacombs. Harry, not to be outdone, followed with the story of his own first visit there, leaving Callie free to turn her watchful eyes on the guests, since she'd heard it before. Mary moved a heartbeat too soon to clear Professor Wingate's plate; Callie saw Bingham flash her a glance of warning, and she retreated to her post beside the huntboard, duly chastened but unshaken. Dorcas had chosen well.

By the time the lamb came, Wallace and Harry were still carrying the brunt of the conversation, with occasional droll interjections from Zeus. Callie watched her father try to draw out the redhead seated beside him—Cobham was his name— but the boy was too cowed by his cutlery to do much more than nod. Zeus did manage to get Tom Gregory, a shy but brilliant third-year scholar, to discourse on his thesis topic of the Homeric epithets of Aphrodite. And Toby Lassiter surprised everyone, perhaps most of all himself, by recounting a truly funny anecdote about hiring a donkey on Crete. Most of the conversation, however, was conducted by Harry, Zeus, and Wallace, while Ormond ate sulkily and upon occasion made some caustic comment. As for Mick Harding, he never said a word.

Yet he didn't seem at all nervous, like poor Cobham. He sat very still, eating what was set at his place methodically, without evident enjoyment; he drank his water, but he seemed very self-contained. Something about him seemed to get Ormond's goat. As Mary and Bea set the trays of cheeses and fruits on the table, the earl's son brought up the matter of religion again.

"Damned fine brandy," he said, swirling it in his snifter, watching the legs run down the glass. "Is it 'twenty-five, Miss Wingate?"

"'Twenty-nine," she said, glad to correct him.

"Ah. I should have known. Are your objections to drinking a tenet of your church, Hardwick?"

Mick Harding was peeling a pear with spare, delicate motions. "I have no objections to drinking."

"Yet you don't drink."

"A matter of personal choice."

"But *are* you Presbyterian? I heard you say you are Scottish."

Professor Wingate cleared his throat. "A man's choice in religion, it seems to me, should be as private as his reasons for declining brandy."

Ormond flashed his very attractive smile. "Beg pardon, sir. I consider myself rebuked. But I wasn't prying for the sake of prying. If Mr. Hardwick—"

"It's Harding," Zeus broke in rather impatiently. "Mick Harding."

"Really? I wonder, Mr. Harding, that you didn't correct me yourself."

"I did not think it worth the bother," Mick Harding said, his eyes behind his spectacles very dark. Callie felt like cheering: Good for you, Scotsman!

Ormond feigned another smile. "Well. As I was saying, *sir.*" The sneer was barely veiled. "I merely wondered, if you were a Presbyterian, what your views might be on the Young Pretender."

"Funny you should mention that, John," said Christopher Wallace. "I ran across him in Rome."

"Did you?" Zeus chimed in, with considerably more interest than Callie supposed he had in Prince Charles Edward. But of course, he was protecting Mick Harding—not that Harding seemed to need protecting. "What was he like?"

Wallace inhaled amontillado. "He surprised me. I found him quite cultured, really. Very well-spoken. Extremely gracious. Not at all what you'd expect from a—" He stopped abruptly, meeting Harding's gaze. From a Scot, thought Callie; that was what he'd been about to say. "From a man of his peculiar upbringing," he finished a bit lamely.

Ormond chewed a grape, then swallowed. "Well, of course. He's been educated on the Continent."

Callie cast a sidelong glance at Harding. Ormond's comment, of course, had answered Wallace's unspoken insult. Would Harding rise to the bait? He didn't seem about to. Her father was smiling indulgently at Ormond. "Now, now, John. Surely you don't believe you'd have any better education at Paris or Rouens."

"Certainly not, sir. *Au contraire,* I meant that universities abroad tend to teach those airy manners that are able to conceal the lack of real substance."

"I can think of a few Oxford students," Toby Lassiter said benignly, "on whom some sort of manners would not sit amiss."

Ormond jerked up his head. "Perhaps it is mingling with inferiors that rubs off."

Callie looked pleadingly at Harry, who cleared his throat, then chuckled. "Go easy on that brandy, John," he suggested. "Your tongue is running ahead of your brain."

Of all those at the table, only Harry's pedigree could match Lord Ormond's. Callie watched the haughty young man; you could almost see him weighing whether to continue the battle. Just at that moment, Professor Wingate intervened. "Do you know," he said, slowly turning his own snifter, "I believe that's what gives Oxford its unique character—gives, in fact, the English system of education such enormous strength. Look at us here. The sons of noblemen, the sons of bakers and brewers, all come together to worship at the altar of knowledge. It really is most extraordinary.'' Callie unclenched her fingers from her wine glass. This was a familiar theme, and one on which her father could and did discourse at length. Ormond should have time enough to cool off before he was done. ''Consider,'' her father went on. ''I am myself the son of a London butcher—a clever man, certainly, and one I am proud of, but one who lived most of his life in what could charitably be called poverty. Yet he took care to make certain I received the best education in the world, right here at Oxford. Education—that's the great leveler, I always say.''

''I'm not at all sure leveling is what is needed in England,'' Ormond noted caustically.

Professor Wingate laughed, wagging a finger at him. ''Perhaps not, from your point of view. But progress marches on. One cannot stand in its way. Learning is the key to the future. In the England to come, an educated man will be able to make his own way, regardless of his father's earnings or occupation.''

Shy young Cobham spoke up. ''Do you honestly believe that, sir?''

''Oh, absolutely!'' said the professor, beaming at him. ''Why, we've proof enough of its truth right here in this room!''

Callie had a sudden glimpse of what was coming. ''Father,'' she started to say, but he spoke right through her.

''Where else but at Oxford could the daughter of a poor butcher's son meet and engage to marry the offspring of an earl?''

There was a moment of absolute silence. Callie felt a blush crawling up her cheeks, straight to her hairline. ''Father,'' she whispered, pained, ''I thought we had agreed—''

''Come now, dear child, there's no cause to keep the news secret any longer, is there?''

Harry stood in his place. ''Absolutely not,'' he said cheerfully. ''Callie, I told you as much.''

''But we agreed not to announce it for three more months!''

Her father touched her bright hair. ''What better time and place,'' he asked softly, ''than here, amongst our dearest friends?''

Callie felt her gaze drawn against her will to Ormond; he

was tight-lipped as he turned to Harry. "Am I to under-stand—"

"Well, the cat's out of the bag," Zeus broke in hurriedly, just as Christopher Wallace stood up, too.

"I gather there's to be a wedding!" he declared with genuine benevolence. "Congratulations, Harry, you son of a gun! You've won yourself a prize!"

Harry grinned, moving around the table to stand behind Callie, bending down to kiss her still-flaming cheek. "So I have," he agreed. Then the room erupted in a flood of eager questions: When? Where? By whom? Harry waved them all down, his arm around Callie's shoulders. "We haven't set a date. Mother and Father were married in April, so I thought perhaps then." Callie did her best to repress a shudder. The last thing she wanted was to be wed in the same month as the earl and countess of Godshall, who on her one and only visit to their estate, scarcely a fortnight before, had made little secret of what they thought about their son's choice of a bride. Harry had seemed completely oblivious to their standoffishness—but then, sensitivity to the feelings of others was not Harry's strong suit. Briefly, piqued by this premature pronouncement, she wondered what was.

"A toast is in order," Tom Gregory decreed, raising up his glass. "To the happy couple!"

"To Harry and Callie," Wallace echoed, followed by a series of clinks. Callie, with Harry's arm wrapped around her, saw Zeus touch his glass to Toby Lassiter's. He was doing a brave job of joining the congratulations, but she knew his heart wasn't in it. He'd been the one who urged her to hold off on announcing her betrothal. His words rang in her ears: *So long as you and he keep it in the families, there's no irreparable harm. . . .* Well, he'd said it best: the cat was out of the bag. She felt a rush of anger at him for making her doubt her own choice. Really, what sort of harm did he imagine she could suffer from Harry, who loved her enough to stand against convention, oppose tradition? Defiantly she raised her hand to cover Harry's as it caressed her cheek.

"If you want April, love, you shall have it," she told him softly.

"Splendid!" he declared. "The twenty-third is a Saturday, and the chapel is open. I went ahead and inquired of Father Pickering."

"Did you really? How enterprising," she murmured, ignoring her brother's sigh of despair.

"The twenty-third of April," said Professor Wingate, his joy cloaking the entire table. "Why, that's Shakespeare's birthday. I simply can't imagine a more auspicious date."

2.

When the rush of felicitations had subsided and the men brought out cigars and pipes, Callie headed for the kitchens. Tobacco smoke made her queasy. Besides that, she felt rather drained. The strain of trying to keep Lord Ormond reined in, on top of the usual upheaval of a large dinner party and her father's unexpected announcement, had left her limp.

Dorcas and the maids had the washing-up well in hand. Callie remembered to compliment Mary on her evening's work, and the girl took the praise in stride, neither feigning false modesty nor showing evidence of a swollen head. This one could be a real gem, mused her mistress, who was all too well acquainted with the difficulties of finding good help. Dorcas, up to her elbows in scalding water, beamed at Callie through a haze of steam.

"Well, mum," she said, "we'd all of us just like you to know, we couldn't be happier for you and Lord Godshall."

"Thank you kindly, Dorcas."

"Just imagine—a wedding," Bea sighed, dreamy-eyed. "Such excitement there'll be!"

"So much extra work," her practical mother noted, deflating her daughter's romantic bubble. "A houseful of gifts, people

coming to call day and night, supper for his relatives . . ."
Callie hid a wince. "Not to mention invitations and flowers,
and the wedding gown—who's to make your gown, pet?"

"Lord, I don't know. Harry will have some opinion, I imagine. But it's all such a long way off."

"Not so long as all that," the cook said briskly. "First
thing tomorrow you'd best get started on your guest list; those
engravers take a long time at the invitations. Then you'll need
to get to London for fittings for your gown, pick out a ring,
and order your trousseau—and where on earth are you to live
once you're wed?"

"With Harry's parents, I guess." The thought made Callie
nauseous even without cigar smoke. "Do you need any help,
Dorcas?"

"Heavens, no, dearie. You run along back in there with your
betrothed."

But Callie didn't return to the dining room; she went through
the door that led into the garden instead.

It wasn't much of a garden, really; the plots here along
Magdalen Street were too narrow to fit much greenery within
their walls. But it had fresh air, which Callie sorely needed,
and a sufficient slice of night sky to show the big three-quarter
moon. The faint scent of roses swam toward her from a late-
blooming climber some previous tenant had planted there. She
went and sat beneath its arching branches, idly twisting one
blowsy pink bloom from its stem.

In a way, I am glad it is done with, she thought of the
wedding announcement. Harry had been pressuring her ever
since her return from Scotland to make the betrothal public. If
not for Zeus buzzing in her ear, she likely would have acquiesced long before now. That visit to Harry's parents really had
unnerved her however. She'd felt like the unfortunate Cobham,
awkwardly out of her depth—the countess seemed so cold and
imposing; Harry's two younger sisters had flitted about, full of
talk about hunts and balls and receptions at court; and the earl
had been as dour as could be. The countess had looked truly
appalled when Callie mentioned her drawing, though Harry
later explained that was only because his mother thought she

was paid for her artwork: "Like a common draftsman. Though I must say, I wish you hadn't told her," he'd added.

"But why shouldn't I have? My art is most important to me."

"Of course it is, sweetheart, now. But you'll hardly have time to pursue that sort of thing, will you, once we are wed?"

Well, if he thinks I intend to lay down my sketchbooks to go trotting off to hunts and balls like those silly sheep sisters of his just because he is marrying me, he is badly mistaken, she thought rebelliously—and then sat up with a start as she saw him standing just in front of her with his pipe in his hand.

"What a dreadfully fierce expression you were wearing, my sweet." He slipped onto the bench beside her. "I do hope I'm not the cause. I know you must be cross with your father. Still, what's done is done. And you must admit, the moment did seem apt."

"What, to have my engagement to be married used to illustrate one of Father's lessons in social history?"

He grinned at her in the moonlight. "Ooh, you are prickly. There is no disputing the point he made, is there? We *are* living proof of the democratizing influence of education."

"Tell that to John Ormond."

"I said already—John is suffering from a splintered heart. He'll get over it." He reached for her hand and warmed it between his.

The small, intimate gesture soothed her. "I am sorry, Harry, if I seem out of sorts. But you must understand, what the future holds for you is very different from what is in store for me. There will *always* be Ormonds all too ready to remind me I o'er-reached my place in marrying you."

"Don't tell me you'll believe them!"

"No, of course not! Well, not intellectually," she amended. "But social tradition is so deeply ingrained. I haven't Father's faith it can all be erased simply by a few generations of interbreeding." Then she blushed, wishing she hadn't said that. Harry had brought her hand to rest upon his thigh. She tried in vain to withdraw it. "Anyway, you cannot honestly tell me you won't be bothered by such attitudes."

"Why should I be? I shall have the cleverest, most beautiful wife in all of England, social standing be hanged."

She blushed again. Still clasping her hand, he was doing *something* in his waistcoat that seemed most peculiar. "Harry, what in the world are you—" she started to say, and then stopped as he pressed a small velvet box into her palm.

"Here. I've been carrying this about for ever so long, waiting for this moment."

She met his gaze. His dark eyes were bright in the moonlight. "What is it?"

"Open it and see."

She untied the ribbon and pushed at the lid. Inside, against a bed of pearly satin, lay a ring, a gold one set with an enormous stone. She lifted it up, and it seemed to flash fire. "Rose opal," he explained.

"Lord, it is beautiful!"

"I'm glad you think so. Some silly folk believe them unlucky. But it reminded me of you, so full of fire and light." He stroked her fiery hair. "Won't you put it on?"

"You put it on for me."

He slipped it onto her finger. She held her hand out, delighted, and watched the interplay of rose and blue and green and magenta in the glow of the moon. "Well," she said shyly, "this certainly makes it official."

"You like it? You wouldn't rather have an emerald or diamond?"

"Oh, no! *Everyone* has one of those."

He laughed. "I expected that was what you'd say."

"Besides, it was for envy of an opal that Marc Antony exiled the senator Nonius."

"I must confess, I was not aware of that." He kissed her finger, then brought his arm around her shoulders. "Oh, Callie. We are going to be so happy."

She nestled against him, gratified by the extravagant gift and by the handsome things he'd said. Fire and light. . . . His fingertips stroked her cheek, turned her chin toward him. His kiss was sweetly tender, but she felt herself stiffen in his grasp, knowing what was to come.

"Callie," he murmured. "Callie, I love you so. I want you so."

She kept her voice blithe. "And it seems you shall have me."

"Aye, love, but when?"

"The evening of the twenty-third of April."

"Christ, it is a lifetime till then!" He let his hand slide down her cheek, over her throat. "Why torture ourselves with waiting? The date is set; everything is made official."

She felt the unaccustomed weight of the ring on her finger, the touch of his fingers at the swell of her right breast. His breath in her ear was harried and hot. Still she tried to maintain calm. "We shall face enough uphill struggles as is, love, without my hiding a babe beneath my gown at the altar. Can you only think what your mother would say?"

"There are ways to prevent such mishaps," he whispered.

"And you know them?"

He drew back a little. "Well. One can't help overhearing . . . you don't imagine Ormond would be saddled with a bastard by his light-o'-love."

"How very jolly for Ormond."

His arm tightened around her. "This has nothing to do with him. It is only about you and me."

"Exactly! You and me, and not a premature heir to the earldom of Godshall."

He was exasperated. "I just told you, I can prevent—"

"Harry, I'll be yours in eight months! Can you not honor me enough to be patient that long?"

"I honor you beyond all reason, Callie! Don't you know that? Why else would I incur public censure by marrying you?"

"Oh, I do beg your pardon. I rather thought public censure was what *I* am trying to avoid."

His face was red with anger. "Dammit, enough of these games! If you loved me as I love you, you couldn't bear to wait, either!"

"If you loved me as I love you, you would not challenge me to compromise myself."

He was silent for a moment, then sighed. "A little liberty,

Callie. That is all I am asking. Surely what I've given you is worth that."

Did he mean the ring, she wondered? If so, he thought her honesty cheaply bought. But perhaps she underestimated him; perhaps he meant his love. She brought her mouth up to his. "How much liberty?" she whispered.

His hand clamped to her breast, eager, yearning. "As much as you will give me."

"And you'll stop when I ask?"

"As God is my judge."

With some trepidation, she let him kiss her again.

It started as gentle as the last one, but within seconds, he'd started shoving at her bodice and pulling her into his lap. You *are* going to marry him, she reminded herself, but somehow all his panting and heaving, the scrabbling of his brusque hands, chilled her heart rather than warm it. Such an *awkward* business, she thought—so many limbs and joints between them, and none moving in graceful ways. She endured it all as best she could, but when he tried to push her down on her back atop the bench, she put her hands to his chest.

"Harry. That's enough."

"God, sweetheart, don't tease me!"

His grip on her was iron. "I'm not teasing. You said you would stop."

"That was before you aroused me so!" He thrust the crotch of his breeches against her leg, pushing up and down.

"I *mean* it, Harry. I want you to stop."

For a moment he wavered. Then he sat up abruptly, his face like stone. "As you wish. But I think you owe me an apology."

She felt her mouth drop open. "I apologize to *you?* In God's name, why?"

"For leading me on." His upper lip was thrust out; he sounded like Zeus at age five.

"That simply isn't fair, Harry! You promised you would stop when I asked you."

"You may have *said* stop, but your behavior was saying something else again."

Callie fought down an urge to laugh. If he'd read her body's responses to his overtures as come-hither, then men were even more vain than she'd always believed. He pointed to the ring that flashed on her finger. "Does that mean nothing to you?"

"It surely hasn't bought your way beneath my skirts! And if you think it has—" She moved to wrench it off.

He stopped her, clenching her hand. "Wait." He breathed in deeply. "Wait. I . . . I am sorry, Callie. I only thought, well, it would please my pride, you know, to think you desire me as I do you."

He was that honest, at least. She took pity on him. "Women are different from men that way, love. You must know that."

"Are they? John says his mistress was always at him, wanting it."

Her fine mouth tightened. "Was she? Then perhaps you should go look her up, while she's at liberty."

"Oh, Christ, Callie. I didn't mean . . . now, see how you have got me all fuddled? Why *would* I want a creature like her, when I have you?"

"To help you bide the time till April." He stiffened. "Lord, it was only a jest! Oh, Harry. Let's not row on this of all nights. Go back inside. Drink some brandy. Help my father wallow in his triumph."

He stood, a little reproving. "He only wants the best for you, you know."

Only an English aristocrat, Callie reflected, could deliver that line with such utter confidence. "I do know that, Harry. And you know you mean the world to me." She stood on tiptoe to kiss him.

Gratified, he offered his arm. "Shall we?"

She did laugh then. "Heavens, Harry, I can hardly rejoin Father's students looking so disheveled!"

"You look beautiful," he said gravely. "You always do." His hand wandered toward her bodice again.

She pushed it away firmly. "Do make my apologies, dear, and say that I've retired. Plead my untoward joy at the announcement of our nuptials."

He cocked his blond head. "Sometimes I suspect that you are laughing at me."

She sobered instantly. "No, Harry. At our circumstances,

often enough, and always at myself. But I take you very seriously.''

He pushed a strand of bright auburn hair back from her face. ''You're an odd little bird, Callie Wingate. Not like Mother or Sarah or Grace at all. That is why I love you so, I guess.'' He bent to kiss her—a chaste kiss, swift and soft. ''Good night, then. Sleep tight. Dream of me.''

''You're all I've ever dreamed of.''

The comment seemed a bit treacly to her even as she said it, but he set off whistling for the house, already filling up his pipe again.

3.

She followed after him a few minutes later, hoping the interval would be sufficient to make it less obvious that they had been together. But there wasn't much use in it. When she'd closed the doors as silently as she could, there was a pause, and then a little burst of giggling from Mary and Bea in the kitchen. Dorcas promptly shushed them, but Callie could tell from her tone that she was smiling.

So this was what betrothal would be like, she mused as she headed up the back stairs—a difficult sort of limbo, with neither the freedom of the unpledged nor the pleasures of marriage. Well, it wouldn't last forever. And Father had been so happy . . . her heart warmed within her, recalling his bliss. That alone had made her embarrassment more than worthwhile. There were not many men, she knew, who, widowed and immersed in their careers, would have taken pains to keep their children involved in their lives so intimately. The aloof, cerebral Oxford don was a cliché, but William Wingate, detached though he might seem at times, had always made her and Zeus feel their opinions were valued and their talents honored. He'd never parked them with nursemaids or shipped them off to boarding schools; their tutors had been the finest students he could find;

and every summer they'd gone out with him to explore the world. She was unspeakably glad that her forthcoming marriage to Harry would repay him in part.

She passed the upstairs sitting room and then Father's study, moving with practiced efficiency despite the shadowy darkness among the busts and amphora and tables full of pottery shards that lined the hallway. Besides mementoes of the family's own journeys, the Wingate home invariably contained hundreds of items sent to the professor by his colleagues for dating or study: vases, marble arms and legs, sea-tarnished coins, scraps of fabric, even a mummy or two. That one's new, she thought to herself, noticing the pedestaled statue in the corner near Zeus's room—and then stifled a scream as its head swiveled her way.

"I beg your pardon."

"Christ, you gave me a start!" She had a hand on her racing heart. It was Mick Harding, she saw now, in the moonlight—not on a pedestal at all, but a great deal taller than she had imagined him. "What in the world are you doing?"

"Your father asked me to have a look at this." He nodded toward the table before him.

"A look at what? You need a candle."

"I have one." He lit it, to prove so. "This one. The Leda."

Callie nodded in tardy comprehension. "Lord Bertram sent it to him last week. He'd bought it in Tarabulus. First-century Greek."

"Oh, no. Cretan. And far, far older than that."

"You think so? How can you tell?"

"The marble is certainly Cretan. Look at the color. And the folds of her gown . . . they come to points; they aren't yet rounded. The technique had not advanced so far. The same with the feathers on the swan's wings." He reached out and stroked them, with long, blunt-fingered hands whose touch was astonishingly delicate. Through Callie's mind there flashed a sudden recollection of Harry pawing at her bodice. How different Harding's hands were from his. She tore her gaze away, up to his face, framed by the tight curls that had made him seem an ancient statue.

"You forget one thing."

"Which is?"

"The story of Leda is indisputably Greek."

He shrugged that off. "Such legends have to come from someplace. There's a growing body of evidence supporting the existence of an Aegean civilization predating the Hellenistic Age."

"What sort of evidence?"

"Shipwrecks. Coinage. Isolated finds and such." He stroked the Leda again.

"And you think it may have been based in Crete."

"It is a possibility I intend to explore."

She nodded. "It would be quite a discovery to make. If it's true."

The candle flickered in a whisper of wind. Mick Harding's long fingers caressed the statue's cool stone robe, the violent wings beating the sky behind her, her face—curious but not yet frightened—as she turned to see the great white bird at her back. Callie suddenly shivered. "God, it must have been terrifying for her," she whispered.

He looked at her with bemused surprise. "It is only myth, you know. Don't tell me you believe in deities who flew down from Olympus in the guise of giant waterfowl to force themselves on mortal maidens."

She flushed in the candleglow. "Of course I don't. But one wonders, doesn't one, whatever could have put such odd notions into their heads? Ravished by a swan. . . ."

"No doubt further linguistic studies will eventually prove the myths to be remnants of ancient tribal totems. Clan of the goat, clan of the swan, that manner of thing." His voice was crisp, detached.

"No doubt," Callie agreed, but her mind was with the girl as those massive wings enveloped her, as that outlandish bird's heart pounded against hers. What prayer do you offer when the great god himself batters between your thighs?

Zeus's voice rose up from the stairwell. "Harding? Harding?" He rounded the landing. "Oh, there you are! Father thought perhaps you'd gotten lost."

Mick moved toward him. "Forgive me. Your sister and I were just contemplating your namesake's dastardly deed."

Zeus glanced at the statue. "Ah, yes. Nasty business, that.

Must have left a mess of feathers, don't you think? Aren't you coming, Cal?''

"I'm going to my room."

Harding turned back to her with a little bow. "In that case, let me say what a pleasure it has been to meet you, Miss Wingate, and offer my sincerest congratulations on your betrothal."

"Thank you, Mr. Harding. Good night."

Zeus was smiling as he came and kissed her. "Do forget all those wretched things I've said about Harry in the past, love. I'm sure you'll be very happy."

"Yes," said Callie. "I'm sure we will be."

Callie had a third-story bedchamber that looked out over the garden. The rooms below were larger, but she'd chosen this one for the western light. A set of screens closed off the area by the windows, which she used as her work-space; it was cluttered with half-finished drawings, with stubs of charcoal and pencils and pots of paint. The maids knew better than to intrude there; not even Professor Wingate ventured to disturb her things.

It was stuffy so high up, though, when the days were warm. She went and wound out the twin casements as far as they would go. The breeze brought with it the faint scent of the late roses, and a distant wave of men's laughter from the dining room. Callie had fallen asleep to the sound of such laughter all her life. She wasn't sleepy now, despite what she'd told Harry; instead she felt restless. She paused at her easel, contemplating the squat clay pot she'd started sketching that morning. But she didn't feel like working on that, either; it was an ugly little pot, of interest to her father solely on account of its lack of grace. She scanned the shelves to see what else awaited her attention—shards of an oil cruet from Egypt, a Roman lamp, an arm her father thought might be Venus—but nothing seemed appealing. Perhaps I'll read, she thought, and stretched across her bed, reaching for the volume of Pascal's philosophy that Zeus had recommended. But she hadn't her brother's gift for language; French was hard going for her, and she managed no more than five pages before setting it aside.

Why *am* I at such loose ends tonight? she wondered, kicking off her shoes. There was the engagement announcement, yes, but she'd known that was coming, sooner or later. Still, her disquiet centered on Harry; she could tell from the way she caught herself trying not to think of him. Hardly an auspicious attitude to mark the start of our betrothal, she decided, and sat up resolutely, determined to settle in her mind exactly how he had offended her. The situation with Ormond was awkward—but he'd been fine in handling Ormond. He'd recounted no stupid stories at supper, hadn't drunk too much champagne, had been appropriately ardent but respectful in the garden. . . .

In the garden. That was what her memory was trying to glaze over—but why? Yes, he'd expanded his assaults against her virtue, but in the end he'd abided by the limits she set.

Into her mind there flashed the image of the statue of Leda, the sweet, perplexed expression on the girl's face as she twisted her head to see what was coming at her through the air, and a small, nagging suspicion formed itself, refusing to be discarded: *You did not want him to stop.*

"Oh, I most certainly did!" she said aloud, in annoyance, and bounced up from the bed. She'd meant every one of the well-reasoned arguments she'd propounded against their un-sanctioned coupling.

But you wish that reason hadn't swayed him, said the voice in her head.

Balderdash! she rebuked.

You wanted his passion for you to be so strong, so all-encompassing that he would not, could not stop himself, would take you as the swan took Leda—

"Nonsense!" she cried angrily. No decent woman would wish for such a thing! And no English gentleman would ever behave in such a scandalous fashion—certainly not Harry, with his breeding and crust.

Certainly not Harry, that pestilent voice agreed.

Oh, for the love of God, she thought in disgust, and went to finish drawing the wretched little pot.

But the voice would not be squelched even with a frenzy

of sketching and rubbing. *Admit this, then,* the voice taunted serenely, *Harry lacks passion.*

Harry adores me, she retorted, reaching for her rag; she'd botched the shading on the handles. Why the devil else would he be marrying me? *He's* the one with money and position and a bloodline. I . . . why, I've got nothing he needs.

Except a father who could substantially advance his career. The voice didn't need to add that; she'd thought of it herself once or twice, early in their courtship, when his unlikely advances had puzzled her. But Harry had no need of a career; sooner or later, he'd be earl of Godshall. He took his studies the same way he took everything else in life, with a sort of blithe half-attention. He had no passion for antiquities; he might have taken up law or politics or banking just as readily.

As he might have taken up Elizabeth Harrell or Margery Bennett instead of you.

Oh, do shut *up,* she told the voice, and fought back an urge to hurl the pot at the wall. She wasn't getting anywhere with this sketch, yet her fingers were itching to work, to drown that voice in something that would seize her attention. Her eye caught on a canvas leaning against the shelves that she'd stretched and sized earlier in the week, in preparation for an oil painting of the Temple of Apollo at Delphi, meant as a birthday gift for Zeus. She was not in the mood, though, for chill stone and greenery. She wanted to paint. But what? She went to her notebooks piled in the corner, and began to page through them. They were all helter-skelter, glimpses of Rome interspersed with Cornish barrows and Florentine landscapes and Venetian balconies. So much to paint, she thought, sighing, and so little time . . . and even less, once she was married to Harry. *You'll hardly have time to pursue that sort of thing, will you, once we are wed?*

Defiance billowed up in her. She grabbed her set of private sketchbooks, the ones filled with subjects which her father did not approve—living, breathing beings, brief renderings of fellow humans' unimaginable lives. A drunken Greek peasant falling off his donkey. A couple on the Ponte Cavour in Rome,

*entwined in one another's arms, his hand sliding beneath her
skirts in the midst of Carnevale. A flower-seller in Sicily, an
old woman awash in a sea of white lilies. A naked boy diving
from a cliff in Spain, his browned body a flash of life against
sere black rock.*

This last sketch reminded her of something. She reached
lower in the pile for the sketchbook she had taken to Scotland
that summer, and shook from it a loosened page.

The man in the wild, tangled garden of that ruined castle in
Ayr—Langlannoch, the Gaelic guide had told her father it was
called. God, she'd forgotten how powerful the image was. She
studied it now, taking pleasure in her own deft capturing of
the lines of the delicate ruin, the leaves of the apricot tree, but
most of all of that savage creature, tongueless and nameless,
who'd confronted them there. His thighs were massive, like tree
trunks; his chest was broad as a church door; the expression on
his face, impassive and enduring, seared her heart anew with
its barbaric grace. And oh, the line of his waist curving into
his groin, the proud mass of testicles and manhood. She shut
her eyes, retreating into memory, and recalled the colors: the
blue-black of his sweat-damp hair, the bronze of his skin fired
by the dying sun. Her noble savage . . . *this* was what she felt
like painting, boxed in as she was at that moment by Harry's
boorish lovemaking, Zeus's disapproval, and her father's insensate pride and tormenting voice. Here was a man, she thought
dimly, eyes still clenched shut, who never would be swayed
by reason, who would seize what he wanted and let the consequences be damned. . . .

Opening her eyes, she reached for her palette and found she
was trembling. She could count on her two hands the number
of illicit paintings she had actually done in her life, most of
them portraits of children, none of them in any way offensive
except in their deviation from the subjects that her father thought
proper for a lady to paint. This, however, was another matter.
This was a nude, a full, frontal male nude—and if the savage's
image was enough to make her tremble at its memory, what
in God's name would Professor William Wingate say if he ever
discovered a full-color rendering of its forbidden glory?

Her tubes of paint beckoned, daring her to try to recreate—
nay, to create. To become God. For no one else in the world,
not even Zeus, who had been there, had seen the savage through
her eyes. For some reason she thought of the unknown sculptor
who had chiseled the statue of Leda that had traveled so far,
across so many centuries, to reside in the hallway below.
Immortality—that was what the Gaelic axe-man's haunting
image seemed to dangle before her. A painting to last through
the ages.

But could she do that? Could she rise to such a challenge?

Her hand snaked out, touching the smooth birch of the palette,
thumb curving through the hole. Her fingers hovered over the
stone jar of brushes. She found her favorite, the long, thin
camel's hair with the slanted edge. She daubed cool white,
deep Theban blue, blinding yellow, warm umber brown, onto
the birchwood. She set the canvas on her easel, tossing aside
the unfinished sketch of the unholy jar.

She mixed linseed oil with rich black, closed her eyes, opened
them, made a swift, sure line, and then another, and another.
She began to paint.

When dawn eroded the sky, she had developed no more than
the barest skeleton of underlayment: the shadow of the breached
garden wall, the mosque-like tower looming above it, the trunk
and foremost branches of the apricot tree. And yet she lay down
the brush in satisfied exhaustion. So far, what stood on the
canvas matched what shone in her memory, and no artist could
ask a better start than that. The man himself, his sinew and
strength, would come later. Already her hand was aching to
go on—a very good sign. But she needed sleep, did not want
to risk marring this work with addled perception. It was time
to stop.

She stuck the brush into oil of turpentine, set a soaked rag
over her palette, cleaned the paint from her hands, and crawled
into her bed.

Lord, she prayed drowsily, make me worthy of this painting—and then had to smile sleepily at that absurdity. God, like
her father, probably would find no virtue in the noble savage's
image. Well, if worst came to worst, and her transgression was

found out, she could always paint a bloody fig leaf over the offending portions and claim it was Adam.

She rolled over and slept, dreamless, until Mary backed into her room far too soon, with chocolate and muffins and a sweet, ripe pear.

4.

"He may be as brilliant as everyone says, but he's dead wrong about Xerxes," Zeus declared, leading the exodus from the lecture hall, so intent on argument that he barged straight into a pair of sedate dons who glared at him balefully. "I do beg your pardon," he told them, making a blithe bow but not breaking stride.

"Settle down, young man," one of them warned.

"I will, sir. Thank you. But listen here, Cobham. I've *read* Ptolemy. There's absolutely no mention—"

"He never claimed there was a mention. He—"

"He said one could discern the dates of the dynasty."

"He said one could *infer* them. There's a bloody big difference."

"Infer or discern, he's dead wrong either way. If you set the abolition of the kingdom of Babel in 484 B.C., as you simply must if you know your Ctesias, then the date for the departure from Sardis *has* to be no earlier than 480. It's completely unambiguous if you follow the texts!"

"Intellectual excitement," Harry murmured to Callie, holding tight to her hand. "I'm pleased to say I've never suffered from it myself. Turns fellows into damned fools."

Callie looked at her brother, locked in animated argument with young Cobham, who in a month at the university had lost a great deal of his timidity. It was precisely intellectual excitement that the callow redhead had to thank for that, she thought, but merely smiled at Harry. It wasn't his fault, really. In his milieu, one was taught not to display too much enthusiasm for anything.

Walking backward across the Quadrangle, Zeus appealed to his sister: "You agree with me, don't you?"

"Don't bother your sister," Harry chided, "she has weightier matters on her mind than some dead Persian king. As I was saying, love. Mother thinks that green you like will make Sarah and Grace look sallow."

And, of course, to the countess the appearance of her daughters meant far more than the bride's own wishes. Callie swallowed a sigh. "What does she want, then?"

"She thought perhaps rose?"

Of course. Safe, well-bred rose, just like the attendants at every other wedding Callie had ever been to. Dead, dull, dusty rose. Whereas the green ... the green had been animated, iridescent, a shifting silken shimmer of seafoam and sunlight. "If your mother wants rose, then she must have rose."

Harry kissed her cheek. "Thanks, love."

Damn. She really had liked that green.

They'd reached Peckwater Hall. "Continue this over a pint?" Zeus asked Cobham, who shook his head.

"I'm for the library. But I'll check Ptolemy for you, if you like."

"No need. I know I'm right. What about you, Toby?" Zeus asked the fifth member of their party.

"Might as well. Coming, Harry?"

Harry glanced at Callie. "I'll see my intended home."

"Suit yourself." Zeus jangled his purse. "I took two pounds from Tom Gregory today on a wager—whether Aquinas counts chastity a natural or a theological virtue. The rounds are on me."

Callie laughed and kissed him. "He should know better than to bet with you. Don't be late. And don't get too drunk." She watched him head across the quadrangle with Toby Lassiter, already arguing again. "Sure you don't want to go with them?" she asked Harry.

"You know how much I like your brother. But really, he's only a boy." His hand slipped around her waist, guiding her through the gate. "Is your father home?"

"He's taking supper with the dean."

"Good," Harry said, and paused to kiss her in the shadow of the ancient stone arch. His fingers stroked her breast through her soft wool cloak as he pressed up against her. Over his shoulder, she saw a gaggle of students pass, most of them managing to avert their eyes.

"Harry." She pushed him off. "That can wait."

"Not for long it can't." But he fell into step beside her. "Chilly for October, isn't it?"

It was chilly and damp. A smattering of raindrops splashed them as they emerged from the arch. He drew his cape up over her protectively. "Oh, by the by," said Harry. "For the wedding trip. Mother and Father went to Bath. Granted, it isn't Paris, but Mother says it is lovely in April. And, of course, the royals always visit in springtime. What do you think?"

"I've never been," Callie confessed. "What does one do there?"

"Take the air. See and be seen. There are gaming houses." He offered her a peppermint; she waved it away, and he popped it into his own mouth.

Bath. She disliked the very name. "I thought perhaps Florence," she ventured.

"Oh, God, not Italy! All those swarthy little men ogling you—and that folderol about language. I detest having to work to make myself understood."

"Well, then, what about Paris? You speak French."

"But who wants to honeymoon in a country full of snobs? You know I'm not one for traveling abroad, love. Let's start our life together here on good English soil."

And end it here, no doubt. For an instant, Callie's pilgrim nature rose up in revolt. Then she remembered how much Harry, too, was sacrificing. "I'm sure Bath will be splendid."

He grinned. "Oh, it will. And Mother thinks she can get Countess Newberry's villa for us—she and the girls in the big house, and you and I in the garden cottage. It should be very cozy.''

''Your mother will be there?''

''Oh, she goes every year, to take the waters for her sciatica.''

Cozy indeed. The wind was whipping the raindrops. With a faint sense of dread, Callie raised a question that had been troubling her. ''Harry. Where will we live?''

He looked faintly surprised. ''Why, at Godshall House. Where else? It has ninety-eight rooms; we shan't be cramped.''

''No, but . . . don't you think it would be pleasant to have a small place of our own?''

''I don't know how I'd afford it. I don't come into Grand-father's money until I'm twenty-five, you know. When you add in staff and all that, even a small place in London is quite dear. And it's not as though you're bringing a dowry.'' She stiffened slightly inside the cloak, and he laughed, hugging her closer. ''I wasn't bemoaning the fact, dear, just observing it. Besides, you've got to learn to run a household.''

''I *do* run a household.''

''And very nicely, too.'' He kissed her nose. ''But I mean a real one, like Godshall House. Father *is* getting on. His grippe was quite severe this winter last. He won't be here forever, and when he's not, *you'll* be countess. It's quite complicated handling all those servants, and the social obligations besides. Especially when you haven't grown up with it.''

''You make me feel daunted.''

''Nonsense. You are sharp as a tack. And Mother is very eager to begin your instructions.''

Heart sinking, she tried again. ''But don't you think, Harry, just at the very beginning, the privacy our own house would afford—''

''We'll have the entire west wing. No one will overhear us of nights, if that's what's worrying you.'' He pinched her side, leering comically. She laughed despite her misgivings. His hand stroked the heavy opal on her finger. ''Besides. I am having a surprise installed there for you.''

''What surprise?''

''I'm not telling.''

''Please?'' she begged, standing on tiptoe to kiss him.

"Well, if you do that again . . ." She did. "It's a room for you to paint in. Adjoining your dressing rooms."

Callie was astonished. "Oh, Harry! I thought you did not approve of my painting!"

"I don't mind you painting, so long as it doesn't interfere with your responsibilities. I think you'll like it. It's very light and airy. I'm having the wallcoverings taken down, and the whole thing newly plastered and washed white."

"What direction are the windows?"

"Westerly, of course."

She squealed with delight. "How on earth did you know?"

"I didn't. I asked your brother. I wanted it to be just right."

Callie felt deeply ashamed of her earlier qualms. That he'd gone to such trouble filled her with tenderness toward him. She squeezed his hand, no longer noticing the wind and rain. "Oh, Harry. You simply cannot imagine . . . I'm so happy. So grateful. Really, I'm overwhelmed."

Pleased with himself, he shrugged. "It isn't such a big thing, really. And it will be easy enough to turn it into a nursery once the children come."

The front of the house was dark when they arrived. "May I come in?" Harry asked.

She hesitated. "It really isn't proper, not with Father out."

He leaned into her on the doorstep. "I know. That's why I want to so badly."

"Well—just for one brandy. I'll have Bingham stay."

But it was the butler's night out, so instead they had Mary, stolid and impassive, standing guard over Callie's virtue from beside the drawing-room doors.

Harry moved close to her on the sofa, putting his arm around her. Callie blushed, sneaking a glance at Mary. "Don't mind that cow," he murmured in her ear. "She hasn't the nerve to say boo to a mouse; you think she'd tell your father?"

"Tell him what?"

"About this." He kissed her, pushing her back against the sofa cushions. He smelled of peppermints, which was better than pipe smoke. His hand trailed down her throat to cup her breast. Callie thrust it off; he replaced it.

"Harry—"

"Relax!"

"I can't!"

"Servants are meant to be ignored," he whispered. "I can see that's the first thing Mother will have to teach you." Callie looked again at Mary. She had her eyes trained straight ahead. Harry's fingers hooked on the edge of her bodice, tugging it down, reaching for her nipple. Squirming with embarrassment, Callie wriggled away.

"If you're finished with that brandy, Harry, perhaps you'd better go."

"I've a better idea. Mary." He sat up, finding his glass on the table beside him. "Fetch me another."

"Very good, sir."

He fell on Callie the instant the maid turned her back, pushing her down on the sofa, his hand scrambling beneath her skirts. He'd located the lace edges of her drawers, for God's sake, before she managed to fight free.

"Harry!" Callie scolded.

"Well, you can't blame a fellow for trying," he grumbled, and sneaked another kiss and a good grope at her breasts before Mary returned with the brandy, setting it on the table without so much as a raised brow and going back to her post. Harry reached for Callie again, but the look in her eye warned him off. Sighing, he felt in his waistcoat for his pipe. Mary brought a taper; he sucked the stem, drew in smoke, and let it out in a cloud. "So. Ready for tomorrow?"

"What's tomorrow?" Callie had just discovered that the tip of one of her breasts was exposed, and was simultaneously trying to tug her bodice up with discretion and wondering whether Mary had seen.

He turned to her, looking appalled. "Surely you haven't forgotten! Mother is driving over with the invitations."

"Good Lord." She had forgotten. "What time?"

"She'll be here for tea. You did tell Dorcas." Callie's woeful expression confirmed his fears. "Damn, Callie! Well, it doesn't matter. We can take her to Tasker's; they do a nice spread. She'll like the currant cakes.''

''No. No, Harry, she must have tea here. There's time yet to arrange it.'' Her mind was flying. Tea with the countess. Were the good linens fresh? They'd need flowers, and the silver set, and Dorcas would have to spend the entire morning baking. . . . What a dreadful bother. How could she have forgotten? ''Mary. Could you please go tell Dorcas the countess will be having tea with us tomorrow?''

''Very good, miss.''

The cook would be, and very rightfully, wroth. Someone would have to do the shopping as well; there was next to nothing in the pantry. And Zeus—she would have to warn Zeus. What was her father's schedule? Friday—he had a lecture at ten. But hadn't he told her something about a meeting afterward? And, Jesus, what would she wear?

Harry was slowly shaking his head. ''I can see you'll need a secretary. I told you two weeks ago—''

''I *know,* Harry. I'm sorry. It's just . . . I've had so much on my mind.''

''If you'd rather do Tasker's—''

''Absolutely not. I'll be ready. Truly I will.'' And so she would be, if she started right now.

He was still eyeing her with reproach. ''My own mother. It's not as though she calls every day.''

''I *said* I was sorry.'' The dining-room floor would need to be waxed. . . .

He moved close to her. ''So you should be. I can think how you could make it up to me, though.'' His palm closed on her thigh.

''Tomorrow?'' Dorcas's voice was a screech from the doorway. ''She's coming here *tomorrow?* By all the blessed saints, child, what can you be thinking of, to spring this on me?''

Callie rose from the sofa. ''Forgive me, Dorcas. Lord Godshall told me ages ago; it simply slipped my mind. If we all pitch in now, though—''

''Pitch in! I've got the damasks out to the laundress; what am I to do about that?''

Harry stood up, too. ''Well. I can see I'd better go.'' His

tongue grazed Callie's ear. "Really, you ought not to let her speak to you that way, love. It's most insubordinate." Mary stood ready with his hat and cloak, and held them for him. "Shall we say four o'clock?"

"Might as well say doomsday," Dorcas muttered in mutiny.

Callie trailed after him to the door, feeling shamed and helpless. "I really am sorry, love."

"It just goes to show, doesn't it, how much you have to learn yet?" Then he smiled indulgently, as one might at a kitten. "Never mind, sweetheart. You do the best you can. Mother will understand."

5.

The tea was a disaster.

Callie knew it would be, from the moment Harry's mother swept into the house in her velvet and ermine, followed by two impeccably liveried servants bearing handsome ribboned boxes. "Where is your correspondence room, Miss Wingate?" she'd demanded, her sharp blue eyes taking in the rather worn upholstery on the wing chair in the corner, the statues lined up on the hall table, made of hammered copperbalanced atop horns, that Callie's father had brought back from Istanbul, and the framed drawings crowded on the walls.

"My—" Callie turned beseeching eyes on Harry. "I—"

"You can just leave them on the table," he instructed the servants.

The Countess Godshall ran a gloved hand over its pocked surface. "A most . . . unusual piece."

"Water buffalo," Professor Wingate said from the drawing room doorway.

The countess jerked up her lorgnette. "I beg your pardon?"

"The horns. Water buffalo."

Harry's mother cast a long glance at the base of the table,

edging back from it a bit. "Really. You don't say. I don't believe I've had the pleasure. . . ."

"This is Callie's father," Harry said quickly. "Mother, Professor William Wingate. Professor Wingate, my mother."

The democratization of education led Professor Wingate to extend his hand. The countess eyed it rather as she had the buffalo horns, then laid her gloved fingers in it. "How do you do."

"It is a very great honor, milady, to meet you at last."

Callie felt a flush of pride in her father. He might be only a butcher's son, but he knew what to say. One didn't hold a post here at Oxford as long as he had without learning how to placate gentry. Bingham, she was sure, would also pass muster; he moved with just the right near-invisibility to stand behind the countess as she shrugged off her wrap. There was a moment of silence. Callie knew Harry's gaze must be boring into her back. "Did you have a pleasant journey, milady?" she asked, her voice sounding faint.

"Tolerable enough for this time of year, in this damp." She was eyeing the sketches on the walls again. "Are all of these yours, Miss Wingate?"

"Good heavens, no. That one is a Giotto." It was her father's pride and joy, purchased in Tuscany for far, far below what it was worth—a gorgeous Virgin and Child. The countess's eyes moved over it without appreciation.

"This, however, is." Professor Wingate indicated a charcoal study Callie had made just the year before in Athens, of a head of Dionysus crowned with fruit and greens.

The countess squinted at it through the lorgnette. "Is this your brother?"

"Lord, no, Mother," Harry said quickly. "It is Dionysus. You know. The Greek god of wine."

"You don't say. How very . . . unusual."

That was the way it went. Professor Wingate did a yeomanly job at keeping conversation going, but the gap between Callie's family and her betrothed's loomed ever larger to her as the afternoon progressed. The silver tea set, worked over by Bea with painstaking care until far past midnight the evening before, looked somehow worn and tawdry; the tablecloth, fetched back from the laundress's at no end of trouble—and, no doubt, expense—had, close to where the countess's cup was set, what was undeniably a spot. Of the vast array of tempting savouries and sweets the cook had frantically prepared, Lady Godshall only nibbled the edge of a watercress tart and ate half a tiny currant cake. We ought to have gone to Tasker's, Callie thought in despair, glimpsing Dorcas's set face through the kitchen door as Mary cleared away.

What was odd to Callie was that her father seemed to take no notice of the awkwardness that, for her, hung so heavily in the air. Granted, the countess was all the professor had ever wanted in an in-law; granted, too, he was not and never had been the most sensitive of souls. But couldn't he feel the weight of the woman's disdain for his household? How could he mistake her terse replies to his genial overtures, read anything but gross contempt into the way she kept her skirts close, and sat on the edge of her chair?

"Well! That went splendidly, don't you think?" he said to his daughter, when, limp and drained, she'd finally shut the door behind Harry and his mother.

"Oh, Father. Honestly," she said, and left him staring in her wake as she ran up the stairs in tears.

He surprised her by coming after her, all the way to her bedroom. "Calliope?" he said tentatively, rapping at the door.

She went and opened it, rubbing her tear-streaked face with her kerchief. "Oh, Father. I didn't mean you. You *were* splendid, really you were." And Zeus, who'd had a devil of a head on him that morning after being out till all hours, had had the uncharacteristic discretion to stay out of the way. It could have been worse, she supposed.

Professor Wingate sat in a wickerwork chair. "My dear child, I think you are taking all this far too much to heart. In so many ways, you are that woman's equal—nay, her superior. Imagine not knowing a Giotto!"

"Giotto doesn't matter in her world."

"That fault is hers, not yours. Believe me, the time is coming, is nigh upon us, when mere happenstance of birth won't suffice to confer superiority on a person."

It was a doctrine he had taught her all her life, and it was a doctrine Callie was less and less sure of. "My *correspondence room?*" she sniffed.

He smiled. "She is simply ignorant of the reality of other people's lives."

"As I am ignorant of hers! Yet I'm expected to learn it, while she goes on looking down her nose at me and mine! What makes hers more worthwhile?"

"Custom," he said. "Simply custom. That, too, will change."

"I'm not certain I have the strength to be the instrument of such change."

"Do you love Harry?"

Callie looked down at her hands, saw the glimmering opal. "Yes."

"Then all will be well. Calliope, when I think how far you and Zeus have come, in one generation, from your mother and me.—" He smiled once more, shaking his head. "I am quite overwhelmed."

She raised her gaze. "It was a step up, wasn't it, for Mother to wed you?"

"It would have been a step up for your mother to marry a goatherd," he said, and laughed. "Her father hadn't more to his name than a set of bagpipes and the faded glory of his clan."

Her green-gold eyes glinted. "What made you marry her?"

"Well." Something very like a blush spread across Professor Wingate's cheeks. "I—she was bright, and quick. There was no mistaking her native intelligence. She simply wasn't learned. If we had had more time . . ." Now he was looking at his hands. "I don't imagine it was easy for her, leaving her way of life, her people, her home. There were times I wondered . . . whether taking her from Skye was just. But now, when I look at you and Zeus, I know I did the right thing."

He so seldom spoke of her mother. Callie felt a rush of gratitude to him for this unprecedented confidence. "I know you did, too, Father. And I'm sure the countess did enjoy her visit, especially meeting you. You were wonderful, truly. It's . . . it's the little things I worried about. The fact I hadn't got a correspondence room. And that spot on the tablecloth."

"What tablecloth?" Professor Wingate asked blankly.

Callie sighed and went to kiss him. "Never you mind. It doesn't matter a bit."

He stretched out his long, thin legs and stood, striding to the door. "If you ask me, what you need is a good night's sleep. I'll take Zeus to supper at the House, why don't I, and have Dorcas send you up something on a tray."

"Very well. But don't trouble Dorcas. If I'm hungry, I'll come down myself and fetch something." There were, heaven knows, enough watercress tarts left untouched.

"That's settled, then." He paused with his hand on the doorknob. "Your brother said something to me when he came in last night—granted, he was in his cups. But it's been troubling me. He rather implied you might be marrying Harry to . . . well, to please me."

"Father! That's not true!"

"I certainly hope not. I won't pretend it doesn't satisfy me, this betrothal, for any number of reasons. Harry's a fine young man. And I like the thought that I'll never have to worry for your future comforts. I am only too aware of what it is to be impoverished. Even more than that, I am absolutely committed to the progress of social change. And there's no surer way to effect that than by just the sort of intermingling—old power with new brains—your marriage represents. But above all, my dear, I want you to be happy. Does Harry . . . make you happy?"

"Of course he does."

He nodded thoughtfully. "I should think that would be able to surmount everything else, don't you?"

When he'd gone, Callie unbuttoned the small bone buttons of her peach satin wrapper, stepped from the voluminous skirts, and tossed it over a bedpost.

Pulling on a smock, she stepped behind the screen that hid the windows, undraped the canvas on the easel, and stared at it. She'd made much progress in a month; in truth, it was likely that this painting had led her to forget the countess's impending visit. She'd worked on it each night that she hadn't any obligation to her father or Harry, and had, in fact, declined two invitations to concerts from the latter just to stay at home and paint. She had the background nearly done now, the sky and the tower and the garden, and had the first strokes of the savage's figure in place. Of course, the background was the easy part. Still, she thought objectively, she had done a fine job on the ruined wall.

Now it was time to get down to business. She laid out her palette, closed her eyes for a moment to recapture the scene, and mixed a thin brown wash to lay in the torso and legs.

Frozen power, she thought, remembering the man's preternatural stillness. Like an ice-covered river, or a snow-crowned volcano—all that energy seething just beneath the surface of his skin. The curve of that thigh—God, she could see it so clearly in her mind, but the exact shape continued to elude her brush. She painted over it and over it, frowning, consulting her sketch, then wiping the results with a rag. She would never get it, never find that careless, breath-snatching beauty, never manage to define with her poor skills what had made her heart stop at the sight of the naked man-beast.

And then, abruptly, almost accidentally, she did. She heard the sound of voices from the drawing room waft through the window—her father and Zeus, and someone else, one of the students, returning from their supper—and her hand jerked just a bit as she turned toward the noise. When she looked back at the canvas, there it was: his right leg raised on the wall, thick with muscle, harnessed with sinew, the suppressed potency crying out from the paint's faint sweep. "Oh, God," she whispered, stepping back, awed. She was afraid to touch it, afraid to go on, terrified that she might spoil the line.

But after a moment, pride steadied her. She had done it. She had gotten that leg; only one more to go. She mixed more paint; she closed her eyes; she remembered. Her brush touched the canvas with graceful certainty.

"Who was here last night?" Callie asked her brother at breakfast.

"Last night?" Zeus winced as Bea drew open the drapes to the sunlight. "What was last night? Tuesday? Thursday?"

"Friday. The countess was here for tea. Good Lord, Zeus, how much did you drink, to not recall the day?"

"Not so much," he said offhandedly, but his bleary eyes belied it. "I only just woke up. Now, let me think. Ah, yes. We had supper at the House, Father and I. Then we went to one of old Fingle's tedious lectures. God, what a bore he is—and thinks he knows all there is to know of Greek to boot. Then Father had something or other to do, so I and some of the boys went to the Black Dog. Got into a jolly good argument with Cobham about the nature of the soul. He's a bit of an animist, did you know that?"

"No. I didn't." Callie concealed a sigh. "So it was Cobham who came back with you."

Her brother nodded, yawning, and then shook his head instead. "No. It wasn't. It was Harding. I ran across him and Father coming along the quad. Rather late for Father to be out and about, I thought, but they were dissecting Celtic symbols, so I lingered. That one's the real thing, he is. Lord, the stuff he knows! He must have done nothing but study and read since he was in short pants. Why? Did we wake you?"

Mick Harding. Callie thought of him standing in the shadowy hallway contemplating the Leda, of his long, fine hands. Odd that his voice should have been the impetus for her to find that leg. She'd scarcely seen him since the dinner here more than a month before. He did not seem a part of the ebbing and flowing circle of her brother's friends.

Zeus, his question unanswered, yawned again and stabbed an egg, sending the yellow yolk seeping over his plate. "How did it go with the countess, anyway?"

In her excitement over the painting, Callie had nearly forgotten the disastrous tea. "Not . . . well," she admitted.

"Can't say I'm surprised. Oil and water." He sopped a corner of toast in the egg-yolk.

"I don't see why you say that. Father says the day is coming—"

"I know what Father says, and it's hogwash."

Callie looked at him across the table, surprised. "Don't you believe you are an earl's son's equal?"

"The question, rather, is whether an earl's son is equal to me. Especially Harry."

She laid down her fork. "If you intend to start in on Harry again—"

"I just don't see why, when you are surrounded by hundreds of brilliant young men, you have to choose such a—"

"You think it makes one brilliant to spend one's evenings drinking one's self into distraction, discussing the nature of—"

"I think it jolly well helps! When did you ever hear Harry Godshall discuss anything more weighty than the cut of one's coat?"

"Father seems to think him a fine enough student."

"Father has got what he wanted out of Harry." He saw her flush with anger, and quickly raised a hand. "Don't bite my head off, Cal! Just answer this one question honestly: Did it never strike you as peculiar that despite all the old man's theories of equality, he pushed like hell for you to marry into the nobility?"

"That is because he believes what he preaches!"

Zeus shook his head. "I wish I could think so. But if you ask me, he's naught but a fraud. It pleases his pride to have you marrying up, and that's all. He's vain as a crow that's got a peacock to roost his eggs."

Callie reached for the jam. "Perhaps you think I should marry a fishmonger."

"If it were the right fishmonger, I wouldn't quibble. That's precisely where Father and I differ, Cal. I believe that what sort of man a fellow is matters one hell of a lot more than where he stands on the social ladder. Whereas Father wants everyone to aspire to the gentryhood."

"There's nothing wrong with the sort of man Harry is," Callie said curtly.

"No?" Her brother met her eyes for a moment, then averted his gaze. "Pass that jam, would you?"

The way he'd looked at her. . . . "Do you know something, Zeus?"

But he'd backed off. "I know a great deal, my dear. On what subject in particular?"

"You know what I mean! About Harry."

"Certainly. I know he drinks more than I do, and a better drink at that."

"That's all?"

"And there are wagers as to whether his thesis will ever be completed."

"He works on that thesis all the time!"

"Is that what he tells you he does?"

She set her chocolate cup down with a clank. "Dammit, Zeus! Tell me what you know."

But he shook his head, grim. "You'd not credence it if I did. You'd put it down to envy, or whatever it is you mistake my feeling for him as."

"And what exactly is your feeling for him?"

"I think he's a snake. But don't mind me. I'm sure he's every woman's dream."

"Why don't you just go to hell, Persues Wingate?" Callie snapped, shoving back her chair and fleeing from the room.

6.

The frostiness that conversation with her brother engendered
cost Callie dearly. They'd been so close all their lives—best
friends, truly—that quarreling with him put her all on edge.
She missed an appointment with the dressmaker for a fitting,
earning her another cross reproach from Harry; she neglected
to take stock of the wine stores, and the household ran out of
both brandy and sherry on the selfsame night. The sole thing
that could hold her attention was her painting of the savage;
she worked on it every free night in a sort of frenzy of creation,
so intent on its perfection that the list of sketches she owed
her father for his lectures stretched far too long. She meant to
start on them, she honestly did, but in her few precious hours
of exemption from wedding plans and daily duties she found
herself drawn irresistibly to the canvas she kept draped on her
easel.

It was an outstanding portrait, by far the best she'd ever
done. She hadn't always been sure; there were moments in its
execution when she despaired of recreating that stunning tableau burnt forever in her memory. But she was nearly finished
now, except for some details of the garden and the angle of

the axe the man had carried, and each time she viewed the canvas she was newly amazed at what her brushes had done.

She ached to share it with Zeus, who was, after all, the only person in the world to whom she could safely show it. It was so raw in its power, so bold in its symbolism—the garden, the savage's provocative stance, the suggestive axe—that she shuddered to imagine Harry or her father or, God forbid, the countess or anyone else laying eyes on it. Yet it was so damned *good!* If I were a man, she thought during nights in despair, this painting would make my reputation. But because she wasn't, it was doomed to remain covered in muslin, hidden from the world's view.

It was Zeus, after a fortnight of chilliness from Callie, who made the first gesture of reconciliation. The occasion was Halloween night. He'd made his usual elaborate defenses against the children who roamed the town after dark intent on mischief, including a truly horrifying caricature of a demon in the drawing room window, illuminated from within by candles. From her rooms Callie could hear the gratified, frightened screams of the mischief-makers he surprised as they passed by. But they died away before midnight; that was when she answered his knock on her door and found him holding the goblin. "My worser nature," he announced, and flung it on the floor. "There, you see? I cast it aside and come craving forgiveness. It's bloody lonely having you be cross with me, Cal. Sometimes I think it's only the prospect of losing you forever to Harry that makes me so sharp-tongued. I take it all back. He's a peach, a gem. He's the only man on earth worthy of my sister. He's the absolute tops. He—"

"All right, Zeus. You needn't lay it on so thick."

"I can come in, then?"

She glanced over her shoulder at the canvas. Just moments before, inspired perhaps by this night of spirits, she'd at long last captured the exact position of the axe. And she was *dying* to show it to someone. "Very well," she told him. "But cover your eyes. I've a surprise for you."

"Likely a box on the ears," he mumbled, but did as he was told. She took his elbow and steered him past the screen until he stood just in front of the painting.

"You can look now," she said.

He took his hands away, and his jaw literally fell open. It took a good two minutes for him to find his voice. "Jesus, Cal," he whispered in awe. "Holy blessed Jesus."

She flushed with pride. "You like it?"

"Like it? I'm—God, I'm overwhelmed."

"You know who it is?"

"Of course I do; I'm not an idiot. Though looking at this makes me feel like one. What I wouldn't give to be able to paint like that!" He moved a few steps back, to the right, to the left, all the time eyeing the portrait intently. "It's flawless," he announced. "More than flawless, really. You've made more of it than I ever saw. The line of the axe—Christ, it's the same line his penis would make, isn't it, if he had an erection?"

"Zeus!" She colored again. "As if I'd know about that!"

"But it is! And you've got the garden perfect—that impression of order run to utter havoc. And his musculature, his chest, his thighs . . . his loins. Lord, those loins! He looks as though he could sire all mankind, doesn't he?"

"It is good, isn't it?" she asked happily.

"Good? It's incredible! It's glorious! I feel like throwing myself at your feet." He did so, then got up. "Honestly, I'm honored just to be a member of your family."

"You're not praising it so much just because we quarreled, are you?"

"You know I'm not." She did. He walked around it again, examining it from all angles, then looked at her with his green eyes alight. "You have got to exhibit this, Cal."

"Exhibit it?" She swallowed a laugh. "Lord, don't be absurd. Exhibit it where?"

"I don't know! A gallery in town—any one would take it. At the college of art—anywhere! God, it cries out to be seen!"

Callie took off her paint-smeared smock. "I can't exhibit it. You know that."

"Why the devil not?"

"You said yourself—the line of his axe. His loins."

"I said they were perfect."

"You know what I mean. It's not a proper subject for a woman."

"Oh, hang all that!" He was restless with impatience, pacing back and forth. "I know Jesse Greenwall at the gallery on High Street. I've bought him enough pints over the years. He'd show it in a minute, I know that he would." He reached for the canvas. "Let me take it there now."

"Zeus, no!" She blocked him with her arm.

"Oh—sorry. It's probably not dry. Well, in the morning, then. I'll take this, and a few of your sketches—only the best ones. Where's that study you made of the old woman selling lilies in Sicily?" He began to paw through her pile of sketchbooks. "And the one of the priest and the boy at the basilica in Rome, with all the doves rising behind them—you know the one I mean?"

"Zeus." She broke into his excited stream of speech, taking the notebooks from him. "Stop it, Zeus. You know I can't. Father doesn't even know I made those sketches. And as for this. . . ." Rather helplessly she looked back at the portrait of the savage, only to be struck anew by wonder. Had she really made that, conjured his wild, splendid presence out of memory and the strokes of her brush?

Zeus had sobered a bit. "Come now, Callie. You may say what you like about Father—I know I have—but he respects art enough to recognize genius when he sees it. He won't stand in your way."

That was probably true, but somehow the knowledge only made Callie more unsettled. She sighed, turning away from the painting. "It isn't just Father," she said reluctantly.

"Oh, no. It's that damned Harry Godshall, isn't it, and his stiflingly blue-blooded family—"

"Zeus . . ."

"It is he and his useless, insensate kind, who couldn't themselves create anything more far-reaching than a seating plan for supper—"

"Zeus, you have no right—"

He silenced her with a shout. "I have every right! I may not be sure what I believe about God or the gods or whatever force it is animates our souls, but I do know this: It or He or They never meant for you to squander this talent making little charcoal copies of clay pots! Who do you think you are, to throw their gift back in their faces this way?''

"You needn't be so overdramatic," Callie said, her voice trembling.

"Oh, I do beg your pardon! I'm not being *proper,* am I? The finer sort of folk never *emote,* do they? They never raise their voices, never raise their sights. Why, they never do a damned bloody thing!

She started toward the door. "I think you'd better go now."

"Oh, Cal." She heard the hitch in the words and turned to see him standing in front of the portrait with tears streaming down his cheeks. "Have you any notion of what I would give," he whispered, "to be able to paint this way?"

Her heart melted toward him. It was easy to forget at times how young and uncertain of himself he was beneath his brittle facade of sophistication. "Zeus, there are so many things you are good at."

"Not so good as this." He wiped his face on his sleeve, looking for all the world at that moment like the little boy she'd had to comfort when he'd scraped his knees. But he'd recovered himself; he laughed and shrugged."Well, there it is. You can mark all my bad temper down to infantile jealousy."

Callie stood with her hands clasped at the front of her gown. "I won't lie to you and say I haven't wanted the world to see this painting," she admitted. "But the plain truth is, I'm not brave enough to cope with all that would entail. If only I had your swagger."

"Or I your talent. But life never does seem to work out that way. It is only fools like me who are willing to bare ourselves to the public."

She nodded toward the easel. "And creatures like him, of course."

He, too, studied the savage. "What in God's name do you suppose he was thinking of, standing there so very still?"

"Raw meat," Callie said, and giggled.

"Aye . . . or going home to his woman and begetting another mewling bairn on her. He's likely got a score of them."

"No doubt," she agreed, and busied herself gathering up her tubes and brushes to hide her blush.

"Here, I nearly forgot what I came to tell you." He took the turpentine and swirled the brushes for her. "Some farmer over in Avebury has turned up a great cache of Roman stuff with his plow—coins and brooches and I don't know what else. Father's going off with some of the students to catalog it. Want to come along?"

Callie nibbled her lip. "I don't know that I should. There's so much still to be done for the wedding—"

"Harry is going."

"Is he? Well, it is different for the man; all he needs is to show up at the church on time."

"Do come, Cal," he urged her. "It could be the last chance you and I ever have to work together. After all, I don't suppose Harry will want you traipsing about all over the country once you are wed."

Her green-gold eyes slanted toward him. "You really don't like him, do you?"

"I don't mind Harry. I only mind what he does to you." He glanced again at the painting, and she saw the muscles beneath his thin flesh grow tight. Poor Zeus. In some ways, she reminded herself, I am the only thing like a mother he has ever known. Little wonder he hates to see me married. He would have objections no matter whom I chose.

"It won't be so very different after the wedding," she said gently. "I won't be abandoning you and Father."

"It will be completely different," he replied, low and stubborn.

She sighed to herself. But perhaps he was right. Perhaps she owed him this. "I'll come to Avebury." It would make a muddle of her already overburdened schedule. It would be bloody cold on the plains in December. And so close to the holidays. . . .

She was glad for her decision, though, when she saw his taut face light up. "Will you? Oh, Cal. I am so glad."

7.

Callie sat on her stool, her sketchbook propped on her easel, and watched covertly as Mick Harding painstakingly dusted layer after layer of brown earth from whatever object he'd discovered in the cold Ayrshire soil. He lay flat on his stomach, arms extended over the edge of the furrow the farmer had been digging when his plow struck gold—or actually, gilded tin. It was absolutely uncanny how he could stay in one position for so long, only his long hands moving with the steady *swish, swish* of the whisk broom. Watching him made her itch; she stood up abruptly and paced across the field, rubbing her arms within her long woolen sleeves.

His head—just his head—swiveled toward her as she approached him; the broom kept brushing. "Cold?" he asked in bemused sympathy.

She nodded; it was easier than explaining why she felt like moving. "Why do these farmers never turn up anything at spring planting?"

"They don't plow so deep."

Surprised, she came closer. "Is that true?"

"Oh, aye. In autumn you must turn the haulm under."

"What's the haulm?"

"Whatever's left after the harvesting. The stalks and roots and such."

"Oh." Callie knew nothing of farming, and was mildly astonished he did. "Why do you turn them under?"

"They enrich the soil as they rot. Rather as he did." He nodded toward the surface he'd been busy laying bare, and Callie gasped, seeing a skull gaping up out of the ground.

"Jesus!" Repulsed, she stepped back, and then, curiosity getting the better of her, came forward again, bending down. "Who is he?"

"I don't know yet. Perhaps nothing more than an unchurched Areburyman. But perhaps . . ." The whisk swished toward the top of the skull, uncovering another fraction of bone and something more—a band of rusted iron circling the forehead. "Perhaps a Roman," Harding said with satisfaction, finally getting to his knees. "Professor Wingate!" he called toward the opposite end of the ditch, where Callie's father was crouched with Zeus and Tom Gregory. "We have got something here!"

Callie's father stood and strode across the field, which she noticed now was covered half with stubbles of barley and half with smoother ground—the part the farmer had plowed before stumbling on his treasure. "What is it?" he demanded, brushing dirt from his gloves.

Harding gestured toward the iron band. "Looks like a soldier. First century A.D., from the make of the helmet."

Professor Wingate leaned closer. "There's no insignia there."

"No, sir. But the bolts here . . . and this has to be copper." He pointed with a blunt-tipped finger at, to Callie, at least was a scarcely perceptible tinge of green against the blood-red rust.

"Mm. Quite so." The professor straightened again, surveying the field. "Odd place for a burrow, don't you think? No sign of a mound."

"No, sir. I suppose over the years it could have been plowed down."

"I suppose it could have." Professor Wingate turned his sharp gaze on his pupil. "Any other ideas?"

"Well, sir. The way the artifacts are scattered—how far down the row do they reach now?"

"Zeus just measured again. Two hundred and fifty-seven yards."

Mick Harding grunted. "They could have been spread by a farmer less observant than Master Shadloe."

"In a nearly straight line? Come, come, Harding. You disappoint me."

"Then there's only one conclusion."

"Yes. Quite."

Callie felt like striking them both. *"What?* What is the conclusion?"

They turned to her, nonplussed. Harding took pity on her first. "He must have been running."

"Running?" she echoed.

"Aye, running. With a great load of stuff on his back. It was slowing him down, and so he started casting it off—there where your brother is standing. And he wasn't doing it haphazardly, either. That's why the coins were first to go, and only later the richer stuff, the cups and brooches."

"That also explains," Professor Wingate observed with satisfaction, "why there aren't any pots."

Callie had already noted that, with great relief. "But what does a lack of pots prove?"

"If it were a regular burial," Harding said patiently, "there would have been pots for the oils and herbs of sacrifice."

"And there's no sword," Callie's father said, while she was trying to digest this.

"At least not so far," Harding agreed. "The only question is, was he a thief stealing his company's treasure? Or was he the last noble remnant of his legion, desperate to keep the empire's riches from falling into enemy hands?"

"Oh, you'll never know that," Callie told him, a little heady at the vignette of wild flight her father and his student had constructed.

"We very well might. Think, Calliope," Professor Wingate urged. "If he was killed by his legion, wouldn't they have retrieved the treasures he so reluctantly abandoned?"

"Wouldn't the enemy have as well?" she countered, glad to have figured out that much.

"Not necessarily. Let's plot the circumstances. A raid by

the Gaels—say, at night. Swooping down on an encampment. What would their objectives be? Death and destruction.''

Callie looked back at the gilded cup, set on a stump, that she'd been sketching. "Even a barbarian would have stopped for *that*.''

"Only if he'd *seen* it. This is a night raid. A solitary figure breaks free from the camp, running with all his might. He's pursued. Someone hunts him down and kills him, then turns to search for other survivors. The body and the goods are left where they fell, to be sunk in the earth by a good steady rain.''

"You cannot possibly conjecture all that from a bit of bone and a few scattered trinkets," Callie protested.

"No," Harding agreed, busy with his whisk again. "But we might from this." He'd uncovered the top of the skeleton's ribcage, and reached between two bones for something black and hard—an arrowhead. "Native, wouldn't you say?" He held it out to the professor, who nodded his head.

"Without a doubt. Excellent progress, Harding. Keep up the good work.''

"Thank you, sir.''

Professor Wingate stuck the arrowhead in his coat pocket and started toward the top of the furrow again. Callie was silent for a moment, watching Harding stretched out on the frost-rimed ground. Then she said, with what came out as a surprising note of resentment, "You don't really *know* any of that.''

"Of course not," he agreed, not turning his head.

"It could have been wild animals that scattered those things. Or . . . or thieves. Or a mudslide.''

"Certainly.''

"So what is the point of making up that whole story about him fleeing from his encampment in the middle of the night?''

"Occam's razor," he said shortly.

Callie blinked. "I beg your pardon?''

"John of Occam. Fourteenth-century Scholastic—''

"I know who he *was*.''

"Then you must know his most famous principle: *Essentia non sunt multiplicanda praeter necessitatem.* Or, briefly put, the simplest explanation is best." He had found something amongst the bones; she saw him lean forward slightly and pry at the earth with a small sharp pick.

"I hardly think all that rigmarole you and Father dreamed up could be the simplest explanation!"

"It is the simplest one that fits all the facts." He got the object loose. Sitting up, he dusted it with the hem of his greatcoat and then tossed it toward her. "Look there. Beryl. Almost the color of your eyes."

She picked it up. It was a brooch, Roman, finely worked with acanthus leaves winding about the central stone. The remark about her eyes had caught her off-guard; she would not have thought he could have known their color, with his own gaze so often trained on the ground. She looked back at him; already he was at work again. "I'll show Father," she said, and hurried off along the ditch.

On her way she passed Harry, who was sitting at the side of the ditch with his hat tilted back to catch the thin winter sun on his face. "Hallo, love. Bloody cold, don't you think?" he greeted her, barely opening his eyes. "What's the crown prince of antiquities turned up now?"

"Harding, do you mean? A beryl brooch."

"Hmph. Trust him to find it."

The sight of him leaning lazily there in the sun provoked her. "It helps if you dig," she said pointedly, and marched past.

Maybe it was Zeus's whisperings, but she'd been disappointed in Harry on this expedition. Had he always been so lackadaisical at his work, she wondered, and she'd simply never noticed it? Or was he—she gritted her teeth—so secure in his sinecure now he was marrying the professor's daughter that he felt his academic success was assured no matter how little he did? He only ever seemed to come alive at their inn in the evenings, when he'd sit by the fire with Tom Gregory and drink brandy, while Zeus and Cobham and the others discussed the day's finds.

Her father was dictating the origins and dates of a handful of coins to Zeus, who wrote each down in his notebook. Callie waited until they were finished before showing them the brooch. "*Very* nice," Professor Wingate noted, and passed it 'round to his students. "And indisputably Roman. Observe the eagle wings worked into the filigree. The stone is likely Irish, from County Down. Thus we have a fine example of reciprocal trade—the raw stone travels to Rome to be worked, then comes home again, or close enough, to clasp a conqueror's cloak. Professor Rushland will be interested. Make a sketch if you will, please, Calliope."

She went back to her easel, set the brooch atop it, and began to work. The sun had disappeared completely now, and low white clouds set in. A tangle of hedgerow lay beyond the ditch, and sparrows twittered in and out from its branches, darting bravely forth now and again to glean seeds from the rubble of the field. It was familiar and peaceful to sit in that setting and sketch, accompanied by birdsong and the soft whisks and chinks of the students' tools.

She was nearly finished when she became aware that Mick Harding had left the ditch and come to stand a little way behind her, watching what she did. She half-turned, just to acknowledge him, and he nodded at the sketchbook. "You are very good at that."

"I should be by now; I have had enough practice."

"It takes more than mere practice to make an inanimate thing come alive. Did your father teach you?"

Callie laughed. "Lord, no. He can't draw a teacup. That's why he needed me to take it up."

"Do you ever draw just for pleasure?"

"Now and then. When I've time."

"What are your subjects then?"

Naked men, she thought of telling him, but quickly banished the giddy notion. "Just . . . this and that." She was spared any further delving by her father, who suddenly clapped his hands and called from the far end of the furrow.

"Let's cover it up, shall we, and end early today? For those of you interested, I thought we might spend the afternoon examining the stone circle beside the village and, perhaps, the barrow up on Silbury Hill."

Harry caught Callie's eye, rubbing his gloves together. "That's more like it, I'd say. Heathen sacrifices, Druidical ceremonies. . . ."

"The Druidical angle," Mick Harding said quietly, "has been pretty well proved false."

"Shut up, Harding, why don't you," Harry told him, "and let us have our fun."

The stones were something to see. Callie had caught glimpses of them from her room in the inn and the edge of the field where they were digging, but it wasn't until she paced around the whole huge circle that she caught a sense of the scale of this ancient monument. Though many of the slabs were fallen or broken, enough remained to foster a deep sense of awe as one walked into their midst. "That's where they burned the virgins," Harry called as she crossed to a smaller circle inside the large one, that was centered with a huge tablestone. He sat on a hunk of rock half sunk in the earth and lit his pipe, while Callie moved gingerly among the monoliths beneath the lowering sky. Soft snow had begun to drift down onto the stones, only to melt instantly as the flakes met the ground's captured heat. The grass beneath her feet was lush and green; she shivered, wondering how many centuries of spilled blood had made it grow that way.

Zeus darted out at her from behind a slab, making her jump. "Nervy?" he asked, and laughed. "It's splendid, isn't it? Much better than Stonehenge, I think. Speaking of which, Mick says that book by Dr. Stukely claiming it to be a Druid snake-worshipping temple is a pile of rubble, if you'll pardon the pun."

"Does he? And what does Mr. Harding believe it is?"

"I haven't any idea," said the gentleman in question, coming up behind Zeus. "It's so much easier to debunk the theories of others than to come up with one's own." His spectacles were steaming up in the snowfall. He took them off to rub them on his sleeve, and she saw his blue eyes reflecting the sky's stormy gray.

"I read somewhere it was the site of Arthur's last great battle." That was Cobham, his red hair wild beneath his wool cap.

"Every crossroads in this corner of England claims that," Zeus noted. "Inigo Jones wrote it was a Roman temple."

"I believe we can safely discount that," said Professor Wingate, who'd come to join them. "There is nothing at all analogous in the ancient world. Indeed, distribution of stone circles seems limited to regions of the earth where the Gaels once held sway—which would seem to argue for the Druidic connection."

"I've seen them in India, sir," Harding demurred politely.

"Have you really? Then perhaps Stukely *is* wrong." The professor pulled his hat down against the snow. "Well. Who's for the barrow?"

Harry had left his perch to slip his arm around Callie's waist. "Who's for brandy, and a fire?"

"I'd like to see the barrow," Callie said uncertainly. She was enjoying the scholarly bickering.

"Good God, Cal, it's nothing but a hump in the ground." Harry was stomping his feet. "I've got frostbite."

"I'm going back to the inn," Tom Gregory announced. "These places give me the willies."

"There, you have company, Harry." Callie gave him a quick kiss. "We won't be long."

She saw him glance toward Harding, definitely displeased, but he only said with a shrug, "Freeze to death, then, if you like. It's your prerogative."

The barrow, only a few acres south, *was* a hump in the ground, but a grand one, rising out of the flat plain like some giant's great grassy footstool. "Why do you suppose the ancients made everything so big?" Callie asked Zeus as they reined in their horses.

He shrugged. "Boredom. Nothing else to do but hunt and fish."

"I think . . ." It was Mick Harding's voice, coming from Callie's other side. She turned to him. "I think it was the only defense they had against their fear. The world must have seemed terrifying to them. Storms and meteors and eclipses, disease and death—and all with no explanations. Perhaps they felt if they could make something big enough, imposing enough, they could trick nature into believing they had some measure of control."

Zeus scratched his chin. "I like that theory, Mick. You ought to write it up for your thesis."

"It doesn't apply to Greece, alas," Harding told him, smiling. "They'd advanced enough there to build on human scale."

"What's inside it?" Callie asked, stepping back to better contemplate the barrow.

"A body and weapons and grave-goods, if it's anything like the smaller ones Stukely has excavated," Zeus told her, kicking the side of the grassy mound.

"Only one body?" Callie said dubiously.

"It could be a tribal chieftain—a king," Mick Harding noted. "Or a number of warriors lost in a battle. Someone will dig it out and find the answer someday."

"Imagine how long it must have taken to build it," Callie marveled, pacing along the edge. She closed her eyes and pictured it: score after score of wild, skin-clad men hoisting stones and earth above the flat plain. Her Scottish noble savage would have fit right in.

Professor Wingate was beckoning to them from the far side of the mound. "Time to go and try to catch up to Harry," Cobham said without rancor, but Callie shot him a frown— which he missed seeing—anyway.

She rode back to the village beside Zeus, contemplating the day's work. "There is something different about this expedition," she said aloud, and her brother nodded in agreement.

"That's Harding's influence—or, rather, that of those French antiquarians he reads. This new vogue of trying to understand the hopes and fears and aspirations of the peoples you study is very seductive. You can see even Father's fallen under its spell."

"Well, I can't say I give it much credence. After all, what can a passel of modern scholars possibly know about the feelings of folk who lived thousands of years ago?"

"You think people have changed so much?"

"Why, of course they have! They've progressed! We no longer offer human sacrifices, or flaunt our fallen enemies' heads up on sticks."

"And that's the measure of progress." He sounded wry.

"That, and everything else mankind has accomplished— literature, music, art. We're a million miles removed from those half-starved Gaels who huddled in their miserable hovels, terrified by thunder and lightning, and worshipping trees!''

''I must say, I'm inclined to agree with your sister,'' Mick Harding announced; he'd ridden up beside them. ''The process of civilization may sometimes seem slow, but there's no doubt it's advancing.''

''On the surface, perhaps,'' Zeus said mildly. ''But tell me the truth, Cal—don't you ever, deep in your soul, feel the impetus to bend your knee to a mighty oak?''

''Oh, not I.'' She laughed at the notion.

''Or make a wax figure of Harry's mother and melt her over a candle?''

''Zeus!'' Enormously embarrassed at hearing this in Mick Harding's presence, she spurred forward to the safety of her father, who was expounding to Cobham on the distribution of long and round barrows in Brittany.

8.

They were late for supper. Harry and Tom Gregory had already begun eating. As Callie slipped onto the bench beside her fiancé, she saw his brow was flushed, and the bottle of claret on the table before him nearly two-thirds gone. "Considering the quality of the food here," he drawled, "we thought we'd best eat it hot; hope you aren't offended. Though it doesn't seem to make much difference. This sauce is utter swill."

Callie cast a quick glance at the innkeeper's wife, who was serving them, hoping she hadn't heard him. Her broad, lined face was impassive, but as she handed Callie her leek soup, a bit slopped over the edge of the bowl onto Harry's sleeve. "Clumsy cow," he muttered, mopping it with his napkin.

"Beg yer pardon, m'lord."

"Harry!" Callie hissed, and quickly took a sip of soup. "Oh, my! This tastes fine!"

"Just what one needs to take the chill off one's bones," her father agreed, smiling at their hostess.

"In that case, we ought to take some out to the soldier Mick uncovered," Zeus noted with a grin.

"Take the roast instead," Harry proposed. "It's tough enough to chew on for eternity."

"Harry!" Callie poked his side. "How much have you had to drink?"

"It's not how much; it's *what*. You've never in your life tasted brandy so foul as they served us here."

Callie looked again at the innkeeper's wife, ready with a small, apologetic smile, but the woman had gone back to the kitchens. "Please, Harry, don't be so rude," she begged him.

"Why not? What the devil difference can it make?"

"I'm sure she does the best she can. The soup is really quite tasty."

"I'm sure you'd think so."

She stopped with her spoon halfway to her mouth. "And what is that supposed to mean?"

Zeus had been watching them, frowning. "I say, Harry," he broke in now, a bit loudly, "you and Tom ought to have come seen the barrow. It was quite imposing in the dusk, with the snow coming down."

"And I suppose Master Harding elucidated all its enigmas for you, according to the latest Continental theories."

Harding looked at him, a little surprised, from behind his glasses. "I don't know much about Gaelic grave ritual. It's outside my field of expertise."

"Really? Nice to hear you admit *something* is."

What on earth had gotten his goat? Callie wondered. It was getting damned tiresome flashing smiles of apology for him. Fortunately, her father stepped in with a brief lecture on Roman methods of iron manufacture, to which Harry listened quietly, if sullenly. Unfortunately, Professor Wingate concluded by deferring to Mick Harding. "Perhaps, Mr. Harding, you could explain to us how you were able to put a date to our dead soldier's helmet so readily."

"Oh, Christ," Harry declared, shoving back the bench so abruptly that Callie and Cobham, seated on it with him, were very nearly unseated. "I need some air."

"I'll say you do," Zeus murmured. Harry grabbed his cloak from its hook and stormed out the door. Callie hesitated, eyeing her half-finished supper, then sighed and went after him.

The snow was falling again, big flakes drifting onto the courtyard. Callie glanced about uncertainly in the darkness,

then heard the scratch of a match and saw the little flare of fire
as Harry lit his pipe. He was hard against the side of the inn,
underneath the eaves.

"Harry, what is wrong with you tonight?" she demanded,
coming toward him across the cobblestones.

"Odd. I've been wanting to ask the same question of you."

"Of me? What do you mean?"

"Do you think I didn't notice you making eyes at him all
day?"

"Making eyes at *whom?*" Callie asked, astonished.

"At your father's little Scottish pet. Master Harding."

Callie laughed. "Oh, honestly, Harry. I don't know what
you're talking about."

"Don't you?" His voice was low and harsh. "I was watching
you, you know. You couldn't keep your eyes off him."

"That is just plain silly." In one way, Callie found herself
pleased at his display of jealous pique; in another, she was
appalled by his childishness. "He'd found something interesting, that's all. I'd have paid as much attention were it Zeus
who found it, or Cobham, or you." Though that, her mind
registered, wasn't likely, considering he'd not been digging.

"You were watching him before he ever turned up that
skeleton."

"Harry, I was *working.*"

"You were staring at him."

"It may have looked that way from where you were sitting.
But really, Harry, why would I look at him?"

"I don't know. Why did you go with him to the barrow,
instead of coming back here with me? Perhaps you like his
type—the nameless, penniless provincial."

"That's rather hard on him, don't you think?"

"You see? There you go, taking his side—"

"I wasn't taking anyone's side! There isn't any question
here of taking sides. I'm in love with *you,* Harry. I am marrying
you."

He turned away from her. "That's what you say . . ."

"I don't see how you can doubt it," she told him, assaying
humor, "with the gown and flowers and all already chosen."

"I just wish I could be sure of your love." There was a wistfulness to his voice that was entirely new.

She felt the weight of the opal on her finger. "I hardly see what more I could do to prove myself true."

"You could come to my room tonight," he said, still looking away.

"Tom's sleeping in your room," she said, after a pause.

"He'd go sleep with one of the others. I know he would, if I said the word."

"And how would he explain that?"

"How should I know? He'd say I was drunk and snoring too loudly. Christ, Callie. If that's all that's standing in your way . . ."

But it wasn't. She had a horrible, half-formed suspicion that all his odd behavior that day might have been calculated to this end. That nonsense about Harding—no one, not even the most mistrustful suitor, could have read anything improper into her behavior toward him. He seemed more a randomly chosen pawn. Lord, she didn't like to think such thoughts about Harry; they made a pain wrench in her belly. "Harry," she began, and then stopped, not knowing what to say.

He'd knocked out his pipe and put his arms around her. "I want you, Callie. I want you more than I can say. I am burning for you here, inside." He rubbed up against her, thrusting her to the wall. "I want to prove my love to you, show you how I feel." His mouth closed over hers, persistent, demanding, and his hand found her breast, fondling it beneath her cloak. "Say yes. Oh, say yes."

He did not seem so drunk now, in the cold night air, but still, she did not want to anger him. Neither, though, did she relish losing her virginity in a clandestine coupling on the inn's rough beds. Perhaps she might assuage him with some further liberties. She stood, unmoving, in his embrace while he groped at her bodice, loosening her breasts from the cloth. "Callie," he whispered, parting the sides of her cloak, burying his face in her flesh. "Oh, Callie. Oh, Callie—"

Over his shoulder she saw a shadow at the doorway to the inn. "Stop it, Harry," she hissed.

"I can't stop. I need you too much. Come to my room."

She felt tired and hungry, and annoyed. "No, Harry. I won't."

"Why not?" he wailed, stomping off a few steps. "What have I got to do to show you what you mean to me?"

"Wait till April," she said, this time humorlessly.

"I wonder sometimes at your lack of passion," he said angrily. "Perhaps you're one of those women—there are some, you know—who lack the capacity for pleasure."

She wanted to strike him. "Because I won't tumble with you into the nearest bed? I wonder sometimes what you expect of me. I'm a well-brought-up girl, a decent girl—"

"Bourgeois," she thought she heard him murmur, and her wrath waxed hot.

"What? What did you call me?"

"I didn't—"

"If I'm so dreadfully common, Harry Godshall, why would you want to marry me?"

"Now, Callie. I don't—"

"Maybe in your illustrious circles it's considered daring and arch and alluring for a woman to be promiscuous, but it's not in mine!"

"Who said anything about being promiscuous? All I want—"

"I know bloody well what you want!"

"There's no need to be coarse," he said reproachfully.

"Coarse? *Me?*"

"Oh, just forget it, then," he told her, backing away and waving a hand. "I only thought, I'd hoped, your feelings for me might match mine for you."

Now, how had that got turned around? "Harry, I—"

"Forget about it," he said again. "If your virtue means more to you than I do, I'll stop pressing. Lord knows I wouldn't want you to betray those quaint morals you hold so dear."

"Oh, damn you, too," Callie called after him as he swept past her and back inside the inn.

On the verge of bursting into tears, she stood alone in the darkness. Was she wrong? Was she being foolish? Perhaps among Harry's friends it *was* natural to expect one's fiancé to engage in sexual relations. Maybe, just as Harry said, she was being prim.

The trouble is, she thought, straightening her bodice, I don't *feel* like making love to Harry. In fact, the notion of it made her quite queasy. What was it he'd said about women who lacked the capacity for pleasure? *Maybe I am like that,* she thought forlornly. Lord knows I've gotten little pleasure enough out of his kisses and fondlings. Maybe there *is* something wrong with me.

She hugged herself within her cape, the snow falling cold and wet on her cheeks. She could hear laughter through the inn's windows, shuttered though they were against the winter chill. She could picture the scene within: her father leaning back in his chair, well-fed, nursing his port and waxing expansive on some topic or other; her brother, bright and changeable as quicksilver, flashing wit; Cobham, shyly droll, and Tom Gregory, aloof but attentive; Harding, still and mostly silent; and Harry, sullenly sucking back more of the brandy he despised. It was all comfortable and well-worn, and all too familiar. On this night, with her emotions hopelessly tumbled, she wanted to be part, not of that constrained little group, but of something grander, something more—something wild and profound, where the small question of whether or not she should give in to Harry would shrink to infinitesimal size.

Beyond the courtyard wall, the circle of standing stones beckoned, crowned with white in the darkness. She moved toward it slowly, only half aware that she was going there.

The ring was so huge that from the center she could scarcely see the stones along its edges. The smaller circles were more distinct. Cape sweeping on the thick snowy grass, she glided toward the closer one, with the tablestone in its middle. Wind whimpered over the empty plain. Callie felt the weight of decision rising from her shoulders, butting up against that cloud-laden sky and then bumping through to where the cold stars glittered in the great hidden vastness of the universe. Her footsteps quickened, lightened. Really, what did one more sacrificial lamb matter in this place where there had been so many? If that was the price Harry asked for peace, for an end to this ceaseless bickering, she would give in to—

"Oh!" It came out as half a scream, half exclamation of wonder. On the flat slab before her, a figure rose up from the snow, stood atop the rock, and turned to her in a swirl of black cape. For one heady instant she thought it was a Druid come back from the dead.

"I beg your pardon." The voice was undeniably human, and familiar. It was Mick Harding's voice, though the strain of Scot in it seemed unusually strong. "Is that you, Mistress Wingate?"

She came a little closer. "What in the world are you doing out here?"

"I . . . found the air in the inn rather hot."

"I should think you'd find lying on a stone in a snowstorm exceptionally cold!"

He laughed a little. "Not so bad as you'd think. They hold the heat in them, you know." He moved to one side. "Here. Feel."

She came and put her hand on the slab. At first she felt nothing but the snow's cold wetness. Then, slowly, a lingering warmth enveloped her palm and fingers. Surprised, she smiled.

"With stones as big as this," Harding said from above her, "I sometimes wonder how old the glow might be that's at their core."

"You've a poetic streak, haven't you, for a man of science?"

He snorted. "I? Not likely. I meant it quite literally. I imagine someday we shall be able to determine it with a thermometer. But you haven't told me what brings you to wander out among the spirits of these stones tonight."

"You didn't ask," Callie said. "Like you, I found the inn too warm."

"You've a very warm family." She lifted her chin. "That is to say, your father and brother have made me quite welcome. At Oxford. And here."

"Oh, Father likes students who care about their work. And Zeus likes everybody."

"I feel quite honored, then," he said wryly.

"No, I meant . . ." Callie felt flustered. "Zeus admires you a great deal. He's spoken to me of it several—many—times." She paused uncertainly. "Well. I ought to leave you your privacy."

"I'll walk you back," he offered.

"That's not necessary."

"Unless, perhaps, you'd care to join me up here?"

"Oh, I don't think—"

"Quite so," he said quickly—so quickly that she felt a little sorry for him. Great gangling, bespectacled, studious wretch, did he ever even speak to women?

"Well . . . perhaps for a moment, then. Just to admire the view."

He gave her his hand. His strength was unexpected, shocking. "My!" she breathed as he pulled her lightly upward, then steadied her with a touch on her elbow. As they stood side by side, she was struck again by his height, which went largely unnoticed when he was sitting at a lecture, or stretched on the ground. She scarcely reached his chest. She blinked snowflakes from her lashes, and turned in a slow circle. The darkness was enveloping, the hush pervasive. "I see why you like it."

"Here. Try this." Again he gave her his hand, helping her to kneel. He knelt down beside her. "Like part of the earth," he said softly, "becoming slowly robed in snow."

"You see, you are a poet," Callie said, but she leaned back, too, until her face was flush to the sky. The big white snowflakes fell with caressing softness on her cheeks and hair. "Actually, I feel like one of Dorcas's plum-cakes, getting sprinkled with sugar." Then she tensed; he was leaning above her.

"I'll wager you taste sweet," she heard him whisper, and then something brushed her mouth: his tongue, intent on capturing a snowflake. Astonishment held her perfectly still. His lips touched hers. "You do."

This was the man she'd felt pity for, for his awkwardness with women? "I beg your pardon!" she huffed angrily, trying to rise. But he kept her pinned to the stone by her shoulders.

"I just have to know . . . can such sweetness last?" He kissed her again, not quite so gently. *What do you think you are doing?* Callie wanted to say. But his touch had sent a tremor through her like the shifting of stone; she had never, *ever,* when Harry kissed her, felt anything like this. He had his hands on either side of her face, his thumbs stroking her cheeks. "Ah," he murmured, sucking in his breath. At the sound of the gratified sigh, Callie could feel the skin tightening on her breasts, and a rush of heat low in her belly, as though the rock beneath them had suddenly let loose its fire.

She had to fight this; she could not let this go on! "Mr. Harding," she began, struggling to sit up again. But somehow his leg had moved across her skirts, holding her tight to the stone.

"Mick," he whispered. Callie beat back an urge to laugh. Imagine such circumstances bringing one to a first-name basis! But there was nothing laughable in what he did next; as smooth as the drift of the snow, he opened her cloak and put his mouth to her throat. "So soft. So white." In a single quick motion, he pulled her bodice down to bare her breasts.

Her nipples went rigid in the rush of cold air. He covered her with his cloak, fanning it out around them. Callie was thinking, absurdly, *It took Harry a year and a half to work up to this point.* He raised himself to pull his gloves off with his teeth, one after the other, flinging each aside with a toss of his head. Then he kissed her again, his weight hard against her bosom. Callie shivered violently, but not with the cold. Really, this would not do. It was the quiet ones, Dorcas had always said, that you had to watch out for. But—oh, God, he'd put his mouth to her breast! He was pulling at its tip with tiny little nibbles that sent the heat within her flaring up, dangerously close to flame.

"Don't," she whispered, and was appalled at the sense of longing that slipped out with the word. "Please." But that, too, had the sound of yearning. For answer, he only cupped her tingling flesh in his hands—such big hands, so delicate, so deliberate. *I imagined this moment,* Callie recalled, *not so long ago. But who could ever have imagined such a swell of feeling? Not capable of pleasure,* she thought derisively, and wanted again to laugh. *So there, Harry Godshall!* He put those long, strong hands on her shoulders and bowed his head to her breast once more. Tentatively, Callie touched his curly black hair with her fingertips. He smelled clean and sweet, like snow and grass, like fresh linen—no thick sweat of tobacco, no brandy marred his breath.

He responded to her touch like a violoncello to the bow; she felt his whole body quiver, resonate with need. She liked the sensation. She put her hand to the plane of his cheekbone, and he raised himself up and kissed her mouth again, his tongue probing her lips to part them and then thrusting inside her, tasting, exploring her warmth. Callie circled his neck with her arms, pulling him close. The snow drifted over and around them, until she felt she'd be content to lie there forever and be buried by it, so long as he would go on kissing her that way. They were a part of the sky, of the stones and earth, wild and natural. And it seemed only natural, too, that he should lay his hand atop her skirts and stroke her belly and thighs; that his palm should seek to part her knees and journey upward, to rest where no man had ever touched her, and trace there small, tight echoes of the great stone circles that enclosed them both. Her sighs were the wind; his hard loins were the continents shifting, and the heat in them seemed to have waited centuries, aeons, for this moment, to be joined and unleashed. Even Harry's outraged gasp, when it came, registered at first as merely part of the maelstrom that held them in its matrix. Not until he said, very clearly, "You duplicitous slut," did Callie pause, with a catch of her breath.

Harding pulled away from her a little, the rhythm of their passion abruptly halted. Harry stood beside the tablestone, light from the lantern he clutched falling across Callie's bared breasts, her flushed skin. She saw Harding push his tangled black hair back from his forehead and search the stone slab for his spectacles; without them, his blue eyes were wide and bewildered, like a startled child's.

"All that talk of your virtue." Harry was shaking his head. "All that—that crap you fed me, calling *my* friends promiscuous, telling me I'd have to wait until we were wed. . . . and all the time you were cozying up with him, is that it, Callie?"

"Harry, I . . . no."

"When I think of all I was willing to give you—I was going to make you a countess! I was going to give you *my family name!*" He was pacing back and forth below them, hands clasped at his back with the lantern swinging. "And now I find you with this—this son of a cleric! What could he *possibly* have that I don't? What skewed, twisted logic could bring you to *this?*''

His voice was getting louder, rising above the wind's croon. Harding was settling his spectacles into place. "Really, the fault's all mine," he began.

"You shut up!" Harry snapped at him, and he did. Harry pointed a finger up at Callie. "My mother was right about you."

She rolled her eyes. "Your mother—"

"You're not fit to talk about her!" he broke in with fury. "I don't want to ever hear you mention her again! She warned me you would end up shaming me, humiliating me, and so you have! Did it ever occur to you how far out on a limb I went to ask you to wed me? Have you any notion of the sneers and abuse I endured from my friends?" He was shouting at the top of his lungs. *"Do you know what it will cost me to cancel this wedding?"*

"Rather less than marrying me would, evidently," she murmured.

He struck her then, a sharp slap to the face that sent her rocking back on her heels. Harding quickly moved between them. "There'll be no more of *that,*" he said, his voice low and even.

"I ought to bloody horse-whip you!"

"I'd like to see you try."

Harding's calm only fanned Harry's rage. "Oh, you're all alike, you people, aren't you? Nothing means anything to you. You think that you can tear us down, destroy us and raise yourselves high, just because you've got a bit of learning. But you won't, because you haven't got our natural gifts. You've got no manners, no dignity, no breeding—"

"All of which," Callie interjected, "are certainly on display by you here."

"Is this some sort of jest to you?" he demanded angrily.

"No, Harry. Not at all. But even you must admit, if we are so unsuited to each other as you say, better to find out now than after we are wed."

"What is going on here?" None of them had heard Zeus coming, drawn from the inn by Harry's outraged bellows.

"What is going on," Harry announced icily, "is that I just found your sister *flagrante delicto* with this—this scum."

"Callie! Were you really!" There was no mistaking the unabashed delight in Zeus's voice.

"You see? It is just as I said!" Harry cried. "None of you take anything seriously!"

Zeus composed his face in the lamplight. "That is to say, shame on you, Cal. I don't suppose this means the wedding is off."

"You're damned well right it does," Harry growled.

"Oh, dear. What a pity. Father will be broken-hearted."

Harry glared at him suspiciously, but Zeus managed to look vaguely distraught. "I wouldn't be so bloody cocky, my boy," Harry told him, "if it were *my* sister whoring about."

That roused Callie. "It wasn't—I didn't—nothing like that happened!"

"Maybe not tonight," Harry said icily. "But I'm sure it has before, and will again. Make my apologies to your father, Zeus, but under the circumstances I'm sure he'll understand that I am leaving here in the morning."

"Certainly," Zeus told him, with a little bow. "And do accept my condolences for my sister's behavior."

"Hypocrite," Callie hissed at Harry. "It's not as though you weren't willing should I whore with *you!*"

"You'll pay," he shot back. "I don't know how or when, but you'll not get away with this." Then he stomped off across the plain with the lantern, leaving only the gentle hiss of the falling snow to break the silence.

Callie glowered at her brother in the darkness. "You've got your damned nerve, haven't you, apologizing to him for me?"

"Oh, come on, Cal. You know I felt like dancing a jig. Let me help you down from there. Really, I couldn't be happier for you." He swung her off the stone slab, giving her a quick kiss. "And as for you, Harding, you old scoundrel—Harding? Harding, where are you?"

"He's gone," Callie said. She wasn't sure how she could tell, but she knew. And with him had vanished all the headstrong magic of their moments together. "Oh, God." Her knees buckled. "God, what have I done?"

"Got rid of that dreary Harry once and for all," Zeus said with satisfaction. "And with Mick Harding, of all people! How, pray tell, did it happen?"

"I don't know." She felt dazed. "He just ... I ... we ... it did."

"You surprise and delight me, sister."

"Zeus, this isn't funny." Harry had been right about that, at least. "The betrothal—all those wedding invitations, and the gifts that have come, and the gowns ..." She thought of Harry's mother, and her insides fluttered. "There will be an awful stink."

"There, you see? You're just not cut out to be a countess; they never say things like that."

"And Father. He'll be so disappointed in me!"

"Father is a big boy. He'll get over it." Zeus put his arm around her and led her toward the inn. Callie suddenly felt cold, frozen inside and out.

"I wish I'd never let him touch me!" she burst out abruptly.

"What's done is done," he soothed her. "It is all for the best."

"Harry was so angry, Zeus. And you heard what he said about getting back—he'll slander me among all his friends."

"You may have ended your chances of finding a suitor amongst his set," her brother acknowledged. "But frankly, Callie, who cares?"

Callie's future, so assured short moments ago, yawned in front of her, vast and empty. What would she do? How would she go on from here? "I've made a dreadful mistake," she sobbed, breaking down completely.

"You've saved yourself from one, rather." Zeus tucked his arm more closely about her. "Chin up, love. Now suppose you explain to me how you wound up out there with Mick Harding."

Oh, God. "I don't want to talk about it," Callie whispered, and fled to her room, going up the back stairs.

9.

When Callie came down to breakfast the following morning, very late and very fearful, the common room was deserted except for her father, who was smoking his pipe, and the inn-keeper's wife, who was clearing the trenchers away. "Mornin', miss!" the woman said brightly. "Ye must have slept well. Bring ye some eggs 'n' porridge, shall I?"

"I'm really not very hungry." Callie tried to read her father's pensive face. How much did he know, and from whom had he heard it?

"A nice cup o' tea, then." Still smiling, she bustled out with her tray. Callie slipped onto a bench as far away from her father as she could, and shuddered as he cleared his throat.

"Well," Professor Wingate said.

"Good morning, Father." Callie suddenly wished she'd asked for food after all, if only to have something to do with her hands.

"Harry came and spoke to me this morning. He told me the two of you are no longer engaged to be wed."

Callie's tea came. She grasped it with both palms, like a lifeline. "Did he say why?"

"He noted only that he had cause to believe your affections

resided elsewhere.'' That seemed fairly mild, Callie thought with relief. ''Do they?'' her father continued.

Harding's taut mouth at her breast, his hand parting her knees . . . Callie quickly took another sip of tea to hide her blush. ''It was more that . . . I realized they didn't rest with him.''

Professor Wingate leaned back in his chair. ''Is there any reason to believe this is just a lovers' spat—that you and Harry will resolve it?''

''Oh, I don't think so.''

Her father let out a sigh. ''Then I suppose we must discuss where we go from here.''

Callie wished she could disappear from the table, be carried off by the innkeeper's wife like one more soiled napkin or sticky cup. ''I'm so sorry, Father.''

''So am I.'' He sounded sad. Callie dared glance at him again, from beneath her lashes.

''You have every right to be furious with me—''

''I'm not sure I do. As I recall, you begged me back in September not to announce the betrothal for another three months. That would have been about now. You must have had doubts even then. I ought not to have forced your hand. There would not be so much mopping up to do.''

Somehow it made it worse that he was being so kind. Someone, somewhere, ought to punish her for her dreadful lapse in reason on that rock last night. But perhaps Harry would. Apparently he'd been discreet enough with her father, though. Of course, he needed a decent mark in Professor Wingate's course to graduate. What a wretched thought, Callie realized— a thought more worthy of Zeus. What she'd done to Harry had been horribly cruel.

And yet some small part of her soul was singing like a bird. *I am free, I am free. . . .* Finished with the countess, with the glum earl, with silly Sarah and Grace—even the numbing thought of all the preparations to be undone, the social ties to be unknotted, could not quell that voice. Zeus was right, she recognized with shock. *I did not want to marry him.* And maybe nothing more than that lay behind her willingness to climb up onto that sacrificial slab with Mick Harding the night before.

She felt a swell of relief race through her with the bracing tea. That was it, of course. She'd sabotaged her own betrothal, seen the opportunity to make certain Harry would not find her suitable for marriage and seized it.

Although it was true, she'd had no way of knowing Harry would show up there.

Still, unconsciously, that must have been what I was thinking, she decided. It was far more comfortable believing that than pursuing the question of why she'd responded to Harding in such an uncharacteristic way.

The innkeeper's wife had come back in with the teapot. Callie suddenly found she felt quite normal—actually, quite famished. "Is it too late for that porridge, Missus Darrow?"

"La, no, pet! Let me just hot it up a bit," the woman said cheerfully, and bustled out again.

"Harry's gone to London, to break the news to his family," her father was saying. "His mother will take care of the official announcement. But you will have to send out notes, of course, and return the gifts." His gaze rested on her ring. "I'm not certain what the proper course of action is in regard to that."

Callie looked down at the glittering opal, hearing Harry's voice: *Some silly folk believe them unlucky* . . . "I'll send it back to him," she decided promptly. Proper or no, she did not want any reminders of this mess lurking in the bottom of her jewelry chest.

"As you wish. And under the circumstances, I think a letter of apology to the countess is called for."

Callie cringed, but nodded. All of this *was* her fault; she could hardly expect not to have to pay. "I'll write it directly, this morning." And after that, the voice inside her was warbling ecstatically, you are free, you are free. . . . Setting down her teacup, she flexed her fingers. She had a sudden urge to grasp a brush and palette with them. "You are being so understanding, Father," she said softly. "More than I deserve."

He shrugged and emptied his pipe. "I've said before, Calliope, all I want is for you to be happy. I would ask, though, that you be more . . . *careful* next time. The university is such a small community. There will likely be a lot of talk. I should not want your reputation to suffer. Whatever the reasons that you've broken it off with Harry, I don't want you branded a flibbertigibbet.''

Such a quaint choice of word—so typical of the professor. She smiled at him. ''Of course, Father. I . . . I've learned a lot from this. Honestly I have.''

He nodded. ''Then there is nothing to regret in it at all, I suppose. I'd best go see how the excavation is coming along. Left to their own devices, those young men might manage to overlook King Arthur's grave. Will you be out to join us, or would you prefer to spend some time alone?''

Callie thought of Harding, stretched out motionless on the cold ground beside the ditch, plying his whisk. It would be awkward to see him, but no less awkward this evening, or tomorrow. And her reaction to him, the emotions he evoked, might help settle in her own mind whether she'd been using him last night to rid herself of Harry, or if there might be something more between them. ''I'll come out,'' she told him, ''just as soon as I finish my letter to the countess. And, Father, thank you so much for not being angry with me.''

He kissed the top of her head on the way to the door. ''It is times like this I feel the lack of your mother most keenly,'' he said ruefully. Then he turned back. ''By the by; I had another early morning visitor today. Mick Harding. He's left us as well. Something about a family obligation he'd let slip his mind. Pity, isn't it? I've come to quite rely on that young man.''

Mrs. Darrow had brought in a tray laden with platters. ''There, then!'' she declared, setting it on the edge of the table. ''I fetched the porridge, and eggs, and a rasher, and toast and jam, too, just in case.

''Thank you,'' Callie said feebly. Her father's news certainly settled the question of how Harding felt toward her, rushing off like a coward, without even the decency to see her again.

Faint-hearted, she surveyed the staggering array of food before her, and found her appetite had, once more, disappeared completely.

10.

"You are moving your lips," Callie said with indignation.

"I am reading Shakespeare." Zeus, reclining on the red velvet sofa that Callie had temporarily spirited away from the upstairs sitting room, grandly turned a page. "*Othello,* to be exact. I like to speak the words as I go. 'Is this the noble Moor whom our full Senate call all in all sufficient? Is this the nature whom passion could not shake? Whose solid virtue—'"

"Very well. I'll portray you with your mouth open, like a jaybird."

Zeus threw the book aside and grabbed an apple from the painstakingly arranged bowl on the table beside him. "But it's so bloody *dull,* lying here hour upon hour without moving!"

"Forty minutes," Callie said, consulting the mantel clock. "And this is only your second sitting."

He let out an anguished groan. "How many do you think it will take?"

Callie dabbed vermilion and violet on her palette, attempting to capture the tone of his jacket. "I don't know. I've never painted anyone from life before."

"Well, can't you make a sketch of me and work from it, the way you did with your savage?"

"That would defeat the purpose. I want to try something new." He'd changed the angle of his arm again. Callie sighed and set down her brush. "Oh, Zeus. I know it is tedious. But you said you would. And you know there's no one else I can ask."

"Only because you are too cowardly to tell Father that you want to try portraits."

Very deliberately, she took up her brush. "Don't you think I've caused Father enough grief of late?"

That silenced him for a good five minutes, during which she did her best to block in the jacket. When he did speak again, it was, for Zeus, quite gravely: "You don't regret it, though."

"I don't regret not marrying Harry, no. But I jolly well regret all the rest of it."

"Mm." He was eyeing the apple in his hand. "For someone who never wanted her son to marry you in the first place, the countess certainly raised quite a brouhaha."

"There's an unattractive phrase; did you hear it in a tavern? If you are thinking of eating that apple, kindly put the notion out of your head. But yes, I found it rather galling that among other things, she demanded Father pay for her daughters' gowns."

"Money well spent," said Zeus, and sneaked a nibble, chewing with tiny motions.

"I wish Father thought so."

"I'm quite sure he does, now that the Godshalls have shown their true colors. Imagine calling on the dean to demand his resignation over something so trivial."

"Father was fortunate the administration didn't cave in, considering the amount of money that family has pumped into Oxford."

"They've had to, to be certain their precious Harry earns his degree."

Callie laughed, which nerved him to take another nibble. "Careful, or I'll paint you with that thing in your mouth, like a suckling pig."

"Well, I for one think it would be worth the loss of Father's post to keep you out of that woman's clutches."

"Don't say that, Zeus. Not even in jest. He lives for his work. He'd be lost without it."

"There *are* other universities, you know."

"Not like this. Not for him."

"I suppose you're right. But that's just his damned snobbishness—which is what nearly got you married to Harry." He was still again for several minutes. "Do you regret the other?" he asked curiously.

"What other?" She was concentrating on his cravat.

"You know. Mick Harding."

She didn't answer at first, partly because he wasn't moving while he was waiting and partly because she wasn't certain what to say. "All in all," she finally responded carefully, "I rather wish there'd been some other engine to the parting of the way between Harry and me."

"Lord, there's a convoluted construction; you ought to sit in on Professor Canning's grammar lectures. What I want to know is, are you sorry you let him kiss you? And . . . whatever else you were doing?"

"Zeus, please." She'd spattered cobalt paint.

"I could challenge him, I suppose."

She laughed out loud. "To what? A war of words? Your knowledge of Greek lyric poetry versus his?"

"Pistols." She looked at him; he seemed serious. "I've been practicing with Toby Lassiter. They're not so hard to handle. I can hit a pie-plate at twenty paces, seven times out of ten."

"Good God, Zeus. If I thought you were in earnest, I'd . . . I'd cut off your hands."

"He offended your honor."

Callie blushed, but decided she'd best scotch that sort of talk for good. "The offense was mutual. He didn't force me, Zeus. It was just . . . it happened. Let's not speak of it."

"I'll give him this: he hasn't."

"Not to anyone you know."

"Oh, no. Not to anyone, I'm quite sure. I've made enough enemies here that if he had, someone would have thrown it up at me."

"I hope you're right." And Callie guessed he truly was— although she found it disconcerting that the passion which had shaken her so much that night should have proven, to Mick Harding, not even worthy of a boast. Cold fish, she thought contemptuously, and then shivered a little, remembering too clearly that his caresses had been anything but cold. Perhaps from the way she'd responded, he thought her loose-moraled, and so despised her. Though that seemed most unfair, really, since she'd only been following his lead. Well, that was the difference between men and women, she supposed. Dorcas had always warned her that, hard though fellows pressed for it, they turned against a girl whose virtue was too easily won. Best to mark it all down, as she'd told Zeus, to something that just happened, some bizarre conjunction of the time and the place and the alignment of the stars . . .

Zeus had risen from the sofa. "Where do you think you're going?" she demanded.

"I've a meeting."

She glanced again at the clock. "At this hour? It's nearly midnight!"

"Can't be helped." He crunched the apple, coming to stand at her side. "Oh, I say. It is coming along nicely. I look useless and degenerate, just as I really am."

Snow was tapping at the windows, pushed by keening winds. "A true degenerate would never venture out on a night like this. Wouldn't you stay? I'll warm some wine—"

"But you wouldn't let me drink it, would you? It would change the angle of my Adam's apple." He kissed her paint-stained cheek. "You can work on the sofa while I'm gone."

"What sort of meeting could you possibly have this time of night?" she demanded, and then caught her breath: "Oh, Zeus! Is it—are you—have you found a girl?"

"Maybe."

"Well, she must not be a very nice one, if she's holding such assignations with you!" she said as he headed for the door.

"Perhaps she's just like you," he said jauntily, turning to blow her a kiss. "Sometimes these things just . . . happen."

"Oh, you!" She stopped just short of hurling the palette after him.

She wondered if perhaps he was only jesting, and had just

been bored with the sitting. But a few minutes later, above the wind, she heard the closing of the front doors. Going to the window, she looked down on the street below and saw her brother pause to pull up the hood of his cloak, then head off in the swirling snow along Magdalen Street.

Thoughtfully, she went back to her canvas. So Zeus had himself a lover. *Lord, I do hope it isn't some tavern-wench,* she mused—*or that if it is, he is properly careful. The last thing Father needs is another scandal right now.*

Still, she found as she mixed tints for the scarlet sofa that she envied him. On a night so raw as this, it would be splendid to lie in your true love's arms . . .

Or in Mick Harding's. The memory of his embraces, suddenly hot in her heart, made her pull the drapes against the snow. She wanted no more reminders of that night, of the way the flakes had drifted around them, covering them, concealing them, drawing forth the stone's submerged warmth beneath their bodies as they lay entwined.

The color was all wrong; it was more like blood than velvet. She thought again of Zeus's wild proposal: *I could challenge him.* . . . She did not want him dead—but oh, Christ, what she would give for some hint, some slight acknowledgement by him of what they had shared!

She'd seen him twice in the month since Avebury. Once, in passing, after a lecture, when her father had hailed him and he'd come to speak to the family—did she only imagine it had been reluctantly? And once, agonizingly, he'd been to dinner at the house with the other students, except of course Harry. He'd been as still and silent as usual, and after the salad course Callie had fled upstairs.

It would be so much easier, she thought, if he'd spoken to her of it, even if he'd laughed and proven rueful, or apologized. But his blue eyes behind his spectacles when she'd seen him had been utterly distant, almost as though he had no memory of that night. If she hadn't known he didn't drink, she might have thought he'd been intoxicated, so drunk he didn't remember what had passed between them. It was damnably awkward, getting no clue whatsoever from him as to what she should feel.

Fool, she told herself. As if his distance isn't message enough; as if it isn't clear how *he* feels about it. It never happened, according to Mick Harding. The fact he'd turned her whole life upside-down was as inconsequential as another squat, ugly Roman pot turned up at a London excavation. That she'd made more of it was her fault, or, rather, Harry's. If his lovemaking hadn't been so distasteful, Harding's would not have proven in such contrast, and she'd not have succumbed to him so readily. I need more experience, she decided. I ought to have asked Zeus if his serving-maid had a stout brother available tonight. Of course, it was different for men; they were expected, even encouraged, to engage in dalliances, even the most unsuitable ones, in order to sow their wild oats before they settled into marriage. But in a woman such behavior would spell certain doom.

She couldn't work in this mood, not even on upholstery. She dutifully cleaned her palette and brushes, draped the portrait, and took off her smock. In the corner stood her painting of the Scottish savage, long since dry, secreted behind a stack of sketches. On impulse she pulled it out and stood it against the wall, standing back to contemplate it.

The passage of time hadn't diminished her opinion. It was magnificent. *He* was magnificent, that nameless soul whose barbaric glory had first impelled her to stretch the limits of her art against her father's will. He stood naked with the axe on his shoulder, reeking of wild manhood, blatant as a god in his masculinity.

She never could regret that she'd painted him. What she did regret, she thought, clawing into her nightdress, was that she'd never find a mate to match him, not among the Harry Godshalls and Mick Hardings of her small, constrained world. If he'd been on that rock, with his bold thighs and sinuous shoulders, she would have opened herself to him in the snow like a Lenten rose.

And what would you have talked of after? she asked herself, nearly laughing. Of the hart he'd slaughtered that morning? How the salmon were running? What insult the neighboring tribe had visited on ours most lately, and how it best might be avenged?

Perhaps of our children. She softened, stretching in her bed amongst linen sheets—not, perhaps, of the quality enjoyed by Lady Godshall, but still quite fine, and ironed by Bea to a mere dozen wrinkles or so. He likely sleeps on skins, she thought, and tried to imagine the tickle of hide beneath her. It was not unpleasant.

Oh, Callie. She flopped over and beat down the pillows, trying not to think of what Zeus might be enjoying that night.

11.

It was the fourth evening in a row that Callie had come down to dinner and found only two places set. Her father was sitting at the table, sipping sherry and perusing the letters page of the *Oxford Gazette*. He smiled when he saw her. "There's a rather pithy piece in here by young Cobham on the corn laws. Did you see it?"

"Not yet. What on earth is Cobham doing writing on the corn laws? I shouldn't think he knew a granary from a grammar."

"You forget, his father is a crofter. And now here he is, contributing to national debate in the pages of the foremost journal of the day. Really, education is a splendid thing."

"Mm. What's for dinner, Mary?" Callie asked the stolid-faced maid who brought the consomme.

"Mousse of salmon, miss."

"Zeus's favorite. Where is he, Father, do you know? He's been quite scarce at meals of late."

The professor was chuckling at his reading. "Oh, tsk, tsk, Cobham; that's quite actionable, really, that bit about Pelham. 'Ready to do anything called for by anyone who has power enough to make himself dangerous'—and yet so nicely put.

He might have a future in politics, that young man.'' Then he looked up at Callie, blinking. ''Did you say something, dear?''

''I asked did you know where Zeus was. He's not joined us at dinner all this week.''

''He told me this morning he had a meeting to go to. Said it would run quite late.''

''Oh.'' Another *meeting*. ''He's been to quite a few of those lately, hasn't he?''

Her father was chuckling again. ''Yes indeed, a *definite* future. 'Together, the two Pelhams seem determined to govern this nation's export policies with all the care they might lavish on a boot-blacking—' '' Callie sighed audibly. As if Professor Wingate would ever be aware of anything so mundane as the fact his son had got himself a lover. He looked up. ''What's that, pet?''

''Your soup is getting cold.''

He eyed his plate. ''So it is.'' Folding the paper at last, he took up his spoon and began to eat. Then, to Callie's astonishment, he brought the subject up himself. ''I shouldn't fret too much about your brother if I were you. This sort of thing's to be expected, isn't it, at his age?''

''I . . . I suppose it is.'' Would wonders never cease? ''Do you know where he goes?'' she asked hesitantly.

''Oh, yes.'' He nodded, swallowing. ''To the Black Hart.''

It was one of the less reputable tavern-houses in town. Callie had never been inside, but she'd passed it often enough, and heard the bawdy songs and laughter that spilled from the doors. ''And you aren't concerned?''

''Why should I be?'' He frowned at the soup. ''There's too much dill, don't you think?''

''It tastes fine to me.'' Since he'd brought it up, Callie felt emboldened to press on. ''But really, don't you think these sort of attachments can prove . . . dangerous?''

''Oh, no. No. Not so long as he's reasonably discreet.''

Callie found herself the slightest bit irate. Her father had been so eager for her to wed a nobleman, but here he was conscioning Zeus's dalliance with a tavern-wench! ''There's the matter of the family's good name,'' she said stiffly.

He eyed her askance. ''Come now, Calliope. Young men

will sow their wild oats. Frankly, knowing your brother, I'm grateful he's chosen to do so in such a time-honored way.''

"Really." Her voice was cool. "I'd no notion your moral scruples were so supple.''

Mary presented him with the salmon mousse. He took a moment to taste it. "Dill again," he said morosely. "Do ask Dorcas to be more light-handed with it, pet, will you? But it's not really a matter of morals, is it? It's more the thrill of adolescent rebellion, running against the established grain. How old is Zeus now—eighteen?"

"Sixteen," Callie said through gritted teeth.

"Well. Starting a bit young, I suppose, but he *is* precocious. All we can do is wait it out. Believe me, any opposition from me would only strengthen his course.''

"I very much wonder would you be so understanding if it were I behaving in such a way," Callie could not help saying.

He glanced up, surprised. "I'd like to think I would, of course. Though that's hard to imagine."

She stabbed at the ethereal mousse with her fork. Life really was unfair. What *was* the male equivalent of a tavern-wench, anyway? She ought to put the professor's expansive mood to the test. Callie had a sudden urge to show him the portrait of the savage, say to him: *Here, look at this! This is the man of my dreams! What would you say if you found me making love to him?*

Oddly, her father's stern face bore a faraway smile. "As I recall, it was in just such a mood of rebellion that I first encountered your mother."

"Father!" Callie cried, appalled. What a comparison to make!

"What? It was. I don't see where there's so much difference between that and Zeus's current affection. Though I rather hope he won't make a lifelong attachment of it.'' And he laughed.

"I'd no idea," Callie said bitterly, "that you thought so little of Mother."

"Thought so *little?* My dear, I've just put her in company with the royal family!"

She stared at him in amazement. "There's a member of the royal family drawing pints at the Black Hart?"

"In a manner of speaking, certainly. Don't you think?"

"In *what* manner of speaking?"

"Well, I daresay the prince pays the rent by now, with as much time as Zeus spends there. Fortunately, the ale is very cheap."

Callie put her hands to her forehead. "The prince? Father, what in the world are you talking about?"

"Why, Charles Edward, of course. The Young Pretender."

"Doesn't he live in France?"

"He did the last I heard. And I trust he'll have the good sense to stay there, despite the shenanigans of Zeus and his friends."

Very dimly, Callie began to see the light at the end of this labyrinth. "You mean . . . Zeus has become a Jacobite."

"I prefer to think he's toying with the notion. Though he does have a tendency to go overboard. That is what we must guard against. I'm contemplating inviting Dr. Tensby to dinner next Friday. He has the most reasoned argument I've heard against another restoration of the Stuart dynasty. But then again, perhaps it would be best not to interfere. Such youthful passions most often burn themselves out." He started. "Oh! I see why you took umbrage when I mentioned your mother. I didn't mean to imply my love for her would have ended—only that it was in the same spirit of wild adventure I went to Scotland in the first place. And of course a Gael was scarcely what my mother had wished for in a daughter-in-law. At the time, as I recall, she was trying to interest me in the young widow of a neighborhood grocer. 'But she comes with a *shop,* William!' I can still hear her say."

"He's a Scot, isn't he? Charles Edward, I mean," Callie said slowly. She was thinking of her savage. Was there some call in her and Zeus of that Northern blood?

"Well, he's the great-great-great-grandson of Mary, Queen of Scots. But since she was half French and at least an eighth English, I should consider the matter of his heritage an open one. Nonetheless, Dr. Tensby believes it is in Scotland that any Stuart uprising will find its most dedicated adherents. Your mother's people always have chafed beneath English rule."

Callie was thinking of her carefree brother. She'd never in

her life heard him voice any political opinion, except for general disgruntlement with the current regime. Everyone said the same sorts of things about George the Second—that he was under the thumb of the Pelhams, that he was German and dull-witted, that through his negligence the great landowners gobbled at the public trough. But for Zeus to become a Jacobite, one of the rabble-rousers who advocated overthrowing the Hanover line—a line brought in from abroad upon the death of James the Second to assure a Protestant succession—really, it was most unlikely. "We aren't even *Catholic,*" she noted plaintively.

"If you ask me, this sort of thing alternates by generation," her father said, wiping his mouth with his napkin. "I bucked the London bourgeoisie by my free-thinking. Where else would Zeus look to rebel against his upbringing but by embracing a return to Papist tradition? But surely you've already considered all this."

Callie, torn from her fantasy of Zeus frolicking with a barmaid, hastened to assure him: "Oh, certainly. Yes."

Mary, seeing they were finished, stepped up to clear their plates. "Cheese or a sweet, sir?" she asked her master.

"Is there dill in the sweet, too?"

Perplexed, she answered, "I don't think so. It's a berry tart."

"I'll just have my port, thank you." He looked down the table at Callie. "Somehow, knowing you've been worried about this makes me wonder if I ought to be taking it more seriously."

Callie, for her part, felt infinitely relieved. Jacobism was naught but talk and more talk, and that, no doubt, was what Zeus liked about it. The Hanover line was entering its thirtieth year. No one of reason could possibly believe in the restoration of the Stuart kings. And she'd no longer be tormented by jealousy of her brother's passion, certainly! "Oh, no, Father. You're right. I'm sure it's just a youthful whim. I'd like the tart, Mary, please."

At Zeus's next sitting, Callie painted swiftly and silently until her brother's fidgeting made further work unproductive. Then she used a pale, creamy ocher to add one detail to the portrait—one that would be easy to paint out again. "That's enough for tonight," she announced.

"Thank God." Zeus stood and stretched his legs. "May I see it?"

"Of course. I'm not one of those portraitists who hides a work from the subject until it is done; I've always thought that an affectation."

He crossed the room to her easel, crunching an apple. "You must be nearly fin—" The apple caught in his throat; he coughed, and she politely pounded his back. "Zounds! What's that you've put in my hair?"

"An ostrich plume. Do you like it?"

"I hate it. I look like some bloody fop!"

"That's odd," she said, wiping her brush on a rag. "It's the same sort of feather Charles the First has in his hair in that portrait we saw at St. Peter's in Rome. I thought that would please you."

His gaze met hers, then slid away. A moment later, he laughed. "So you have found me out. How?"

"Father told me."

His jaw dropped. "Father knows?" She nodded. "And—is he angry?"

"Bemused would be more like it."

"Oh. Well. Of course, he would be. For Professor Wingate, going backward never could be progress."

"I don't see how it could be for anyone," she said gently.

"No? Then you don't have your eyes open, Callie. Haven't you any sense of the mess England is in these days? The poverty and crime in the cities, the corruption in government and the courts, the canker eating away at our sense of morals, our acknowledgement of what is right and wrong. And do you know what it can all be traced to? The fact that a hundred years ago, we killed our rightful king."

"Now, Zeus. You speak of corruption. No one proved more venal in governing than the Stuarts."

"Great men make great mistakes," he told her stubbornly.

"Catholic kings ruling a Protestant people are a recipe for disaster."

"And foreign kings ruling the English are exactly the same."

"The Stuarts had their second chance at the Restoration. If they could not compromise their religious principles sufficiently to accommodate—"

"What king worthy of that title *would* compromise his principles? First you call them venal, and now you accuse them of too much adherence to their faith!"

Callie was astonished and a little embarrassed by his vehemence; her brother was not often so sincere. "Well," she said, and worked her brush through turpentine. "King George is a Stuart, after a fashion. His grandmother Elizabeth—"

"He has no more right to sit upon the throne than a pig— and he is no more fit."

That frightened her. "You mustn't say such things, not even to me! They are certainly treasonable."

"Someone must speak out, before that German swine drags the whole nation down into the mud with—"

"Zeus!" The brush clattered to the floor as she clapped her hands over her ears. "Stop it! I don't like to hear you talk like that!"

"Oh, I'll do more than talk," he murmured with a small, tight smile, "before all this is through. What, pray tell, does Father make of my new avocation?"

She always had been honest with him. "He says it's but a youthful passion, one that will burn itself out."

"Does he?" Again that little smile. The expression, far more than his usual cheery cynicism, made him look old beyond his years; his clear green eyes were bright and intense. "And what do you think?"

"Until Father disabused me of the notion, I thought you'd taken up with a barmaid. I . . . I find now that I wish you had."

He laughed at that. "Poor Callie. You must be worried indeed. But there's no need for it." He patted her shoulder, rather as though she were a child who'd had a nightmare. The gesture irked her.

"No need to worry? From what I gather, you are sitting in a public-house openly discussing the overthrow of the government!"

He dropped his voice to a whisper. "We do so very quietly.

And we keep the shutters well-closed.'' His eyes were twin-kling.

Callie could not remember ever having been so furious with him. "Oh, this is all some sort of grand charade for you, isn't it? A chance to play with pistols and hurl words about, and never mind the consequences to anyone else, to Father or to me!''

His aspect changed abruptly. "No, Callie, it is not a cha-rade," he told her gravely. "I'm afraid I find, to no one's surprise more than my own, that this is a cause in which I believe to the deepest fiber of my being. I have no choice but to follow it. To do otherwise would be to deny my soul.''

"You'd plunge the nation back into the horrors of civil war?''

"A great wrong has been done. It may take further wrongs to correct it.''

"God, Zeus.'' She shook her head. "This is not like you.''

"It is now.'' He kissed her quickly. "I have a meeting to go to.''

"Zeus—'' She put out her hand to him, but he headed toward the door. Halfway there, he turned back.

"I nearly forgot. I have a commission for you.''

"A *what?*''

"A commission to do a portrait. Of Lord Delaney.''

Callie knew him, barely. He was a young dandy she'd seen at concerts and plays. A Catholic, she seemed to recall. "How in heaven's name does Lord Delaney know I paint portraits?''

"I told him, of course. And when he stopped by one day, I brought him up to see your work.''

Callie's gaze flew to the painting of the savage. "Oh, Zeus. You didn't show him . . .'' She trailed off in horror.

"And why not?'' he asked impatiently. "It is your master-piece.''

She was cringing at the thought of anyone viewing that painting, and possibly discerning the stark longing she had put into every brush-stroke. "You had no right to do that!'' she cried angrily. "Don't you ever *dare* bring anyone up here again!''

"I was only thinking of your art, Cal. It's a bloody shame to keep your talents hidden. Lord Delaney was most impressed."

She shuddered. She would never again be able to meet that young man's eyes. And, God in heaven, what if he told his friends? She imagined the whisperings: "Professor Wingate's daughter . . . aye, the redhead . . . this great huge portrait of a naked Scotsman . . . drawn from life, her brother says . . ." It made her want to throw the damned thing on the fire. How could she have been so rash as to paint it in the first place? And Zeus . . . "You betrayed my trust," she said shortly.

"I was trying to do you a good turn."

"Don't do me any more!"

"I'm sorry," he said after a moment. "I didn't know you'd take it so to heart." The clock began to chime, ringing in the eleventh hour. "I . . . I really have got to go."

"Go on, then."

"I will. Don't be angry with me, Cal. It's just that I'm so proud of you."

She looked at him. The strange, fierce light was gone from his eyes; he was once more her little brother, who'd begged her to let him crawl beneath the covers with her when they were children, to stave off the hobgoblins who haunted his sleep. "All right, then," she said grudgingly. "But if you ever, *ever*—"

"I won't," he promised quickly, and blew her a kiss.

But he'd made that vow before. When he was gone, she took a knife and slit the canvas carefully from the frame. But where to hide it? Her constant revisions had made the paint too thick to roll it into a bundle; it had to lie flat.

She eyed her bed; it was the only place big enough. Sandwiching the portrait between two stiff sheets of clean canvas, she slid it under the mattress, against the hard wood frame. She would miss having it about for inspiration, but really, it was safer like this. *And you've always wanted to sleep with him, anyway.* She laughed to herself.

Later that night, when she slipped beneath the blankets, a chill wind was howling at the casements. She thought of the miserable huts that she and Zeus had seen in Ayrshire, and wondered how the Gaels withstood the clime. Her savage—

was he huddled in one tonight, with his wife and children and perhaps a sheep or cow? Or were they in some corner of the ruined manor, surrounded by relics of a distant grandeur they could never understand? She imagined him turning to his wife amongst the heap of skins they used for blankets, the soft breathing of the bairns at their feet no deterrent to his need. He would reach for her; she would submit in silence. And the wind would whistle through the chinks in the walls . . .

Her nipples had gone taut beneath her nightdress. Low in her belly, she felt a stirring of heat at the image in her head. She wished, futilely, that she'd gotten Zeus to ask his name; she would have liked being able to call it out to him in her dreams.

She put a hand to her breast, tentatively brushing its hard tip. That was how Mick Harding had touched her; this was where his mouth had lingered, awakening the fire in her she had never known existed. Now the oddest things could stir it, remind her of the wild wonder she had known at his hands— the cold kiss of a snowflake, the hiss of chill water hitting the hearthstones, the thought of that Gaelic savage coupling with his wife.

Well, half her blood was born to that. If her father hadn't, in his youthful passion, gone to Skye, her mother would have wed a piper or crofter, and their children have been full-fledged Gaels. *I might even have met him,* she thought of her savage, *if that had been my life. Of course, I wouldn't have been me, then; I'd have been half me and half someone else. Or I might not have been at all.*

It was hard to fathom, harder even than Zeus's attachment to the Jacobites, and it made her head spin. She went to sleep, and dreamed of the soft padding paws of wolves against mosaic floors.

12.

"I'd like a word with you, please."

Behind his spectacles, Mick Harding's blue eyes had gone narrow and wary as Callie approached him. Now, as she spoke, he looked about the room as though to find the nearest route for escape. "Here?" he said faintly. "Now?"

All around them, the audience for the recital—two Italian violinists brought in to Christ Church for the evening at the behest of the dean's wife, who was given to foreign influences—was filing through the wide doors toward the refectory, where tea and cakes and sherry would be served. "I don't see why not." Callie was surprised by her own steadiness—but then, she'd rehearsed this innumerable times in the past month, while she'd waited for an opportunity to confront him.

Her father, having reached the doors, had turned to look for her. "Calliope?" he called.

"Go ahead in, Father. Mr. Harding and I have something to discuss." She met his guarded gaze, daring him to deny it. Her father waved and went on, carried by the movement of the crowd.

Though the old stone church was frigid in mid-March, Mick Harding's brow was beaded with sweat. "Miss Wingate. Calliope.'' Her expression forced another correction. ''Miss Wingate. You are right, of course. I should have spoken to you before now—''

''Mr. Harding. If you've any notion this is in reference to a certain highly regrettable incident now several months past, you may disabuse yourself of it.''

''I may?'' he echoed, looking simultaneously relieved and perplexed.

''Oh, most certainly. I haven't given it another thought.'' That had sounded right while she practiced; now, suddenly, she wondered if it made her sound promiscuous, to dismiss it that way. But it was too late for corrections in her script; she was far too nervous to proceed spontaneously. ''This concerns my brother.''

If he'd looked relieved before, he now appeared absolutely giddy. ''Zeus?'' he said, and his voice cracked.

''I haven't any other, have I?''

''No. No, you haven't.'' He touched her arm. ''Shall we . . . would you like to sit?''

He must not touch her again; that had nearly unnerved her. If there had been any other student she could have been sure of, she never would have confronted him. But Toby Lassiter was the only name Zeus had mentioned, and he was too close to Harry. If their pistol-practice together had no bearing on the subject, she didn't dare arouse Lassiter's suspicions. It had to be Harding, alas. Slight though the brush of his hand on her elbow had been, she had felt a tremor surge through her. Dammit, Callie, this is for Zeus, she thought, and steeled herself. ''I prefer to stand.''

''As you wish.'' He waited. Callie did, too, for Doctor Canning and his wife to circle around them as they stood in the aisle. Perhaps I ought to take him up on his offer, Callie thought; she'd forgotten, as she always did, how tall he was when one stood beside him. Only his quality of stillness, that strange, unmoving repose, made him seem smaller, inconsequential, really, from further away. But it was too late now.

She took a breath. ''I'm sure that in many ways it is very gratifying for you and your friends to have ensnared Zeus.''

He blinked behind the spectacles. ''My *friends?*''

An odd word for him to have seized on. "Well. Your fellow conspirators, or however you prefer to think of yourselves."

"Miss Wingate—"

"Let me finish." But he'd thrown her concentration off. She gathered it again, squeezing her hands into tight fists. "For young men who have naught to lose—or so much that they can afford it—this no doubt seems an innocent frolic. But Zeus isn't like that. For one thing, he's much younger than the rest of you, though it's easy to forget that, I grant you, from the way he acts. The point is, it simply isn't fair to involve him. Especially, I should think, for someone like you, who has taken such pains to gain my father's good graces." She blushed. That, too, hadn't been in her script. But she couldn't help thinking He'd not be in Father's good graces if I'd opened my mouth about that night on the rock. Come *on,* Callie! "You ought to be ashamed of yourself," she finished rather lamely.

He passed his hand over his brow, pushing back his heavy black hair. "Miss Wingate. I regret to say I'm at an utter loss as to what you are speaking about."

"Don't you pretend with me!" she hissed in fury, and then composed herself as a passing student eyed her curiously. "I am speaking about your damned Stuart rebellion."

"My Stuart—oh, my dear Miss Wingate." To her chagrin, he laughed. It was a lovely laugh, honestly amused, not at all mocking. "I very much fear you have mistaken your man."

She hadn't meant to bring this up, she honestly hadn't, but his show of innocence provoked her. "In light of how abominable your behavior toward me has been, you might at least have the decency to be truthful! I'm not about to give away your secret. I only ask that you discourage Zeus in his enthusiasm." Lord, now she'd offered up a quid pro quo, her silence for his letting Zeus go, when she'd been so determined not to let that wretched night of excess interfere. She imagined how she must appear to him: desperate, overprotective as a mother hen.

At least he'd stopped laughing. The expression in his azure eyes, or so she imagined through those thick lenses, was pitying. "Miss Wingate," he said, his voice very low. "I glean from this disjointed conversation that your brother has embraced the Jacobite cause. You have my condolences for that. But I assure you, I have no more interest or concern in politics than a flea in a fish.''

"You're Scottish, aren't you?" she demanded.

"I do hope in your painting you don't employ so broad a brush. What if I am? Coincidence of birth ought not to brand a man a rebel.''

For the first time, Callie felt a twinge of doubt. "You don't espouse the Young Pretender's cause? Everyone says, especially Doctor Tensby, that Charles Edward's support in the event of rebellion will come from the North." Her father *had* had the professor to dinner; unfortunately, Zeus had been to a meeting. But Tensby's scholarly dissection of the Jacobites had certainly convinced Callie that they must be mad. Initial resentment of the Hanovers' foreign ancestry had long since faded among the vast majority of the English. Even the excesses of Lord Pelham and his brother, with their highhanded manipulations of the Parliament, were not enough to urge a return to Stuart despotism amongst sensible men. At least, that was what Tensby said.

"Miss Harding. My field of study is ancient Greece. Whatever weak devotion I can summon to any cause rests there—with Aristotle and Sophocles, with men of rational thought. My long-held belief that such thought died out centuries ago is only reinforced by my homeland's absurd history. Have you any idea what the burning question in Scottish politics has been over the past fifty years? How the election of bishops ought to be governed. Does this seem the sort of nation equipped to overtake English might?''

There was no doubting his sincerity, even for Callie. *Cold fish,* she thought, remembering her earlier instincts. He doesn't care about anyone or anything, not in the present day. And that jibed perfectly with how he'd treated her: *as though it never happened.* For him, she thought, withering inside at her mistake, it didn't. He doesn't give a damn.

And now her mistake had compromised Zeus. Inside her heart, she panicked. But to a man like this, a man lacking in emotion, she dared not show vulnerability. She forced her own laugh, and not a bad one. "Dear me. I have been foolish." She met his eyes, bravely, not quavering. "I do hope, Mr. Harding,

I have your assurance of confidentiality in this matter.'' He owed her that, dammit. Hadn't she proved discreet?

He was smiling, shaking his head. ''If you imagine me trotting off to tattle to the Crown that your brother is a traitor, you truly do misunderstand me. I don't care if Zeus raises the standard for the sultan of Araby; it doesn't touch me.''

Nothing did, did it? ''Thank you,'' Callie said, and fled from him, to where her father was waiting with almond cakes and tea. God help him, Mick Harding was a most unnatural soul.

13.

The air that night was cold enough to set a cap of ice across the cobblestones, but the breeze in the afternoon had brought the first promise of spring: a westerly breeze, soft as crocus petals, silky on one's face like Aegean wool. Mid-March, Mick Harding thought in disgust, his boots crunching across Magdalen Street. In Greece, windflowers would already be covering the hills in a sweet blue haze.

He wanted to be there, in the bright harsh light of Mediterranean sunshine, in that land where there was stone and wood and scrub grass and very little else, where nights were briefer and, God knows, warmer, and could be spent in the anonymity of some small taverna, drinking black coffee made thick with sugar and devouring Aeschylus or Euripides. To sit surrounded by swart, bickering men who downed cup after cup of noxious turpentine-scented wine and wonder how in the gods' names such a race could have produced the greatest thinkers ever known on earth. Aye, that was what he wished he were doing. For that matter, he thought, catching himself as his boot heel skidded on the stones, he would prefer to be doing practically anything at this moment other than what he was, which was heading for the most notorious inn at Oxford on this bitter night.

The sign of the Black Hart groaned on its chains, sounding like an augur of doom. The windows were unnaturally bright, long rectangles of yellow lamplight in the winter gloom. The door swung open, letting out a burst of voices and two men so drunk they had to cling to one another on the icy cobbles. The stench of beer struck him like a blow as they passed.

He hesitated, the hood of his cape drawn up to ward off the lamplight. I must be mad, he thought, his legs actually aching to turn and take him home, to the solace of his small scholar's room lined with books, and the chair—too short, too hard, but blessedly familiar—by the window facing east that caught first light. That had been a break, to get that window; it served to cut down considerably on his expenses for candles. But none of his housemates, those so-called students who spent their nights carousing in places like the Black Hart, had seen any advantage in a room that confronted the dawn.

He pictured again Zeus's thin, intense face that afternoon as the boy had asked him—begged him, really—for this meeting. "It won't take but a moment of your time," Zeus had insisted.

"Then let's talk here."

"No. No, I can't. Just be at the Black Hart at eleven." Then he'd darted off, like the gadfly he was, back to the loud, cheery company of his friends who were leaving the lecture, rejoining their argument without a pause, in midstream.

He'd never known a family like the Wingates, had not imagined such families existed. He remembered crossing the threshold of their house last September for that first supper and surveying with astonished eyes the hodgepodge of artwork on the walls, the bits of bone and statuary lining tabletops and mantels, inhaling the mingled smells of dry earth and linseed oil and roasting lamb, and thinking, *So this is a home.* It was a revelation to a man raised in the drab, interchangeable interiors of Presbyterian rectories.

And they were so at ease with one another—the professor and his children. He recalled catching the girl's wordless appeal to her brother at some juncture, and the way Zeus had instantly risen to his feet to come to her aid. He remembered the professor basking in pride as he watched his daughter. He'd never in his life seen an expression like that in his own father's eyes.

Well, best not to think of his father just now, as he was about to violate one of the old man's sternest precepts and set foot in the Black Hart. Perhaps it was sheer perversity—"Dinna e'er let me hear, Michel, that ye hae ta'en up the woeful sin o' drinkin'!"—that had made him leave the sanctuary of his room this night. Or perhaps it had been Zeus's unaccustomed expression, the previously unglimpsed solemnity with which he'd made his plea. Mick had seldom seen him with anything but a sneer on his very young face.

Or perhaps he felt he owed the fellow's sister a debt. He veered away from that thought with a force that propelled him through the Black Hart's door.

Inside, he blinked, lamplight bombarding his glasses. The place was thronged; he saw a sea of faces turn to view the newcomer, determine if he was a friend, and then return to mugs of ale. His back stiffened. If I've no comrades among you, he thought, it is only because I've better ways to make use of my time. Rich men's sons, content to squander away these priceless years of learning . . .

But they were not all rich men's sons. He glimpsed James Cobham's carrot-red head amongst the crowd, and took a step toward him. He liked Cobham, admired his mind, wished he knew some way to tell him so.

"Well. See who's here."

The low, silken voice drew Mick's chin up. It was Toby Lassiter, seated next to John Ormond, who had his boots perched on the table. "Hallo, Lassiter," he said cautiously.

Ormond leaned forward abruptly, boots thudding onto the floor. "I told Toby once I'd do a jig stark naked if I ever saw you stand a body to a pint, Harding." His voice had its familiar well-groomed drawl. "Care to make a dancer of me?"

"Not tonight, thanks."

"Skint as any Scotsman," he heard Ormond murmur with contempt.

Mick hoped the cold night's ruddiness would hide his flush. "Seems to me you've pints enough," he told the earl, pushing up his spectacles to eye the row of empty mugs on the table. "I might buy you a book, though. That would be more to the point."

"Ooh," Lassiter cooed, laughing as he cocked his head to look up at Mick.

Ormond was unperturbed. "The library at my estate contains four thousand volumes. I rather doubt anything you might afford, Harding, could amplify it."

Mick could picture that library, long rows of books in rich leather covers embellished with gold—and likely the pages sitting still uncut. He contemplated mentioning that, then reconsidered. Men as wealthy and petty as Ormond were dangerous. Why the devil had he acquiesced to Zeus Wingate's invitation to this damnable place?

"Mick! Mick!" He heard the hail and saw Zeus standing on a bench in the back of the room, waving madly. Grateful, he made a bow to his tormentors.

"I'm sure you're right. Good evening, gentlemen." He moved toward Zeus, shoulders braced against the Parthian shot he was certain would come.

And it did, from Ormond. "Such admirable manners," he told Lassiter nonchalantly. "Of course, courtesy can be acquired free."

Mick kept walking. There wasn't sense in doing anything else.

Zeus's smile was honest and shyly surprised as he shook Mick's hand. "I wasn't sure you were coming. I know you don't frequent this sort of establishment. Can I buy you something?"

"I don't drink."

"They have cider, or coffee."

"I can't stay long," Mick said, more brusquely than he'd meant to.

"Certainly. As you wish. But I do appreciate your coming. You know Cobham, of course. And this is Lord Delaney—"

"Edmund," said the young man being introduced, extending his hand. Mick shook it, too, with a feeling that he was surrounded.

"And Zachary Fleming, and Eral Thinnes—" Zeus went around the table, while Mick stood awkwardly, wishing more than ever that he'd stayed at home. "And Duncan Farquar. One of your countrymen," Zeus finished, beaming.

A thick-necked Scot, poorly dressed, his handshake firm and

earnest, Farguar was just the sort of fellow, Mick thought wryly, that gave Ormond ammunition for his jibes. And his accent was thicker than his neck. "Pleased I bae, Master Harding, to meet ye, especially in light o' wha' Zeus here has turned up." He made room for Mick beside him on the bench.

Mick remained standing. "And what, pray tell, has Zeus turned up?"

"Do you know, Harding, it is the most astounding thing. I'm not sure you recall that at Father's introductory dinner back in September, Cal and I mentioned a ruined manor we'd stumbled on in Ayrshire."

"Who?" said Mick.

"My sister. Callie." Zeus eyed him oddly.

"Oh. No. I can't say I do."

"No? Well, no reason why you should. But it was the most fantastic place, half mosque, half Norman fortress, beetling out over this great huge desolate cliff high above the sea. Anyway, Cal and I brought Father back there the next day. He was as intrigued as we were, couldn't figure what to make of it. I can't really describe—" He searched the top of their table, which was littered with papers. "But here, you can see. Callie made a sketch of it." Mick took the drawing he was handed, examined it without comment, and passed it back the same way. "Father was so intrigued, in fact," Zeus went on, "that he set Duncan here, and Zachary, to researching the house for a term project. They've spent the past six months up at Edinburgh and Scone and Perth, combing through old records and histories."

"You have my sympathies," Mick told the two students.

"Ach, 'twar nae sae bad as that," Duncan said comfortably. "The Scots bae nae much for the keepin' o' records, as nae doubt ye ken."

"And wait till you hear what they found out," Zeus said excitedly. "Go on. Tell him, Zach."

Zachary Fleming, thin and soft-spoken and so unassuming one would never have guessed he was heir to a dukedom, smiled shyly at Mick. "May I say first, Mr. Harding, how very greatly I enjoyed reading your abstract on the war with Xerxes, which Zeus was kind enough to share with me."

"Thank you," Mick said briefly. He was getting impatient, and wished he'd sat down.

"Come *on,* Zach." Zeus was itchy as a three-year-old with a secret.

"I am getting to it." Fleming took a notebook from the mess on the table. "Duncan and I have more work to do, of course. But as it stands now, we've traced ownership of the house, Langlannoch, back through the fifteenth century. It seems there were two branches of the ancestral family, and ownership of the manor bounced back and forth between them. In addition to the idiosyncrasies of Scottish inheritance customs, with which I'm sure you're familiar, the situation was further complicated by a number of lawsuits and yet another branch of the family hailing from France. The senior line, which held the house most often up until 1521, was surnamed Faurer. That's French, too, of course, though we haven't been able to dig back deep enough to find the founder of the family's fortunes. Someone on the family tree, somewhere, must have been a crusader or married an Arab princess; the Moorish details of the architecture, or what's left of it, are absolutely authentic. And there's a mosaic floor in the great hall that's every bit as fine as the ones at Ravenna, though nonrepresentational, interestingly, in the Muslim fashion."

"Interesting indeed," Mick said dryly as Fleming turned a page in the notebook. "I do hope there's lots more."

Zeus murmured something in Fleming's ear, and Fleming flipped ahead in his notebook. "A separate branch of the family," he read, "which occupied the manor for the following century or so, was surnamed Harding." They all looked at Mick.

"Harding," Zeus repeated with emphasis. "That's your name."

"So it is. Mine and several thousand other Scotsmen's."

"Read him the part about the Berkeleys," Duncan suggested.

Fleming searched his notes. "Ah. Here it is. 'A legend current in Ayrshire claims the name Harding was brought to Langlannoch by a cadet son of the English Earl of Berkeley who married into the family early in the fifteenth century.'"

They were all looking at him again, like a circle of small,

sincere owls. Mick fought back an urge to laugh. "Am I . . .
missing something here?" he asked delicately.

Zeus leaned forward in his seat. "Don't you see, man? You
could be related!"

"I suppose I could be," he shrugged.

Fleming thrust the notebook at him. "There's much more
here than I read. All sorts of heroic tales of the family. Some
of them date back as far as the fifteenth century. There's one
Lord Faurer who singlehandedly roused the populace of the
Isles to defend their lands against incursions by Henry the
Eighth. And the women! There are nearly as many stories about
them. They're said to have the power of healing—their enemies
say of witchcraft. Duncan tracked down a portrait of one of
them hanging at Blackfriars in Perth."

"The fairest lady," Duncan interjected, his round face
dreamy, "that I e'er hae seen. Hair black as midnight, skin
white as roses, breasts like—"

"And just what," Mick broke in, "has become of this illustrious clan?"

"They've died out," said Fleming.

"Wait!" Zeus cried. "We don't know that! You and Duncan
still have research to do."

"Well, there's little question about the Faurer branch, at
least," Fleming noted. "We can document that the inheritance
passed to the Harding line in 1521, when the last Faurer died
without issue. He'd wed a MacShane from Portree," he added
as an aside to Mick, "and she drowned on their honeymoon.
He never married again. That's the sort of family it was. Everything to extremes."

"They must have been charming houseguests," Mick murmured. "But really, I fail to see what any of this has to do
with me."

Zeus took a breath. "We thought, that is, I thought, well,
Fleming and I did, really, that you might like to examine more
closely the possibility that you're related to these Langlannoch
Hardings. Since they're so very noble and famous."

"Since they are," said Mick, "don't you think someone,
sometime, would have mentioned it to me if we were kin?"

"These Scottish clan histories are extremely complicated,"

Fleming told him, frowning. "What with all the intermarriage, the difficulties in transliterating names from Gaelic, the arbitrary systems of recording dates, familial connections get lost all the time. It wouldn't be at all surprising, really, for you not to know."

"Gude Laird, man." Duncan Farquar's eyes were round and shining. "Ye might e'en be the heir to the place!"

"And what would that get me?" Mick asked curiously. "You say yourselves the manor's a ruin. Is there a title?"

"Not beyond the lairdship," Fleming acknowledged.

"A fortune?"

The English earl's son laughed at that. "No, no. There were lands, but they've been sold off. And any chattels besides the house itself have long since disappeared."

"Well, then." Mick spread his hands. "I fail to comprehend—"

"You're a man of history, Mick," Zeus said urgently. "This place can't help but intrigue you. Duncan and Edmund and I are planning to do some further research on the house, perhaps some excavations, this summer. You could come with us—"

"I'll be in Greece. I leave the first week in May."

"Oh. Pity. But still, before you go you could file suit in the Orphans Court. Do they have an Orphans Court up there, Duncan?"

"Orphans 'n' Widows, aye."

"Of which," said Mick, "I'm neither."

"Oh, that's just what they call it. It's for anyone, really, with a claim for an inheritance."

Behind his glasses, Mick's gaze narrowed. "It's rather a far leap, isn't it, from 'you may be related' to filing a claim for the property?"

Cobham spoke up. "You want to get your claim in there first, though, Harding, just in case there are others."

"Bludy right," Farquar confirmed. "Strike while the iron bae hot."

There was still space on the end of the bench by the Scotsman. Mick folded his legs and slid them under the table; it was a tight fit. He put his elbows on the plank, curled his fists, and leaned his chin on them, closing his eyes. "Let me see, now," he murmured, rocking back and forth a little. "Let me just see. What you're after is the claim, which would provide an excuse for you to be poking around that property. But you could have that just as well, Zeus, with a letter from your father or the dean to the local constabulary. You'd only need me if for some reason you didn't want to trouble either your father or the authorities."

"I told you, Zeus," Cobham muttered, "that this wouldn't work; he is far too—"

"Hush, James." Zeus leaned in so close that his high forehead nearly brushed Mick's. "Very well, then. Here it is in a nutshell. We'd like to file that claim in your name to give us access to the place. There's a decent natural harbor just off the cliff, and the surrounding countryside is next to deserted. We want to run in arms and men there to—"

"Christ, Zeus!" Fleming cried, jumping up and clapping a hand over his friend's mouth.

Zeus yanked it off. "Support the Stuart cause." Defiantly he met Mick's gaze.

"Sure 'n' we bae done for now," Farquar groaned, slipping down on the bench.

"Why do you assume that, Duncan?" Zeus demanded. "Mick has two choices. He can turn us in to the Crown—"

"Though frankly," Cobham put in, "we'd rather you didn't."

"Or he can give us what we ask. So. How about it, Harding? Which will it be?"

One by one, Mick considered the circle of faces, some openly apprehensive, others, like those of Zeus and Cobham, preternaturally calm. He'd grown accustomed to the din in the tavern, and now despite the clink of mugs and deep shouts of laughter he could hear, or imagined he could hear, their heartbeats racing like wild drums.

Slowly, Mick pushed himself to his feet. "You neglected to mention my third choice."

"Which is?" Zeus asked eagerly.

"I can do nothing. I can go back to my rooms, to the extremely interesting volume of Plato I've been reading, pour myself a cup of water, drink it, and wash this evening away."

"You will nae turn us in?" Farquar asked anxiously.

"For what? For being idiots? Even at Oxford, I've never heard of that being against the law."

"But you won't join us, either," Zeus said slowly.

"Good God, no. I'd sooner join in at cricket—and you've no notion how I detest sports."

"You've got to be for one side or the other." That was Cobham, taut and curt. Mick wagged a finger at him.

"Master Cobham, you disappoint me. I was wont to think from reading those epistles you pen to the *Gazette* that you were a rational man. I am under no constraint to be anything at all. I won't turn you in because I don't give a damn, and I won't join you for that same reason. Now, if you'll excuse me, Plato is waiting." He made a small bow and turned to go. At his back he heard Farquar snarl:

"Why, ye traitorous scum, I ought to—"

"That's enough, Duncan," Zeus said quietly as Mick walked away.

He had an intuition that Zeus might follow him, and so he hurried his steps, slipping and sliding recklessly across the frozen cobblestones down Magdalen Street. Quick though he went, Zeus was quicker. He must have cut through somebody's garden, for he was waiting by Mick's front steps. He looked slight and small in his overgrown great-coat, like a boy who'd swiped his father's clothes. Mick sighed when he saw him, and started 'round to the back gate.

"Wait! Please wait." Mick didn't, so Zeus came skidding after him along the icy walk. "I suppose you think we're all idiots—"

"Didn't I make that clear?"

"And perhaps we are. Cobham *told* us it was a mistake to approach you—"

"You ought to have listened."

"Well, you know what Heywood wrote: Naught venture, naught have. I didn't come after you to change your mind. Really I didn't." They were almost to the kitchen door. Mick felt him catch his cloak. "But I do want to explain—it isn't just for the harbor that I thought you might want to do this. This house—Langlannoch—it's like something out of a dream.

It's rather hard to know what to compare it to. It just rises out
of the rocks there like some barbarous temple. And the gardens,
all overgrown and lush, like Eden after the Fall. It's nothing
but a shell, that's true, but it has a way of seizing the imagination.'' Mick was staring at him stolidly. ''I'm telling you the
truth, man! It does! Duncan and Zach felt it, too! It's as though
there's some great story, some romance, knit into the very
stones themselves. Dammit, I am not explaining it well. But
Callie made a painting of it. She managed to capture its spirit.
I wish you could see that.''

Mick let go of the door latch. ''Perhaps I should.''

''I can't show it to you. I promised.'' At Mick's raised
eyebrow, Zeus went on to explain. ''There's a man in it, this
sort of wild heathen we saw there, and he's naked. She's worried
for her reputation. You know how women are. They think they
have to be so careful—'' He stopped abruptly, flushing, as
though he'd just remembered seeing Mick with her on the rock.
''And perhaps she's right. I mean, she is a good girl, a nice
girl.'' He stopped again, torn. ''But it's a shame. Because the
picture is a masterpiece.''

''I would be curious to see it. I am a great admirer of your
sister's talent.''

''I wish I could show it to you. But I did promise. I just
don't dare . . .''

''You might ask her to let me see it.''

''Oh, no, she'd never—she wouldn't show it to you!'' Zeus
giggled nervously.

''Mm. Pity. But it doesn't really matter. It wouldn't change
my mind.''

''I don't suppose you have a brother with Jacobite tenden-
cies?'' Zeus asked, only half jesting. ''Or perhaps a cousin?''

Mick shook his head. ''It's just my father and me. And he
is even further removed in sympathies from your cause than I
am. If that's possible.''

''I see.'' Despite his disappointment, some of Zeus's innate
high spirits were reasserting themselves. ''Well, we'll just have
to find ourselves another Harding, one more pliant. As you
said, it's not an uncommon name.''

''If you want my advice, you'll stay away from the place.''

There was a sharpness to Mick's tone that made Zeus look up. "Will I? Why?"

"It's in Ayrshire, you said?" Zeus nodded. "I'm not much acquainted with that part of the country, but I do know the West Scot Gaels can be wild. There's more than one instance of them massacring English travelers. They don't like strangers. They stick to their own kind."

"I've heard that too. But I imagine we'll look harmless enough, a handful of Oxford boys with notebooks and shovels. Thanks for the warning, though."

"If you're wise, you'll heed it."

"Oh, I never claim to be wise. Do you . . . will you really keep our secret?" It was Mick's turn to nod. "Well. I appreciate that. More than I can say. Really, all of us do."

"It seems the least I can do, since anyone with sense knows the Young Pretender's supporters won't have long to live if they're ever fool enough to bring him over the Channel."

"What I love about history," Zeus told him, grinning, "is its way of defying sense. Enjoy your Plato."

"What?"

"You said you were reading Plato."

"Ah. So I am." Zeus held out his hand, and after a moment Mick grasped it. "Good night."

"Sleep tight!" Zeus sang out, and trotted off down the walk, dancing a little from one side to the other to warm his feet. Mick watched him go until the blackness swallowed his fair hair. Then he set his key to the boarding-house door and slipped inside. The kitchen smelled of cabbage and mutton, appropriately cheap. He groped his way up the back stair to his room, lit the candle, and sat in his chair, looking out over the sea of rooftops cresting and waning beneath the thick-spread stars. Well, I was certainly wrong about that, he thought, and started to laugh. Despite his earlier misgivings, it had proven to be a very interesting evening indeed.

14.

Callie knew the moment she turned the door-latch. Behind her, Zeus was burbling happily about the atrocious revival of Otway's *Venice Preserved* they'd just witnessed, and her father was grumbling that he'd found a hole in his favorite glove. James Cobham, whom Zeus had asked to the play, was knocking his walking stick against the curbstones, and someone's coach rumbled by in the road so fast that all of them jumped. But as Callie told the constable who came later, the moment she turned the door-latch she felt something just wasn't right.

"Come on, Callie," Zeus urged her, "don't leave us standing here when we might be having a sherry." When she still didn't move, he gave her a bit of a shove. "Daydreaming again, are you?"

"Hush!" she said sharply, peering into the vestibule. The lamp beside the doors to the drawing room cast faint, flickering shadows along the crowded walls and tabletops.

By now, even Professor Wingate had noticed the delay. "For heaven's sake, Calliope, don't stand there blocking the way!" He started to push past her, and she grabbed his arm.

"Father, don't! They may still be inside!"

"They? They who?"

"Look there!" She pointed to the end of the hallway.

Zeus, craning, demanded, "Look at what?"

"At the umbrella stand!"

"Aye, there it is!" he said cheerily.

"Don't you see? It's been knocked over!"

"Has it? I suppose it has."

It took Cobham to make sense of what she was saying. "You think there's been an intruder?" he asked.

"I most certainly do!"

"Oh, honestly, Cal." Zeus laughed. "What have we got to steal?"

"I don't know, but I'd swear on my life someone's been in here. Look at the tables! Everything on them has been moved—shifted all about."

"A marauding redecorator," Cobham said dryly, wryly, and Callie turned on him.

But before she could speak, her father noted briskly. "Well, there's one sure way to find out. Dorcas! Dorcas!"

"It's her night out," Callie told him.

"Oh. Who's in, then?"

"Bea or Mary. Mary, I suppose."

"Mary! Mary!" the professor called into the echoing house.

The lengthy silence that followed unnerved even Zeus. "You don't reckon they've done her harm," he said uncertainly. "Perhaps we ought to fetch the—"

But there she was now, coming toward them with stolid, unhurried steps, reaching for Professor Wingate's coat. "Evenin', sir. Hope you enjoyed the show."

"Yes, yes. It was dreadful. Mary, has anyone been here in our absence?"

The girl's dark, disinterested eyes blinked. "Here, sir? You mean—in the house?"

"No, in the hemisphere," Zeus muttered, rolling his eyes.

Callie nudged him. "Yes, Mary. In the house. You see, the stand there is overturned."

Mary looked at it. "So it is. Now, how could that be?"

"You've been here all the time we were gone?" the professor asked, and she nodded.

"Aye, sir, every minute of it."

"And you heard nothing odd—no strange noises?"

"Not a peep. Mind, sir, after I'd got the washing-up done I sat by the fire, 'n' I may have drifted off a bit, but there's no harm in that, I hope." Her gaze shifted toward her mistress.

"No, Mary, of course not," Callie told her. Now she looked again, the girl did have an air of being just roused from sleep. Her hair was tousled, and her cheeks had more color in them than they usually did.

Zeus had crossed to the drawing-room doors and stepped inside to light the lamps. They saw the glow of light, then he reappeared. "Nothing amiss in there. I'll check the other rooms. All of you, wait here."

"Oh, Zeus. If anything is out of place, what makes you think you'll notice?" Callie demanded.

"Mm. Perhaps you're right. You'd best all come with me. Mary, do pop out to the stables and have Joe run and bring the constable, will you?"

"But what should he tell him?"

"That we think there's been an intruder, of course."

"An intruder!" Mary's bland face looked almost animated. "An intruder here! Imagine that."

They found no more evidence of a break-in until they came to Zeus's study. That had been fairly well ravaged; books were tumbled from the shelves, and the drawers of his desk were turned out. "Good Lord," whistled Cobham.

"Don't touch anything," Professor Wingate warned as his son went to straighten the mess of papers. "We'd best leave it all the way it is for the constabulary."

Just then they heard his knock at the door. "I'll bring him up," Callie offered, and hurried downstairs.

The officer of the peace was burly and brawn and, Callie thought, reassuring in his very presence. He went through the house from top to bottom, with her accompanying him, then sat them all down in the dining room and accepted Callie's offer of a cup of tea.

"Well! You say nothing's missing," he noted cheerily, nodding four times for sugar. "More'n likely 'tis no more than someone's notion of a lark. Unless—would you say, sir, you have enemies?"

"Only intellectual ones," Professor Wingate said, and laughed. His rooms had been untouched, even though a highly valuable Etruscan statuette had been in plain view on his credence. Of course, as Zeus had remarked, to steal it one would have to have known what it was.

The officer turned to Callie. "Beggin' pardon for my forwardness, mum, but—any disappointed suitors?"

"Hah!" Zeus crowed, highly amused. "Can you imagine Lord Harry—"

"No, not really," Callie told the constable, glaring at her brother.

"Are you quite sure? This is the sort of petty shot at revenge we often see in that sort of thing."

"Quite. That was some time ago. And he's a gentleman—not the type of man to trespass."

"Oh, mum, you'd be surprised the kinds of things we see. I know the gentry grumbles 'bout how the universities these days be open to anyone—but God's truth, we've more trouble wi' the blue-bloods than wi' the good honest boys from the lower classes." He glanced quickly at Cobham. "Beggin' your pardon, sir."

"Oh, I am lower-class," the student hastened to assure him.

"Hmph! Glad to hear of that."

"What puzzles me," Zeus mused, "is how the fellow got *in*. You're quite sure, Cal, that the door was locked."

"Absolutely."

"No mystery there," the constable said briskly. "More'n likely he just strolled in the kitchen door."

"But Mary was here," Callie protested.

The constable leaned toward her. "La, they all say that," he hissed conspiratorially, "but when it comes down to't, they were busy wi' Tom or Dick or Johnny, if you know what I mean."

"Not our Mary," Callie said firmly.

He looked for a moment as though he'd dispute it. Then he let it pass. "Well. I'll make my report to the captain, then," he said, draining his cup, " 'n post a man to watch the house—"

"Oh, surely that's not necessary," Professor Wingate demurred.

" 'Tis the safety of your family, sir, I have in mind."

"Nonetheless. As you said earlier, I've no doubt this was only a prank. A few neighborhood boys out for a bit of havoc, nothing more."

"Still, Father," Zeus began, "don't you think—"

He broke off as the professor looked at him with unaccustomed sharpness and said firmly, "No guards. It isn't necessary. I'm quite certain it was only a prank."

The constable nodded, getting to his feet. "I'd have a talk wi' that Mary," he muttered in passing to Callie, "if I was you."

When the front doors closed behind the man, Zeus turned to his father. "I do think you are being a bit cavalier," he said with reproach. "If you won't think of yourself, you might at least think of Callie."

"Actually, my boy, I was thinking of you when I turned down the constable's offer."

"Of *me!*"

"Well, of you and your friends. While for obvious reasons I neglected to mention it to that gentleman, I can think of one very good reason for an unknown person or persons to enter this house and conduct what was evidently a fairly thorough search of your personal effects. Can't you?" Zeus stared at him with wide green eyes.

"My God," Cobham muttered, just as Callie realized it, too.

"Up until now," the professor continued, "I was inclined to look upon your flirtation with the Jacobite cause benignly. As I told your sister, boys will be boys. If, however, your activities have been sufficiently lacking in discretion to attract the attention of agents of the Crown and tempt them to ransack my house, I believe myself justified in demanding that you find other living quarters. In the meantime, I'll not have a constable posted outside to record your comings and goings. Calliope, have Mary bring sherry to me upstairs. Good night." He strode from the room, pausing at the door just long enough to sniff, "Cavalier with your sister's safety, indeed!"

Zeus's jaw was hanging open. Cobham was laughing quietly.

"Well! The old man is more perspicacious than it sometimes appears!"

Callie wasn't laughing; she was frightened. "Oh, Zeus! You don't really think that's what it was, do you—someone spying on you?"

He didn't seem to have heard her. "I will, then!" he told the air behind his father. "I *will* find another place to live—see if I don't!"

Callie clutched his arm. "Don't be rash. He was angry, that's all. Upset. It isn't something that happens every day, you know—having your house broken into."

"But to imply that it's *my* fault—"

Cobham patted his shoulder. "Come on, old chap. Let's get a couple of mugs and get to work straightening up the chaos." He steered Zeus through the doorway, but Callie's brother turned and looked at her, that strange fierce light in his eyes.

"I'll move out before I'll give up the cause. He may not believe that, but I swear it. I mean it, Cal. Tell him that for me."

Callie went up to her own rooms slowly. As she passed Zeus's door, she heard him talking with Cobham, their voices hushed and low. She considered stopping to calm her father, but decided against it. Let him cool off first; she'd never seen him so wroth. She paused before entering her bedroom. Though she'd stood inside while the constable examined it quite thoroughly, the notion of a stranger pawing through her belongings was unnerving. There had been no sign, however, that the intruder had come in here.

Or was there? She hesitated at the threshold. She'd told the officer nothing had been disturbed, but how could she be certain? True, she often left her nightdress lying in a heap, but had she done so that morning? And her easel—had it been knocked to that odd angle by the constable? Had she put it that way to better catch the light? Or had some unknown person touched it, tampered with it? She eyed the untidy heap of sketchbooks by the window, the stacked canvases, the jars of brushes. Had he been here or not? It was impossible to tell.

Uncertainty made her skin crawl, sent small stabs of chill poking at her spine. Impatient with her fears, she strode across the room and set the easel straight again. She wouldn't give in to this sort of nonsense; she had work to do. As for Zeus and his cronies, she could only hope he'd had the foresight not to leave anything that could be incriminating lying about his rooms.

15.

Zeus didn't move out. There were no more suspicious incidents, and though relations between him and his father remained somewhat strained, Professor Wingate's attention alighted on another, more pleasant subject. He had been invited by the president of the Royal Society to mount an exhibition on Greek mythology at Oxford, the opening of which would be attended by His Majesty, King George.

"Perhaps you will be knighted, Father," Callie teased him when he told her of the honor.

"Don't be foolish. What is important about the invitation, Calliope, is that it signals our sovereign's awakening interest in scholarly pursuits, which can only prove a boon to Oxford and to the nation as a whole."

"And you never even contemplate the notion of a knighthood?"

"Naturally not. Come, now! We have work to do!"

Professor Wingate proposed that the exhibition, while displaying a comprehensive collection of the most pertinent artifacts available, should also include a detailed study of the evolution of the more important gods and goddesses through Greek history—surveying, for example, the development of

Hera from primitive nature-goddess to the queen of the heavens and consort of the great god Zeus. For this segment—really quite a new field of study—he was relying on Mick Harding. "It is bound to ruffle some feathers," Zeus noted as his father proposed this one evening while the family supped, "if you choose a first-year student for so major a part of the exhibit. What about Toby Lassiter instead?"

"Lassiter's a fine pupil. But if he has any intellectual honesty, he is bound to agree with my choice."

Callie and her brother exchanged glances. Then Callie ventured, "It isn't always simply a matter of that, Father. The students get jealous—"

"Do they? Well, they ought not to. No sense in it, is there? More asparagus, Mary, please." Then he looked at his daughter. *"You* agree, don't you, that he is the obvious candidate for preparing such a display?"

"Oh, I . . . scarcely could be judge of that."

"I gave you that essay of his on Dionysus to read."

He had. She'd found it lucid and witty and highly challenging in its novel propositions. What a radically different opinion she would have of Harding if she'd only ever read his writings! "And it was splendid," she said, only a little reluctantly. "Still, Father, I'm inclined to side with Zeus. Harding has many more years in which to vie for honors. Let this one go to a senior student. There's no need, is there, to go stepping on toes?"

Her father sliced his asparagus with brusque efficiency. "I am surprised at you, Calliope—at both of you. How in Olympus' name are we ever to create a system ruled by merit in this nation if we insist on taking such considerations into account? Harding deserves the honor; he has worked twice as hard and has already twice the learning of any of my other students. Lassiter and the other upperclassmen can assist him, if they like. As will you, of course, Calliope, in any way you can."

That was what led Professor Wingate to schedule an appointment for Harding to come to the house and discuss with Callie what he might need in the way of sketches to support his exhibit. She so dreaded the encounter that she postponed it twice, until the May opening of the exhibit was less than a month away. Finally she ran out of excuses and sat, toes tapping nervously, with her father in the drawing-room, waiting for Harding to arrive.

She peered through the window and watched him coming up the street, head down, his shoulders hunched inside his coat, oblivious to the swooping sparrows and tufts of violets and forget-me-nots that heralded the spring. She heard him rap at the door, heard Bingham usher him in, heard his footsteps in the hall and then the door swinging open. "Mr. Harding," Bingham announced. Professor Wingate stood and greeted him. Callie busied herself dipping her pen and flattening the page to which her notebook was turned.

"How do you do, Miss Wingate?" he asked politely, formally.

"Very well, thank you, Mr. Harding." She did not look up. "And you?"

"Very well, thank you."

"How is your work progressing, Harding?" the professor inquired.

"Quite well, sir, I believe. Though time constraints will force us to confine the exhibit to the major gods and goddesses."

"Just as well. Don't want to frighten the royals off with too much detail, do we? Lassiter proving helpful to you?"

"Very helpful, sir."

"There, I knew he would," Professor Wingate said with satisfaction. "No conflicts between you?"

"Oh, no, sir. Not at all."

"Good, good. You spoke of time constraints. Would some additional assistance be welcomed?"

"Actually, sir, another of the students has signed on. Lord Godshall."

"Harry?" Callie blurted in surprise, looking up at last. "Good God," she said. "You've grown a beard."

He put a hand to his chin, coloring faintly beneath the scraggly black growth. "Actually, just haven't shaved, rather. The . . . the time constraints."

The professor was peering at him. "By Jove, I did think you looked rather different. Thought perhaps you'd got new spectacles."

"No, sir. It's just the whiskers."

"Mm. Well. Sensible, isn't it, when you think about it?

Having a beard, I mean. Damned waste of time, shaving. I ought to give whiskers a try."

"You did," Callie reminded him. "Three summers past, in Damascus. You couldn't stand the itching."

"Did I? Well, Harding. What can Calliope do for you?"

Harding pulled a list from his breast pocket. "I've jotted down what I intend to cover. I don't think we need the illustrations to be all-inclusive—representational, rather, I'd say. Though I did hope to do a fairly detailed sequence on Dionysus. But no doubt you already have many sketches I could use."

"No doubt," Professor Wingate agreed. "Take him upstairs, Calliope, and have him look through the notebooks."

"Up . . . stairs?" Callie swallowed. "To my rooms?"

"That's where the notebooks are," he said logically. "When you're finished, Harding, come back down and you can give me a report on where you stand."

"You aren't coming with us?" Callie did wish her voice would stop squeaking.

"No point in that, is there?" He started from the room.

Callie darted a glance at Mick Harding. Damned if she wanted to be alone with him in her rooms. "Bingham," she told the butler, "do send up some tea. Mr. Harding, this way."

Wordlessly he followed her along the hallways and up two flights of stairs. When she paused outside the doors to her room, though, he cleared his throat. "If you'd prefer, Miss Wingate, I could bring the notebooks downstairs and look at them there."

"No sense in that; there are far too many. I merely stopped for breath."

"I thought you might feel my presence an intrusion on your privacy."

"I will let you know when you are intruding on my privacy, Mr. Harding." She turned the knob and went inside.

The blank white walls were awash with sunlight. A vase of lilacs she had cut in the garden that morning stood beside the bed, a blotch of blue-violet against the white coverlet. Their scent filled the air with faint, bright sweetness. At least she'd picked her nightdress up, Callie saw with relief.

"You haven't any pictures hanging," he observed, surprised.

''No. I find them distracting when I work. This way, please.'' She led him 'round the screen. He stood for a moment contemplating the chaos there, the mess of canvases and sketchbooks and paint-pots and boxes of charcoal. ''It's not a neat business, you know,'' she said rather defensively.

''No. I only wondered . . . where do I begin?''

Skirts rustling, she moved toward the sketchbooks. ''This one is Greek. And this, and this, and this—'' She stacked the relevant ones, and he began to page through them, now and again laying aside those with drawings that suited his needs. Callie perched in the windowseat, wondering where the tea might be. ''If there's an asterisk in the bottom right corner, it means I've already prepared an enlargement for one of Father's lectures,'' she noted.

''So it would be best if I selected those.''

''Well . . . it would spare me the trouble of copying more.''

''Quite,'' said Harding.

''Of course, if there is something you really need—''

''I'm sure my needs can be satisfied with what you have prepared.''

Covertly, she watched him turn the pages. The short curl of black beard made him look subtly older, more distinguished. She could imagine him a few years hence delivering his own lectures at the college. Her father certainly felt he had a brilliant future here. That reminded her of something. ''Is Harry proving . . . useful?''

He looked up blankly. ''Who?''

''Harry. Lord Godshall. You said he'd joined you—''

''Yes. So he did. Lassiter told me he'd expressed an interest. And he's been quite useful. Arranged for the earl to lend several statues I'd been coveting for the display.''

''And you didn't find that . . . peculiar?''

He laid down the sketchbook he was holding. ''Actually, I did. The earl is famous—or infamous, rather—for not loaning his collection to anyone.'' He blinked behind his spectacles. ''Oh. I'm sorry. Did you mean—'' Callie had flushed red, with an admixture of embarrassment and anger. Really, how could the man be so dense? ''I suppose you are referring . . . to what happened at Avebury.''

"Never mind," Callie muttered.

"No, I . . . I ought to tell you. The truth is, I felt sorry for him. Sorry about the whole thing, really. And since he wanted to help—it seemed a chance to make amends."

"Sorry for *him,*" she echoed bitterly.

"For . . . yes." He picked the sketchbook up again. "This is quite remarkable, this one you've done of that Leda."

"But it doesn't suit your thesis," she noted, the words curt.

"No, it doesn't." He stared at the drawing. "Miss Harding. I—"

There was a knock, and Mary's dull voice. "Tea, mum."

"Bring it in," Callie said.

She cleared a space atop her worktable. Mary set the tray down and started to go, but Callie told her, "Wait, please. You may as well stay, in case there's something we need. I hate to have you running up and down all those stairs."

"Very good, mum." She retreated to the doorway.

Callie poured steaming tea and offered a cup to Mick Harding. "You were saying?"

"I? Oh. Nothing, really."

"Sugar? Cream? Lemon?"

"No, thank you. Just plain."

After that he paged through the books more quickly. In an hour's time he'd found two dozen sketches, each already enlarged, to illustrate his topic. Callie located the enlarged versions in her haphazard system of filing, made a neat package of them with string, and handed them over. "You're sure there's nothing more you need?"

"Quite. I . . ." He glanced at Mary. "I'm sure their quality will greatly enhance the presentation. I'm very grateful to you."

"I consider it part of my duty to my father to assist his students. Speaking of which—Mary, the professor wanted another word with Mr. Harding. Will you show him down?"

"Yes, mum. Mr. Harding, this way."

He shifted the bundled sketches. "Thank you again, Miss Wingate."

"I'm just glad we were able to conclude the business so promptly," she told him coolly. "I do trust you won't need to call on me again."

16.

A brilliant day for the opening lecture of Professor William Wingate's exhibition on "Ancient Greece: Birth of the Gods," Callie thought with satisfaction—and a brilliant crowd. Carriage after well-equipped carriage rolled into the quadrangle through the west gate, discharging lords in powdered wigs and ladies wearing gowns more suited to a ball at Windsor than to the academic world. "I don't see how they will balance on the chairs," Zeus observed as he watched one woman swoop toward the doorway in her stiff, wide skirts, pause, and then edge through sideways.

"They have plenty of practice." Self-consciously she smoothed down the skirts of her own new gown of sea-green watered silk, ornamented with ruched Cluny lace at the bodice. She'd thought it so elegant when she'd put it on that morning. But now, beside these ladies' rich garments, it seemed downright plain.

"You look beautiful," Zeus said softly, and she smiled at him gratefully.

"Thanks. The audience is a bit intimidating, don't you think?"

"Father will be in his element. Look, there's the king."

Callie turned where he was pointing, and saw a coach marked with the royal arms disgorge King George himself, shortish and stout, clad in deep blue and leaning on a stick. "Not an overly attractive personage, is he?" Zeus murmured, and she whirled on him. "I know, I know," he forestalled her, holding up a hand. "My role today is to keep my mouth shut and keep out of sight. Don't fret, Cal. I won't spoil Father's big chance."

"I just want everything to go well for him," she whispered, hands clenched into fists at her sides. "He's worked so hard."

"We've all worked hard. We have done all we can. Now it's in Father's hands."

"Or God's," Callie murmured.

"Or *the* gods'," he corrected her, and gave her a swift kiss. "I am going to secure a place amongst the student rabble. Kind of Father, wasn't it, to insist on standing room for us poor scholars? If some crackpot shoots a pistol at His Majesty, at least I'll have a few dozen witnesses to vouch it wasn't I."

"Oh, Zeus! How can you even jest about such a thing?"

He waved jauntily and headed for the entrance to the hall. Callie nibbled her lip and turned for the side door, the one that led to the chamber where Professor Wingate was making final preparations for his lecture. She saw him sitting in a corner, reading over his notes one last time, quite debonair in his scarlet doctor's robes and square black velvet hat. Toby Lassiter was there wearing the university's gold-laced nobleman's gown, and she saw Cobham in his sleeveless commoner's cope. Mick Harding looked taller than ever in his academic robes. His beard had grown thick and curly over these past two months, she noted; with the spectacles, it made him look fiercely grave.

"Callie?"

She turned to find Harry standing beside her in his own gold-laced gown and black tippet. "I just wanted to say . . . how very lovely you look," he said almost shyly.

"Why—thank you," she told him, surprised.

"And . . . well . . . to apologize to you. All that business about getting your father to resign—that was Mother's idea, not mine. I tried to talk her out of it. I never wanted to make trouble for you."

Callie found herself touched. He was so tentative, so unsure of himself—really, quite unlike the old Harry. "It doesn't matter now," she said gently. "I think you've proven that by working so hard with Father to make this exhibition a success."

"I enjoyed it. Your father is a remarkable man." He took a deep breath. "Sometimes I think it was the biggest mistake I'll ever make in my life, Callie, ending it with you. And I just want you to know . . . that I wish you well. I honestly do."

"Why, thank you, Harry," she stammered.

"I mean that. I want you to be happy, even if it can't be with me." Regret shone in his eyes. Hastily he bent and kissed her softly on the cheek. Then he hurried away.

Well! Callie thought, staring after him. Will wonders never cease? Harry Godshall eating crow—wait until she told Zeus! She put her hand to her cheek where he'd kissed her, then glanced up to see Mick Harding staring at her quite fixedly. Self-conscious, she crossed the room to where Cobham and Lassiter were preparing to carry the easel loaded with her sketches into the lecture hall.

"They're all in order?" she asked anxiously, eyeing the curtain-draped pile of drawings.

"In perfect order," Lassiter assured her. "Harry just went over them one last time."

"Still . . ." Callie hated to think the rhythm of her father's speech might be disrupted by any confusion in the illustrations. "Let me just check again."

"Too late," Harry announced, peeking through the doorway to the lecture hall. "His Majesty's just sat down. Mustn't keep him waiting."

"I'd best go sit down, too." Callie went and kissed her father, straightening his cravat. "Good luck, old pet."

"We make our own luck," he told her, then motioned for Cobham and Lassiter to wheel the easel in.

Callie slipped around to the hall and into her reserved seat behind the ranks of countesses and earls and dukes and duchesses, just as the applause that greeted the appearance of Dean Wurthing began to die away. Some of the women's headdresses towered so high that she could barely see. Craning her neck, she glimpsed the dean as he introduced her father, who walked in looking perfectly at ease, uncowed by his illustrious audience. He took a moment to introduce Mick Harding as his chief assistant, and then Cobham and Lassiter, who stood by the easel ready to display the drawings on it, one after the other. Then Professor Wingate surprised and rather alarmed Callie by mentioning her.

"I'd very much like to thank my daughter Calliope," he said from the podium, smiling at her across the heads of the crowd, "who prepared all the paintings and sketches which you are about to see. And now, let's get to it, shall we?"

Callie knew the words of her father's speech by heart; she'd even written out his notes for him, since her penmanship was clearer than his. This left her free to observe the men and women around her, to see what their reactions might be. King George himself was beyond her view, hidden by a head of white-powdered hair swept up nearly a foot and crowned with ribbons and roses. Somehow Callie was not surprised when the obstructing hairdo half-turned and she recognized the sharp features of Harry's mother. Well, of course she'd be here for Harry's sake. It had been sweet of him, truly sweet, to make that little speech to her. She felt quite guilty for all the wretched things she'd wished on him all this time.

Mick Harding had briefly left the podium, returning with a wheeled platform which held a bronze statue of Zeus, lent by the Duke of Clareborough. The ease with which he pushed it along took Callie by surprise; she knew from experience how heavy such pieces were. The platform allowed Professor Wingate, with Harding's help, to turn the statue around to display the acanthus leaves decorating its base. The nude statue had been carefully draped with a scarf, to spare offense to the ladies in the hall.

"Oh, how I'd *adore* one of those in my dressing room," Callie overheard one of the women whisper, and she bit back a smile. This exhibit was bound to fuel the gentry's fever for Greek antiquities, already raging hot. It was rather a pity that all her father's years of research and learning should be reduced in this noblewoman's eyes to an *object* for her boudoir. Still, the lecture was going awfully well. She shifted in her seat, trying to see around the countess head to King George, to find out if he was fidgeting or sitting still, but she couldn't tell.

There was some sort of rumpus in the student section. Hearing raised voices, Callie whirled to look with her heart in her throat. Surely Zeus respected his father enough to stand still and quiet. But then she glimpsed him actually hushing the offenders, the expression on his thin face positively ferocious. Good for you! she cheered her brother silently, and turned back to her father. He'd reached the section on Dionysus, her favorite part.

"A perfect example of this synthesis of numerous tribal spirits can be found in the figure of Dionysus—that is, 'son of Zeus,' in the Thracian dialect. He originally appears in Greek mythology as a nature god of fruitfulness and vegetation, especially the grapevine—hence, distinctively, the god of wine. His numerous cult titles include the familiar 'Bacchus,' which Mr. Harding"—he nodded at Mick—"has suggested to me might be traced to the Thracian verb 'to shout,' from the loud exclamations of his worshippers, as well as 'Bassareus,' thought to derive from the fox-skin garments worn at the Thracian Bacchanals. Dionysus can be considered in two distinct aspects: as a popular national god of wine and good cheer—" Here Cobham and Lassiter revealed a sketch of the round-cheeked god of revelry, taken from a frieze Callie had seen at Sardis. "And as a foreign deity imported from Thrace, worshipped with mysterious ecstatic rites." He paused for breath, and to indicate another change of sketch. Another flurry of loud voices had arisen in the student section. Callie turned to scowl at the sound—where the devil was Zeus? This was the very meat of the lecture. In the sea of faces, it took her a moment to locate her brother. Then she saw him standing, staring open-mouthed at the podium in the front of the hall. The murmur of voices surrounding him grew louder. Why doesn't he quiet them? Callie wondered in fury. What was he gaping at so fixedly? Suddenly she glimpsed Harry in the throng of students. He was beside John Ormond, and both of them were grinning in a most peculiar way.

The hubbub had distracted Professor Wingate. He glanced toward the students, then down at his notes, clearing his throat. A rumble of comment was running through the hall. "Well, I never!" Callie heard a woman cry, and just a few seats ahead of her, a wigged and powdered lord clapped his handkerchief over his wife's eyes.

Something was very wrong. Everywhere the audience was rising from its chairs. Callie's father stood befuddled at the lectern. Through the surging tide of silks and velvets and lace, Callie saw Cobham, motionless as bronze, gazing dumbstruck at the easel. And then she saw the painting that was mounted there.

It stood out in that company of plain gray sketches like some vast exotic bird in fantastical plumage: the Ayrshire garden in the height of summer, leaves and flowers and curling tendrils unfurling in a riot of bright yellow and red and green against the delicate spires of the ruined house, and there, his arm curled 'round the axe, one leg on the breached wall, Callie's noble savage in all his unclothed splendor, a rippling mass of bronze skin and taut muscle and black hair.

"How—" Callie started to say, and then realized it didn't matter, not now. All that mattered was to cover the offending portrait. But Cobham and Lassiter seemed frozen with shock, unable even to draw shut the curtain on the easel. And her father still hadn't grasped what had occurred. Callie felt herself shriveling inside; one after another, the men and ladies were turning to stare at her with hostile, outraged eyes. Oh, Cobham, *please,* she begged silently, *please* cover it up!

Then, as if to answer her prayer, she saw the red-robed Mick Harding, his black head towering above even the ladies' wigs, striding toward the easel. He was no more than halfway, however, when a hoot went up from the pack of students, and a shrill voice cut through the clamor: "It is he! By Christ, look! It is he!"

The forest of faces swiveled toward the podium en masse. Mick Harding had stopped, a red-robed, long-legged insect trapped in the amber of the crowd's stares. He stood beside the portrait with the new growth of black beard covering his chin, his spectacles clutched in his hand.

"Oh, dear God," Callie whispered, and swayed on her feet.

"It is Harding! It is!" someone shouted out triumphantly.

Across the room, the subject's gaze, guiltily defiant, blazed out at his portraitist. Then he whipped the curtain over the painting, hiding his nakedness.

Callie sank into her seat, awash in utter shame, and heard a low, harsh chuckle from over her shoulder. "Yes indeed," Harry Godshall murmured, leaning toward her with that same small, malicious grin, "I wish you only the best."

Part II

Edinburgh, Scotland.
March, 1745

17.

I am doomed, Callie thought mirthlessly, to live in houses with bad gardens. One aged hawthorn tree, a fistful of jonquils, and two lonely crocuses pushing through the brown grass were all this place had to boast of. Not a single rosebush graced the high wall; no gay thickets of columbine or fritillary sprang up like sweet fresh surprises between the paving stones.

She turned and paced in the opposite direction, back toward the house, contemplating its grim square outline against the dull sky, the small narrow windows sadly out of proportion to the graceless whole. All in all, the prospect was so lacking in charm that it was nearly worth sketching. She pushed that thought from her mind. The university had lovely homes for rent closer into town, near Greyfriars Church and the Parliament Hall, but Professor Wingate had chosen this time to live with a bit more distance between himself and his students. Callie could hardly blame him for that. After Oxford, they all needed a little space.

She guessed at the time and then sat on the garden bench and waited, watching a stubborn song-thrush trying to tug a worm from the ground, until the bells of St. Giles disproved her hazard. Only ten o'clock. Christ, but time crawled in this place! Restless, she went inside and found Dorcas rubbing imaginary spots from the silverware. "Could I make up the beds for you?" Callie offered. "Peel vegetables perhaps?" The cook grunted something that Callie took for no. "Well, can I help with the polishing, then?"

"I don't need help, thank you."

" 'Twill make the work go faster," Callie said, too brightly.

Dorcas glared. "If you're implying I can't handle the load myself—"

"Oh, Lord. Of course I'm not—"

"Good! For I defy any soul to say my housekeeping standards have slipped one notch since we left England!"

"Of course they haven't—"

"Despite the fact that I am doing with these two hands the work that eight hands used to."

"Quite so," said Callie, and quickly escaped up the back stair to her room.

You couldn't blame Dorcas for grumbling. She hadn't wanted to leave Oxford, and especially her daughter Bea, behind. But wages were low in the North, and Professor Wingate's new salary only allowed expense enough for one house-servant. And Dorcas had been absolutely adamant that must be she. For she still blamed herself for the hiring of Mary, plain stolid Mary, whose stoicism had finally collapsed into a torrent of tears as she confessed that yes, yes, she had let Harry Godshall's driver make love to her in the gardens on the night the Wingates' home had been broken into, knowing all the time that Harry was inside the house, alone. "You've got to understand," the poor girl had blubbered. "No man had ever said such pretty things to me before, nor treated me so fine."

That was when Harry had found and taken the portrait, leaving the mess in Zeus's study to divert suspicion. How he'd found out about it in the first place they could only surmise. Zeus thought perhaps Lord Delaney might have told John Ormond, who would have told Harry. He blamed himself for that part in the business. And James Cobham had proffered Callie an abject apology for not having noticed Harry slipping the painting into the stack of sketches on the easel. Toby Lassiter had stopped by as they were packing up the house to say the same thing.

Well, thought Callie, flopping down on her bed, there was fault enough to go around, but in the end, she had painted the damned thing. Ultimately, it was thanks to her and no one else that she was stuck here in Edinburgh with too much time on her hands.

She looked at her hands. Ten months—nearly a year now—since she'd held a paintbrush or stick of charcoal. Nearly a year spent unlearning the habits of a lifetime, teaching herself not to appreciate nuances of shadow and light, the sky's blue, a willow-tree's gray-green. Try as she might, though, she could not help seeing the planes of a face, the line of a rooftop, the crook made by the branches of a hazel tree. Ten months, and her fingers still had not stopped itching. She was beginning to doubt that they ever would. Still, giving up her art seemed a small enough penance for having ruined her father's life.

He had blamed himself, too, though in a vague, diffuse way, for allowing her too much freedom, for failing to provide her with a proper moral grounding, for letting her view too many undraped male statues in Athens and Rome. He'd been impossibly noble and understanding in the aftermath of the aborted lecture; he was the one who'd questioned Mary, patiently and persistently, until she broke down and confessed. He'd presented the resignation the dean demanded, set about finding another post, and uprooted his family and career to the far less prestigious University of Edinburgh with only one brief speech of reproach to the daughter who'd disgraced him. Her cheeks flamed as she recalled his plaintive words: "I simply don't understand, Calliope, how you could have done such a foolish thing."

So she had given up painting. She missed it with a dull, constant craving like that of an opium-eater for his drug. She was glad for the pain, for no matter what her father said or didn't say, she knew it was her fault and hers alone that he was teaching Homer to provincial freshmen instead of basking in the success of his exhibition to King George.

* * *

"I saw," said Zeus, "the most amazing thing today."

Professor Wingate went on reading his gazette. Callie pushed at her salmon, admiring, against her will, its lush, blushing color against her white plate. Zeus cleared his throat. "I *said*—"

"I heard you," said Callie. "What was it you saw?"

"An entire field full of yellow narcissus, down in The Meadows. Quite took my breath away, really. You ought to go and look at it tomorrow."

"Ought I to? Why?"

"Well, as I said, it's just . . . just breathtaking."

"Mm." Callie swallowed a bite of fish. "I know what narcissus look like."

"Of course you do. But this—the sheer scale, the profusion—"

Her gold-flecked gaze slanted toward him. "Makes you wish you were a painter, does it?"

"As a matter of fact, it does."

Their father looked at them over the edge of the newspaper. "Zeus. Stop badgering your sister."

"I wasn't badger—"

"Whatever you call it, then."

Zeus folded his napkin with a flap. "I just don't see how you can sit there, Father, and watch her squander her God-given talents—"

"Which are hers, to use or not as she sees fit."

"It's a waste, an utter travesty! You ought to be encouraging her, Father, to leave the past behind—"

"I have always held," the professor noted, "that one can learn a great deal from the past."

"But she—"

"*Would* you please," Callie broke in, annoyed, "stop speaking about me as though I'm not here? Father's right, Zeus. It simply isn't any of your business how I spend my time. I don't bother you about your silly little meetings with your Jacobite friends."

"How very kind of you," her brother said, grinning, "to

characterize them that way. There's one tonight, you know. Perhaps you'd like to come with me? We usually have quite a few female guests. Something about men plotting rebellion seems to excite them.''

''It doesn't excite me.''

''Perhaps you've other plans?''

''Actually, I have. I plan to bathe, and then to comb out my hair, and then to indulge in a hand or two of solitaire.''

Zeus threw up his hands. ''Do you hear that, Father? She's become a hermit. She will never marry. She'll be an old maid, and I will have to support her when you're gone.''

''On what,'' Professor Wingate said dryly, ''I simply can't imagine.''

''That reminds me.'' Zeus grinned again, winningly. ''Can I borrow five shillings?''

His father raised a brow. ''What's become of your salary from the bookshop?''

''You know, I'm not at all sure. I either ate it or drank it.''

''Perhaps you read so much while on duty,'' Callie suggested, ''that Mr. Dunning doesn't feel you deserve to be paid.''

''If I'm not familiar with the wares we offer, how can I be of service to our clientele?'' Zeus reached for the coins his father held out, but then the professor pulled them back.

''I do trust my pocket-change isn't being used to foment revolution, Zeus.''

''Only very indirectly,'' Zeus assured him, and gave Callie a quick kiss on his way to the door. ''Don't wait up for me.''

Callie pushed the salmon across her plate and back again with her fork. Her father glanced at her. ''He's right, you know,'' he said softly. ''You really must get out of the house.''

''Worried I'll be an old maid?''

''Worried you are unhappy.''

''Well,'' she said after a moment's silence, ''what if I am?''

''You must not go on punishing yourself, Calliope. You made an error in judgment—''

''*There's* an understatement. Must we talk about this?''

''I believe we must. You've been a virtual recluse since we moved here, my dear. You've made no friends, joined no social circles—''

"I will, Father. I just need more time."

"How much time would you suggest I allow you?"

"I—" Until the memory of the jeering lecture crowd receded; until she stopped seeing Harry's wicked smile in her mind. "A little more. That's all."

He rang for Dorcas, and when she came, asked for coffee. "There's a concert of the collegiate choir on Friday evening. Will you accompany me?"

Her gaze dropped to her lap. "I can't."

"Very well. Tuesday evening, Professor McPhee is presenting a lecture on symbolism in the *Iliad*. How about that?"

"I think not."

"There's a performance of *The Frogs* next month. You used to love Aristophanes."

"I—"

"Late next month."

She smiled up at him. "Well, then. Perhaps. Will you excuse me, Father, please? I have some sewing I must do in my room."

Here, as at Oxford, she'd taken the room beneath the rafters—not for light this time, but for the lack of it. Illuminated by a solitary dormer, her bedchamber was so dark most of the day that one could scarcely dress, much less draw. She went and sat by the window now, leaning on the sill. The dying sun cast long shadows of the trees and houses. She watched two children chase each other through a neighboring garden. Their high, wild laughter as they ran reminded her of long-ago races with Zeus.

There were swans in Duddingston Loch; she could just glimpse their graceful arched necks above the black water. For some reason she thought of the face of that statuette of Leda, turning at the pounding of wings. Life was like that. You never knew what was coming up behind you. After that time with the swan, she mused, I'll wager Leda spent the rest of her days looking over her shoulder, just to be prepared.

At least Leda had the comfort of knowing her misfortune wasn't of her own making; she had simply been too lovely for the thunder-god to resist. Whereas I—Callie buried her face in her arms, trying not to think of everything she might have done to avert this disaster. As for Mick Harding, if at any time over the months he'd been her father's student, had been received in their home, had been alone with her, he had simply said, "Do you know, I believe we have met before?" Then he'd have confessed to being at Langlannoch, and Callie certainly would be embarrassed, but they'd likely have had a good laugh about it, and it would make a splendid anecdote for Zeus to tell, and of course she never would have worked on the portrait, for it wouldn't have been proper once she knew who he was, or knew that she knew him.

And how *hadn't* she known him? How, in the name of everything that was holy, had her acute eye, taught by years of hard training to observe and commit to memory the slightest variance of form and shadow and shape, failed her so utterly, so completely? God, it was galling! She slammed her fist against the windowsill, making the old panes rattle and shake. Night after night she'd spent refining every aspect of that painting. She'd agonized for two weeks straight over Mick Harding's left thigh. For months on end she'd stared at the image of his manhood. Yet all that time she'd been supping with the man, working beside him—kissing him, by Christ!—and she'd never recognized him.

Zeus hadn't either, true—but Zeus wasn't an artist. And yes, Harding hadn't had the beard when she'd first met him at Oxford, and yes, folk did say clothes made the man, and yes, everyone knew how hard it was to place people one saw out of context, like the woman from the bakeshop encountered on a visit to the doctor. Still, her acquaintance with the savage she'd painted had been so lengthy, so intimate, so intense, that it cut her to the quick to realize she hadn't known who he was in the flesh.

In the flesh. Alone in her garret, she blushed deep crimson to remember all those nights she'd spent with him, the way she'd captured every inch of his body with her brush-tip. All the romantic claptrap she'd indulged in, creating that persona for him: the noble savage, the Gaelic chieftain sprung from ancient rootstock, the gloriously inarticulate embodiment of nature's blunt, brute strength.

And all the time he'd been naught but another bookish Oxford boy, so bereft of natural instinct that he likely couldn't bear to see the center of a beefsteak red.

Well, so much for playing Pygmalion. She wondered briefly what the mythic sculptor had found when Aphrodite brought his creation to life. Perhaps Galatea proved impossibly silly, or a nag or gossip; perhaps her voice had been grating, or her breath foul. That was the trouble with those antique Greeks— everything was based on appearance, and appearances could be so deceiving. Look at poor hapless Zeus, swooping down from Olympus to ravish nymph after naiad after virgin, and never finding enough beyond a shapely pair of hips or bee- stung lips to keep him there. The gap between perception and reality, as with her savage and Mick Harding, could be impassi- bly wide.

It was interesting, in a way, to do this sort of thinking. She'd always been so busy with her hands, so quick to reach for her sketchbook, that her mind hadn't been free to wander quite so aimlesssly. Perhaps, she thought, if I work at it long and hard enough, I'll think of some reason why I should go on living.

For really, without her art, getting out of bed in the mornings scarcely seemed worthwhile.

18.

Another day, and the same view from her window. It was a fortnight later, and nothing, Callie thought, had changed, except that the ancient hawthorn at the foot of the garden was stirring from sleep, sending out small curved leaves among its vicious spines. Who could tell? By May Day, it might blossom. And I, thought Callie, I will still be here staring at it. *Or perhaps,* something inside her whispered, softly, seductively, *perhaps you won't.*

At breakfast that morning, Zeus had proposed a dozen different excursions they might go on. His efforts to get her to bestir herself had grown more frantic lately; he seemed able to sense the growing depths of her despair. It might have been because she no longer cared enough to put up much of a facade. She'd rejected his suggestions, one by one, while their father read his gazette in silence and ate boiled eggs.

It gnawed at her to see him this way. Something truly had gone out of him since Oxford—some joy in his work, in sharing with his students the knowledge he'd accumulated over his lifetime. Perhaps it was the death of his dream of equality through education. Harry Godshall's nasty trick had seen to that. When push came to shove, the dean had listened to both sides of the story and then backed the aristocracy over the parvenu.

Something has gone out of me, too, she realized, watching as a mother a few houses away carried her baby into their garden to play. The child toddled over the green grass, arms stretched out to the sky. Once upon a time, Callie had greeted springtime with that same innocent joy. Now it made her want to bang the shutters closed against the sparkling sun, against the patterns of light and dark slipping through branches and leaves, against the offhanded loveliness of the young woman as she stooped to gather the baby to her breast. The world's burgeoning, careless beauty only ripped at her soul, made her fingers ache for the work she had forbidden them.

Her father's unhappiness was her fault. Try as she might, she could not shake that thought from her mind. In losing him his post, she had lost him his reason for being. Guilt coursed through her with every beat of her heart.

He'd have been better off, she mused, pulling at a bit of loose paint on the pane with her fingernail, if I had never been born. I have brought him nothing but disgrace and shame.

He'd be better off if she died.

Callie had never thought much about death—what person her age did? But the notion surrounded her now each day, as she wandered in the garden, as she picked at her meals, as she sat hour after hour at her high window, watching the world from afar. She played with the idea the way she'd once toyed with charcoal and paper, sketching and resketching its consequences in her mind.

If she were to die now, while still so young, people would feel sorry for her, instead of disgusted by her. She'd be an object of pity, almost a martyr. "Poor thing," people would whisper at her funeral. "So much promise—why, she was once engaged to marry an earl's son, can you believe that?" She'd lie in her coffin in her unused wedding gown, with flowers in her dead hands, and everyone would cry and mourn.

And talk about how she'd disgraced her father. Unfortunately, dying wouldn't solve that.

The fleck of paint broke loose from the pane under sudden

pressure. *Unless . . .* The thought came out of nowhere. *Unless you were to kill yourself.*

Afraid, she tried to pull back, to argue with the realization that had exploded in her mind like a star. "What would that prove?" she whispered out loud.

That you were mad, reason hissed back. *Deranged. Insane. Not responsible for your actions . . .*

Not responsible for having painted that portrait. God, it was perfect. Of course.

She had begun to shake; her shoulders and her knees were shaking. No one could blame her—or, more importantly, her father—for the mess she'd made, if they thought she was mad. In fact, perhaps I *am* mad, she thought, staring at a bit of blood on her fingertip; the shard of paint had pierced it. Look at what I've done in the past year and a half: thrown over Harry for no earthly reason, practically offered myself to Mick Harding, a virtual stranger, and spent weeks, *months,* perfecting a portrait of a naked man. Now I haven't stirred from this house since we moved in last June, I've no interest in the things that used to occupy me, I spend my days alone, talking to myself—good God, I really am a lunatic!

She moved away from the window toward her looking-glass with uncertain steps. *Look at yourself,* sang the voice in her head. Her hair was its usual mess of tangled russet curls; her face was gaunt and hollow, skin so ghost-pale from lack of sun that it seemed nearly translucent. Her eyes were enormous, great pools of greenish-gold, but dull, lacking inner light. *Not like beryls at all . . .*

It had been a very long time since she'd done more than idly glance in that mirror. Lord, she thought, studying her wan, unfamiliar reflection, I look the madwoman's part.

Her father might not notice, but Zeus certainly had. That must be why he was trying so mightily to interest her in life again. Next thing you knew, he'd be trotting her off to an asylum to try the latest methods of treatment—water therapy, or purges, or whatever was the rage this year. Callie shuddered all the way to her toes, imagining how awful that would be. She and Zeus and her father had toured Bethlehem Hospital in Lambeth a decade or so before, in the interests of science.

She'd had nightmares for years afterward of the howling, sad-eyed lunatics there.

I'll never let them take me to such a place, she vowed. I'd sooner die!

If you are mad, you can't stop them.

Resolve, hard as crystal, formed in the face the mirror echoed. Oh, yes. I can.

Like clear water, the answer to her dilemma, to her senseless existence, flooded her soul. If she killed herself, she'd be safe. And more than that, her family would be freed of her stigma, of the shame she had visited on them. God, she thought, her whole body trembling, the dean might even give Father back his post at Oxford! This was how she might make things right again.

But how to do it? She mulled the matter over. She couldn't abide blood, so that eliminated knives and guns—not that she knew how to use a gun anyway. Hanging? She'd seen a hanged man once in Sicily, his blank eyes bulging, clothing stained where he'd voided himself at the moment of death. No, that was entirely too messy. Someone in the family would have to find her, and she wouldn't wish that on them.

Poison? That had possibilities. But what sort of poison? Arsenic, she'd heard, was dreadfully painful. Nightshade? Wolfsbane? She didn't know enough about such plants to ensure success. Nux vomica, folk said, induced wretched convulsions. Opium, perhaps? That was what Professor Strachley's wife had taken a few years back, when, rumor had it, she found herself with child when her husband had been away in Rome for more than ten months. Zeus and Callie had gone with their father to the funeral. She'd looked pale but lovely lying in her coffin, in a bed of rosy silk.

Callie had even taken opium once, for a toothache. She could recall the sensation of delicious lethargy it induced. There had been no pain. And one could buy tincture of opium at any druggist's. She let her mind drift, remembering the soft slip into numbness, the sweet sensation of release.

She could go and buy it now. She watched from the window as the neighbor's baby fell face-down on the lawn; its mother ran and snatched it up, cradling it gently. That was all death was, wasn't it—finally being at peace, quiet and cold, against the breast of the earth? Rational people like herself and Zeus didn't believe in hell, in the punishment of sinners. Death was the natural consequence of life; it was nothing to fear.

Already moving with a sort of exalted dullness, she put on a black day-dress and her best black stockings. She slipped into her shoes, combed and tamed her curls in a chignon. She fastened jet earrings and pinned a cameo at her throat. Zeus and Father will miss me, she thought vaguely. But they will get over it, in time, just as we all got over Mother's death. And really, it's the only way.

Dorcas was dusting in the front hall; she looked up, startled, as Callie came toward her and took her cloak from the wardrobe. "Going out, are you?"

"To the bookshop, to see Zeus."

The housekeeper nodded uncertainly. "Well. That's good, then. Good for you, isn't it, to be out and about?"

"Yes. I've been here too long, haven't I?" Callie tied the laces of her cloak with steady hands.

Dorcas stood with her duster clutched to her breast. "I'll come with you, shall I, to show you the way?"

"No need for that. He's told me where it is."

"But you don't know the city, pet. Let me send for one of the neighbor's boys—"

"It isn't necessary. I'll be fine." Callie smiled. "Oh, and Dorcas. One other thing. I've got a bit of a headache."

"Oh, I've powders in my room—"

"I don't want to take yours. I'll buy some on my way, if there's a druggist near."

"There's one right up by Potterrow, on your left. You can't miss it."

"Good," said Callie. "I'll be back, then, in a little while."

Dorcas watched her from the doorway. "Mind the pickpockets!" she called in her wake.

It felt odd to be walking on something besides wood floors, going someplace besides across her room and back. Callie stepped carefully among the cobblestones. Along Crichton Street, the air was filled with dust from the new houses being built all around George Square. Edinburgh was prospering under the Scottish union with England. Callie wondered, watching the workmen busily laying brick, what made Prince Charles Edward think he'd find a warm reception here.

There were flower-sellers all along Grassmarket, hawking nosegays of violets and primrose. Callie saw one, an aged crone whose ugliness made her bouquets even more glorious, and felt her fingers itch. That would be a finer sketch than the woman with the lilies . . . but she would do no more sketches. The void that decision had made in her life was what had driven her from her room, she realized. She could not draw now. And if she could not draw, she did not want to live.

She was headed toward the university, and the streets were filled with students carrying books, talking with their heads close together, their voices young and gay. Like Zeus, she thought, and then cringed as a knot of them stared at her. Did they know who she was? Had they heard the story? Edinburgh was a long way from Oxford, but universities all over Europe were linked together in innumerable ways. Terror of gossip, of whispers, was part of what had kept her in the house all this time.

Loud laughter rang out. She whirled around and saw two young men just behind her, grinning. Their eyes met hers. Did she only imagine that the laughter had been aimed at her? She quickened her steps, pushing through a bevy of students, hearing the babble of their voices. They were talking about her; she was sure of it. Ducking her head, she rushed past—and straight into the broad chest of a swaggering fellow with a stack of books under his arm. He steadied her solicitously. ''Professor Wingate's daughter, aren't you?'' he asked, polite and smiling.

''I—'' Callie blushed, trying to move past him. He caught her sleeve, spun her 'round, and started yanking at his hose.

''Care to do a portrait of me?''

''Oh, God!'' Hand at her mouth, Callie broke free and began to run. Howls of laughter chased her up the street. She'd been right—they did know. Everyone knew. Lord, her poor father, poor Zeus—how had they endured it? Desperately she searched the shop signs for the druggist's caduceus.

There it was, only a little way ahead. Frantic, sobbing, glancing over her shoulder to see if she was followed, she yanked

open the door and darted inside. The sharp scents of sulphur
and herbs struck her as she slammed the door shut, jingling
the bell. The druggist, short and fat, was at his counter, and a
customer, a tall man all in black, stood before him. They both
looked at her when she came in, the tall man turning slowly,
the thick jet-black tail at the nape of his neck sweeping across
his coat.

Spectacles shielded his cobalt-blue eyes. His black beard
had grown longer, more like the one he'd worn in the portrait,
that she'd captured so deftly, so perfectly. I am mad, Callie
thought, staring at the apparition before her. He . . . cannot
. . . be here . . .

"Your change, sir," the druggist announced, rolling his eyes
a little.

The customer was frozen, a statue, unmoving.

Callie swayed on her feet. "Oh, dear Lord—"

19.

Callie felt naked, raw, like knuckles raked across rock. Her insides were a cauldron of anguished emotion, shame, rage, grief, and bewilderment churning together in a volatile stew. And the sight of this man, this man who, across the months at Oxford, might have stemmed all this suffering simply by admitting who he was—this man who stood now, so still and calm in his neat black suit, not even blinking, who'd been the cause of her ruin and that of her father, was the match that ignited the morass. *"You,"* she said, her voice low and quavering, and with that word the last of her control snapped. "You *bastard!"* she screamed at him, and hurled the nearest thing to hand, her purse, straight at his head. Her aim was off; he did not even duck as it sailed past him and the now bug-eyed druggist, to shatter a heavy bottle of some rose-hued elixir on a shelf. "Hey! Hey, lady!" the druggist cried, aghast. "See here, ye cannae—"

"How dare you come and show your face here?" She threw her parasol as well; it smashed a whole row of bottles. The druggist looked as though he'd have an apoplectic fit right there on the spot. But Callie didn't even notice; she was consumed, she was burning with fury. "Haven't you done enough to us, you *inhuman* creature, that you must dog us even here?'' She grabbed for something, anything, to make him move, God damn him, to wipe that blank, stark expression from his eyes. Her groping hand settled 'round a tin of powdered talc; she flung it hard as she could. The druggist barely managed to deflect it from his wares.

"Sir," he pleaded desperately to Mick, "d'ye ken the lady? Can ye nae control her? She'll lay waste my whole shop!"

At last Mick Harding seemed to shake himself, like a waking giant, and took a step forward. "Miss Wingate—"

"Don't you come near me. Don't you touch me!" she seethed at him, letting fly another tin. It clipped his shoulder, but he didn't flinch.

"You have to get hold of yourself," he said in a low voice. "You are making a spectacle—"

"Do you think that I care? Could I possibly make any greater spectacle than the one you've already been responsible for?" She backed away from him, circling a little table piled with soaps and salts, putting it between them. "Go away. Get out!"

"Dinna gae, sir!" the alarmed druggist cried. "Keep her here; I'll run 'n fetch the watch—"

"He is going for the authorities, Miss Wingate. Do you want to be arrested?"

"I don't care, I don't care!" She started to push the table over toward him, but he blocked it with his hand, thwarting her effortlessly.

"Really, Miss Wingate, this sort of behavior is most unseemly."

"Is it?" Her tawny curls had worked loose from their chignon, and wreathed her small, wretched face like a great cat's mane. Sheer hatred had brought life to her eyes again; she felt like the fabled basilisk that killed with a glance. She could will him dead—but he wasn't mortal, was he? He was something less, a great unfeeling hulk of clay. "Is it really?" Just beyond him, to the left, was a display of razors. If she could reach it, reach him, she'd cut his throat, by God, and see if he bled.

"You know it is. What would your father say?"

"Don't you *dare* mention my father!"

"I fear I must, Miss Wingate. How else am I to make you

see how foolish you are being?'' His muscles never moved, but she saw his blue eyes blink like an owl's, toward the door and back. He is reasoning to stall me, she realized, waiting for the city watch.

But that wouldn't work. She let her head drop as though she meant to acknowledge he was right, then kicked the table at him, hard as she could. She had the satisfaction of hearing the breath go out of him in a gasp as she scrabbled across the scattered glass shards and goods to the razors, caught one up, and flicked the blade at him as he turned 'round.

He swallowed heavily. ''My dear Miss Wingate. Callie. I beg you, don't do anything rash.'' His gaze shifted to the door once more. He is trying to trick me, Callie thought, into thinking the watch is there. But I won't be fooled. She took a step toward him, then jerked her head up as the door's bells jangled at her back. Dammit! She raised the razor up, but his hand closed over hers, yanking it down again.

''Callie. Callie.'' It was Zeus's voice, choked with the tears that streamed down his face. ''Oh, Callie, love. How could you?''

With great gentleness, Mick Harding wrested the razor from Callie's clenched fist and lifted her off her feet. ''Come on,'' he told Zeus tersely. ''We've got to get her out of here.''

He hailed a passing hack and thrust her into the back, then bundled Zeus in with her. ''Where to?'' the driver asked.

The whistles of the watch could be heard approaching. ''Anywhere,'' Mick Harding told him. ''Anywhere. Just drive. Fast.'' He jumped into the coach, and the man clucked his tongue to set the horses off at a brisk clip.

''I'm ... so very sorry,'' Zeus told Mick, holding tight to Callie's hand. ''I know we've inconvenienced you—''

''It doesn't matter. I'm only glad you arrived in such a timely fashion. But what brought you there?''

''I told our housekeeper to send word to the shop where I work if Callie left the house. She ... hasn't been well, you see. Not herself. And then when Dorcas said the druggist's, I feared—'' He put his arm around Callie where she lay huddled, limp, against the side of the carriage, all the rage gone from her. "Oh, Cal." His voice was tragic, broken. "How could you even think of such a thing?"

"How do you know what I was thinking?"

"Because I know *you*. My poor dear Callie, don't you know how lost I'd be without you? How lost Father would be?"

He stroked her wild hair, but she shrank from him. "You would be better off . . . both of you."

"Never! Never!" He pulled her tight to his chest, and Callie burrowed against him, her face stained with tears.

"They laughed at me," she whispered, anguished. "The students . . . in the street. They laughed and stared, and one of them said . . ." She shuddered at the memory. "Zeus, they all knew."

"And what if they did?" he demanded fiercely. "What do you care what they think?" He looked up at Mick again, apologetic. "It's been hard on her—Father losing his post, and the move . . . and she's given up drawing. She blames herself. . . ."

"Quite," Mick Harding said crisply.

The word sparked Callie's dormant fury. "You needn't speak about me as though I can't hear," she told her brother angrily. "And you are wrong. I don't blame myself, not completely. I blame *him* a great deal. He's out to ruin my life, our lives, don't ask me why. First Harry and then the portrait, and now this—what is he doing in Edinburgh, anyway? Hounding us, I'll wager. Go on and ask him, why don't you? What *are* you doing here?" Her eyes met his, but he looked at Zeus as he replied:

"There was a memorial service for my father at St. Giles this morning. He died last month. The music gave me a headache, so I found that druggist's. I'll go home to Ayrshire tomorrow."

For a moment the only sound in the carriage was the rattle of wheels. Then Zeus said softly, "You're no longer at Oxford?"

"The dean revoked my scholarship."

"God. I'm sorry. But with your credentials, some other university—"

"My living stipend was paid by the Presbyterian church. Once they got wind of what had happened at Oxford, they cut it off."

"Christ! What a stupid waste! I am sorry about your father."

Then he brightened slightly. "But perhaps your inheritance will enable you—"

"Zeus!" Callie interrupted, shocked.

"I'm not being cold-blooded, only practical! It's a damned tragedy for a scholar of his talents to go to waste. You can't deny that's true."

Callie said nothing. Across the carriage, Mick Harding smiled slightly. "You Wingates are forthright. But my father was as poor as the proverbial church-mouse. There's no inheritance beyond Langlannoch. And you've seen the shape the house is in."

"So you truly are the laird of Langlannoch. Why didn't you tell us that night at the Black Hart?" Zeus asked curiously.

Mick took off his spectacles and rubbed them clean on the edge of his cravat. "All that wild nonsense you were dragging up about the family—great heroes and stalwart heroines—it's got no meaning today. It's so far in the past. And I'm content it should stay buried there."

Callie looked at him; without the glasses, his eyes were the brilliant blue of gentians. She had never once thought what impact the unveiling of the portrait might have had on him, how it would have affected his career. The way his black beard waved was precisely the way she had painted it. "What were you doing there that day?"

He knew what she meant. "At Langlannoch. Fixing the roof, or trying to. The kitchen ceiling leaks. My grandmother still lives there. My father's mother."

Callie could scarcely believe anyone would live in that great ruined hulk. "Why didn't we see her?"

"She keeps to herself. You'd have seen her if she wanted to be seen."

Zeus cleared his throat. "We owe you an apology, Mr. Harding."

"Do you?"

"Aye. For the way we talked about you that day. We didn't think you knew English." He flushed a little. "As I recall, I said some harsh things about the Gaelic race."

Harding shrugged it away. "I've told you since, I share your feelings. A most irrational people."

"But you didn't speak up," Callie said suddenly. "You might have let us know you understood us."

For one instant his blue eyes touched hers; then they glanced off again. "Now and then, tourists come upon the place. They always want to know its history, about the family. It's quite tiresome, really. So I long ago took to feigning ignorance. It's so much simpler that way."

Callie looked straight at him. "Do you drop your drawers to all of them? Is that part of your charade?"

A slow red flush crawled up from the edge of his beard straight to his forehead. "The string on them broke," he said. "They just . . . fell. And I was so . . . I didn't know . . . you were—" He stopped, and swallowed. "It just seemed simpler not to move. That was all. And I never imagined I would see you again." She well believed it. "I am sorry for that."

"Well, it seems we are even, at least," Zeus told him, "having both offended each other. Except that we are in your debt again now, for your having been in that shop today. God, what odd coincidence! It is almost enough to make one turn to religion. Oh, I do beg your pardon." He was looking at Mick. "I fancy you must be one of the faithful, what with your father and that grant from the church."

"I never shared my father's faith. It was . . . one of many things we argued about."

The carriage had slowed. They'd long since left the city behind them, Callie saw through the window, and were way out past Holyrood Park; she could see Arthur's Seat not far off. "Any further directions, then?" the hack driver called back to them, sounding annoyed.

"Back to Clerk Street," Harding told him, leaning out to be heard. "Number ten. The rooming-house where I'm staying," he explained, settling back in. "I'll get out there, and you can take the hack home again."

They rode in silence as the coach turned 'round. Clerk Street was narrow and dark, lined with cheap students' quarters. Callie watched the house numbers from her window, counting the doors until Mick Harding would be gone from her life once more—this time, she hoped, for good.

The driver whistled and reined in. Harding pushed open the

door, then reached into his pocket. "This should cover half the fare." He held some coins out to Zeus, who sat without moving. So he offered it to Callie instead. But she was looking at her brother, recognizing that he was pondering something.

"Zeus," she started to say, with a sinking feeling. He cut her off, his voice once more bright.

"See here, Harding. I say. How about coming to supper?"

Callie went pale. "Jesus, Zeus, leave well enough a—"

"No, I mean it. Father would be ever so glad to see you. He's often wondered, all of us have, how you are getting on."

"Speak for yourself," Callie muttered in rebellion. "I scarcely think it is appropriate—"

Her brother turned on her, his gentle face surprisingly stern. "Stop thinking only of yourself, why don't you, just for a change? Father has been suffering too, although I doubt you'll have noticed, wallowing in self-pity as you've been."

"I have *not*—"

But he'd looked back at Harding. "He has been most unhappy. And he has so much respect for you. . . . He's teaching Homer to first-year boys. I fear it's killing him."

"I—" He was sitting awkwardly, with one leg out of the coach door. "That is really very kind of you, Wingate. I appreciate it. But I'm afraid, as your sister says, it would hardly be appropriate."

"Damn what my sister says! She set out this afternoon to kill herself; do you think her opinion ought to hold any weight? It seems to me there's blame enough in this situation. We might as well all share it—and share what bloody solace we can with one another. It's been a raw deal all around. Father's not much better off than Callie. Who knows? You might be able to spark life into him again."

Callie wanted to protest, but what he'd said about their father stalled her. Perhaps she had been selfish. Still, she'd only wanted what was best for him.

Mick Harding still had a foot outside the hack. It was uncanny how he could stay in one position so long. Little wonder he'd been such a fine model.

"Bae anyone gettin' out?" the driver called in despair.

Harding was looking at her. She averted her gaze.

"Bae *anyone*—" the driver started again.

Harding pulled his leg in. "If you honestly believe I can be of some service, I will join you for supper. I appreciate the invitation."

Zeus's grin was huge. "Splendid! Thanks! Chalmers Street, please!" he shouted to the driver.

"*Chalmers Street?*" the poor man echoed. "Bae this some sort o' jest?"

"Fifteen Chalmers Street," Zeus told him briskly. "Don't worry. We are good for the fare. At least—have you any money, Callie?" he asked in a whisper.

Feeling rather like a fox cornered by hounds, she shook her head. "I threw my purse at *him*."

"Well, the druggist can use it to pay for for the havoc you wreaked. Harding, I'm afraid we'll have to be even further in your debt. Growing tiresome, isn't it, this adding and sub-tracting from the ledger, figuring who owes whom?"

"We are all going to owe the driver," Mick Harding told him, showing the coins he still held in his palm. "This won't be nearly enough."

"Christ! What a trio of vagabonds." Zeus laughed outright. "It goes to prove, doesn't it, that intelligence is never justly rewarded? What are we to do?" He scratched his head. "Well. Perhaps Dorcas has some egg money stashed away somewhere. I do hope so!"

20.

Dorcas did, and seemed glad enough to pay it, though a bit muddled as to what had become of Callie's purse. "Told you to watch out for pickpockets, didn't I?" she scolded, with a crossness born more of nervous fear than of anger. Her keen gaze swept Callie's face, then skewered Zeus. "Found her, then, I see."

"Yes, yes. False alarm, Dorcas, dear. No need to mention anything to Father, is there? People do get headaches, after all. Look who we've trotted home with! You remember Mr. Harding."

"That I do." Her lips were tight as she scanned him, up and down. "What's he doing here?"

"Tut, tut, what sort of greeting is that? He's come to supper, of course. Is Father home?"

"Not yet."

"We'll wait for him in the drawing-room, and have a drop of claret."

"Orangeade for Mr. Harding, Dorcas," Callie put in quietly.

Zeus laughed. "Quite so. I'd forgotten. The notion of not drinking is so foreign to me."

"Actually," Harding spoke up, "I'd prefer the claret."

Zeus's eyebrow stretched. "Freed from your father's sober influence at last?"

"No, no. Nothing like that. It's simply been a very trying day."

"So it has." Zeus considered his sister. "Run along upstairs, Cal, why don't you, and put on something a bit less funereal for the meal? I do dislike looking at you in black."

It would serve him right, Callie thought, mounting the flights to her room, if I didn't come back down at all. Imagine asking that man to supper! And how uncouth of Harding to have accepted! As though I ever shall be able to look at him again without thinking of . . . she was flushing already, picturing the line of his loins, the deep hollows of shadow alongside his groin that she'd captured so well. Really, it was most insensitive of Zeus to expect her to sit at table with him after all the trouble he'd caused.

If not for him, came the nagging thought, *you wouldn't be supping this evening. You'd be lying cold in your bed, and the whole house in mourning.*

The notion made her shiver. She went to the washstand and splashed chilly water over her face and neck. I wouldn't really have done it, she argued back. I would have come to my senses.

You'd have bought the stuff. You'd have had it here. Sooner or later, you'd have used it.

Well, I just may go back tomorrow and buy it anyway! she thought defiantly, and toweled off her face. From across the room, she stuck her tongue out at the mirror.

And then slowly moved closer, studying the image there.

She looked like a harridan, hair all tangled in knots, skin still so ghostly pale and stretched thin over her bones. Yet something had changed since that morning, something about the eyes. They were not quite so dull and dead; a bit of gilt enlivened their green depths again. Well, little wonder, she thought, the way you let loose your spleen on Harding in the druggist's shop. Christ! What a sight she must have been, screaming and calling him names and hurling things about! The memory made her cheeks flood scarlet—and for a moment the wan image in the mirror shimmered with lost beauty, reflected a life that had been filled with careless wonder and joy. Callie stared into her own eyes, transfixed. "So you are in there still," she whispered. "I had wondered . . . whether I should ever see you again."

That afternoon, Harding had seen her at her worst. This evening . . . Callie hesitated, then began to pull the pins from her hair. She didn't dare ask Dorcas for hot water, not with the extra work a guest for dinner meant, so it would have to be cold.

She spilled the pitcher into the basin and plunged her head in, gasping as the frigid water tightened her scalp. She used her rose-attar soap, lavishly, so her curls would take the scent, then rinsed and toweled them. For a moment she wavered over lighting the fire—it wasn't really cold enough, and wood cost money. But without it, her hair would never dry in time.

In the golden glow of the flames, she combed through the tangled ends and then brushed the whole thick, rippling mass until it gleamed like russet satin. She stood for some minutes in front of her open wardrobe, pondering what to wear. Her newest gown was the sea-green silk made for the exhibition, but she had too many awful memories of that day. The dark blue slubbed linen was too plain; so was the coffee-brown serge. Oh, what she would have given for a godmother like those in fairy tales, to conjure up for her a dazzling new gown!

But she had such a dress. Tentatively she reached for the sturdy box on the highest shelf. Her wedding dress, in which she was to have married Harry. She took the box down and raised the lid. Up wafted a cloud of fine copper-gold damask, wreathed in the fragrance of the rose sachet Bea had tucked inside.

Slowly she lifted the gown by the shoulders. She'd never even had the final fittings for it. But as she ran her hand over the lustrous silk, she knew this was what she wanted to wear. She wanted to float into the drab drawing-room so absolutely dazzling that Mick Harding would need more than claret to steady himself. She wanted to erase from his blue eyes forever the humiliating pity she had seen there today.

This evening, he would see her at her best, or as close as

these months of misery would allow her to be. By God, she'd fix it so he would never feel sorry for her again!

She eased her arms into the billowing sleeves and twisted to fasten the long row of hooks up the back of the bodice. Christ! She'd forgotten how low-cut the dressmaker had insisted it should be. She'd meant to put her foot down at the later fittings. But perhaps, she thought, smiling slyly down at the round swells of her breasts above the tight-drawn silk, it was better this way—though Zeus would certainly wonder what she had on her mind.

What *did* she have on her mind? Only that Mick Harding should not feel sorry for her? Or did she hope, with silk and roses and white flesh, to reawaken whatever dormant madness had seized him when he'd kissed her on that snow-covered rock, and touched her with his hands like fire?

Well, if that happened, all the better. Damn his bloody sang-froid—look at how calm and in control he'd been at the drug-gist's. The only chink she'd ever seen in his wall of reserve had been there on the rock that night. She would enjoy glimpsing it again. By God, he'd soon learn her misfortunes hadn't bent her so low as to be cowed by a penniless Scottish scholar, no matter how illustrious his ancestors may have been. She'd tease him all through supper, dare him to make advances—and then send him packing back to his miserable Ayrshire ruin again. After the way she intended to play him, he'd steer far clear of Edinburgh for a long time to come.

Back to the looking-glass she went, to ponder her image as she once would have eyed an unfinished painting. What further gilding? Perhaps her amber ear-drops, and the cameo that had been her mother's, on its black-velvet band. Her hair . . . she would need Dorcas's help to do anything elaborate. It seemed rather a shame to put it up; the way its long, sheeny weight caught and traded the shimmer of the damask was quite ravishing. Of course, to leave it down was out of the question; that simply wasn't done.

And who says so? she thought bitterly. Women like Harry's mother, those brittle ladies of fashion who had come to the exhibition in their ermine and pearls? I am a lost cause to them already, and have been since they saw the portrait. Why should I go by their rules? Eyes flashing defiance, she pushed a wayward strand back over her bared shoulder, where it merged once more into the rippling russet mass. Then she marched downstairs.

Dorcas caught her in the corridor, and grabbed her wrist. "Why, you brazen thing! What are you doing wearing that? You get right back up to your room and put on something decent—and braid your hair while you're at it. You look a right little hussy!"

"Just the image I was after," Callie told her, and broke free to sweep into the drawing room.

Her father and Mick Harding were deep in some discussion; the professor glanced up, smiled vaguely, said, "Good evening, Calliope. How nice you look," and went back to talking: "Still and all, I find the 1514 Aldine edition of the *Iliad* immensely superior to anything published since. Don't you agree?"

But he'd lost his audience. Mick Harding had risen from his chair, claret cup in his hand. "Miss Wingate," he said, and had to clear his throat. "How do you do." He clearly wasn't used to drinking; the wine had made his blue eyes bright and put spots of red high on each of his cheekbones. He set his cup down with a clink.

Zeus had let out a long, low whistle under his breath. Callie ignored him as she flounced down on the sofa at an angle that afforded Harding a clear view into the front of her gown as she bent over to straighten the bow on her shoe.

He sat down quickly, hurriedly. "What an interesting outfit," Zeus murmured. "Are you going hunting?"

Callie ignored him. "Forgive me for interrupting, Father. What were you saying?"

"Oh, just comparing translations of Homer with Mr. Harding. It really is splendid to have his path cross ours again with such serendipity. I only fear I'll drive him off by talking too much. But I have missed his quick mind, haven't you, dear?"

There was a briskness, a vivacity to his voice that had been too long absent. Zeus was right, Callie thought; seeing Harding is good for him. "His mind? Oh, yes," she drawled. He was sitting stone-still, his knees spread, staring at his hands. She had to hide a smile. This was quite fun, really, this role of *femme fatale*. "I'm sure Mr. Harding knows how much time

I've spent admiring his . . . mind. Pour me some of that, would you, Zeus, pet?'' She waved toward the claret. "And I see that Mr. Harding's glass is empty.''

"No more for me," Harding said, with something like alarm.

"Cal!" Zeus hissed at her, but she just leaned back against the cushions with her claret, the edge of her tongue tracing the rim of the silver cup. He'd done that, hadn't he, to her mouth with his tongue? Was he remembering that night? His knuckles were white against his knees, and he had not raised his head.

"Such an extraordinary smell," Professor Wingate said, nose probing the air. "What do you suppose Dorcas has made for supper?"

"That isn't supper; it's Callie." Zeus's voice was disgusted. Trust him, she thought, to spring to Harding's defense! But men always stuck together. It was high time she stuck up for herself.

"Speaking of Homer," she began airily, "I must say, I always have wondered what Helen of Troy might have looked like, to drive all those men wild. What do you imagine, Mr. Harding? Do you picture her fair or dark? What color were her eyes?"

"I've . . . never given the matter any thought."

"Haven't you? How odd. How about you, Father?"

"Why, I've always pictured her looking like your mother, Calliope. You know, with your green eyes and red hair—"

"How very sweet of you to say so. But I'm sure Mr. Harding has his own idea of beauty. Anyway, Father, my hair isn't red, not really. It's more copper-colored, Mr. Harding, wouldn't you say?" She pulled a long strand forward and twirled it between her fingers. "Or russet, men sometimes tell me."

"Fox-colored," Zeus muttered.

"Helen was the daughter of Zeus and Leda," Callie murmured dreamily, still twining her shining curl. "Mr. Harding and I once had a most interesting discussion on the subject of Leda. But perhaps he doesn't recall."

Dammit all, why didn't he look up at her so she could properly enjoy this? Taunting him was proving all too easy. Why, he was tongue-tied, couldn't say a word! "Supper," Dorcas declared mutinously from the doorway, glaring at Callie.

"Oh, what a pity," she purred, rising in a rustle of silk. "Just when the conversation was going so well. Mr. Harding, won't you take me in?"

"You," Zeus whispered at her back, "are going to get yours."

"I'm sure I don't know what you mean. Mr. Harding?" He still had not moved from his chair.

"Never fear, Calliope," the professor said heartily. "We'll all have plenty of time to enjoy conversing with Mr. Harding."

"Oh, yes. I hope he won't be rushing off this evening."

"He *won't* be," Zeus hissed. "You missed all the discussion, Cal, while you were getting—dressed. We've worked everything out already, haven't we, Mick?"

"I—I must say, Wingate—"

"Zeus. You really must call me Zeus now."

"Zeus. Since I've had some time to reflect, I fear I've been too hasty in accepting your proposition."

"Nonsense, my boy!" Professor Wingate said, beaming. "You'll be doing us a great favor, especially me!"

Callie looked to her brother and then to her father. "What favor is that?" she asked, suddenly suspicious.

"It's very kind of you to say so, sir," Mick Harding put in quickly. "And I do appreciate your generous offer—"

"What offer?" Callie felt absolutely undressed as Harding slowly raised his big head to meet her gaze. He looked abjectly miserable—just as she'd wished. Why, then, did her bare skin abruptly feel so cold?

Her father smiled expansively, offering her his arm. "Well, my dear, as you know, I've yet to choose a professorial assistant. I'd been conducting interviews, but somehow no one seemed quite right. Mr. Harding has spoiled me, I believe."

"Has he?" Callie slipped her hand through the crook of his elbow with a sinking sensation in her belly.

"Yes, indeed. So I've gone ahead and offered the post to him. Since he finds himself at such loose ends, so to speak. It's the perfect answer to my dilemma."

"I can see that." Callie cast a baleful look over her shoulder at Zeus—why the devil hadn't he told her sooner?—and saw

him mouth at her: *Just wait . . .* Wait for what? Behind her
brother's back, Harding was rising to his feet. Christ, but he
was tall!

"Professor Wingate," he said haltingly, "I really do think,
upon further consideration, that I must refuse your—"

"No! No, I won't hear of it. You are a breath of spring in
what has been a very dreary household, Harding, and I absolutely insist that you remain in it."

"Re*main?*" Callie echoed in dismay. "What do you mean,
re*main?*"

"Well, my dear, since the stipend I can offer Mr. Harding
is appallingly low, and since we have that spare bedchamber
below yours, I thought it only fitting to invite him to stay."

"Stay? How *long?*"

"Professor Wingate, you are truly most kind, but under the
circumstances—"

"I'll brook no argument—none! My daughter, after all, is
responsible for the loss of your scholarship at Oxford."

"I?" Callie cried. Her father tucked her arm more firmly
into his, heading for the dining room.

"Yes, you. And this is one small way of making amends."

"Oh, Jesus!"

"You buttered your bread, didn't you?" Zeus whispered.

Professor Wingate held out Callie's chair, then beamed at
the three young people from the head of the table. "It should
prove a most edifying experience, Mr. Harding, having you
join us this way."

God, what a night! Callie slammed shut the door of her
bedroom and stomped toward the wardrobe, desperate to peel
off the alluring gown she'd been so eager to don. She'd left
the men as soon as she could, when they'd taken their port to
the drawing room, but she hadn't wanted to have it look like
she was slinking away. So through five long courses *and* coffee
and cheese, she'd been stuck across the table from Mick Harding, all her boldness deflated at the horrifying prospect of his
moving in.

In her house! At meals, day after day, when she'd practically offered herself to him like the roast veal on its platter, garnished with rosewater and amber and silk instead of parsley and leeks. Oh, Christ, it was so humiliating! What must he think of her now? Furious, she pulled off her shoe and hurled it, clattering, across the floor.

She froze in terror. Lord, his room was just below hers. He could hear her walking. He would hear her bathing—hear her bedsprings creak! What if he was down there now? As quietly as she could, she slipped out of her other shoe and tiptoed to retrieve its mate.

Of course, her father hadn't noticed her chagrin; he was too delighted to be discoursing again on all his favorite subjects. Zeus had been less than helpful, too. Having sat by and let her seal her fate, he'd joined in the conversation wholeheartedly, sending an occasional smug smile her way.

Now that she thought of it, once Harding had stopped protesting that he couldn't stay on, he'd settled in quite easily as well, even winning Dorcas over with compliments on the meal. Yes, indeed, the three men had been as cozy together as kittens; only she, in her seductress's garb, had been out of place, blushing whenever anyone addressed her, taking tiny nibbles of her food, and all the time trying desperately to hike up her neckline without being too obvious about it. She ripped open the hooks along her back with angry hands, stuffed the offending gown into its box, and jammed on the lid.

Well, there was nothing to be done for it now. She'd made a fool of herself again—amazing, really, how Harding brought that out in her—and she was stuck with the consequences. He'd said he never thought about what Helen looked like. Perhaps he hadn't noticed how she was dressed.

But she didn't believe that, not for a minute. She had been too blatant, bending over to let him glimpse her breasts, decorating herself like a shop-window—"Come buy! Come buy!" And all those innuendos she had thought so clever: *I'm sure Mr. Harding knows how much time I've spent admiring his . . . mind.* She'd acted cheap and available, just as she'd meant to, believing she would never have to see him again. And now she'd be living with him every day.

Perhaps not, though. Her behavior when she first came in had plainly unnerved him; he'd tried to back out of his acceptance of her father's hospitality. He might have the decency to stay only a few nights, then make some excuse and be gone. Surely she could avoid him for a time; she'd have Dorcas bring her meals up, and only venture downstairs once he had left the house.

Yet if she steered clear of him, her father was bound to notice. And the one saving grace in all this mess was that Professor Wingate remained blissfully unaware that he had raised an idiot daughter. Between the druggist this afternoon and supper this evening—why, Harding must truly think her mad.

She perched on the windowseat, staring out at the hulk of Castle Hill in the distance against a sky spangled with stars. A fat full moon had risen over the towers, flooding the ancient stones with silvery light. Her only hope lay in the chance that Mick Harding really was like her father—that most of what went on in everyday life passed him by, while his mind soared on loftier planes.

Even her father, though, she reminded herself, had come down to earth once, when he met Laurie MacCrimmon. What sort of courtship could theirs have been, the professor and the piper's daughter? She yearned with all her soul to know, but knew she never would.

She was at the mercy of Mick Harding's discretion. Whatever he did or said the next time she encountered him would dictate where they went from here.

He's proven his discretion before, she realized, when he held his tongue for all that time about being at Langlannoch. Maybe she was worrying too much. Maybe he didn't give a damn.

She looked down into the garden, slowly buttoning her night-dress—and then leaned forward, staring. Something new had sprung up in the hard soil near the hawthorn, something surprisingly tall. She stared at the plant's silhouette. What sort of Jack-and-the-beanstalk magic was this? It was the size of a tree, but capped, like a tulip, with a pale flower.

Not a flower—a face. As she peered down, loose hair tumbling over the white nightdress, she recognized Mick Harding. He was standing with his hands behind his back, planted firm as an oak—and he was staring at her. Quickly she ducked out of sight. At least he hadn't heard her throwing her shoe.

She crawled into bed and lay, still as she could, beneath the covers, wondering how long he'd go on standing there.

21.

Having Mick Harding in the house disrupted everything. Callie couldn't come down to breakfast without putting up her hair, was always wondering if her bodice laces were straight or her petticoats showing or a bit of fennel leaf stuck in her front teeth. It was true that often enough in the past, she'd stayed with her father and his students at villas and rooming houses all around the world, but that had been neutral ground, home to none of them. This was altogether different. Now he was always in *her* sitting room when she wanted to curl up with a book there, in *her* kitchen, passing the time of day with Dorcas and nibbling cheese, when she craved a snack, in *her* garden every time she longed for a bit of fresh air. It was infuriating—and what made it worse was that neither Zeus nor her father seemed discombobulated by his presence one bit. On the contrary, dinner-table discussions were once again lively; Professor Wingate trotted off to the university to wrangle Homer into his freshmen with new spring in his step. And Zeus—well, really, it was rather hard to tell about Zeus. Since Mick's coming he'd been slipping away to meetings nearly every evening, with something slyly satisfied about him. When his father teased him about the Jacobites and Bonnie Prince

Charlie, he still bantered back, but Callie thought she sensed in him a certain guardedness. Perhaps he is simply growing up, she mused, and learning that if one insists on engaging in illegal conspiracies, it is wiser not to go around boasting of it.

In the newspapers her father took—the Edinburgh *Journal,* the *Free Briton,* and, tardily, the *Daily Courant*—there was much back-and-forth about the prince and his champions; indeed, they seemed to delight in passing on the latest rumors. There was talk of papal backing for a huge invasion force to be sent across the Channel that summer; of treaties between Charles Edward and King Louis of France, abetted by the sinister Cardinal Tencin; of a massive conspiracy of Jesuits to be spearheaded by the prince in restoring Catholicism world-wide. But to Callie, who read them more or less faithfully, these articles and letters seemed to contain a hint of wistfulness, as though the men who penned them glimpsed in the person of the Young Pretender some last vestige of the glory of former days. Even those writers who decried Charles Edward's cause took pains to compliment his charm, his skill at arms, his *savoir faire,* his quick mind and exquisite manners—all those attributes so notably lacking in the Hanovers now occupying Britain's throne.

"Oh, I say, look at this, Zeus," Professor Wingate said one evening over jellied veal consommé, handing him the *Journal.* "The letter by the MacMillan chap, at the bottom of the page. He compares your Bonnie Prince Charlie to King Arthur."

"Does he really?" Zeus grabbed up the paper.

"There are certain superficial similarities," Mick Harding conceded, breaking apart his bread. "Certainly the Celtic origin, and the aura of Christian mystery surrounding Camelot—one could reconcile that quite easily to Catholicism nowadays."

"I like it," Zeus declared, scanning the paper. "That's just what the movement needs to attract adherents in England. Appeal to their latent national pride—'Britain for the British! Throw out these parvenu Germans.' "

"But it's all wrong," Callie noted, setting down her spoon. "He has got it backward. Prince Charles isn't Arthur; he is Lancelot, the great knight from the Continent, dashing and holy and pure. The miracle-worker. And the Scots are Guinevere, whom he seduces away from her spouse."

Zeus was staring at her, entranced. "Oh, dear God, Cal. That is even better. It has just the right illicit air; it appeals to one's libidinous instincts. You ought to write it up and send it in. If you won't, I will."

"As I recall," Harding said dryly, "Lancelot's adultery with Arthur's queen destroyed Camelot and ushered in the Dark Ages—not, perhaps, the image you Jacobites wish to conjure."

"But I suspect," the professor put in, "very much what would happen were Charles Edward to invade. What I simply cannot fathom, Zeus, is what you and your fellow malcontents have against the status quo. The nation is thriving. Didn't you read the agriculture ministry's report on wool exports last year? Or see the coal-extraction figures? Have you been to market lately and seen how the corn laws are holding down the cost of bread?"

"We are becoming a race of little clerks," Zeus said mournfully, "scratching pens and stamping stamps and pushing papers about, none of us thinking, none of us *creating* anything."

"Well," said the professor, ringing for Dorcas to clear the soup away, "you are never going to effect rebellion so long as people's houses are warm and their bellies full."

"I would like to believe," Zeus told him rather stiffly, "that the British, or the Scots at least, have more soul than that. That there is in their marrow some ineffable yearning toward the higher ideals. Mick, what do you think?"

Harding seemed a bit embarrassed to be thus appealed to. He sat very still, hands on the napkin folded on his lap. "You know I am inclined to agree with your father. An atmosphere of reason and peace is more conducive to the nation's prosperity than one of partisan strife. Fifty years of union between Scotland and England have shown us that much. And to resurrect religion as a barrier—well, I simply do not know of any road less likely to lead to rational behavior. God has caused more wars than Satan ever could."

"An odd sentiment for a parson's son," Professor Wingate remarked.

"I was always puzzled by my father's faith," Harding admitted. "He was by no means a stupid man, yet he seemed to find genuine solace in the church. Whereas from an early age it was quite clear to me that religion of any sort is pure rejection of reason. Excepting, of course, a strictly pro forma religion, such as that of the ancient Greeks."

"Mm. Quite." Professor Wingate dug into the chicken with a carving knife.

"And your mother?" Callie asked.

Harding turned blue eyes to her. "Pardon?"

"Your mother—where did she stand on the question of reason versus religion?"

He hesitated. "She was . . . the least rational person I ever knew."

Callie suddenly wished she hadn't posed the question; there was something raw and pained in his deep voice. Zeus sensed it, too, and hastily changed the subject.

"But don't you see, Mick, if you follow your argument, that the rejection of the Stuart dynasty was truly irrational? For Parliament to depose and kill kings strictly because of their religion is madness! And to pass over the true heirs on those same grounds, to go grubbing up Protestant claimants from overseas and hand the crown to them—"

"You are simplifying, my boy," his father said mildly. "Though you may have a point."

"Of course I do! How can we even pretend to be a rational nation when this great, grave act of insanity and bigotry looms in our past? The way to restoring reason lies in restoring the Stuarts to the throne."

Professor Wingate eyed him with some pride. "You've been refining your arguments, young man. That was very nicely put."

"Thank you," Zeus told him, grinning. "I'll have a drumstick, please."

Zeus didn't stay for coffee; he rarely did anymore. Callie accepted a cup when Dorcas offered it, though. It was a mannish drink, but she liked its bracing flavor, and the rich color, like good garden loam. Mick Harding let his cup be filled as well. The professor, however, waved Dorcas away—"None for me, thank you. My stomach's been a bit churlish all day. Could I have chamomile instead, in my study? I've fifteen essays on the travels of Ulysses to read."

"I'd be happy to help, sir," Harding offered, starting up from his chair.

"I'll have the first go-round at them; you can take your shots in the morning. I'll likely turn in early. Good night, Calliope." He came and kissed her.

"Good night, Father."

So she was stuck alone with Harding. It had happened once or twice before in the month he'd been with them, and always, as if by unspoken agreement, one or the other of them had promptly withdrawn. She thought this time it was his turn to get up and go, but he just sat, stirring sugar into his cup. Annoyed, Callie determined to drink her coffee as fast as she could and then disappear. She took a big sip, and nearly choked on the scalding brew. "God, that's hot!" she cried, her napkin to her mouth.

"Hot and strong," he agreed. "She makes the best coffee in Britain. I have told her so. It reminds me of the coffee in Greece."

That reminded Callie of a bone she'd meant to pick with him. "What did you mean when you called the Greek religion pro forma?"

He raised his gaze from his cup, surprised. " 'Pro forma.' From the Latin—"

"I know what it *means;* I wanted to know what you meant."

"Oh. Just that . . . well, you know. That whole o'er-arching system of deities, the innumerable cults in all their minutiae, the Protean nature of the gods and goddesses, the utter lack of dogma—really, nothing to grab onto there, is there? Just a sort of pleasant, mild polytheism, gods like one's uncles, either chummy or a bit menacing, and the goddesses much akin to the sort of women a fellow fantasizes about when he is ten or twelve, perfectly lovely but unapproachable. . . ." He trailed off, looked away, and quickly took a gulp from his cup.

"You don't think they believed in it?"

"Good Lord, of course not! How could they? What was there to believe in? There's no clear-cut morality, no set of laws, no creed. It's no more than the rational Greek's stab at wishful thinking—glorified nature-worship, animism taken to the utmost degree. It made for charming stories, of course, but religion? That was no religion. Homer and his ilk did not believe in Zeus and Athena and Dionysus the way my father believed in God."

"Are you certain of that?"

He smiled briefly. "Certain enough to have written a treatise contrasting the two systems for my admission to Oxford. And they let me in."

"When we were at Delos," Callie said softly, "we visited the ruins of a house, quite a big one, in the hills. Father said it must have been the home of one of the administrators of the temple; he seems to have been well-off. There were mosaics in the bath, and statues, and everywhere he'd had his name and that of his wife carved in. Then when we went to the temples, we found in one of the courts a prayer-stone with the same names engraved. They'd lost their son, the man and wife, their two-year-old son, and in their prayer they importuned the boatman who would row their boy across the river Styx to help him in and out of the craft, because his walking was unsteady and the shoes in which they'd buried him were new." She looked up at him. "It did not seem the prayer of a people whose religion was perfunctory to me."

"Oh, well, perhaps the common folk. But the intellectuals—"

"You said your father was intelligent. Yet he believed in God."

He took a draught of coffee. "You've chosen an odd side to back in this, considering that I gather you were planning to do yourself in a few short weeks ago." Callie flushed. "Did you think you were condemning yourself to eternal damnation? Do *you* believe in God?"

"Well, not in all the trappings, no. Not Satan and saints and Mary being a vir—not in those sorts of things. But in something, yes. Some sort of force, some beginning."

"Primus motor—the Prime Mover." His smile was indulgent.

"Something like that, yes! A power that created the world's beauty, made the sky blue and the grass green and gave lilies of the valley their scent. I mean, it didn't have to be like that. It might have all been gray and brown and dull, or red and violet and clashing. It very easily could have been."

"I've never heard the argument for God's existence reduced to color theory. It's very primitive, rather Egyptian or Syrian." He paused, considered. "Or Celtic, I suppose. One can't get more down-to-earth than worshipping oak trees."

"It is easy for you to sneer, when you clearly don't believe in anything."

"Oh, but you're wrong. I do. I believe in reason, in man's ability to think and plan and control his baser impulses. I worship at that altar. I daresay your father would agree with me. I thought that you did, too, before I found you contemplating suicide."

"Actually, that would have been an act of reason. I'd thought it out quite carefully—its effect on Zeus, and Father's career, and all of that."

"If that's true, you weren't thinking rationally."

She set her cup down with a clatter. "What would you know about it? What acquaintance do you have, you stuffy scholar, with misery and despair?"

"Emotion, by definition, is irrational."

"Oh, you are impossible!" She stood up with a swish of skirts and started for the doors. His voice at her back brought her up short.

"And I do have some nodding acquaintance with those feelings. My mother killed herself when I was ten years old."

Callie turned, her hand at her mouth. "Good Lord. I'm so sorry."

He shrugged, looking down into his coffee cup. "So while I may never have experienced such sentiments myself, I can testify to the effects of suicide on survivors. However you calculated what your family would feel, you did not weight it enough." He drained the cup. "Really, that's splendid coffee. If you'll excuse me, Miss Wingate, I have some reading to do.'' He pushed his chair back, stretched to his full height, and walked past her, down the corridor and up the stairs.

A few nights later, Zeus did linger at the table. He called for coffee and cream-cakes and talked his father into staying as well, even though the professor still had reports to grade; the end of term was drawing near. He was at his most witty and charming, telling tales of the customers at the bookshop that made even Mick Harding laugh out loud. Callie was absolutely, positively certain he was up to something. She watched with narrowed eyes as he deftly wound the conversation 'round past the exceptionally fine spring to upcoming final examinations to what sort of summer weather might be expected to—what the devil, Callie wondered, was he aiming at?

''The weather was quite lovely in Ayrshire last summer when we were there,'' Zeus noted in an offhand tone, passing the plate of cream-cakes. ''Just as I like it, not too hot nor too wet. Is it always like that there?''

The appeal had been made to Harding, who took a cream-cake and nodded. ''Generally. Though some summers lately, my grandmother says, there have been dreadful storms.''

''Sweeping up from the Channel.'' Zeus nodded. ''It was just that sort of storm that helped Drake destroy the Spanish Armada.''

''Oh, there are those. But Grandmère says the ones in August are much worse—those that come off the Atlantic. The hurricanes. Of course, those only hit Langlannoch once or twice in a hundred years.''

Zeus took a bite of cake, dusted sugar from his shirt-front, chewed, and swallowed. ''Spend a lot of summers there, do you, Mick?''

''Not anymore. I did when I was a child.'' He almost looked at Callie, then didn't. With his mother? she wondered. Did he regret having confessed about her? ''But since I've been in school, I've tried to go overseas whenever I had the chance— Turkey or Greece or wherever. I'd go to Grandmère at the start and end of holiday, but that was all.''

''Headed abroad this year, then?''

Harding shook his head. "Can't afford it."

"No, nor we neither, I reckon. How about it, Father? Will we be able to travel?"

"Afraid not, my boy. Maybe next year."

"Pity. I'll miss grubbing about in the dirt." That made Callie snort inelegantly into her coffee. The men looked at her.

"I didn't ever realize you were so fond of grubbing," she told her brother.

"Well, it's more the adventure of the thing—uncovering the past, learning about other cultures, living out of one's trunk. I really shall miss that." He realized Callie was eyeing him askance, and held the cake-plate out to her. "Another?"

"No, thank you." What was he driving at?

"You'll still be going to Langlannoch, though," he said to Harding.

"Oh, yes. I've written Grandmère to expect me in mid-June. With the extra time, perhaps I'll finally get that kitchen roof leak bunged."

Zeus nodded glumly. "You'll have a change of scene, at least. I don't know what in the world I'll do with all my free time. Mr. Dunning cuts his staff down quite severely over the holiday. He's already said he won't be needing me." He sighed. "Everyone tells me the city gets beastly hot, especially down here by The Meadows. Not much to look forward to, I fear." He poured himself more coffee, took cream, and then raised his blond head. "I say, Mick, here's a thought. Perhaps we all might go along to Langlannoch with you."

Behind his spectacles, Harding's gentian-blue eyes blinked. "But that's impossible."

"Is it? Why?" Zeus had leaned forward with unwonted eagerness. So that's what he's been wrangling for—an invitation to Langlannoch, Callie realized. But what was in that for him?

Harding seemed, for a change, almost flustered. "You've seen the place. It's a wreck, a ruin. It's not set up for guests."

"Oh, we're not guests," Zeus told him cheerfully. "Besides, we're quite accustomed to making-do. I'm sure we've stayed in worse accommodations in our time. Remember, Father, that place in Sicily with the fleas?"

"Don't badger, Zeus," the professor chided.

"I wasn't badgering. I was just remembering how intriguing Mick's house was. You said so yourself."

"Mm. Most extraordinary piece of Eastern-influenced architecture I've ever seen in Britain, that's true enough."

"*And* you said you could spend years studying it."

"It's just an old house," Harding said.

"With some remarkable features," Professor Wingate noted, smiling. "Those minarets, the mosaic floors, the frescos . . . don't sell the place short, young man, just because it is yours. Familiarity need not breed contempt."

"No, sir," Harding murmured. "And I don't mean to be rude, Zeus. But it really isn't possible."

Professor Wingate pushed back his chair. "I'd suggest, Zeus, that you spend the summer brushing up on algebra. Your tuition next year may be gratis, but passing grades certainly won't be."

"Yes, sir. I only thought Mick might appreciate the opportunity to return your own hospitality."

"Zeus!" Callie was appalled at the transparent blackmail.

"What?" her brother said with wide-eyed innocence.

Harding was sitting stock-still, but a spot of color had flared on each of his cheekbones. "What did you say, Zeus?" the professor asked; he'd been searching for his glasses and had missed it.

"Oh, nothing. If Mick says we aren't welcome, well, that's that."

"Quite so," his father said crisply. "Has anyone seen my spectacles?"

" 'Round your neck," Zeus told him.

"Oh, yes. Quite. Thanks. Well, I'm off to my study."

"Professor Wingate. Wait." Mick Harding took a deep breath. "Of course I would be honored if you and your family came to stay at Langlannoch, for as long as you wish."

"Mr. Harding." Callie glared at Zeus. "Just because my brother has the manners of an ape, you must not feel obligated—"

"But he's quite right, isn't he? You have opened your home to me. This is the least I can do to show my gratitude."

Callie had been following Zeus's finagling so intently that she really hadn't stopped to think what such a visit would mean for her. Returning to that lost, tangled Eden where she'd first seen Harding, and made the sketch on which the portrait was based . . . "Well, *I* shan't be going," she announced.

"Why not?" her brother inquired. "I daresay the country air would do you a world of good, Cal. You might even feel like drawing again."

"I'd bloody well like to know why you're so keen on going," she hissed at him.

"Scientific curiosity. I already said."

"Stop it, you two," their father said mildly. "That's quite a generous offer you've made, Harding. It occurs to me such a visit would answer a dilemma. I've wanted to give Dorcas a holiday to go back to visit Bea. If we could spend a fortnight in Ayrshire—"

"Oh, a month," Zeus urged. "Surely Dorcas deserves that much."

"But if Dorcas goes to England," Callie began, heart sinking.

"You certainly can't stay here alone," Zeus concluded in triumph. "You will have to come."

"I really think, Father," she cried, "poor Mr. Harding has had his hand forced!"

"Have you, Harding?" the professor inquired.

Mick Harding had recovered his aplomb. His expression was that of a man condemned to the gallows for a crime he didn't commit, but his emotions were in check. "Not at all, sir. If I seemed less than eager, it was only the novelty of Zeus's proposal. It has been . . . a good many years since we've had guests at Langlannoch."

"And we won't be putting your grandmother to trouble?"

"Oh, no. I daresay we will scarcely see her. Grandmère likes her solitude."

Callie determined to give it one last try. "Mr. Harding is just being polite, Father, which is more than Zeus was!"

"Mr. Harding tells me we are welcome, Calliope. Are you accusing him of being uncandid?"

"Of course I'm not accusing . . ." Cornered, she rolled her eyes.

"Very well, then. Mr. Harding, we accept your invitation with pleasure. Let me go tell Dorcas. I'll wager she'll be quite ecstatic." Professor Wingate shifted back his lanky shoulders, standing taller. "It does make one feel enlivened, does it not, having an outing to look forward to?"

22.

So much, Callie thought, was a matter of perspective. Take Langlannoch. She craned to see beyond Zeus's shoulders to the manor, the salt breeze whipping her hair. Approached this way, from the north, from the village of Ayr, along the sea road, the great house seemed more, well, intact than it had when one came upon it from the high crags of the south. It was at once grander and less exotic, more like a late Norman castle appended with a few Eastern touches, the minarets and the soft buff-yellow stone that reminded her so much of the Holy Land. The wild gardens, at this distance, were no more than a rich haze of green. If she and Zeus had first come at the place, two years ago almost to the day, by this angle, they might very well never have ventured inside the gate at all—and what then?

Perspective. She glanced across the open wagon at Mick Harding, and then quickly away. Ayr had been, in respect of him, rather a revelation. Everyone knew him, called to him from shop doorways and along the narrow streets: "God 'n Mary bae wi' ye, Yer Lairdship!" "God bless ye, Yer Lairdship!" "God rest yer dear father, Yer Lairdship! Mourned we war, faith, to larn o' his death!"

"They speak English," Zeus had noted, astounded.

"Most do, aye," Harding acknowledged. "The old folk less. My father had it taught in the schools from when he became laird."

"Quite rightly," Professor Wingate said with approval. "He had an eye to progress, your father."

"But they didn't speak English to me." Zeus was still perplexed.

"Oh, they wouldn't, to a stranger. The Gaels as a race are quite adept at feigning." Harding smiled briefly. Something had changed in his voice since they'd reached his home country; the lilt in it had become richer, more noticeable, quite unconsciously. A little girl picked a bunch of wild gillyflowers from beside the road and ran to give it to him, shy but eager.

"God 'n Mary bae wi' ye, sir."

"Thank you, Fi. It is Fi, isn't it? Mrs. MacGregor's daughter?"

"Aye, sir! Fancy yer rememberin'!" She bobbed a curtsy as the wagon rattled away. "Mum says gi' her best to yer grandam!"

"I will, Fi. Thanks." He'd waved his hand and settled back in his seat, staring at the gay blossoms self-consciously.

"Forgive my asking, Harding," said Professor Wingate, "but what rights do you retain as laird of Langlannoch?"

"None, not really. Not under English law."

Zeus's eyes were eager in the bright morning sun. "But a good many, I'd wager, by local tradition."

Harding waved a hand. Did Callie only imagine that the gesture had something faintly, negligently regal to it? "A few nominal fees and tithes. Some of the farmers insist on bringing 'round sheep and chickens and such. One old man hauls a sheaf of wheat up to the house each harvest—the 'first fruits' thing, you know."

"What about the system of justice? Are you the officer of the peace?" Professor Wingate inquired.

"We've had an English sheriff up to Ayr since the union. My father hadn't lived here since—he hadn't been in residence for a good ten years."

"Who calls out the clan?" Zeus asked curiously.

"There isn't any clan as such. My family . . . never proved very fecund. No lady of Langlannoch has had more than one or two children in four centuries."

"How very odd," said Professor Wingate, clearly intrigued. "I once read of a parallel circumstance among the dukes of Loigne. The writer of the essay concluded it was because their castle lay in bogland; he thought perhaps the fumes prevented conception. He did note, though, that there were rumors among the peasant populace of infanticide."

"Good Lord, Father," Callie murmured, embarrassed.

"Heavens, child, Harding's a rational man. He knows I'm not insinuating his ancestors were murderers." And he reached across the wagon-bed to rap Harding's knee. "Who knows—perhaps you'll be the one to break with tradition, spawn a whole dozen cubs!" Callie slid back on the hard wooden seat, blushing furiously.

Of course she'd known the man was laird of his ruined castle, but she'd never thought of that as being on a par with Harry or Lord Ormond. That is, he hadn't two shilling pieces to rub together; he'd worn the commoner's gown at Oxford, and he had none of the English gentry's rarefied airs. Still, it was something to see the honor and respect he commanded in the village, though evidently reluctantly.

"Someone must call them out." Zeus was still following some train of thought that had escaped the rest of them. "The men of the region," he amended. "In the event of warfare."

"The British commander at Kilchumin, I believe, has the authority," Harding said with an air of abstraction. "But they've never been summoned in my memory. You English tend to find us undisciplined soldiers."

You English. There it was again, the subtle shifting to the other side. She looked at him again. He'd taken off his glasses to rub away the road-dust; the breeze was riffling his thick black hair. Except for the pallor of his skin and the black Oxford suit, now grown shabby, he was very much the bronzed warrior she'd once painted, and had imagined huddled in the ruins of Langlannoch, coupling with his wife.

They'd reached the gates. The wagon-driver hopped down to push them open, tilted back his wide hat, and surveyed the garden's tangled, overgrown madness. "Culd stand a bit o' cuttin' back in here, culd ye nae?" he observed, then led the horse onto the drive, or what of it hadn't been reclaimed by creeping mats of greenery. "Come up wi' a few o' my lads, shall I, Yer Lairdship?"

"You know my grandmother prefers it this way, Collum." The laird of Langlannoch ducked to avoid a low-hanging snare of roses, seemingly unaffected by their rich spice scent. Callie, however, turned her face skyward and let them sweep over her skin in a rush of petal-soft sweetness. When she lowered her head, Harding was staring at her. "You'll get marked by thorns that way," he said, and then turned his attention to the driver. "I would, however, like some help with the kitchen roof. You might tell Liam and Davey, and see if they can put a crew together. Six or eight men, for a week or so. I can pay a little. Very little."

"They'll be glad o' the work, m'laird." He whistled the horses to a halt before the gaping front doorway. "Here ye bae, then, m'laird."

"Thank you, Collum." Harding jumped down from the wagon-bed, then turned to offer his hand to Professor Wingate. Zeus swung Callie to the ground. They left Collum unloading their baggage, and followed Harding into the vast, echoing hall.

Perspective. It was different to walk across that rich mosaic floor, defaced and dirty though it was, and know the man whose ancestors had planned and installed it. "How old is the house, Harding?" the professor inquired, his voice echoing weirdly across the stones.

"Early fourteenth century, I think."

"Ah. The time of the Bruce."

"Yes, I suppose it would have been."

"And was the builder a Crusader?"

"I'm really not certain."

It was odd, thought Callie, that a man otherwise so well-versed in history should be so careless of his own. Then she jumped as a huge gray cat appeared out of nowhere, padding soundlessly across the mosaic to rub against her skirts. "Well! Here's a friendly fellow," she exclaimed, and knelt to scratch his ears.

"Still here, are you, old thing?" Harding frowned absently at the cat. "That would be Grimkin."

"The two hundred 'n fifty-eighth Grimkin," said a voice from the shadows out of which the cat had sprung—a woman's voice, rich and low-pitched, with a strong undercurrent of Gaelic. "Taken a shine to ye, missy, he has."

"Come out of the dark, Grandmère," Harding chided, bemused, "before our guests think you a ghost."

The voice laughed. "Aye, that bae me—the wraith o' Langlannoch." She stepped forward, though, into the slanting rays of sunlight pouring through the high casements. "I bid ye welcome, gude m'laird." She made a low, graceful curtsy that left her genuflected at her grandson's feet.

"Good God, Grandmère, get up!" He tugged her by the arms. "What will the professor think?"

"Ye ken I cannae rise until ye bless the house, Michel. Ye bae the new laird."

"Grandmère . . ."

She pushed his hands from her wrists. "Speak the blessing, Michel."

Harding cast an apologetic glance at Callie's father. "I don't remember it."

She raised her bowed head. "Dinna remember it, ye say! There bae a fine lie, when I taught it to ye myself. Dinna remember it? Hah!"

"Grandmère . . ." His embarrassment was palpable. *"Please.* You know I don't believe—"

"But I do, Michel. Speak the blessing, or I'll stay on my knees on this chill, drafty floor until I die o' the ague!"

Harding let out a long, slow sigh that seemed to waft toward the vaulted ceiling. "All right, Grandmère." Then, very quickly, he rattled off some lines in what Callie assumed was Gaelic but realized toward the end was French, a French so antiquated that she'd scarcely recognized it.

"Amazing," she heard Zeus murmur.

The woman prostrated on the floor pushed herself up briskly, dusted the palms of her hands, and then embraced Harding, kissing him on both cheeks. "Welcome home, my darlin', darlin' laddie."

He returned the kisses, mumbling: "You will find one way or another, won't you, Grandmère, to make a fool of me?"

"Ach, ye do that all by yerself, Michel." She winked at Callie over his shoulder. "But ye maun introduce me to our guests."

"As I was trying to, before you launched into all that nonsense. Grandmère, this is Professor William Wingate, his son Zeus, and his daughter Calliope. Professor, allow me to present my grandmother, Margaret, Lady Harding."

"Maggie," she corrected him, as the professor bent over her hand.

She wasn't *anything* like what Callie had expected. Lady Harding was as lean as a whippet, taller than Zeus, with fair, pale skin that seemed almost untouched by time, and a magnificent mane of black hair that gleamed white only at the temples. How old was she? Callie wondered. If Harding was twenty, and his father had him at, say, twenty, then she would surely have to be at least in her fifties, even if she'd been a child bride.

Zeus was enchanted by her; Callie could tell by his sudden shyness, the way his words, usually flippant, came slow: "Lady Harding, I—"

"Just Maggie! There bae ceremonies I dinna stand on, 'n those I do." She gave her grandson a sharp glance.

"I am honored to meet you," Zeus managed to stammer, and kissed her hand.

"Ach, he bae a fair-tongued wonder, bain't he, Michel?" Zeus blushed, and she laughed and actually ruffled his blond hair. Such intimacy would have earned anyone else a withering glance. But for Harding's grandmother, Zeus had only a dreamy smile.

Lady Harding took a step toward Callie. "Now ye, Calliope."

"Callie," she said faintly.

"Callie." The woman's eyes, a paler blue than Harding's, scrutinized her from head to toe; she actually circled 'round Callie, who stood motionless, self-conscious and perplexed.

"That hair," Lady Harding murmured, and touched Callie's russet curls. "That hair has Scots red in it, has it nae?"

"My late wife," Professor Wingate told her, "was a Mac-Crimmon, from Skye."

"War she, now?" The woman turned to her grandson and beamed. "Ach, she bae lovely, lovely. Highly suitable, Michel. Ye hae done well."

"Highly suitable for *what?*" Harding asked, with a bit of a squeak.

"Why, for yer bride, lad!"

Harding and Callie both erupted at once: "But I'm not—" "But she isn't—" Mortified, Callie felt her cheeks flood red.

"Nae? Ach, my mistake," Lady Harding said easily. "I thought, Michel, ye wrote in yer letter—"

"Grandmère, you know I did no such thing!"

"Well, then, ye maun forgive an auld woman's fancies. My memory bae nae wha' it once war." Her eyes, though, were as bright and sharp as a bird's. "Put it down to wishful thinkin'. I wuld like to see ye wed, Michel, before I gae to my grave."

"You'll live another hundred years, Grandmère; only the good die young. Now behave yourself, would you, and show Miss Wingate to her room? Perhaps, Zeus, you might come and give me a hand with the bags."

Lady Harding cackled a laugh that sounded faintly witchlike. Then she crooked a long, thin finger at Callie. "Come along, my dear."

The magnificent front staircases were too crumbled to be safe, so they went through the house to the kitchens, where the biggest hearth Callie had ever seen was glowing and a woman in a white cap stirred something in a pot on a cleek. The air smelled mysterious, of herbs and bark. "Jennet, this bae Miss Wingate, wha' bae come wi' Michel," Lady Harding announced. "Miss Wingate, this bae my Jennet."

The woman smiled at Callie. She had a broad, freckled face and straw-colored hair done up in tight plaits. "Pleased I bae to meet ye, missy. Will ye hae a try o' this, then, mum, afore I bottle it up?"

"Nae, faith, ye make it finer than I do anymore."

"What is it?" Callie asked, sniffing the exotic scent.

"Arrow-poison," Lady Harding said matter-of-factly, and pushed open a door as Callie gasped. "Will ye come this way?"

The upper story was in far better condition than one ever would have guessed from the ruined front hall. As she followed Lady Harding down a long corridor, Callie peeked through doorways and glimpsed bedsteads, couches, queer old-fashioned chairs, even a few tapestries. "These bae my rooms," Lady Harding told her, nodding into a chamber furnished with an elegant cherrywood bed hung with rosy damask curtains. "I hae put ye here, just across the way, for propriety's sake."

"Lady Harding, I assure you, there's no question of—"

"Maggie. It bae gude, plain Maggie."

Callie hesitated. "Perhaps—Lady Maggie?"

"Ach, ye English! Stiffer than boards." Then she shrugged and smiled. "Very well. Lady Maggie, if that suits ye. That bae wha' hospitality bae meant for, nae? To set one's guests to ease." She opened the door, and Callie followed her in.

The bedchamber was utterly delightful, with whitewashed walls and a polished wood floor whose chill was eased with a carpet patterned in roses. There were roses, too, great clouds of fragrant white and red roses in jars and vases set about the place, on the bedstand and the wardrobe and the wide windowsills. The bed was high, and curtained, like the windows, in a fine soft linen, lucent in the late-day sunlight. Lady Harding watched with a satisfied expression as Callie stared at the vision of lush roses and pale linen, entranced.

"Will it do?"

"Oh, Lady Harding—Lady Maggie! It is . . . indescribable. Beautiful."

"Michel mentioned in a letter once that ye war an artist. This bae the prettiest room in Langlannoch, I think. 'Twar in this room that the first laird slept wi' his lady. His name war Michel, too."

"He built the house?"

"Aye, aye. He began work on it the year o' the Bannockburn—1314. But it war nae finished for nigh ten years. He had much fightin' to do, for he served the Bruce."

"Mr. Harding told my father he did not know who had built it."

The woman's fine eyes narrowed. "Michel ken well eno' the story of his family, just as he ken the house-blessing. Dinna let him tell ye otherwise. But ye maun bae weary fro' yer journey. Here bae water 'n' towelin'—I'll gae 'n fetch the soap for ye. I dinna ken until I saw ye which soap best wuld suit ye.'' She reached out her long-fingered hand and stroked Callie's cheek. ''Wha' bae yer favored scent?''

''I . . .''

''Ne'er ye mind; I smell it on ye: attar o' roses. I'll send ye some 'round.'' She turned to go.

''Lady Maggie—''

''Aye?''

''Was that truly arrow-poison?''

''Aye, aye, sae it war.''

''But what on earth for? You aren't fighting anyone, are you?''

''Ach, not now. But potion-makin' bae like anythin' else—ye maun keep yer hand in it, or ye'll find yerself forgettin'. Care for a bath, wuld ye?'' Callie was on the verge of denying it, but her face must have showed her longing; it had been a four-day ride from Edinburgh. Lady Harding laughed. ''I'll send Jennet up wi' the tub, then, 'n water. Make yerself to home.''

''Thank you,'' Callie said, but she'd already gone, silent as the ghost she'd jested she was. Callie turned toward the bed—Lord, it looked soft and inviting after that journey—and started in surprise as she saw the gray cat, Grimkin, curled up in the midst of it, calmly nattering at a paw. ''Perhaps she turned into you,'' Callie whispered, and felt even more unsettled when the cat opened its wide gold eyes to stare at her.

''Cal!''

She nearly screamed at the voice so close to her ear. ''Jesus, Zeus, don't give me such a start! What is it about this house that makes folk sneak about so?''

''I wasn't sneaking,'' he defended himself, setting the trunk he'd carried up beside the bed. ''The door was wide open. I just walked in. Isn't it splendid, Cal? Isn't *she* splendid?''

''Oh, yes, splendid. Did you know what she's brewing down in the kitchens?'' Callie moved quickly to close the door. ''Arrow-poison!''

But Zeus, rather than offended, seemed intrigued. ''Is she

really? You don't say. My, my, your room is handsome, isn't it? And I thought mine was. But yours puts it to shame.''

''She told me it's where the first laird of Langlannoch slept with his lady.'' Callie found herself whispering. ''He fought with the Bruce at the Bannockburn. His name was Michel, too. He built the house.''

''Did he, now? That's interesting. Did you hear that blessing Mick spoke?''

''Heard it, aye, but didn't understand it.''

''Little wonder. It was in perfect fourteenth-century French. Astonishing to hear it recreated in the Highlands of Scotland. It might explain one thing.''

''What's that?''

''It was a Templar prayer.'' Callie stared at him blankly. ''You remember the Templars, Cal. We visited the ruins of their palace on Cyprus. The knights—''

It was coming back to her. ''The knights who fought in the Holy Land, and then were dissolved by Pope . . . Pope . . .''

''Clement the Fifth, in 1307. Seven years before the Bannockburn. The Order of the Knights Templar was originally French. And Michel is a French name.''

''That's rather a far stretch.''

''I'm not so sure. There's been a persistent rumor throughout Scottish history that the Bannockburn was won by Bruce because of his cavalry, which consisted of outlawed Templars fled to Scotland.''

''That bae true.''

Callie whirled to see broad-faced Jennet smiling, standing in the doorway. ''Sorry, mum,'' she apologized, ''but I did knock twice. Brought ye hot water, I hae.'' She stepped into the room with her twin jugs, followed by a boy hauling a copper tub. ''My Gordie,'' she said to introduce him; he ducked his head shyly. ''Set it there, Gordie, 'n run 'n fetch more water. Mind ye dinna spill it.''

Above the sound of the water splashing into the tub, Zeus called: ''The builder of the house was a Templar?''

''Oh, aye, sir. The first laird—Michel Faurer. Nae wonder there bae such a foreign look to the place. Served in Palestine 'n Cyprus 'n I dinna ken where else for twenty years or more, he did.''

''And he fought at the Bannockburn?'' Zeus's voice had risen a little with incredulity.

''Aye, sir. Led the cavalry there, wi' Sir Robert Keith. There bae a tapestry o' it in Lady Harding's chambers; she'll show it ye, if ye like.''

''I would very much like. Historians have been attempting to prove or disprove that theory for the past four hundred years.''

Jennet raised her shoulders up and let them drop. ''Well, sir. They ought to hae asked me.''

Callie was surprised at her impertinence, but Zeus laughed. ''I suppose they ought have! What other wonders, I wonder, does Langlannoch hold in store?''

''Ach, sir, just get m'lady talkin'.''

''I believe I'll go do that.'' The boy, Gordie, had come huffing up with more water. Jennet took the jugs and emptied them in the tub. ''Having a bath, are you, Callie?''

Why should she feel defensive? ''Lady Harding suggested it.''

''You mean Lady Maggie. Where might I find her, Mr.—''

''Jennet. Just Jennet. I'll bring ye to her, shall I? Gordie, two more ought to do it.''

''Aye, Mum.'' He picked up the empty jugs and started out again, after Zeus and Jennet. Zeus turned back at the door.

''Enjoy yourself, Cal. Take a good long time at it. You deserve it.'' She stood staring in his wake so long that Gordie came back with the water, and a little vial he drew from his belt.

''Mistress said gi' this to ye, mum.''

''Thank you.'' He shut the door behind him. Callie uncapped the vial, and the scent of roses in the room redoubled. Bath oil, very richly made.

She poured it into the steaming tub, then unbound her plaits slowly. Zeus was in his element here, and little wonder—it was history come alive for him. Whereas she—she touched a hand to the water; it was almost too hot. I feel very odd, she thought, casting off her cloak and unhooking her gown. But perhaps that was only because of the dreadful faux pas Lady Harding had made at the outset—*Why, for yer bride, lad!* As though I'd ever marry him, she told to herself.

The girl in the village, running to him, with her bouquet. The shopkeepers coming to their doors: *God bae wi' you, m'laird!* The way he'd looked in the wagon, sitting ever taller as they neared his home.

But she knew well enough, from the days when she'd painted, that perspective could be a deceptive thing.

She stepped out of the gown, unlaced her pettiskirts and let them drop. At least Lady Harding hadn't been wearing hoops; Callie trusted she could do without the set she'd hauled across Scotland, just in case, for the duration of their stay. Now that she thought of it, the woman's outfit had been downright anachronistic, rather like the gowns one saw in paintings from late Medieval times.

She shrugged off her drawers and put a toe into the water. The temperature was perfect now; the silky oil caressed her skin.

She sank down onto her buttocks, just soaking for a long while, letting the dust of the road float away on the water. Then she knelt up and reached for the dipper hanging on the tub's side, and let scoop after scoop fall onto her face and hair. She slapped her face with waves of the heady rose scent . . . *You'll get marked by thorns that way* . . . rubbed her shoulders and breasts clean, laved her belly, then stood in the tub to reach her feet and calves. The oil of roses made her flesh gleam bright in the sunlight pouring through white linen; the water sluiced in rivulets over her hips and thighs from the wet weight of her curls. She felt clean and alive and shining, glorious, born anew—

And she had the sudden distinct impression she was being watched.

Startled, she straightened up and glanced toward the door. It was still shut. Then why . . . naked, vulnerable, she turned in a slow circle, thin trickles of water coursing down her skin. The windows . . . at the farthest one she saw, through the billowing curtains, the dark outline of a ladder's staves and rungs, and frozen, partway up, the new laird of Langlannoch, with a hammer in his hand.

She met his gaze. His face bore the most peculiar expression, shamed and craven, like a boy caught thieving, but his blue eyes burned with a fierceness she had never seen in them before. For a long moment they stared at one another, and Callie thought, *I don't know which of us is more surprised.* Then separately, mutually, they came to their senses; Callie lunged for a towel, and he ducked his head and vanished from her sight. She heard the ladder-top rattle against the wall as he clambered to the ground with reckless speed.

How long had he been there? She clutched the towel tight around her, shivering despite the sunlight. And how unspeakably boorish of him to have lingered, staring at her that way! Yet her anger was mitigated by the memory of his anguished face, the shame cut through by what had almost looked to be desire. Perhaps the cold-blooded scholar was not so aloof as he seemed.

Oh, Callie. Don't be silly, she scolded herself, opening her trunk and fluffing out clean pettiskirts. If Mick Harding had any interest whatsoever in making love to you, he's had *tons* of opportunities. You've been living underneath the same roof for nigh on three months now; don't you think you'd have gleaned some inkling of his feelings by now if any existed? He stared at you because men stare at naked women; it is their nature to, even if they are cold as stone.

He hadn't been cold that night in the snow, she remembered, and blushed, realizing that the tips of her breasts had grown hard. At Avebury he'd been hot and pliant and smooth, covering her body like molten lava.

That had cooled, by the following morning, into common flint. If I had not been there myself, felt his kisses, Callie mused, I would not believe that had been the same man. It was as though he'd been disembodied, possessed by the spirits of that ancient, hallowed place.

This house, too, had spirits. *'Twar in this room that the first laird slept wi' his lady. His name war Michel, too. . . .*

Michel. It had a pleasing foreign flavor, that name, far more suited to a laird than plebian Mick. I wonder why he does not use it, she thought. It surely sounds more scholarly.

"Michel Harding," she said aloud. The cat on the coverlet perked its ears, making Callie laugh. "So, you know your master's name!" The creature's great round eyes watched her without blinking. Callie went and sat beside it, absently scratching its ears. "I'll wager you know all the secrets of Langlannoch, don't you? How many lives did Lady Maggie say you'd had—two hundred something? I wonder what triumphs and tragedies have passed right by you while you were curled up napping on the windowsill."

That made her think again of Harding on the ladder. What should she do when she saw him next? Acknowledge that he'd been there, or ignore it? What might he do or say? Really, it was damnably awkward.

In that instant, she felt a burst of sympathy for the man, who'd come to Oxford and discovered he'd exposed himself to his professor's daughter just the summer before. If he'd only said something, she'd often moaned, about having met us . . . but it was not so easy, when you came down to it, to know what to say. In Michel Harding's shoes, she likely would have kept quiet, too.

"Well, I saw him naked first," she told the gray cat, who rolled over and stretched, grand as some oriental pasha. "I suppose now we are no more than even, tit for tat." *But how his eyes had burned . . .*

"Mum?" Someone was rapping at the door. "Dinner bae in half an hour, mum. Shall I help ye dress?" Jennet called.

Startled from her thoughts, Callie shot to her feet suddenly, guiltily, uprooting the cat, who mewled in protest and then leaped from the bed to the windowsill, curling there in a puddle of sunlight. "No, thank you! I'm fine!"

"Very gude, mum." Quiet footsteps padded off. Below the window, someone had come to retrieve the ladder. It swung away abruptly from Callie's view, once again scaring the cat. He glared at Callie balefully, as though this, too, were her fault. "Well, don't blame me!" she exclaimed, rummaging through the trunk for her comb. "It never was my notion to come here at all!"

"How did the roof look, Michel?"

There was a barely perceptible pause in the methodical motions of Harding's hands as he carved the roasted hen. Callie stared at her trencher. "It needs work," he said in answer to his grandmother's question. "Liam and Davey will be 'round in the morning with a crew. We'll have a go at it. Thigh or . . . white meat or dark, Grandmère?"

"You ken I crave the breast, the same as ye."

"Ah, yes. So you do. And you, Miss Wingate?"

"Either," Callie managed to say.

"I'd like a drumstick," Zeus offered, his spirits irrepressibly buoyant. Callie had come down to dinner to find him chattering madly with Lady Maggie in the kitchens; in Harding's grandmother, it seemed, he'd found a kindred Jacobite soul. "Union? Bah!" she'd heard the woman declare while emphatically mashing turnips. "We'll see wha' union there bae, right eno', when our king from o'er the water comes home!"

Harding himself had been late to the table; they'd had their soup without him. "He takes too much on himself every time he returns," his grandmother said fondly. "Ye wait 'n see—

he'll bae clamberin' about the place, fixin' this, fixin' that, the whole while he bae here.''

"A house such as this must require tremendous upkeep," Professor Wingate had observed, sipping lamb and barley broth appreciatively.

Lady Maggie had made a face. "More a matter o' keepin' it fro' fallin' down. But all that will change, too, when—''

Zeus had finished with her: "When our king from o'er the water comes home!"

Harding had come in just then, his hair and beard damp and curling where he'd splashed his face with water. "Mind your tongue, Grandmère, please. Such talk is treasonable—and Zeus, I'll thank you not to encourage her in it." He sat and shook out his napkin with a flap, then nearly knocked over his water-cup reaching for the carving knife. "Dammit. Wouldn't you know, I have misplaced my glasses."

"Ye look more handsome wi'out them," Lady Maggie had assured him, with a sly glance at Callie that made her blush furiously.

"But I'm blind as a bat." Was that some sort of apology to me, Callie wondered? He hadn't been wearing them on the ladder. That was when his grandmother asked about the roof.

"Delicious bird," Professor Wingate said now. "In fact, everything is delicious."

"Jennet does well by me." Lady Maggie smiled. "But it bae nae like the auld days, when we'd hae half the knights in Scotland to a sittin'. Why, I remember once—''

"Did you have a chance to look about the place, Professor Wingate?" Harding interrupted, so baldly that even Callie raised her gaze to him. After a little silence, the professor turned to Lady Maggie.

"You were saying, madam?"

She opened her mouth, but before she could speak her grandson said, politely but firmly, "Professor Wingate is here to study the architecture, Grandmère, not to hear your reminiscences."

"Oh, on the contrary," Callie's father demurred, "I—''

"All of that is in the past." Harding had laid his long, blunt-fingered hand atop his grandmother's smaller one. "It is better to leave it that way."

"Ye hae a rich heritage, Michel Douglas Harding." His grandmother's eyes flashed. "Just because ye try to ignore it dinna mean we all maun."

"It's ancient history, Grandmère."

"Well, for that matter," the professor said judiciously, "so is classical Greece."

Harding smiled. "But the Greeks have numerous lessons in their history that are worthy of today. Whereas the history of my family teaches but one: If you go about bashing everyone in sight for a few hundred years, you will eventually bash yourself into oblivion."

"Oh, now, that's a bit reductive, Harding, surely."

"I'll say sae!" Lady Maggie was indignant. "The blude o' great warriors runs in yer veins, young laddie, 'n the shame bae on ye to shame it sae!"

Harding shoved back his chair. "Talk if you like, then. I'll have my supper upstairs." He took his plate and went.

Callie stared at her meat, wretchedly embarrassed. To her surprise, though, Lady Maggie was laughing softly, raising her glass of wine to his empty place. "Ach, it bae in ye, Michel," she heard the woman murmur, " 'n ye will nae deny it forever. It may hae skipped my son, but I see it in ye."

Professor Wingate cleared his throat. "I do hope, madam, that our coming hasn't caused this conflict."

"La, nae, man. Michel has been at war wi' his heart since long afore ye came. More turnips?"

"Mm. Please."

" 'N ye, Callie?"

"I . . . it truly is delicious. But I'm not very hungry."

"Well, I am," Zeus declared. "For turnips and for stories. You should hear, Father, the tales she has to tell! She knows all about the lairds of Langlannoch back four hundred years. The first laird was a Templar knight; he escaped from prison in France and washed up somewhere—was it Devonshire, Lady Maggie?"

"Aye, Devonshire. 'N the lady he war to marry, many years after, she pulled him fro' the sea. Madeleine de Courtenay." Callie glanced up. The woman's eyes had gone misty, her voice soft and young as a girl's. "It bae writ right there in the chronicles the monks keep on Iona: 'One o' the great luvs o' their time.' That war Michel Faurer and his Madeleine.''

"So the family wasn't Scottish at all," Professor Wingate noted.

"Nae, not then. But their son wed a Douglas, daughter o' the great Archibald, that war regent o' Scotland 'n fell at Halidon Hill, fightin' the third Edward. The son—Rene—'n the girl, Catriona, spirited our young King David off to France. Three boys they had, 'n all but one killed in battle. 'Twar Rene's sister Anne brought in the Harding name. She wed a cadet son o' the earl o' Berkeley.''

"Another Englishman!" Zeus was attacking the turnips.

"Aye, aye—'n another great romance. Though the chronicles say Bayard Berkeley ne'er war a fighter. He'd been a lawyer in England. He showed his mettle, though, when he went wi' Rene to rescue Anne fro' the Tower o' London.''

"She'd been imprisoned there?" Professor Wingate asked, intrigued.

"Oh, aye, for blastin' the place apart to set her brother free.''

Zeus was leaning across the table. "Oh, do tell us about it!''

"Well," said Lady Maggie, laying down her knife, "the first thing ye maun ken bae how Langlannoch war lost afore Annie won it back again. Ye see, Rene had been a scoundrel, 'n had dallianced wi' a niece o' the English puppet king, Edward o' Baliol. She found herself wi' child, 'n claimed the bairn war his—though that ne'er war true. After the fall o' Berwick, though, in '33—''

"Pardon me," Zeus broke in, "but what century are we?''

Lady Maggie turned scornful blue eyes on him. "Why, the fall o' Berwick, boy—1333! Dinna ye ken yer own history?''

"Not the way you do," Zeus said enviously. "Pray go on.''

Lady Maggie did, while the sauce grew cold and the candles burned low in their silver holders. The tales she spun out were magical, unreal—except that she stopped every now and again to say, "That chair there in the corner—that bae the chair the Bruce sat in the night afore he left wi' James Douglas for the Holy Land.'' Or, lifting her glass for more wine, "The decanter war a gift fro' Mary, Queen o' the Scots, when the fifteenth laird war wed.'' Or, even more unnerving, "Should ye hear a wee babe cryin' in the night, pay nae mind. It bae the ghost o' the thirteenth laird. That always war an unlucky number for Langlannoch. Poor thing, he starved to death in the nursery after the English slaughtered the household. That war when the Harding line came to the lairdship—in 1548.''

By the time Jennet brought port and cheese, Callie's head was a muddle of knights and ladies and deeds of derring-do against impossible odds—and she was more perplexed than ever as to why Michel Douglas Harding—''The twentieth laird,'' Lady Maggie said with satisfaction, ''a gude round number, to turn 'round the family fortunes''—should pay so little heed to his clan's history. Her father clearly shared her confusion. ''I don't mean to be intrusive, madam, into your family's business,'' he said, taking a sip of the port and then stopping, staring at his glass. ''By God. That's amazingly good.''

''The count o' Alto Douro sends me a case of his oldest each Christmas. We spent a holiday at his vineyards, my husband 'n I, many years ago. I hae rack upon rack o' it down in the cellars. Michel, ye ken, will nae drink. Neither did his father.'' She made a little face. ''We each of us rebel in our own way. But ye war sayin', Professor.''

Callie's father, still lolling the wine on his tongue, finally swallowed. ''Mm. Yes. Why is it, do you suppose, your grandson seems to care so little for his heritage?''

Lady Maggie contemplated her own wine glass for a long moment, then sighed. ''Ach, I bae to blame for that. My husband died young, ye see. 'Nae my son—Rene, I called him, for my favorite hero—well, I fear I filled his head so full o' talk o' the Hardings 'n the Faurers that I scared the lad! Took to religion, he did—though he war nae the first; the chronicles do say that Madeleine de Courtenay . . .'' Her voice trailed off. ''Sae much, sae long ago. Then when his Darcy died . . .''

''She killed herself,'' Callie said softly.

Lady Maggie's dark head came up. ''Michel told ye that? He maun think much o' ye. Aye, sae she did. 'N she war nae the first o' that, neither. All great families, it wuld seem, hae their share o' great grief. Darcy—la, she war fro' Skye, like yer mother. Nae a MacCrimmon, though, but a MacLeod. Ye

ken wha' they say o' the MacLeods—that they hae fairy blude
in 'em, fro' when Rory MacLeod took one o' the night folk
for his lady. I wuld well credence it, fro' Darcy. She war all
light 'n dark, hot 'n cold, 'n nae in-between. I luved her as a
daughter, 'n Rene luved her, too—but luv could nae save her.
Naught could hae saved her. She said she heard the sea callin'
to her o' nights, 'n one night she walked in. *She* drank—port,
madeira, anythin' to quiet the voices. P'raps that bae why
Michel will nae. He war but ten years auld when she did
herself in.'' She shook herself, like the gray cat, shrugging off
memories. ''Once she died, my Rene war lost to me. He went
all into himself 'n his God—'n little eno' left o'er for the boy.
'N he hated Langlannoch. He wuld nae come here himself,
though he had the grace to send the lad o' summers. I fear,
though, that Michel found it dauntin'. All fallen into ruin by
then, 'n nae company but me, wi' my stories to tell . . .''

Zeus had reached for her hand. ''I should never want anything
more,'' he told her quietly, fiercely.

She smiled sadly, brushing his blond hair from his brow.
'' 'Twar too late for Michel, though. How can ye e'er trust a
soul, when the one ye luv best has done that to ye?''

Callie felt a sharp tang of pain in her heart. To think that
she had almost done the same to Zeus. And oh, God, poor
Mick Harding! No wonder he kept so wrapped up in his work,
turned his back on Langlannoch and all that it stood for. She
tried to picture him as a boy—and caught her breath at a sudden
clear vision of him standing at the seawall, staring down into
the waves that had claimed his mother's life.

Lady Maggie had shot a sharp glance at her. ''MacCrimmon
blude,'' she heard her murmur. ''D'ye ken they say on Skye
that a MacCrimmon sold his soul to Auld Clootie himself to
learn to play the pipes sae well? Ach, a reckless clan yers bae.
Just like mine.''

Callie slept late the next morning, between thick white sheets
in her room filled with roses. She awoke to hot sun pouring
through the casements and a far-off sound that set her heart
beating fast even before her mind could put a name to the

noise. It was the drone of pipes, carrying far on the still summer air. Running to the window, she stared out over the road winding northward to Ayr and saw in the distance some sort of procession, men and women and children, most on foot, some riding, some in wagons, led by a solitary piper in a tall white hat. If they've come from the town, they must have set out at dawn, she realized, watching the distant procession, hearing the high, bleating whine of the piper's chanter. And they had to be coming here—there was no place else within miles for them to go. Hurriedly she slipped into the clothes she would have worn at any antiquities site in the heat of summer—a pale linen shirt that buttoned at the throat, with sleeves that could be rolled up in the sun's blaze, and a skirt, full enough for kneeling, the color of earth.

Jennet was in the kitchens, washing up from the breakfast Callie had missed. "Jennet," Callie said excitedly, "there is some sort of parade coming this way from the town, with a piper!"

"Sae there wuld bae," the cook affirmed, not looking up from her work.

"But what are they—" Callie started to ask, then stopped as she heard Mick Harding's voice from the dining hall, sounding angrier than she could ever recall.

"I won't do it, Grandmère!"

And then she heard Lady Maggie's voice, so gentle that Callie could not make out the words, and then Harding again.

"I don't bloody *care!* They *have* a justice of the peace; let them march on him!" The fury in his voice was frightening. Callie glanced at Jennet, who met her startled gaze with a broad, calm smile.

"Gae on in, then," the cook urged, up to her elbows in dishwater. "There bae bread 'n bacon still on the table for ye."

"I don't like to intrude," Callie said uncertainly.

"La, dinna mind him, pet; he bae naught but bluster."

It sounded like a good deal more than bluster to Callie, but she crept cautiously toward the doors.

Their host was dressed in work clothes—a loose shirt, leather breeches and boots, his thick hair tied back—and he stood at his place with his hands on his hips, facing down his grandmother. "I have told you before, Grandmère, I want no part or parcel of such nonsense! I've come to fix the roof; that is how I intend to spend my day."

"But Davey 'n Liam told ye they wuld—"

"I'll not accept their charity!"

"It bae nae charity to do for the laird," Lady Maggie scoffed. "It bae the warp 'n woof o' the social agreement—ye do yer part for them as laird, 'n they do theirs for ye."

Harding gave his wide belt a yank. "Well, I'm not a party to this social agreement. I'm going up on the roof." He spun on his boot-heel and marched past Callie, who scrambled out of his path. His expression was mutinous, thunderous; he did not even see her there. She turned and watched him stomp out into the yards, his black queue lashing furiously back and forth. Then, timidly, she peered into the dining hall once more.

Zeus was there, and her father; her view of them had been blocked by Harding's angry stance. Her brother beckoned to her cheerfully: "Come in, come in! Every meal at Langlannoch, it seems, comes complete with an explosion by Mick."

"Don't make light of it, Zeus," his father reproached him.

"I'm not making light. I'm just unspeakably jealous. You'd not see me turning down the opportunity to play God."

"What in the world are you talking about?" Callie asked, slipping into her seat. "Good morning, Lady Maggie."

"Gude mornin', pet." Harding's grandmother seemed unperturbed by his display of temper; her blue eyes were merry as she pushed the bread toward Callie, and a pot of honey-butter. "Wuld ye care for tea?"

"Yes, please."

The Scotswoman poured it with a steady hand. The sound of the pipes was growing closer and closer. "There's some sort of parade," Callie began.

"Yes, we know," Zeus assured her. "It's just His Lairdship's loyal subjects, on their way to worship him."

Lady Maggie gave him a fond, bemused glance. "Nay, now, nae worship, but to take advantage o' his wisdom. Twice a year they come—if the laird bae in residence. 'N as I said to Michel, it has been far too long since we had a laird in residence. He'll nae get to that roof this day."

"It seems," Professor Wingate told his puzzled daughter, "that Harding was not . . . forthcoming with us about the system of justice. There is an English sheriff—"

"Bah," said Lady Maggie.

"But except when they must—in capital cases, for example—"

"O' which," his hostess said with complacence, "there bae none."

"They prefer to appeal to their laird. So all those folk are on their way to have their disputes judged."

By now the parade had reached the front yard; besides the pipes' whine, there was a clamor through the open windows of laughter and chatter. "They don't sound especially disputatious," Callie said dubiously.

"Ach," said Lady Maggie, making the syllable deeply satisfied, "that bae on account o' they ken their laird will do right by them." She stood, gathering her skirts. "Shall we gae out 'n see?"

"This should prove most entertaining," Zeus declared with zest as he offered her his arm. Callie gulped down her tea and hurried after them.

There must have been a hundred or more people milling about in the side yard, beneath the oak trees. The piper, his face hot and red, was sitting on a stone, gathering breath. The children were skipping about in frenzied excitement; women clustered around a girl holding a newborn baby in a sling at her breast. Men were lighting their pipes, and Jennet had rolled out a barrel of ale. Overall, the scene resembled a genial country village fair.

"Yer Ladyship!" The din faded a little as Lady Maggie appeared and the folk bobbed greetings. She moved among them easily, accepting condolences on the death of her son, exclaiming over the children and babies, while Callie and her father and brother hung back beneath the eaves, feeling conspicuous and out of place. The truth was, though, that no one was taking any notice of them. "Really, it's a most accommodating system of justice," Callie heard her father murmur, "though completely nonrepresentational, of course. Rather like being whisked back to the Dark Ages, Zeus, wouldn't you say?"

But Zeus hadn't a chance to answer; Lady Maggie clapped her hands, and the crowd turned toward her expectantly.

"My friends," she called out, her voice steady, her pale face glowing, "I bid ye welcome in the name o' our laird! Ye hae come to him for fair judgement o' yer disputes, 'n that ye shall hae."

"How can she be so sure of him?" Zeus murmured at Callie's side.

"Fro' time immemorial," Lady Maggie went on, "ye hae appealed to the laird o' this house for justice." Her strong voice was rather louder, Callie thought, than was needed under the circumstances; it carried easily over the steady *thwack, thwack, thwack* of an axe in the distance. Now it grew even more forceful: "Ne'er in hundreds o' years hae ye been disappointed. Nor shall ye bae now!"

The axe had paused in its chopping. Lady Maggie's words rang clearly through the summer air: "The laird o' Langlannoch will nae fail ye; I give ye my promise!" A great cheer rose up from the folk in the yard. Boys hurled their caps toward the sky, and the piper, his strength renewed, launched into a sprightly tune.

From around the far corner of the house, slowly, came the laird himself, holding the axe he'd been swinging. "Grandmère," he said in hoarse, desperate appeal, "Grandmère, don't—"

" 'N here he bae now!" Lady Maggie called brightly. The piper broke off, with his drones still wheezing. As one, the crowd dropped to its knees.

Mick Harding's face was a study in woe above the sea of bowed heads. He grabbed one of the kneeling men by the collar. "Dammit, Davey, what of the roof? You were supposed to help me with the roof!"

" 'N sae I shall, gude m'laird, after ye hae heard wha' I maun tell o' my black cow 'n Andrew M'Quigan."

"Ye mean *my* black cow," rumbled a fat red-haired fellow from the back of the yards. "Ye ken full well, Davey Johns, ye sold her to me fair 'n square."

"But nae the calf she war bearin'!"

"Wha' fault bae it o' mine if ye dinna ken when a she-cow bae bearin'?"

"Davey ... Andrew. Please." The laird of Langlannoch raised his hands for quiet. Across the yard, his eyes met his grandmother's. He stood motionless for a moment, surveyed the eager, hopeful throng, then dropped his hands to his head, pushing back his hair with a sigh. "All right, then. Let's get it over with; 'tis clear I'll have no peace until I do. Form some sort of line, though, could you? Complainants to the right, defendants on the left. If you've witnesses, mind they be ready when your turn comes 'round. Davey and Andrew, step forth."

"Wait!" Lady Maggie cried, bustling toward the house. "Ye maun hae yer seat o' judgement, 'n yer robe! Jennet, run 'n fetch the robe. Ye, Jock MacKenzie, ye bring out the chair."

"Grandmère," Mick Harding said pleadingly, but she only shook her head at him.

"In for a penny, Michel, in for a pound." He moaned.

So it was that Mick Harding, former Oxford scholar, present associate master of classical studies at the University of Edinburgh, a few minutes later sat in a huge carved chair, draped, despite the growing heat, in a rich cloak of red velvet edged in ermine, listening with his head bent as Davey and Andrew each in turn told his side of the tale of the black cow, replete with gestures and name-calling and exaggerated outrage at the other's lies. Davey, Callie thought, looking on in fascination, was particularly convincing, swearing up and down that it was long-standing custom in the shire for the offspring in such a sale to be returned to the former owner. Each called witnesses: Davey his eldest son, a strapping lad of perhaps eighteen who'd gone with him to Andrew's barn to deliver the cow and agreed with his dad that the beast had shown no signs of parturition, and Andrew his wife, who'd brought ale to the barn and watched the two men toast the completed deal.

Harding summoned his own witness then, one of the oldest men present, with a long gray beard and face wrinkled up like a winter apple. "Andrew, Davey, you both ken Seth Donohoe." The two aggrieved parties eyed the old man suspiciously, but nodded, while Callie noted how Harding's voice was slipping more and more toward the native speech. "And you'd agree

there be no man in Ayrshire better learned in cattle-rearing.''
After a brief hesitation, they nodded again. ''Well, Seth.'' And
then the laird of Langlannoch lapsed into what Callie supposed
had to be Gaelic, to address his witness.

''He's asking,'' Zeus muttered in Callie's ear, ''what signs
there would be at two months' gestation of a she-cow's condition.'' She turned to him in amazement. ''What?''

''You *have* been studying up on your Gaelic, haven't you?''

''Well . . . just a bit.''

There were more questions then for the old man, duly trans-
lated by Zeus for Callie and their father—whether he could
recall any similar disputes in his lifetime, what had been the
outcome, and then, surprisingly, what he thought ought to be
done. When the answer came, Zeus laughed out loud, then
quickly stifled it as Harding shot him a glare. ''What? What
did he say?'' Professor Wingate whispered.

''He suggested they roast the calf here today, to celebrate
the laird's homecoming.'' Andrew M'Quigan's face was as
dark as night. But it brightened considerably when, after a few
minutes' thought, Harding delivered his verdict: M'Quigan was
to keep the calf, by both men's accounts a fine young bull now,
but Davey was to have the use of it at stud any time he chose,
and his pick of the next four calves delivered by the black cow.

''Convoluted in the extreme,'' Professor Wingate muttered.
''Still, they seem satisfied.'' And the two disputants must have
been; they shook hands amicably, then went off to the ale keg
with their arms on one another's shoulders.

''Next case,'' Mick Harding declared.

The makeshift court went on for hours, with the variety of
suits astounding: property lines, water squabbles, short-
weighting at market, shoddy workmanship of everything from
shoes to staves to wagon-wheels. One irate woman claimed
her neighbors' pigs were running through her laundry-yard; her
opponent insisted the woman would not keep her fence repaired.
There were battles over chickens, china, chimneys, chitterlings,
chores, chowder; arguments concerning leases, lending, let-
tuces, legitimacy. Some were laughable; some were certainly
not. Harding listened to them all with the same grave attention,
asked careful questions, and resolved each in satisfactory fash-

ion. In fact, what struck Callie most about the proceedings, which continued on past the dinner-hour, so long that Zeus went and fetched them stools, was the absence of rancor on the part of the losers. "Is it just that the laird has spoken that contents them?" she asked during a lull in which Harding mopped sweat from his brow and downed three pints of ale in startling succession. What had happened, she wondered, to his not drinking?

Her father shook his head. "Haven't you been listening, Calliope? There's no bitterness because his decisions are just. His range of knowledge really is quite formidable."

There was one case, though, in which Harding seemed stymied. It came near the end, when the sun was setting and most of the villagers and crofters had wandered off from the seat of judgment, gathering in little knots to talk among themselves. This dispute drew them back. It was between the girl with the baby, a pretty black-haired girl whose gray eyes were a sea of sadness, and Davey's eldest son, who'd stood witness for his father when the day was still young. Zeus reported their stories in the merest whisper. She claimed they'd plighted one another their troth, she'd lain with him, and the proof was the baby. He declared stoutly that he'd made no promise; she had offered herself to him, she'd been equally forthright with others, and he could never be certain that the child was his.

There were witnesses. The girl's mother, loud and insistent, claimed her daughter had reported the swearing of the promises to her, and anyway maintained her Jessie was a good lass, not the sort of which Davey's son ought to be spreading lies. The son's best friend, bashful and red-faced, reported that at Midsummer last, Jessie had drunk too much and approached him. Jessie, bursting into tears, had cried out he had better have a mind to his soul. It seemed an unhappy morass with no possible resolution. Callie was wracking her brain as to which party she believed when, to her shock, she heard the laird of Langlannoch call, "Mistress Wingate!"

"Me?" She nearly fell off her stool.

"Aye. Would you step up here, please?"

"I really don't see . . ." But Zeus was pushing her forward.

Blushing madly, she stumbled toward the judgement chair. "Really, I—"

Harding's blue eyes entreated her: Help me. Why me? she wanted to ask. But the girl had turned to her, distraught, desperate, and was pleading in Gaelic. The words might have been unfamiliar, but the tone rang clear. The young man stood to the side, stony, simmering. As for the babe, Callie reached for the edge of the blanket covering its head, smiling involuntarily at its small, sleep-sweet face.

"Boy or girl?" she asked the young mother.

"My son." She could speak English, then, when she cared to. Callie looked from the babe to the purported father. Impossible to tell any resemblance between them; the child was too young. She turned toward the young man and searched his eyes. His gaze veered from hers abruptly.

"He's a bonny boy," Callie said softly.

"That may bae, but he bae nae mine."

Callie looked back at the girl. "Where do you say you lay with him?"

The answer came promptly: "In the hedge by his father's house. The one wi' eglantine flowers."

"What night?"

"The Sabbath afore Michaelmas."

"What had he on?"

"His white shirt, 'n his blue serge britches. His belt wi' the thistle on the buckle." Her brow folded into tears once more. "His boots. Nae more."

"What was the last thing he said to you when he left you?"

"He told me—dinna bae afeared."

"Ach, Jessie." The young man's breath came out in a sigh. "If I culd bae sure, lass—"

"The bairn bae yers, Walt! D'ye think I'd lie to ye on this, after wha' we hae shared?"

The crowd was dead-silent. Walt scuffed the toes of his boots on the grass. "But Jamie says—"

"D'ye think I dinna ken why ye will nae wed me? Because I hae nae dowry! Jamie wuld say wha'e'er wild business ye willed him to say!"

"It bae nae for lack o' dowry!" Walt had stood up taller.

His harsh words had awakened the babe, and it, too, started to cry. "La, Jessie, hush the thing!"

She thrust the baby toward him. "*Ye* hush him, then! Ye bae his father!"

He took a step back. "Ach, I ken naught o' babies."

"Ye maun learn, man, for the bairn bae yer own!"

Harding spoke up then. "Do you have a belt-buckle with a thistle on it, Walter?"

"All the town ken I do." His voice was sullen now.

Callie looked at the girl. "Jessie. Do you want money from him?"

"Nae." She shook her head emphatically.

"What do you want, then?"

"I want for him to marry me!"

"Why? Because he fathered your child?"

"Nae!" She laughed. "Because I luv him!" Walt's head came up slowly. "Aye, ye thick, grand lug! I luv ye! Why else wuld I hae gi'en myself to ye in the first place?"

Lady Maggie, looking remarkably fresh despite the long day, came forward. "Bae it the lack o' dowry, then, Walter Coady?"

He flushed. "I dinna—"

"For if it bae, I hae this to gi' the girl." And she unclasped from her throat a circlet of Scottish pearls. "Here, Jessie. Use it as ye please."

The girl held the jewels on the tips of her fingers. "Lady Harding, I cannae—"

"Buy him wi' it, if he bae worth it to ye."

A small laugh escaped her. "Can I buy purchase ye wi' this, then, Walt? Wuld ye gae sae dear?"

His eyes were wide. "They wuld buy a croft, lass."

"Aye, I reckon they wuld."

He stared down at the baby. "He does hae a bit o' me, dinna he, there about the eyes?"

The yard erupted in hoots and laughter. Walt let his arm slide around Jessie's shoulders, and then, to the shouted demands of the crowd, gave her a kiss. The baby started bawling; Jennet was clanging a bell, crying, "Gude fish stew 'n oatcakes for them as wants 'em!" Mugs overflowed with ale, and Callie escaped gratefully to her family, back under the eaves.

Her father squeezed her hand, beaming. "You did well, dear." And Zeus hugged her.

"I was wrong about your painting, Cal. You were cut out for a career in law."

"I still don't see why he needed me." She was flustered and flushed from having been on public display, embarrassed by the details of the couple's intimacy. And yet in her heart there was a glow of deep satisfaction. She *had* done well, by God; they'd gotten to the bottom of the thing, and Jessie's son would bear his father's name.

Lady Maggie came floating toward them over the yards in the twilight. "Sae, now. Michel will hae his roof tomorrow. But first things first, eh? Come 'n hae some stew."

"No wonder your castle's fallen to pieces, the way you throw your jewels around," Zeus teased her.

"Ach, those pearls wuld nae make a dint in this ruin." The mistress of Langlannoch ran her hand over the chinked sandstone wall. " 'Twill take a full-time laird to set the house to rights again. Better buy Jessie her heart's desire; he came a great deal cheaper!" Then her fingertips caressed Callie's arm with the same fond, proprietary air she'd had when stroking the stone. "Ye see Michel has got a heart in him, too."

"I never said he didn't."

The older women laughed. "Nae, but I'll wager ye hae had yer doubts betimes!"

Harding himself was approaching, peeling off his robes, pausing now and again to speak with the villagers as they hailed him. "He ought to run for bloody Parliament," Zeus said enviously, watching his easygoing progress.

"The men o' Langlannoch hae a knack for leadin'," Lady Maggie agreed. "It always has been sae." Callie, too, looked on as Harding, the antique robes draped over one broad shoulder, exchanged a few words with Jessie's ecstatic mother.

"That suits him better than his Oxford gown ever did," her father observed, nodding toward the robe, mirroring Callie's thoughts. "Quite a splendid way of life you've got here, Lady Harding. One would hate to see it die out."

"Aye, sae one wuld. Still, that bae an odd sentiment for a bludy Englishman to express."

"I can assure you, milady, there's no history of mighty warriors in my heritage—nor, for that matter, of poor ones. The Wingates are more known for butchering meat than splitting Scottish skulls."

"Sae ye hail fro' a family o' butchers."

"My father wielded the best cleaver in Spitalfields."

" 'N yet ye grew up to teach at Oxford." She mused on that a moment. "Queer, bain't it, how a house's fortunes can turn in one lifetime. It nearly gives a soul hope."

Hope for what? Callie meant to ask, but the piper, fed and stoked with ale, had taken up his instrument. Some of the boys stabbed oil-soaked cattails into the lawn and lit them; they burned with a smoky gold glow. A cluster of girls formed a circle for dancing, their hands joined, their long plaits and wide aprons swinging in time.

Harding had reached his grandmother's side, and unceremoniously dropped his robes in a heap at her feet. "Contented?" he asked briefly.

"Aye. 'N sae ye bae, too, Michel," she told him, unperturbed.

He looked out over the heads of the crowd, running an absent hand over the damp curls at his temples. "Well. Davey says he and a dozen more will bide here tonight, and start splitting the shingles at first light. If the weather holds, we could finish by sundown. *That* would satisfy me." He rubbed his throat. "God, I'm parched."

"I'll gae 'n fetch ye ale," Lady Maggie offered.

"I believe I'll try that stew, if the native hordes haven't polished it off," Zeus announced. "Father?"

"Mm? Oh, yes. I'll come along with you."

Callie started off with them, but Harding's long fingers curled 'round her wrist forestalled her. "Thank you," he said in a low voice.

"Lord, you would have done fine without me."

"I wasn't sure. It is not a field in which I have any claims at all to expertise."

She waved that off. "No more than common sense, really."

He shook his head. "No. In matters of the heart, it seems

to me, common sense does not apply. But, as I say, I've no direct experience."

His hand still held to her wrist. "Perhaps you will, someday," Callie said, and pulled free.

He barked a laugh. "God, I trust not, considering the muddle it made for those two!"

Callie gazed across the yard to where Jessie lay in Walt's lap, his arms circling her and the baby. "Oh, I don't know. I'll wager they'll be happy enough."

His voice had lost its clipped Oxford vowels; he spoke in the round, slow drawl of his homeland. "I must say, I'm surprised your own experiences have not made you bitter." The moon had come up over the sea; its silver made his blue eyes dark as the water. She stared up at him as he towered above her, uncertain what to say.

But Lady Maggie came back with the ale just then, sparing the need for response. "Here ye gae, darlin'. Callie, ye poor wee thing, ye dinna e'en get yer breakfast; ye maun bae fair starved. Take her for stew, Michel. We maun build a bit o' flesh onto her whilst she bae here."

"I'm afraid I must decline the honor. I have the account-books to go over yet, and a raft of correspondence. Not to mention getting up at dawn to split shingles."

Lady Maggie's face fell. "La, Michel, wha' o' the dancin'? 'N there'll bae toasts, 'n Rory Kennedy has promised a ballad in yer honor—"

Harding had shuddered. "Saints preserve us. No, Grandmère, you have gotten all you will of lairdship out of me this day—and even you will admit it was a great deal more than I intended." He kissed her furrowed brow. "Good night. And good night to you as well, Miss Wingate." He made a bow, then turned and strode into the darkened house, leaving his grandmother sputtering in his wake.

"Ach, I'll hae ye yet, Michel Harding, if I maun conjure the spirits o' the dead to win ye!" She saw Callie's startled eyes, and laughed. "La, it bae naught but jest. Come taste that stew." She pulled Callie across the yard by the elbow, pausing to scoop up and smooth the fur on the robe that her grandson had shed at her feet.

24.

First light brought a wild bevy of axes thudding into hard oak. Callie sat up, rubbing sleep from her eyes, the taste in her mouth an odd commingling of fennel from the fish stew and the dusky herbs that flavored Lady Maggie's ale: borage, hyssop, woodruff. All the household had been up late at the feasting, and when she'd come to bed, drooping with exhaustion, the revelers in the yard had still been going strong. Yet here they were to work already, and no one within half a mile would be getting any more rest now that they'd started. She crawled out from the covers, shook her hair loose from its night-plait, and splashed cool water on her face. "Look out below!" she heard someone cry, and stepped back as an avalanche of broken bits of tile flew past the window, landing with a crash in the yard. There was a ladder reaching past the arching casement top. Self-conscious, she drew the laces on her nightdress tight. If Mick Harding had been looking in again, she had been sound asleep.

How splendid he had been in his robes, listening and delivering his judgments. Hard to reconcile the figure he'd made on the lawn with the stiff, formal scholar she knew. And yet, perhaps that stiffness suited him in his role as laird; perhaps it had been bred in him by centuries of governing. He was what the great lords of England must have been like, she thought, before easy money and frilly manners cut out their backbones. It was impossible to imagine Harry or John Ormond sitting in state to hear such petty squabbles. And yet their ancestors must have, once upon a time.

Like being back in the Dark Ages, her father had said. If that was true, they didn't seem so dark now to Callie. On the contrary, the close link between ruler and ruled made for trust, intimacy, genuine concern—all the qualities so sorely lacking in today's English nobility. Little wonder Harding showed a feel for life in Roman England when we went to Avebury, she mused, taking the precaution of dressing on her bed, behind drawn hangings. He practically lives there now, whenever he is here.

What an odd sort of existence he had led, between Langlannoch and Oxford. And then there was his father, the Presbyterian cleric—that side of his past she still knew nothing about. But she was gaining a sense, she thought, of what had made him the man he was. What possible use such knowledge might prove to be was beyond her ken.

He is like a chameleon, she realized, taking on the color of his surroundings. When she'd first seen him, in the unruly gardens, he had been a savage. Then at Oxford, he'd been the prototypical scholar, book-bound and intense. And last night he'd been laird of Langlannoch, with all the regality that role entailed. How very tiring it must be, she decided, lacing up her boots, to change so all the time. What was he like in his heart, at the core? Or was he so accustomed to playing parts that by now he was no more than their sum?

Another load of roof-tiles came slithering past the window. She yanked tight the bow in her lace and ventured downstairs.

The kitchen was an inferno, the hearth still blazing from the fire needed to prepare so many breakfasts. Yet Jennet, scrubbing pots at the long sink, had a smile on her face. "Gude mornin'! Root ye out o' bed, did they, wi' all this noise?"

She nodded. "Stuff kept flying past my window."

"Ach, 'twill bae a fine thing to hae a dry roof o'er our heads.

Ye bae the first down. Wait a bit, if ye will, 'n I'll set the table in the hall.''

"You needn't do that for me. Can I help you with those dishes?''

"Nah, pet, thanks. Glad I bae for extra washin'-up, if it means Langlannoch hae come alive again.'' She pushed a strand of hair from her face with the crook of her elbow. "Last night put me in mind o' when I war a wee lass, scramblin' to keep out fro' underfoot whilst my mum laid the feasts.''

"Your mother worked here, too?''

"Oh, aye, 'n her mother afore, 'n hers, 'n hers, 'n hers 'n hers besides. We bae part 'n parcel o' Langlannoch. We hae served the lairds for more than four hundred years.''

"My word!'' Callie laughed. "I've known great families in England who cannot keep a cook for a fortnight!''

"Ach, I cannae conjure workin' anywhere else. Though I do wonder betimes will this laird bae the last one.''

"Why should he be?''

"Well, he ha nae much, ha he, to offer to a lass for his wife? Nae money, 'n nae looks to speak of—''

"I don't find him *bad*-looking,'' Callie said in his defense.

"Dinna ye now? Ach, then, mayhaps I bae wrong.'' It took Callie a moment to realize the cook's wide shoulders as she stood with her back turned were shaking with laughter.

"May I ask,'' she said stiffly, "what you find so amusing?''

"La, naught, lass, naught at all. Dinna ye mind auld Jennet. Care for some tea?''

Callie sipped her tea at the work-table in the kitchen, surrounded by the music of the thudding axes, the clatter of boot-heels overhead, and a chorus of shouted orders and suggestions and bawdy jests. The yard beyond the open door was swarming with Scotsmen stripped to the waist against the June heat that was already curling the tips of the leaves in the herb-beds. Now and again a grinning worker, ripe with sweat, would come tramping in to beg a bit of clabber-milk or barley-cake from Jennet, and she would grouse but accommodate him. Callie was just about to venture outside for a glimpse of their progress when Zeus came trotting in.

"Good Lord, Zeus, you're not up on that roof!" she said in dismay.

"Nah. I offered, mind you, but the general consensus was I'd break my own neck or one of theirs. Morning, Jennet!"

"Mornin', Master Zeus. Tea or coffee?"

"I think I'll just have water, thanks. It's so bloody hot!" Jennet fetched him a pitcher, and he sat at the table and drank from it slowly, thirstily. Callie studied his face. He looked subtly different in the slanting morning light, somehow sturdier, less ethereal. Grounded, she thought, and then wondered at the word that had popped into her head. It seemed an odd one to apply to her flighty younger brother, yet just now it fit.

"Have you seen Father?" she asked.

"Passed him in the upstairs sitting room. Lady Maggie's brought him the estate ledgers for the past thousand years or so. Complete records of harvests, husbandry, natural disasters. He thinks he's died and gone to heaven."

"From the looks of it, so do you."

He smiled at her above the pitcher's lip, a child's smile, with nothing in it of cynicism or mockery. "Perhaps I have. You must admit, it's a remarkable place."

"Remarkably noisy, I'll grant you." Someone was thumping with a hammer right above their heads. "What are your plans for the day?" she called over the din.

"Best to stay out from underfoot," he shouted back. "I rather thought I might explore the coast."

"The what?" More hammers were pounding.

"The *coast*. Go down to the shoreline! Care to come with me?"

She still hadn't heard him, but she nodded. Anything to get away from the noise!

She sat with her hands over her ears and watched as he wangled a hamper from Jennet and filled it with tidbits for a picnic—slices of ham, some cheese, bread, strawberries. He slipped it over his arm, then grabbed Callie's hand and led her into the light.

The air was heavy and hot after the cool, dim halls. Callie walked backward across the lawn to the seawall, watching the men scramble over the steep pitched rooves like ants on a rock.

What a sketch that would be, she thought with longing, allowing herself to go so far as to compose it—from there above the side porch up to the tower, then down and across to where Davey and Andrew, side by side, were ripping up the old tiles with crowbars. She raised her two hands, fingers stretched in L-shapes, to frame it.

"Of course," Zeus said hopefully at her side, "if there's something else you'd rather do . . ."

"There isn't." Still, she lingered for another moment, wondering where Mick Harding would fit into the picture. Then she saw him: lips clenched around a bristling rosette of nails, hammer thrust into his belt, halfway up a spindly ladder stretched to the tower. Just the sight of him made her dizzy. *Oh, be careful!*

"Like a monkey, isn't he?" her brother said, following her gaze. "I wonder has he thought that if he falls and dies, there'll be no laird of Langlannoch?"

"God, Zeus! Don't say that!"

"He'd best get started on those dozen bairns, if he's going to clamber about that way."

She couldn't bear to watch; she turned toward the sea. "Where did you say we were going?"

"Down there." He pointed over the wall to the water.

"To the strand? What for?"

"Just for some peace and quiet. And to eat our ham."

She trailed after him down the steep, rough stairs hewn into the face of the cliff. A breath of wind was blowing off the sea; it felt blessedly cool against her face and throat. Zeus pointed off to their right, where the foot of the bluff gave way to low hills strewn with gravel and shingle. "Lady Maggie says Robert the Bruce made his camp a mile or so down that way the year before the Bannockburn. It's where the first laird, Michel Faurer, trained the cavalry that won the battle."

"You don't say."

"And he built the house on this cliff because it's where he and his Madeleine first made love to one another."

"On a *cliff?*"

"It's quite a hot-blooded clan."

"The temperature seems to have subsided a bit in the present generation."

"Oh, I don't know. The penchant for coition on rocks still crops up now and then."

Callie flushed. "Don't speak of that, Zeus."

"Why not? He's an extraordinary man. It's an extraordinary family. They were mareschals of Scotland while Harry Godshall's kin were still farming turnips in Essex. You felt something for him once, Cal, there in Avebury. And you wanted the savage you painted."

"I didn't—"

"Oh, come on. That's what made it so remarkable—the passion in your strokes. Don't you want him still, now he's here in the flesh?"

"Certainly not."

Sighing, he gave her his hand to help her down the last few feet of shifting gravel. "Have it your way. I feel I ought to warn you, though: Lady Maggie says the brides of the lairds of Langlannoch are destined for them, their names written in the stars."

"So?"

"I'd say in the past few years your destiny and that of Mick Harding have been mightily entangled."

It was a thought that had occurred to her more than once since they'd come to Langlannoch. But no reasonable, modern soul believed in that sort of stuff; it was more suited to the days of chivalry and romance, when knights on horseback fought and gladly died for their lady-loves.

She looked out over the strand and for an instant imagined she could see them: Michel Faurer and Madeleine de Courtenay astride a huge black horse, galloping out of the Bruce's encampment with its pennants and quaint tents, thundering up the beach to the cliff. Her hair was black and wild with wind; his eyes were the blue of gentians, and ablaze with desire. . . .

She wrenched away from the tantalizing vision. That sort of thing simply didn't go on anymore; yearning for a love like that was as wasteful as wishing for wings. There were no heroes these days.

Zeus was fumbling with the string of a plumb-line. "What in the world are you doing?" Callie demanded.

"Trying to untangle this."

"Here. Let me." She took the string and started easing out the knots in it. Zeus sat on a rock and pulled off his boots, then rolled up the legs of his trousers. "Going wading?"

"As a matter of fact, I am. Thank you." He took the untangled line and stepped into the water, flinching as a wave lapped him. "Brr! God, it's like ice." He ventured out a few yards more, reared back, and hurled the weighted string as far ahead of him as he could. Then he waited for a few minutes, wound the string back up on his hand, moved ten feet to his left, and repeated the process.

"I suppose you might bonk a fish on the head that way," Callie called to him, "but most folk use a hook."

"I'm seeing if it's safe for swimming."

"Swimming! You couldn't swim in this; your lips are already blue."

He gathered in the line, moved down, and threw it out again. "Lady Maggie says Scottish pirates used to raid English ships and then anchor in this cove. It seems to have silted up since then. Still, I'll wager you could bring in something smallish— a yacht or a schooner—and off-load in jolly-boats."

Callie raised her brows. "Going in for piracy?"

"Contemplating it. I need a change of life." He waded out of the water, rolling up the line and thrusting it in his pocket. "Let's walk on down here to the Bruce's encampment. Do you mind? I rather fancy the notion of standing where he once stood."

They strolled along the shore in the molten sunlight, Zeus carrying the basket. A mile or so down, they came upon a cairn, a heap of stones piled up well back from the sea. "This is it," said Zeus, turning to survey the landscape. "This is where his tent stood. And Michel Faurer would have trained his horsemen down there."

Callie pushed back her tangled russet curls, wishing she'd worn a hat; she was going to sunburn. "Whence this sudden intense interest in King Robert Bruce?"

"He was this nation's greatest hero, wasn't he? Anyone

looking to salvage Scotland from British thralldom would do
well to emulate him.''

Callie turned to him slowly. ''Now, see here, Zeus. You
listen to me. I don't want you enlisting Lady Maggie or Langlannoch in any of your harebrained Jacobite schemes. It wouldn't
be fair, after she has been so very kind and hospitable to us.''

''Who's to say,'' Zeus countered with a smile, ''that she
hasn't enlisted me?''

''Not to mention the fact that the laird would have you by
the ears!''

''What Mick doesn't know won't hurt him,'' her brother
said complacently. ''Come along. We'll picnic back here, in
the shade of the hills. Your nose is turning red.''

After the meal he did some pacing off and measuring and
tinkering about in the cove. Callie was content to take off her
boots and stroll along the shoreline, letting the cold water
nibble her toes. The sea breeze was sweet; strange birds whirled
overhead, and the soft thunder of the waves was lulling after
all that cacophony of hammering. The uproar of the last few
days, coupled with the late night of celebration, had taken their
toll. She felt deliciously drowsy. ''Mind if I nap?'' she called
to Zeus as he climbed over the rocks.

''Not at all, not at all!''

''Then I will.'' She found a patch of cool sand shadowed
by an outcrop of stone and curled up in it, her head cradled on
her arms.

She must have slept a long time. When she woke, the shadows
of the cliff had reached all the way down to the sea. She yawned
and stretched, shaking sand from her hair. The skin on her
cheeks and nose felt hot and tingly. Zeus was nowhere in sight,
but the hamper was beside her. The ham they'd had left her
thirsty. She took the water-skin and drank from it greedily,
then splashed some over her face.

''Zeus?'' she called, but heard only the echoing cry of a
seabird wheeling in the deep blue sky. ''Zeus, where are you?''
She shivered in her thin lawn gown, that had felt so clammy
at midday. The air had turned cold; night was on its way.

''You might at least have taken the hamper,'' she grumbled,
slipping it over her arm and thrusting her boots inside it; she

could go faster over the shifting shingle barefoot. Then she hiked her skirts up in her free hand and started toward the stairs in the cliff. Halfway there, a bundle on the beach caught her eye. She gave it a wide berth, fearing it might be some strange sea-creature, then paused as she saw it for what it was: leather boots and breeches, the latter dark with sweat. Whose were they? She turned in a circle, searching the shore, but saw no one. Perhaps they'd washed up there; they weren't far from the waves.

The disembodied clothes gave her an eerie feeling, though, as if she'd been spied on. She quickened her steps, spinning about now and again to scan the empty beach. In the shadows, the pounding of the waves seemed much louder, like the beating of wings at her back. She sighed with relief as she gained the foot of the stairs; the rising tide was lapping them with white foam. She yanked her boots from the hamper and leaped up onto dry rock to pull them on, turning to sit on the step.

Then she screamed.

The wind winnowed the sound from the air, so even she did not hear it. He was not ten yards from her, rising out of the sea, naked, his body gleaming as the water sloughed down it, his long hair loose and slicked tight to his head. He shook himself in a flurry of droplets that spattered on the foam-strewn water. Still he took no notice of her. He hasn't got his spectacles, she realized. He cannot see. . . .

If only he would turn and go back to swimming, she could make her escape. He leaned over, the cold waves smashing at his knees, and then straightened, pushing back his hair with his hands. Callie stayed motionless, half-crouched, like an animal frozen in the sights of a hunter. And still he did not see her.

God, the gleam of his flesh! It made her belly tighten, made her heart race. That dark vee of curling black hair reaching down to his waist beneath his taut nipples, then spreading out again—and his manhood tightened by the frigid water, the smooth round weights of his testicles skinned hard to his groin . . . *I want to paint him,* she thought in a wash of longing, and then amended herself: *Nay. I want to hold him.* The awful acknowledgement shook her to the bone.

Go. Now, she told herself. But it was too late. She'd flinched,

or sighed, and he raised his head, meeting her gaze. His clenched
hand moved to shield his privates, an involuntary gesture—
and then, in one arrived at more slowly, inched away to his
hip.

"Miss Wingate."

"I . . . I'm sorry. I didn't mean—I fell asleep on the beach.
I only just woke up. I—Zeus and I had a picnic. He must have
left me here. I wasn't spying. I . . ." Her voice died away. He
was coming toward her, dripping wet, impossibly tall. And the
thunder of the waves his wings. . . . "Did you finish the roof?"
The words were high and bright, unnatural. He nodded, his
eyes not leaving hers. They were as blue as the sky. He was
so close she could see the gooseflesh the chill wind had raised
on his arms. And something else had been raised: his manhood
stood stark upright, like a flag.

She grabbed her boots. "I'd best be going. Amazing how
you stand that cold water. Refreshing, though, I'll wager." The
stone stairs cut into the soles of her feet; she bit down on her
lip, hard, at the pain.

Wings beating at her back. His arms enveloping her . . .
"You'll never make it barefoot. Here. Let me." He eased the
boots from her hand. "Stockings?"

He was so close. "There." She nodded toward her left boot,
eyes downcast. He drew them forth, then rolled one up over
his thumbs. Callie watched from beneath her lashes. One thumb
snagged on the silk.

"Calluses," he apologized, carefully tugging it free.
"Here." She hesitated, then raised the edge of her skirt and
held her foot out to him. He slipped the toe of the stocking
over her toes, smoothed it up her calf. . . .

And his hands kept going, reaching all the way to her thigh.

"Oh, God," Callie whispered, the touch of his fingers making her white flesh quiver. "God, don't." Obliging, he withdrew
his hands, then fished inside her boot for the other stocking.
Callie was trembling. "I'll do it myself." She held her hand
out.

"Let me."

The waves pounding on the shore made a tumult. Callie
raised her head and looked at him. He smelled of saltwater,

bracing and fresh. His eyes were like the sea. The skin across his cheekbones was stretched taut as the silk in his hands. The planes of his chin bore a bristle of whiskers. His full lips were parted; he was breathing hard, his chest rising and falling with each inhalation.

She dropped her gaze abruptly. If she looked at him a moment more, in his naked splendor, she would do something she was sure to regret. To her great relief, he let the stocking flutter to the sand. . . .

And laid his hand on her breast.

"No!" she exclaimed, alarmed. But her body had swooned to his touch of its own volition; she felt her flesh melt to the palm of his hand, a perfect fit. He cupped his fingers, sighed, shuddered.

"I . . . want you, Callie." He shrugged, shook his head. "As I have never wanted anything in this world. I want to take you. Now."

"No." Yet even to her own ears, the protest rang hollow. He leaned forward to kiss her. She bent against the unyielding rock, and then, as his mouth closed on hers, closed her eyes, surrendering.

His mouth was impossibly warm, sweetly salty. He kissed her hungrily, anxiously, and she had the certain sense that if she'd pulled away he'd have relinquished his grip, let loose her breast from the tender trap of his fingers. She did not pull away, though. She could not have, for her life.

"Callie. Oh, Callie." He covered her with kisses, her mouth, her eyes, her wild hair. "My sweet, sweet Callie." His fingers fumbled at her bodice, and she was deliriously glad that she had worn this gown, with its simple laces rather than intricate hooks, for in his fervor he would have ripped anything more complicated right away. As it was, he tangled up the knot until she had to push his hands aside.

"Let me."

And he knelt on the rock, watching, waiting, until she worked the laces free. Then he fell on her with an intensity that would have been frightening had her own desire not matched it. "Oh," she sighed as his tongue rimmed her tight nipples, "oh, oh . . ."

"God, you are beautiful." He buried his face at her breast. "Christ. You're an angel. I want to look at you, feel you, touch you everywhere." He'd stripped off the stocking he'd slipped on so carefully, and was running his hand along her leg. Callie arched away, shivering with his intensity. His mouth was at her breast, suckling hungrily; his fingertips were lunging toward the edge of her drawers, and then reaching inside—

"Callie!" The long, drawn-out shout made them both freeze in mid-passion. "Callie, time to wake up!"

"Zeus," she whispered, drenched with regret.

"Perhaps he won't come down."

But he was on his way; in the gathering twilight they heard his footfalls on the stone stairs. "Callie! Christ, you are a sleepyhead."

"Damn him," she heard him mutter. Then his mouth closed over hers again, briefly, with great force. "I'll come to you tonight."

"In the house?" she whispered back with trepidation.

"In your bed."

She laughed, a little shakily. "It will be softer than this rock, anyway."

"Wait for me." He kissed her, his long blunt fingers playing at her nipples. Then, before Zeus made the first turn of the stairway, he turned and plunged back into the sea.

"Callie! Wake up, Callie!"

She tugged her bodice-laces tight, gathered up her stockings, and began to yank them on. "I am here! I'm coming!"

Her brother came hopping down the stairs. "Have you been asleep all this time?"

"Only just woke up this minute," she told him, glad for the twilight that would hide her blush.

"Hmph! Lazy-bones! The roof's all finished, and the work-men gone off home. And where were you? Snoring on the strand. And what a sight you look, all mussed and disheveled!" He reached to brush a curl from her cheek, and she flinched; the gesture echoed one that Mick had made just moments before. He let his hand drop, surprised. "What's the matter?"

"Nothing. I'm sorry. I am still half asleep." She thrust the hamper at him. "Here. You take this." She was cramming her boots on, not even bothering to lace them, and pushing him up the stairs; who knew how long Michel Harding could hold his breath? "I haven't missed supper, have I?"

"No, no. Lady Maggie's waiting on Mick. No one seems to know where he's gone."

"Really. How peculiar. *I* certainly haven't seen him."

Ahead of her, her brother turned, his green eyes suddenly thoughtful. "No one assumed you had."

25.

She asked Jennet for a bath—"All that sand from the beach," she explained apologetically—and sat on the edge of the bed, tapping her toes, while Gordie brought the water. She lit the candles atop the wardrobe, rearranged the nodding roses beside them, took her clothes off, laid out her sheerest nightdress, and stepped into the tub. Her heart was pounding out a wild tattoo: *He is coming. He is coming.* The knowledge made her hands shake; she could not even grip the soap.

Dinner had been excruciating—small talk, dry talk, talk that seemed to go on forever, and all the while sitting not five feet from him, all her senses ablaze. She could smell the sea-salt on his hands as he passed her the oysters, see the rise and fall of his chest beneath his coat. He was taciturn as ever, while she felt compelled to contribute to the conversation, nervous as a child with a secret, a big one, one that must be kept. The knowledge—*He is coming. He is coming*—had tightened her nerves, stretched her very skin until it felt transparent; she was sure if Zeus looked too long at her he would see straight through her. But he was preoccupied with asking questions of their hostess about the manor's days as a haven for pirates.

Lady Maggie had an eye on her grandson. "Ye maun bae

pleased, Michel, now that the roof bae finished.'' He grunted affirmation, swallowing oysters. ''Wha' will ye tackle next?''

Callie thought he glanced toward her, but since she did not dare to look at him could not be sure. He shrugged then, washing down the oysters with the cup to the right of his plate.

''That's my Rhenish,'' Zeus pointed out.

''Is it? Sorry. It tastes good. Pour me some, Grandmère, will you?''

''Mind yerself, Michel. Ye bain't used to drinkin'. Wine will gae straight to yer head after the whole day spent in that hot sun.'' But she passed him a cup. He drank it right down, thirstily, and passed it back for more. ''Ach, Michel—''

''I'm not going anyplace but to bed.''

Callie's blush was so entire and sudden that she felt impelled to feign a small coughing fit. ''Choking on a pearl, Cal? Don't swallow it,'' her brother cautioned helpfully.

''Just a bit of sand.''

''Speakin' o' sand, that war a nice long nap ye had on the beach today, waren't it?'' Lady Maggie asked, beaming at her. ''Ye'll bae rarin' to gae tonight, I reckon!''

Callie's head jerked up. ''What?''

''Why, ye'll bae up till dawn, dearie, after such a sleep. Mayhaps we ought to have a round or two o' whist after supper. D'ye play whist, pet? Michel war quite gude at it once.''

Callie shuddered at the notion of sitting at the card table with him for hours, still not able to touch him, to be touched by him. She made it into a yawn. ''Oddly, I still feel exhausted. It must be this heat. But another night, I'd be glad to play.''

''Pity. Well, Michel, ye can still make it a foursome.''

''Sorry, Grandmère. I'd fall asleep on my cards.''

And so it had gone through five endless courses, with every nonchalant remark made by her father or Zeus or Lady Maggie seemingly sprung like a trap, to catch her unawares. She did not know how Mick could stay so calm; by the time the tart was served, she could not pick up her knife and fork without having them rattle in her hands.

* * *

There came a knock now at her bedchamber door, very soft. Eyes wide, she stared at the portal. "Y-yes?"

"It's I, Cal. Zeus." Her breath went out in a rush. "I thought you might be asleep; I didn't want to wake you. Can I come in?"

"No! Not now!" Too emphatic. "I . . . I'm in the bath."

"Oh. Well, then. I have got this book here you might like to see, from Lady Maggie's collection. Astonishing woodcuts in it, really. You ought to have a look."

"I'll do that. Just leave it by the door." What if Mick saw him hanging about and was frightened off? *Go, Zeus! Go away!*

"All right. Good night, Cal." But no footsteps. Then his voice chimed out again. "You know, a bath sounds quite splendid. I think I'll have one, too. Send Gordie with the tub, will you, when you are done?"

"Yes, yes."

"I'll be downstairs. I'm going to teach Lady Maggie to play hearts."

"I can't hear you!" Callie called, splashing the water. "I am rinsing my hair!"

After a while, she stopped splashing and listened. All was silent, except for the distant pounding of the sea. She did rinse her hair then, and stood up for the towel. When she twisted 'round to dry her buttocks, Mick was standing in the doorway, his blue eyes ablaze.

"It was thus I saw you . . . from the window," he said hoarsely, and closed and latched the door.

Callie clutched the towel to her breasts. Of course he would not knock; he was laird of Langlannoch. He came toward her slowly, seeming to fill the room, crowd her into her corner. "Weren't you expecting me?"

"I . . . yes," she whispered, toes curled on the bottom of the copper tub.

"Why do you look so frightened, then?"

Perhaps her nakedness made her feel vulnerable; perhaps it was the burning in his gaze, the way his eyes raked over her cool white flesh as though he had already possessed it—and yet, she realized, he has. *I have been his ever since I saw him* down below in the garden. This is our destiny. The wonder is that it has taken us so long to get to here.

"Someone's left you some nighttime reading." He held a book in his fist.

"Zeus."

"Thoughtful of him." He tossed it onto the bed. Then he stroked her shoulder, ran his fingers up to her throat. "Are you clean?" She nodded, trembling beneath his touch. "Pity. I would have washed you. At least let me dry you." He pried the towel from her clenched grip, then offered her his hand. She stepped from the tub, her long hair dripping, making puddles. He dried that first, standing at her back. Then he wrapped the towel around her, still behind her, and began to rub. He worked downward, from her face to her shoulders and breasts, his long, strong fingers firm through the thick cloth. He moved down slowly over her belly, her buttocks, the gentle swell of her mound of Venus—Callie caught her breath as his hands pressed there. But he kept moving, along her thighs all the way down to her ankles, kneeling, his heavy head bent against the small of her back.

Then, with his hands on her hips, he spun her so she faced him. On his knees, he stared up at her in the glow of the candles. "This is what you want." He meant it as a question. She nodded once more, wordlessly. "Are you sure?" One last chance for her to deny it.

She wrapped her arms around his neck and kissed him as he knelt before her, kissed him with all the wild longing that had been tearing her soul apart for two endless years. Without another word he stood, lifting her off her feet, and carried her to the bed.

Her nightdress lay there. "Pretty," he grunted. "We don't need it." And he shoved it aside before he laid her down, her wet hair fanned against a nest of white pillows. Then he started to unbutton his shirt.

"Wait," Callie said. "Let me." Now it was her turn to kneel, there on the bed, and undress him. His skin already was more bronze than it had been that morning; the darker hue accentuated the bands of muscle binding his chest and arms. She unclasped his breeches, let them fall, and leaned back, tracing the hollow plain alongside his groin with her fingertips. "If you had any notion how many nights I spent on *this* . . ."

"Spend this one on it, too."

Her green-gold gaze met his; then she bent and kissed his thigh, and felt the whole great length of his body stiffen in surprise. His manhood, red and swollen hard, was by her cheek; she turned her head and kissed it, too. "Oh, Callie. Oh, my." He shuddered. "Don't . . ." But she liked the feel of it on her mouth, the skin so slick and smooth between its ridges, and the round head, like the pad of one's thumb pierced by a thorn. She touched the tip of her tongue to the puckered thorn-hole. "Callie! Jesus!" His knees had buckled beneath him as a pearly bead of fluid gathered there. She licked it away; it was salty-sweet.

"Stop, Cal," he said breathlessly.

"Doesn't it please you?"

"Did Harry Godshall teach you that? Did you do that to him?"

"No! Never! Why in God's name do you bring up Harry?"

He looked down at her in the glow of the candles. "Forgive me. I just . . . I would have liked to be your first."

"But you are."

His eyes, deep blue like the ocean, glinted. "You and Harry didn't . . ." She shook her head, smiling. He let out a long, slow sigh. "I'd hoped . . . but I didn't dare believe it."

"Would it have mattered so much?"

The muscles of his face drew tighter. "You will think me old-fashioned. But . . . yes. You were betrothed to him all that time. I saw the way he looked at you, craved you. And he's the son of an earl. Why didn't you give in?"

"I was waiting for you, I suppose." She took his hand and lay back, pulling him atop her. "I am waiting for you still!"

Laughing, he rolled over and brought his knees up, to tug off his boots. "You hadn't finished undressing me."

She had not heard him laugh very often, and she loved the sound. She wanted to hear it again and again. As he struggled with a boot, she reached for the taut skin beneath his ribs and scrabbled at it with her fingertips. He gasped and doubled up, rolling away. "Christ! What are you doing?"

"Tickling you. Are you ticklish?"

"No!" he insisted, laughing helplessly.

"Here, then, perhaps?" It was the only place Zeus was vulnerable—on his thigh, just above the knee, and you had to dig in a bit. Her touch reduced the laird of Langlannoch to a mass of giggles. He grabbed her by the wrists and pinned them up above her head.

"There! Now tell me, what makes you so bold, Calliope Chloe Wingate? I thought you were a proper professor's daughter."

"I don't know," she admitted, tossing her head. It was true: she felt utterly loosened, unbound, unashamed. "Perhaps it is this place. This house. It has a way of changing one, don't you think?"

"I've no idea what you mean."

"Oh, come, Michel, you know you—" She stopped; he'd stiffened. "What?"

"Why did you call me that?"

"Call you *what?*"

"Michel."

"Did I?" She couldn't recall. "I suppose because it suits you. Mick's no name for a laird."

"It is my name. So that must make me no laird."

"You're every inch a laird." She looked pointedly at his erect manhood. "It's the name that is wrong. I shall call you Michel if I please. Michel. Michel. Mi—" She ended her teasing with a kiss, a long, hard one that left her breathless.

"Mick," he said, finally pulling away.

"Michel."

So he kissed her again, looming above her, his face in shadow but his black hair wreathed with candlelight. He had her wrists pinned still; he shifted on the bed, his tongue tracing a line from her ear to her chin and down her neck. He paused to plant a kiss in the hollow of her throat, then resumed his journey, moving lower, lower, until he seized the tight red bud of her nipple in his mouth. Callie arched up, letting out a moan of pleasure: "Oh . . ."

"So you like that? I seemed to recall that you do." His tongue and teeth were rimming against her in a slow, steady motion that set her flesh ablaze. She strained in his grasp, wanting and not wanting him to release her hands; she loved the force of his grip, the way he'd bent her to his control. How astonishingly different his mastery was from Harry's crude, flawed gropings. Something niggled her memory.

"Would you stop, if I asked it?"

He raised his head, then shook it. "Nay. Not now. I could not." He started to her breast again and paused. "Were you going to ask it?" She laughed, and, satisfied, he sucked the tip of her nipple until her laughter turned to sighs.

"If you promise to leave off tickling, I will release your hands now," he whispered. "Do you promise?"

"Aye . . ." God in heaven, what bliss! He released her, and she pulled him down to her, wanting to feel his weight atop her. He was so warm, so alive, so long and lean and hard. His manhood pressed against her thigh, unyielding, demanding. He slid his hand along her side, shifted, and ran it over her taut belly, down to the tuft of curls that crowned her mound of Venus.

"You are misnamed. You should have been Aphrodite." The goddess of love. . . .

"That's as awful as Mick." Then she gasped; his hand had slipped between her thighs, and his long fingers were stroking the dark softness there.

"Oh, Christ," she heard him whisper. "Christ have mercy." His breath was coming ragged and fast. He brought his mouth up to kiss her, this time with such raw yearning in his eyes that she shivered to see it. To be wanted so . . . it was all she ever had longed for. She parted her knees, her hands stroking his shoulders, drawing him down, inside.

"I don't want to hurt you," he whispered.

"You won't hurt me," she declared with such certainty that he laughed and kissed her eyes.

"Still, your first time . . . I must be gentle."

"I don't want you to be gentle."

"What do you know?" His fingertips searched, probed, soft as air. Impatient, Callie strained against his hand.

"What are you waiting for?"

In answer he caressed the small, sweet knot of her passion with one long finger. Callie's breath escaped her as her tightened sheath released a burst of warm wetness that let his strokes move easily. "That," he told her, smiling at her mouth. "I was waiting for that."

He knelt above her, suddenly grave. The room was very still; the far-off thunder of the waves loomed loud. Callie stared up at him, capturing in her mind for all time this image of him just before he took her: the feral stallion of her covert dreams. Yes, but now so much more—scholar, teacher, doting grandson, laird, and, beneath it all, that lonely bereft boy staring down into the sea. *I will never leave you,* she wanted to promise, but before she could he took his manhood and drove deep inside her.

Her fists clenched as he entered, and her whole body tensed, but she did not cry out: she had said she would not be hurt by him. She had bitten down on her lip, though, so hard she thought she'd drawn blood. He respected her pride enough not to apologize, but simply waited, plunged deep within her, until her tightly-wound muscles slackened slightly. Then he pulled back, soothing her with a kiss, his hand smoothing her hair.

"Again," she whispered.

"Oh, I will." But still he hesitated, his fingers playing against the bud of her desire, coaxing her to readiness. Nothing, however, could prepare her for the sensation of that long, hard shaft piercing her, forcing her flesh apart. When it came again she gasped, jerking backward. "Callie," he whispered. "Callie, your hands—" Her nails were digging into his back, raking his sunburnt skin.

He had to reach back to pull them free, for she was caught in a web of perception, pinned unmoving by the spear of his manhood and a swirl of impressions: heat, weight, pain, delight. She had to close her eyes to try and take it in; otherwise she feared the onslaught would make her swoon. It was too much to bear, to look at him, smell his rich sea-scent, hear his thundering heartbeat and at the same time feel him in such myriad ways. The scratch of his beard, the heat of his skin, the swell of his muscles, the salt haze of his sweat, the caress of his hand, the sweet pressure of his kiss. And, underlying all that, right at the core of her being, the mystical, ineffable juncture of their separate bodies. Two becoming one—

"Callie!"

His sharp voice yanked her back from the precipice of dream. He was staring down at her, his blue eyes startled, fearful: "Christ! I thought I'd killed you!"

She gathered in her wayward senses, concentrated on his taut face. "Kill me some more."

Relieved, he laughed and reared back, sliding from her sheath. Callie felt her very blood swirl up to try and hold him, keep him there inside her. "Don't go!" she cried, clutching his hips with her knees.

"I'm not going anywhere but here." He drove into her, pulled out. "Here. Here." And each word punctuated with another thrust, and with each thrust her tightness eased so that he pushed a little deeper, and the unfamiliar wellspring in her belly flowed and sang. "Here. Here." He was moving faster, harder, panting out the words: "Here—oh! Oh, Christ. Here! Here! Oh, God in heaven!"

"Here," Callie whispered, gathering him in, holding him tight as she could, open to him like a flower. "Here." She could feel him straining in her arms; it was like riding—nay, like being ridden by—a wild stallion, a great bucking brute of a horse in the throes of need. She stroked his sharp shoulder blades, his back, felt him slide his hands down to cup her buttocks, lifting her against him.

And then suddenly the wellspring inside her burst open, leaving her clinging to him, desperate, panting herself in a frenzy of longing, of straining toward some end she had only dimly known existed, the culmination of this shared wild ride. As she moaned her hunger in a rising crescendo, she felt him pause, saw him smile down at her in prideful approval. But only for a moment; then he set on her again, thrusting, driving, yearning. Callie clenched her eyes shut; her mind was a muddle of dark shadows, forms: Michel Faurer and his Madeleine atop the black horse, pounding over the strand, harder, higher, and a hundred other dim shades, the lords and ladies of Langlannoch across all the centuries coupling on this bed. It was as though she held them all inside her—and when the moment of release came, when he made his final desperate thrust and his seed shot forth, searing her with its heat, making her scream his name in wonder at the ecstatic fire in her belly and thighs, it was as if they all cried out to him too, their voices fading slowly as he fell against her, limp and drained.

The ghostly procession, the sense of having been conduit to spirits, left her shivering, shaking. He lay with his cheek against hers, his elbows on her hair. There was sweat on his skin; she could taste it in her mouth. After a long time, he pushed himself up with a groan, as though his muscles ached.

"Callie?" he said, and kissed her closed eyes. She was afraid to open them, terrified of what she might see. If he made light of this, if he laughed or jested, after what she had felt. . . . He took her hand in his, laid it against his pounding heart.

She dared then to look up from beneath her lashes. His blue eyes swam with tears, so far from laughing. "Callie," he whispered, and touched his mouth to hers with infinite tenderness. Then he fell back upon the pillows, still breathing hard, his chest moving in heaves.

Lying beside him, staring up at the scrim of white linen stretched overhead, Callie felt his hand still clasping hers, their fingers entwined. We had so much to say before, she thought, and now we have nothing. But that was all right. When you have just had your world upended, you needed time to reflect.

He shifted, sitting up. "Thirsty?" he asked. She tried her parched throat, then nodded, sitting up, too. He went and brought the pitcher and cup, then stopped, staring at a crimson splot on the bedclothes close by her knees. Callie looked as well. He touched it, turned to her. "Your maidenhead."

"I shall have a hard time explaining *that* to Jennet."

"She will know already. Grandmère, too. Grimkin will have told them." She stared at him, saw he was teasing. But she didn't mind now. He poured her water, and she drank greedily. Though he seemed quite content to stride about her rooms unclothed, she felt self-conscious, and reached for her nightdress. He stopped her, his hand on her wrist. "Must you? I will only take it off again."

"I . . . there's a chill to the air, don't you think?" she lied, and pulled it over her head. He watched with regret.

She busied herself with braiding up her hair, sitting cross-legged on the bed, her thighs still aching with his imprint. He sat across from her, and said nothing for so long that she was casting about for some remark of her own—what did one say, after all, afterward, to one's first lover?—when he cleared his throat. "You're not . . . are you sorry, Callie?" His voice was low and hoarse.

"No!" she said quickly.

"You are so quiet—"

She tried to laugh. "I'm just not certain what to say. What do you usually discuss with your . . . amours in the aftermath?"

He flushed. "I haven't any amours."

"Well—whatever you call them. Your women."

"Don't you understand, Callie? If men had maidenheads, mine would be staining the counterpane with yours."

Wide-eyed, she stared at him. "You mean . . ." Still red-faced, he nodded. "Oh, my. I never imagined . . . well, now I think of it, you don't even drink."

"I did tonight."

"And didn't your grandmother warn you it would go to your head?" He laughed, emboldening her to ask: "Why me?"

"You are . . . very lovely."

"Oh, bosh. There are lots of girls more lovely than me."

"I don't meet lots of girls."

"Ah. So it was a simple matter of proximity."

"No! Of course it wasn't." He sighed, pushing back his hair. "What do you want me to say?" She knew damned well what she wanted him to say. She wondered if he did. "Let me ask you the same thing, then. Why me?"

She twined a red-brown braid over and under her fingers. "I suppose it is because I feel I knew you in another life."

To her surprise, he shrank from her. "Christ! Don't say such things!"

"Lord, Michel, I was only jesting."

"And don't call me that! Please!" He turned his long straight back to her, sighed again, then looked over his shoulder. "I'm sorry. It is just . . . that's the sort of thing Grandmère would say. Fate and all that. Our destiny."

"And you don't think it might be?"

"We make our own destinies," he said stubbornly. "We aren't victims of our stars. That's all a load of rubbish—gypsies and tarot cards and crystal balls. This is the Age of the Enlightenment." Callie thought of the dark shadows she had felt pass through her at the climax of their coupling, but decided against mentioning them.

She looked down at her hands, folded in her lap. He started to yawn, and then, embarrassed, tried to hide it. "I am sorry," he apologized.

"No, no. You must be exhausted—up on that roof all day, and swimming . . ." And now this. She turned the coverlet down for him. "Go on, then. Go to sleep."

"Here, you mean." He sounded alarmed.

"Well . . . that is how it's done in all the cheap novels I am not supposed to read. The hero and the heroine—you know—and then they curl up in each other's arms."

"I don't know that I could sleep, with someone else beside me."

"You might find you like it."

"You might find that I snore."

"I don't mind snoring." She had a terrible fear that if he left now, he would disappear the way he had the last time, at Avebury, and deny that anything had passed between them. If he did, she knew, it would break her heart. She had to hold him here for the night, the way the fairy-folk held their victims for a year and a day. Then he would be hers forever. She looked at him with pleading eyes. "Don't go. Don't leave me."

"Callie, I—"

"The bed is very soft," she rushed on, "very comfortable, really. Such a thick mattress . . . see? And the pillows—"

"I know. I used to crawl in with my mother, when I was quite small."

No wonder he was loathe to stay. Defeated, she turned away—

And felt his hand on her cheek. "All right, then. For a little while." Grateful, she kissed his fingers. He leaned toward her and touched his mouth to hers gently, almost regretfully.

"Are you . . . sorry?" she whispered.

"I am only tired." He yawned again, this time without restraint, and eased between the sheets, moving as though his muscles were aching—and well they must be, Callie thought, remembering how he'd clambered over the roof and swung his hammer all day long. He lay with his back to her. Tentatively she ran her hand over the tight knot at the base of his neck, rubbed it with her palm. He let out an appreciative grunt: "That feels good." His skin was warm and smooth beneath her fingers. His hair still bore the scent of the sea.

She went on stroking his back, and thought he might be asleep when suddenly he thrashed with his leg at the foot of the bed. "What? What is the matter?"

"Something there," he mumbled, sitting up to grope among the covers. "That." The book Zeus had left for her, that he'd brought in and then tossed aside. "What are you reading?"

"I don't know. Zeus gave it me. Said I should look at the woodcuts."

In the guttering glow of the candles, he let the volume fall open, looked at it, then looked at her. "Your brother," he said, "is a most peculiar soul."

"Why? What is it?" She arched to see, then gasped. "Oh, dear Lord!" He turned the page, examined it, turned another. Callie began to giggle, crowding closer to see. "Jesus! Oh, look there. That's physically impossible. Isn't it?"

"One would certainly think so." He turned the book over to see the spine. "The *Kama Sutra*. A manual of lovemaking. Indian, from the 12th century."

"You've seen it before?"

"I've only read about it. What, pray tell, could your brother have had in his mind, to pass this on to you?"

"No doubt he believed it had academic value. Oh, God, look at this one!" The woodcut, beautifully, intricately made, showed a woman bent over backward all the way to the ground, long breasts hanging, her palms spread out behind her, while her lover thrust at her from above, smiling beatifically. "Go on. Turn the page."

Instead he shut the book. "I really don't think it's proper that you be exposed to this sort of thing."

"Be exposed to—who the hell do you think you are? Damn you, give it to me!" Furious, she lunged for it—and saw the corners of his wide mouth twitching. "Oh, you! You know you are dying to see it, just the same as I am."

"Only in the interest of academic research." But she'd seen his lax manhood tighten.

"Really. Then you ought to try to maintain a more objective posture." And she slid her hand onto his thigh.

"Do you mind? I'm trying to study." He shook the book open at another woodcu. Both their moths dropped.

Callie bent closer. "Aren't there too many legs?"

"No, no. Two each, that's right. It's just the juxtaposition—"

"Just the position, I'd say!" She twined her knee over his, hiking up her nightdress.

"What are you doing?"

"Scientific experimentation. This *is* the Age of the Enlightenment." Her back felt as though it were breaking. "God, I can't even come close!"

He nuzzled her breast through the sheer lawn. "Close enough, I'd say." His manhood was stark upright now, and pushing at her thigh. "Finished reading?"

"Oh, no. I think we should see it through to the end."

"I intend to." He rolled her onto her back. The book dropped off the bed.

"You don't think this is a bit . . . plebian, after what we've just seen."

"Novices have to start somewhere." He pushed the nightdress up, baring her belly and breasts. His mouth traced lazy circles over her flesh. Callie sighed with pleasure, arms stretched over her head. God bless Zeus. . . .

He kissed her taut nipples, then reached up for her mouth. Callie felt the fire in her soul begin building, stoking to a blaze.

His loins were hard and smooth as marble, stone with flame hidden at their core. "Besides," he whispered, just before he drove inside her, "we have the whole night to study." She caught her breath as he slipped his arms beneath her knees, tilting her upward as he entered her again. "And I learn fast."

26.

How very quiet the world was before dawn, Callie thought, edging cautiously away from the crook of Mick's arm. Her mind told her she need not be so careful—a cataclysm could not wake him; he slept like a dead man—but in her heart she feared that having him beside her was only a dream, that when the morning came the man who'd held her so tightly, taken her again and again with such hot, sweet passion would disappear. And so she'd lain for hours beneath the welcome, leaden weight of his right leg, remained almost not breathing with his splayed fingers tangled in her hair, his chest rising and falling beneath her cheek, listening to his heartbeat as it echoed the hushed, distant drum of the sea.

But now she had to move; she was dying of thirst, and if she did not use the chamber-pot she would burst. She crawled to the edge of the bed and swung her feet to the floor. The old oak boards creaked, and she froze, glancing back at him in the light of the sole remaining candle. When he didn't stir, she eased herself up from the mattress and inched across the room.

Chamber-pot first. She perched on it, holding her breath—how mortifying if he woke and found her that way! Still he slept on, though in the silence the sound was like a mighty waterfall. He'd used it during the night, with manly nonchalance, standing with legs spread apart and not even pausing in his conversation—what had they been speaking of? And she, watching, enthralled by this intimacy he seemed to take so for granted, had felt love deep and hard within her, certain as stone.

Her own body smelled foreign to her, bosky, like the floor of a forest, the earth at the roots of old trees. There were marks on her skin from his mouth and hands; her nipples were fat and swollen, tender as rosebuds. She remembered how hungrily he'd pulled at them, and shivered as a faint aftershock of desire pulsed through her. *Greedy thing,* she chided herself, smiling, *how could you want more?* But she did; her marrow ached for him.

She drank thirstily, her eyes never leaving him. How splendid he was; with what lean, strong perfection his limbs fitted together! The curve of his back into his buttocks, the long sweep of his thigh, the hollow at the back of his knee, his feet—what magnificent feet! *The Savage at Rest,* she'd call this composition, his skin sheened with sweat, dark against the linens in the candlelight. . . .

He stirred a little and rolled over to face her, arms wrapped over his chest. His manhood hung flaccid; his testicles sagged, loose and brick-red. She curled her fingers, thinking of the taste of his skin there, the prickly feel of it against her tongue. And the feel of *his* tongue! Sometime in the night, in the delirious haze of their pleasure, he had knelt between her legs and put his tongue to her *there,* and laughed as her shy protests dissolved into an arc of sighs. "You come nicely," he'd whispered. "So ladylike. I wonder . . . can I make you scream for it?"

He had. He had made her beg, and shriek, and giggle, and once, when his kisses had been unbearably gentle, he had made her cry. He'd brushed the tears away and held her, and he hadn't asked why she was weeping; it was as if he knew she could not have explained.

"Lover," she breathed in the stillness. "My lover." What a marvelous word. What a marvelous man. Michel Douglas Harding, laird of Langlannoch. Pride buckled her knees. He had chosen *her.* She had brought him to this bed, brought him again and again to the pitch of ardor and felt the hot blast of his seed burst forth. What they'd shared had been as old as the world, and as new as rain. . . .

It was odd to think of all they'd done together with his grandmother sleeping just across the hall, with her father and brother but a few rooms away, reading dry books or snoring in solitary beds. Her father—Lord, her mother had been dead sixteen years; how had he lived without this all that time? It was different when one got old, perhaps, but just now she did not think she could last until dawn without making love again.

The tub still stood in the corner. *I never sent it on to Zeus,* she thought with a twinge of guilt. *I wonder will he know, when he sees me, what I have done? He reads me so well. No doubt he'll be glad for it if he does guess; it will fit in with whatever half-cocked scheme has got him sounding that cove and pacing off the rocks, for his sister to be sleeping with the laird.*

She was getting restless, jumpy, thinking of the other people in her life, of the repercussions from this night of love she'd tumbled to so willingly. The man asleep in her bed—what would his thoughts be when he awoke? Would he regret what he had done to her, with her? Would he blame the wine?

Silly, he adores *you,* she told herself.

Still, through all those mad hours of love-making, he'd not once mentioned the word.

Impatiently, she crossed the room to the window, forgetting the creaking floorboards. *Neither did I,* she quibbled with her conscience, which rose up in revolt: *You would have, if he did.*

Well, maybe he would if I had! she argued back defiantly. Anyway, it was too soon to talk of love; they'd only just that night—

Only just that night *what?* Joined, man and woman, flesh to flesh, time and again; given to one another the priceless, irrevocable gift of their chastity. Taken such keen pleasure in each other that just the memory set her trembling. *If what we shared is not proof of love,* she thought wistfully, *then I don't know what is.*

Look how often Harry Godshall had protested he loved her, when all he'd wanted was what Michel had gotten. Surely acts of love meant more than the mere word; his gentleness, his reluctance to hurt her, all those impassioned kisses—didn't they speak for themselves? He *does* love me. . . .

Or as close to love as he can come.

That was a discouraging thought. She tried to nudge it away, but it kept returning. He had cut himself off from feeling anything for so long. What if the capacity to love was simply no longer there?

Then I have made a grave mistake this night, she realized, and turned to watch him as he slept. Still, I had rather have made love with him than with Harry. For if Michel Harding ever does love, I'll wager it will prove a story worthy of his clan.

Naked, sprawled across the sheets, he looked so defenseless. And yet she knew that time and circumstance had built a fortress 'round his heart that would be hell to breach. So tonight had only been a beginning; though it seemed topsy-turvy, perhaps he needed for her to prove her love so completely before he dared show his.

Then again, perhaps when he woke he would bolt like a rabbit, disappear to Cyprus or Greece, and she would never see him again.

But she didn't believe that. In her inmost soul she felt, had felt for a long time, what her brother had suggested to her out on the strand—that her destiny and Mick Harding's were inexplicably entwined, that the two of them were part of some far larger story whose outlines they could only see as shadows, like the letters on a palimpsest. She'd felt that on the stone at Avebury, and she had felt it again last night at the moment of climax, when Michel Faurer and his black-haired lady and all their descendants had come crowding in on her like guests at a love-feast, celebrating the laird of Langlannoch's inheritance. Lady Maggie's words rang in her ears: *One o' the great luvs o' their time* . . . That same blood ran in Michel's veins. Someday, hundreds of years from now, an old woman might sit in the great hall of this house and speak of her and Michel's love in that same hushed, proud tone.

It did not, she admitted, seem very likely. After all, the times had changed. Mick Harding was no chevalier, and she no titled beauty. In the hard light of day, she was a butcher's granddaughter, and he a gloomy cleric's son—not exactly the stuff of legend.

Still, I'll wager Madeleine de Courtenay never dreamed anyone would remember her, after all these years.

She went back to the bed and sat staring at him. He looks the part of hero at least, she thought with satisfaction. I hope he has lost those damned glasses forever; without them, he's the handsomest man I have ever seen. And he is wise and just and, Lord in heaven, virile. . . .

And as skittish of his heart as a mouse of snakes.

"What am I to do about you, Michel Douglas Harding?" she whispered.

And the dawn wind, curling around Langlannoch's yellow stones, whispered back: *Cleave to him.*

His big hand, the palm thick with new calluses, groped toward her. "Callie?" He was more asleep than awake.

"I'm here." She crawled in beside him, back into the crook of his arm. He flung his leg atop hers once more, pinioning her there.

"Thought you'd gone," he mumbled.

"Where would I go? We are in my bed."

But he was already snoring. Callie lay with her cheek against his chest, listening to the drum of his heartbeat as it sang, like the roar of the sea, like the whispering wind, like the ghostly shadows: *Cleave to him. Cleave to him.*

27.

He was gone when she woke.

Too warm, in a tangle of bedclothes, Callie opened her eyes, heard silence, could not feel his weight beside her. She caught her breath. A dream ... or, worse, he planned to pretend it never happened, just like Avebury. Damn, damn, damn! But as she sat up, wounded and furious, something scratched her hand. She glanced toward the side of the bed where he'd been sleeping and saw that it was heaped with roses; he'd taken them from their vases all around the room and piled them beside her. She laughed out loud at the glorious mess of stems and petals and thorns; it was a gesture worthy of a laird. One perfect blossom graced her pillow. She held it to her cheek, inhaling the rich musk scent, so like the scent of his skin.

Then, with his pledge to her still strewn across the sheets, she jumped from the bed and into the tub. She could not wait for this day to begin.

Half an hour later, wearing a butter-yellow gown of sheer dimity, her hair washed again but not yet dried, and hanging loose down her back, she came into the kitchens. Jennet had just taken a taste of something steaming hot from the kettle on the hearth-cleek; her mouth too full to speak, she nodded a greeting and waved Callie into the dining hall. *He* wasn't there, she saw with a stab of disappointment, but Zeus was, gobbling hotcakes and Jennet's extraordinary jam. He used his foot beneath the table to shove a chair out for her. "Hallo," he said then. "God, your hair dries slow."

"What?" She put a hand to her damp curls.

"You were washing it ten hours ago, and here it still is wet."

"Oh! I . . . I had to rinse it out again this morning. All that sand from the beach." Change the subject! "Are you going back there today, with your measuring sticks?"

He flashed a grin. "Nay. I thought I'd trot off to Ayr, see what there is to be seen. Care to come along?"

Leave Langlannoch? Leave Mick? "No, thanks. I don't relish riding in this heat. I'm surprised you do."

"I figure I might as well work myself into a lather, since I never got to bathe last night."

The tub. "Oh, Zeus. I am sorry. I just . . . forgot all about it."

"No matter. I'd only have to do it again when I come home tonight. I thought perhaps it might have been that book I left you that distracted you." Callie's blush was so sudden and entire that he bit his lip. "Oh, dear. I *am* sorry, pet. I didn't mean it to offend you. I just thought you might find it, well, interesting. In a strictly intellectual way."

"I paged through it." Hell, she and Mick had *lived* it. "As you say, interesting."

Zeus seemed embarrassed now by his little joke. "Quite. There are any number of interesting volumes in the library here—and I don't mean interesting in *that* way. Lots of philosophy, lots of theology—very dense stuff. It would take a soul a lifetime to read through it. Some of the books are extremely valuable. There's a copy of Aquinas's *Summa Theologiae* that must be thirteenth century, and the *Morte d'Arthur* with woodcuts that I swear must be by Dürer. It's not a vast collection, mind you, but it—Callie?"

"Mm? Go on. I'm listening."

"But what are you *doing?*"

Their father had left one of his notebooks and a Cumberland

pencil at the breakfast table; while waiting for Jennet and listening to her brother, Callie had taken them up and was idly tracing the outlines of the row of arched windows above Zeus's head. She liked the way the thick leaded panes subtly distorted the sunlight, making it shimmer and wave like the surface of the sea. "Oh, just drawing those windows."

"That's what I thought. You're drawing."

Callie, realizing his point, looked down at the pencil in her hand. "Well. So I am. Well!" Her fingers curled hungrily on the lead. "It wasn't to be expected, I suppose, that I could hold out forever."

"No, but I feared you would!" He looked at her closely, then away, as though afraid to make too much of this. "Has anything . . . happened, Cal?"

"Happened? What could have happened?" But her voice had trembled. *You could have realized that you were in love; you could have spent the night in your true love's arms. . . .*

Jennet came bustling in. "Sorry, dearie, to hae kept ye waitin', but my preserves war just comin'. Wha' can I get ye?"

Callie looked longingly at her brother's rapidly vanishing hotcakes. "You know, I feel quite famished. I hate to trouble you, Jennet, but could I get some of those? And maybe some meat?"

"His Lairdship had blud sausage. He had an appetite on him this mornin', too, dinna he, though?"

"Blood sausage would be splendid," Callie said. "And . . . some fruit?"

"La, that bae just wha' His Lairdship had," Jennet noted. "Hotcakes 'n blud sausages 'n ripe red cherries."

Callie was blushing again. She leaned over to fix her stocking till it wasn't so obvious. "Where is His Lordship?" she asked Jennet, when she dared to straighten up again.

"Why, right atop ye, mum."

This time there was no hiding her startled red flush. *"What?"*

Jennet giggled. "Ach, I do beg yer pardon! On the rooftop, I meant, mum. That 'n nothin' more."

"Oh!" Callie let out her breath. Jennet went off to the kitchens, shoulders still shaking with laughter. Zeus was looking at her very curiously. She reached for the teapot, holding tight to the lid lest it betray her trembling hands.

Zeus set down his fork. "See here, Callie," he began.

She met his gaze. She didn't know what her face showed, but she knew what her heart beseeched: *Don't make me speak of this yet. Please God, no banter or teasing. It's all too raw, too new; I need time to keep my secret my own, just for a little while. . . .*

And Zeus, bless him, did not fail her. He opened his mouth, closed it abruptly, then started again. "I might be able to pick you up some sketchbooks and charcoal in Ayr. Shall I try?"

"Why, Zeus. How thoughtful of you. I'd like that very much indeed."

He downed the last of his tea. "Right. Well, I'll be off, then."

Jennet had brought the bowl of cherries. Callie smiled her thanks, then sucked one of the scarlet fruits from its stem with her lips, still tender from Mick's kisses. The skin burst in her mouth; the flesh was puckery-sweet.

Zeus had started around the table to kiss her; now he paused, watching as she plucked another cherry from the bowl and unconsciously caressed it with her tongue.

"Right," her brother said again, and blew the kiss to her from a distance. "I'll see you later, pet."

When she'd eaten all she could of Jennet's hotcakes, which was quite a bit, Callie took a handful of cherries and went out to the yards. The sun was bright and blinding; shielding her eyes, she looked to the rooftops. "Mick? Are you there?"

He came around a corner of the closest tower, shirtless, his breeches hanging low with the weight of the tools on his belt. His brown skin gleamed with sweat; his black hair was plastered to his neck. Callie felt her thighs begin to ache.

"I did not mean to abandon you," he called down to her, smiling.

"I know that. I had the thorns to remind me of you."

"Am I so prickly as that?"

She shrugged and popped a cherry into her mouth. He peered over the edge of the gutter. "What have you got there?"

"Cherries." She spat the stone out and swallowed.

"Let me have some." She started to toss them up, but he shook his head at her: "No. Bring them up here."

She backed away. "I don't like heights."

"It is perfectly safe."

"Then why are you fixing it?"

"It's already fixed. I'm just tacking the flashing down. Come up! The ladder's just around here." He led her to it, walking along above her.

"Is that my window?" Callie asked, seeing the second-story casement it climbed past.

"Of course," he said cheerfully. "Come on. I want my cherries."

"Come down and get them."

"I'm not done with my work. You come up. There's a fantastic view." Still she hesitated. "I won't let you fall, goose." When she didn't move, he shrugged and started away. "Suit yourself, then. But I'll be up here all day."

"Wait!" She wanted to be with him. She put her boot on the bottom rung of the ladder, then sprang back as it swayed.

"I'll hold it for you," Mick assured her, and hurried to do so, pulling the staves tight against the gutter. "Just don't look down."

She couldn't bear for him to think her a sissy. Teeth gritted, she began to climb.

One foot atop the other, higher and higher into that sun-blazoned sky. She paused, a little dizzy, clinging to the ladder. "Don't look down," Mick warned again. She looked up at him instead, reassured by his encouraging smile. "You can do it. You're nearly to your window now."

From four rungs up, she could see in through the casement, see the bed where they'd lain together and the roses still heaped. "You had a nice look at me, didn't you, that first time, when I was bathing?"

"A *very* nice look. I damned near fell off the thing." She gripped the ladder even more tightly. He laughed. "Just keep climbing! One foot after the other. That's it." She'd gotten close enough that he could grasp her wrists and pull her up, which was what he did. Her bootheel, swinging free, brushed the top of the stave.

"Mick! The ladder!" It was pushing off from the edge. Safe in the circle of his arm, she watched in dismay as it veered back, teetered upright for a moment, and then began to fall across the lawn. It landed with a *thunk* that made her shiver. "Christ! Now what are we to do?"

"I suppose we are stranded."

"Unless Jennet heard it." Callie looked toward the kitchen door, far below, but the cook didn't appear. "Good Lord. I am sorry."

"Are you? I'm not. At least this way you can't leave straight off."

"Perhaps Father or your grandmother—"

He was shaking his head. "They rode off early to the church, to look at the record books there."

"They could be gone all day! And Zeus is gone to Ayr."

"I know. I saw him ride off, too."

She turned to him, eyes gold in the sunlight. "Then we truly are stranded."

"So we are. Where are my cherries?"

Callie opened her tight fist. They were all squashed to bits. "That's what you get," she said darkly.

He lifted her palm to his mouth, to lick away the sweet juice. Callie felt her knees go weak—a precarious state of affairs, perched on that narrow, sloping gambrel. Grinning, he spat out a stone and ducked his head to kiss her. He tasted of sweat and cherries. "Could we at least," she pleaded, holding tight to him, "move back a bit from the edge?"

He laughed. "There's a flat space over there between the towers—and it's even in shade this time of day. Come on." He yanked her along, clambering over the steep slope surefooted as a goat. She scrambled in his wake, using her free hand to clutch at the shingles, wishing she'd never come up.

But when he swung her over the pitch of the gambrel and onto blessed flatness, her head stopped spinning. She stood well back against the stone wall and took a breath, looking out over the sea. "Oh, dear Lord."

"I told you, didn't I?" He stood beside her, following her gaze, her hand still clasped tight in his.

The sea glinted in the sunlight, stretching out in a vast sweep of blue beneath the cloudless sky. Far in the distance she could see the pine-dark bulk of an island. "What's that?" she breathed, pointing.

"Arran. And Kintyre beyond it." She could see that, too, looking hard: a paler, less distinct bulk rising out of the waves. "And Ireland there." He nodded southward, toward a very faint edge of green separating blue sea and sky. "The Glens of Antrim. You can only see them when the day's so clear."

"I want to paint it," she said, surprising herself.

He smiled down at her. "I thought you might. When I was little, I used to come up here all the time, to watch the sun and the moon rise. You should see the moon rise."

"Unless Jennet tears herself away from her preserves to come out into the yards, I very well might."

He laughed again. "You don't really mind being stuck up here, do you?"

"Would it matter if I did?" But she softened, having him so close. "No. I wanted . . . to be with you anyway."

"And I with you." His mouth was warm and winning; his hands were caught in her loose hair. She felt dizzy still, and not from the height. "I like your gown," he offered shyly.

"This thing? You have seen it a million times."

"I liked it every one." He began to unlace it. Alarmed, she clutched at his hands:

"Are you mad?"

"Mm. About you." There was a bulge in his breeches pushing at her side.

She glanced around uncertainly. "Someone will see us!"

"Who? The cormorants?"

He was right; for out in the broad, open flat, the stretch of roof was utterly secluded. "You are out of your mind," she told him anyway, and then breathed a sigh as his mouth closed on her bared breast. "Oh, Mick!"

"You've made a monster of me. I cannot get enough of you," he told her, drawing her onto the stones at their feet.

His skin was slick and hot; there were ridges along his back where her nails had scraped him the night before. "You'd best keep your shirt on in public," she whispered breathlessly, tracing them with her fingertips, "until those heal. Do they hurt you?"

"I love them. Make some more."

"Do you think you might take off your belt?" His hammer was crushing against her waist.

"I'll take off everything, if you will."

"I sunburn," she warned him.

"I will keep you well covered."

He did, too. He helped her shrug off the dimity gown, and her underskirts, and made a nest of them beneath her. He eased off her drawers, and then he knelt beside her. "Are you sore?" he whispered, his mouth at her ear.

"Aye. Very."

"Where?" He touched the tip of his tongue to her left nipple. "Here?" She nodded, melting beneath him. "Here?" He ticked her other breast. She stretched and sighed. His fingers trailed down her belly to the soft crown of curls atop her mound of Venus, brushed them with exquisite gentleness. "Not here . . ."

Her knees had parted. "Aye. There, too."

He clucked his tongue. "What a pity. Surely not here." His finger reached inside the folds of her flesh, open to the sky, finding welcoming wetness.

"There most of all," Callie said, and pulled him onto her.

He entered her with infinite care, slow and tender. Callie shivered as he slid inside her, just a little way, and clutched the strength of his arms. "Oh," he said in wonder, pressing a little lower.

"Oh," she agreed, wrapping his buttocks with her knees, drawing him in. He arched above her, all his muscles tensed to hold back. She had her eyes wide open; she could see his eyes, endless blue, and beyond him the endless blue sky.

"You," he whispered, and drove into her with a suddenness that made her gasp. "You, Callie. You—"

"Oh, God." Her nails were raking him again; she tried not to hurt him, but he seemed beyond caring as he rose up and then pushed deep inside her once more. Through the fluff of skirts beneath her, she felt the hot stones blazing out their captive heat. "Mick. Mick . . . oh! Oh!" She was ablaze as well, glowing, candescent, and his rod within her was a pillar of fire. "Oh—dear—God!" she cried to his thrusts, her fist at her mouth. Then she went beyond caring; she was screaming his name as he pounded against her, as the whole sky swelled up around them and enveloped them in a pure white haze. "Mick!" she cried, and found she *was* crying, tears of awful joy that burned against her face.

His seed burst out of him like fire. His loins stopped moving, thrusting; he fell against her, his head at her breast. He was panting for breath; their heartbeats were coursing in union, slowing, slowing, as the sky shifted back into place.

He gently kissed her tears once more. They lay together on the stones, beyond words, beyond thought. He had his hand curled over hers at his neck; now he pried her fingers open and kissed them, one after the other, with great tenderness. "Cherries," he whispered. "I am glad . . . you brought them to me."

"Who else would I give them to, when I love you so?"

Her question hung in the clear, bright air. He fell back beside her, looking up at the sky, his hand still clasping hers. They lay that way for a long time, long enough for Callie to realize what she'd said, and grow afraid of it.

He must have realized it too, she thought, as at length he sat up and reached for his breeches. "Callie, I—" he said, then stopped, while she waited with her heart in her throat. "Callie. I—" he said again, and her heart was thumping. "Callie." He kissed her, full on the mouth. "I had best get this done."

He buckled on his belt, looming above her. "Mind you stay in the shade," he cautioned her, "or you will burn." She took her time, though, pulling on her drawers, fastening her pettiskirts, lacing her bodice. Last of all, she tugged on her stockings. He was whacking nails by then. She heard him curse as he hit his thumb.

Don't ask for too much at once, she told herself, smiling. He loves you, too; it shows in all he does, his gentleness and his fire. Be content; don't push him. But she hadn't meant to push him; she'd simply said what she felt. Her love for him

was as wide as this sky, as endless as the ocean. And when he
let himself admit it, his love for her would be, too.

Hammer poised, he glanced at her. "What are you smiling
about?"

She looked back at him, unafraid. "I like the view."

28.

It was a magical day. After another few hours on the roof, Mick pronounced his work finished. "So fast?" Callie asked, actually disappointed. She'd relished watching him wield his hammer, admiring from all angles his lean, hard body gleaming in the sun.

"I had inspiration," he told her, and came to kiss her. She held him back long enough to wipe the sweat from his temples with her kerchief. He made a face. "And I could use a swim. Do you swim?"

"Heavens, no."

"You'll have to learn. All the women of Langlannoch do. Grandmère still bathes three or four times a week in summer."

"In that cold ocean?" She shivered despite the glaring heat.

"It's refreshing. You'll see."

Callie peered over the eaves at the fallen ladder. "You forget. We've no way to get down."

"Oh yes we have." He led her over the rooftop to the base of the far tower, where a small door lay hidden in the shadows.

She laughed. "Ooh, you're a sneak, aren't you, telling me we were stranded?"

"I couldn't have you escaping, could I?" He climbed through

first—it was a tight fit—and then reached back to help her. It was dark and cool inside the minaret; they had to wait until their eyes adjusted to the lack of light. Mick took advantage of the pause to back her up to the stone wall and besiege her breasts. She could feel his manhood, swollen again with desire, thrusting against her. Through the narrow balistraria, scarcely wider than an arrow's breadth, she glimpsed the ocean's blue glimmer. "I want you," he murmured, then cursed as he bashed his forehead on the low ceiling. "But I want that swim, too. Come on."

He pulled her by the hand down the steep winding staircase, through another small door cloaked by a hanging on the outer wall, and down two more flights to the kitchens. Callie was breathless and laughing. Jennet looked up from the crocks she was filling with preserves. "Goin' somewheres, Yer Laird-ship?"

"Swimming," he told her, cramming a hamper with food and drink. "Where are those boys of yours?"

"Gordie's driven yer grandmother and the professor to the church. Ben bae somewhere about."

"Keep him off the beach," he ordered with true lordly insouciance. "I am going to teach Miss Wingate to swim; I don't want to be disturbed."

Jennet shrugged, ladling steaming berry pulp. "Wha' bae she goin' to swim *in*, then?"

"The ocean," he said. Callie giggled.

The housekeeper eyed him askant. "Nae, I meant—wha' clothes?"

"That's why I want Ben off the beach." Blue eyes dancing, he swiped a fingerful of jam from the table where it had spilled, licked a bit, then offered it to Callie. She sucked the warm sweetness, while Jennet watched them with her hands on her hips. "Incomparable, as always, Jennet. Keep up the good work." He grabbed Callie's hand and pulled her through the doorway. Jennet snorted, and mumbled something in Gaelic in their wake.

"What did she say?" Callie wanted to know when they'd reached the gardens.

"She was wishing she was one-and-twenty again." He

shifted the hamper so that he could hold her tight to his side, and they crossed the lawns that way.

Down on the strand, he stripped off his breeches and boots, flinging them across the sand. Callie laughed to see his manhood stark upright. He grinned and came for her, tugging off her shoes, rolling down her stockings. A flash of icy spray spattered toward them. "You don't really think I'm going in there," she said dubiously.

"The trick is to plunge in all at once; that way you don't feel the cold."

She scrambled back against the warm stones. "And neither does one feel it from here."

"Chicken," he taunted, reaching for her laces.

"You swim. I'll watch."

He'd bared her breasts. "Mm. I have a better idea." He sucked one nipple, then the other, until she clutched at him, her breath coming faster. When he slid her arms from her sleeves and unhooked her skirts, she made no protest, only stroked his stiff manhood. He let out a groan, pulling off her drawers and sliding his hand between her thighs, teasing at her there with his callused thumb. The sensation made her mad with longing.

"Take me . . ." she begged him.

"Oh, I will." He arched over her, hands cupping her buttocks. Then he straightened abruptly, lifting her from the rocks, and ran right into the sea.

"No!" Callie screamed, clinging to him as the first wave hit them, sending sheets of frigid water splashing toward the sky. "Mick, don't!" He plunged on, running with her until the water reached his waist. Then he lunged head-on into an enormous swell, ducking both of them under, and came out on the other side.

The cold shocked her speechless. She sputtered, dripping, freezing, furious. "You—you!"

"Close your mouth," he warned, and ducked her under again.

"Damn you!" she cried this time as they surfaced, and swung her fist at him. He laughed and caught her hand, letting go her waist. "Don't drop me!" she screamed, forgetting to fight and flailing for the comfort of his chest.

He gathered her in, holding her tight against him. "You could stand, you know. It's not very deep."

"I don't want to stand! I don't want to be here at all! What a wretched trick."

He shrugged, water streaming from his hair. "Sorry. But I knew I'd never get you in otherwise. Still cold?"

"Freezing!" But as she paused to catch her breath, she realized she wasn't. His skin was warm, and the water really not so bad. Watching her face, he leaned back so he floated with her stretched out atop him. They'd moved beyond the violence of the breakers; the surface dipped and swelled and spun them gently, agreeably. And she wasn't sinking. "Am I swimming?" she asked, startled.

"No. I am."

She curled her arms around his neck, her cheek against his chest. The sun steamed above them, making rainbows of the drops of water on her lashes. Beneath her, his legs were kicking slowly up and down, buoying them on the waves. The motion brought his manhood hard against her thighs; it had gone flaccid in the first rush of sea, but now she felt it swelling. She wrapped her legs around his loins; he foundered for a moment, then found his footing. "I can't swim that way," he said, laughing, and kissed her sea-slick shoulder.

"Forget swimming." She rubbed against him.

"No. You have got to learn. Here." He held her hands, pulling her along. "Keep your legs straight. Kick them." She made a tiny effort. "No, no. Kick with your whole leg, right from the waist. Here." He moved beside her, sliding one hand under her breasts and using the other to raise up her hips. "Kick."

His fingertips were at her mound of Venus. She twisted, parting her knees. "You aren't kicking," he said faintly.

"No? How's this?" She let her breast bob into his cupped palm, closed her thighs around his other hand, squeezing tight.

"Then again," he said, "I may not be the best one to teach you." Abruptly he swung her around to face him, saw her laughing, and scowled. "I ought to duck you again."

She put her hands on his shoulders, sliding up and down against him, and he gave up, guiding his manhood into her sheath with a quickness that made her gasp.

They made love there in the waves, in the strong smell of salt, in the brilliant sunshine, the water lapping around them like a million tongues. Then he carried her to the shore. "Not bad, for a first lesson," he said, "though you were a bit forward with the instructor." She watched as he swam far out into the sea, black hair and bronze skin agleam. When he returned, they devoured the contents of the hamper and then made love again, naked in the gritty sand. That necessitated bathing to wash off, and another brief lesson intermingled with kisses. After that, they lay and dozed together, with the sun crusting the salt on their skin.

By late afternoon, they *had* to head back to the house; there was nothing left to eat, and Mick said he was starving. "After all that huge picnic dinner?" Callie demanded.

"You raise an appetite in me." He nibbled at her breast, holding her in his lap.

"Watch out; I'm sunburnt there."

"How about here?" He ducked his head lower, to her thighs.

"There, too. I am sunburnt just about everywhere, I fear."

"Not here." His tongue delved deep, to the small, hard bud of passion he caressed so adeptly, firing her senses.

"No, not there. Oh, Mick . . . oh. Oh!" He brought her to climax with stunning swiftness, his beard tickling her thighs while his tongue flicked back and forth against her. She came in shuddering waves, fists clenched, sprawled in the sand.

When she could move again, she reached to stroke his man-hood. "Let me reciprocate."

He pushed her hand away, laughing. "Later! Do you want me to starve? And I've got to get you out of this sun."

"Later when?"

"Tonight, in your bed."

"So long from now as *that?*"

"You went twenty years without it; don't you think you can wait for a few hours now? Don't be so greedy, or I'll play whist with Grandmère after supper."

"You wouldn't."

"I wouldn't," he admitted, and kissed her. "Not for the world." Satisfied, she let him wash her once more, dress her, and lead her up the stone stairs.

"How gae the lessons?" Jennet greeted them in the kitchens.

"The lessons gae well," he told her gravely, then sat at the table and polished off all that was left of the ham.

He was ready for supper, though, when his grandmother and the professor and Zeus came home. By that time Callie had bathed again and dressed, and was sitting demurely with a volume of poetry in the dining hall. "Brought your sketchbooks!" Zeus declared in triumph, dropping them into her lap. He bent to kiss her. "God, you've a sunburn! What have you been up to?"

"Nothing much." But Mick came in just then, and the way she looked at him, his answering smile, were dead giveaways. Her brother turned from one of them to the other slowly, shook his head, and grinned, about to speak. "Zeus," she forestalled him.

"Aye?"

"Remember when you were ten and you broke the arm off Father's favorite Athena, and you said if I didn't tell him who did it you would do anything I asked for the rest of your life?"

"Aye . . ."

"Well, I'm collecting. Keep your bloody mouth shut."

"I was merely going to observe that a sunburn suits you. Though I do hope it isn't too . . . extensive." She swatted him with a sketchbook, and heard Mick laugh.

"Did we miss a jest?" Her father, with Lady Maggie on his arm, entered, blinking.

"I was just remarking Callie's color," Zeus said blandly. "Isn't it splendid?"

Lady Maggie came closer. "Mind ye dinna freckle, lass, in our strong sun. I hae an ointment I make up will soothe that red."

"Best make up lots," Zeus murmured. Callie surreptitiously kicked him as they headed for the table.

It was the best meal they'd had yet—or perhaps all that lovemaking put an edge to Callie's appetite. It surely had to Mick's.

"I ne'er knew ye to bae such a glutton, Michel," she chided fondly as he finished off his third plate of stew and dumplings.

"You know how I appreciate Jennet's stew."

"Ye wuld hae had fish wi' it," the housekeeper noted, "but ye banned poor Ben fro' the beach."

"Banned him fro' the beach? Why?" asked Lady Maggie.

Mick and Callie exchanged glances. "I was teaching Miss Wingate to swim," he answered after a pause.

"War ye, then?" His grandmother nodded thoughtfully. "Did I tell ye yet, Zeus, that it bae a rule o' this house each new bride maun need learn to swim?"

"I don't believe you had."

"Oh, aye, it bae. A tradition passed on fro' the first laird. Ye recall, his Madeleine pulled him fro' the sea. If she culd nae hae swum, the house's fortunes wuld hae ended afore they'd begun. Did Michel tell ye that, Callie?"

"He told me the tradition, but not the basis for it."

She frowned at her grandson. "Half a story bae nae story."

"And story's all it be," he answered, though without the undercurrent of anger that had marked such exchanges with her in the past. "No one knows if those quaint old tales are true."

"O' course they bae true!" she said indignantly. "Wuld ye call yer own forebears liars?"

"Let's say, rather, they had the French penchant for exaggeration.

Lady Maggie was glowering. "'N the gude brothers on Iona, then, wha' set it all down in their chronicles—war they Frenchmen, too?"

Mick smiled indulgence. "My illustrious forebears were no doubt making sizeable contributions to the monastery all the time the monks were busy penning their paeans."

"Bae ye implyin'—" Lady Maggie broke off, too offended to complete the thought. "Ach, Michel, bite yer wicked tongue!"

Professor Wingate had been steadily consuming stew, seeming above the fray. But he set down his spoon now, cleared his throat, and said, "I've spent the past few days thinking."

"Of course you have, Father; that's all you ever do," Zeus

jibed, but Callie shot him a withering glance. Now she thought of it, her father had seemed distracted, ever since the morning when all those villagers had showed up for judgement.

"Our hostess has proven such a remarkable font of knowledge on local traditions and customs—" He smiled at Lady Maggie, who beamed back. "And the house ledgers, reaching back hundreds and hundreds of years—I must say, I simply don't know of a comparable record anywhere in Britain. A true treasure. One of a kind. Combined with the visual evidence, the tapestries and paintings, not to mention the architecture itself—well, it's clear to me this is an opportunity that must not slip away."

"An opportunity for *what?*" Mick said, after a moment.

"Oh! I beg your pardon. Cart before the horse again, eh what? I'd like to write a history of the family, Harding. Your family."

"What in God's name for?"

The professor was taken aback. "Why, man, I just explained. The extraordinary completeness of the historical record—"

"Historical? The meanderings of those mercenary monks? Crop tallies? Or do you mean Grandmère's romantic fantasies?"

Callie's father stared at him. "Now, Harding, you know perfectly well that such records, taken together, are more than adequate to prepare a treatise; it is just what that Father Descoux whom you admire so at the University of Paris is doing!"

"But who do you think would give a damn about the thing?"

"I would," Zeus piped up promptly.

Mick's fine upper lip curled. "Besides, of course, immature half-baked Jacobite fanatics."

"Oh, Mick, that isn't really very . . ." Callie's voice trailed off at his furious glare.

Professor Wingate had pushed back his spectacles. "I must say, Harding, I fail to comprehend your objections. If this were any other family's past—"

"But it's not, is it? It's mine!" Mick was jabbing at where his own glasses would have sat, had he not lost them. "And I refuse to subject myself, not to mention Grandmère, to the academic ridicule that would be sure to meet any such publica-

tion! All those family myths are just that—myths! Fabrica-
tions!''

"Ach, Michel." Lady Maggie was wounded. "Ye ken that
bae nae true!''

"Wha' bae nae true," he shot back, caught himself, and
then started again in his best Oxford clip. "What isn't true is
that the Faurers and Hardings have been the unheralded saviors
of Scotland! And anyone who thinks they have, or ever will
be again, ought to be locked up in Bedlam with the rest of the
lunatics!'' He paused for breath, while they all stared at him.

From the doorway to the Great Hall came the sound of
someone clearing his throat. "I do beg your pardon," said a
voice, very English. "I did knock, but there was no answer.
Have I come at an inconvenient time?''

Mick rose to his feet, with a gesture, Callie thought, that
was almost like a warrior's reach for his sword-hilt. "Who the
devil are you?'' he growled at the stranger who had entered
his household.

"Commandant Henley, sir. Chief of His Majesty's garrison
at Kilmallie.''

In the silence, Callie heard Zeus take a deep breath. Mick
started to look down at him, then didn't, turning back to the
soldier. "And what brings you here?''

Henley took a few steps forward, into the light cast by the
table-candles. He was an ugly soul, Callie thought, tall and
lank, with badly pocked skin. "It's more or less a standard
social call, Mr. Harding. To offer my condolences on the death
of your father, and to meet the new . . . owner of Langlannoch.''
He seemed to take care not to say "lord." "We'd heard you
were in residence.''

"Only for the summer," Mick said slowly. "I'll be returning
in September to Edinburgh, to the University. I have an assistant
master's post there.''

"Yes. We'd heard that, too.''

There was something vaguely ominous in the man's de-
meanor, in his crisp English speech. *As though he were our
enemy*, Callie thought, and then wondered: *Now, what on earth
do I mean by that? I'm English, too.*

He made a little bow to Lady Maggie. "Madame. So sorry

to hear about your son." She inclined her head in acknowledgment, but Callie thought she looked nervous, shaken. He turned back to Mick. "You had quite a number of visitors out here a few days past, did you not?"

At least the disdain in Mick's voice was absolutely authentic. "Some idiotic nonsense about settling disputes. Our cook gave them soup and ale and sent them home again."

"Glad to hear you characterize it that way. I'm sure you're aware that the sheriff in Ayr has jurisdiction over all legal matters in the shire. You may not know, though, of a new regulation prohibiting gatherings of more than ten men in the west of Scotland at any time—saving, of course, at church."

"What bloody sort of—" Zeus started to demand. Callie stepped on his boot-toes, hard. The commandant's high-hatted head swiveled toward him.

"It's to prevent any foolish congresses to plot rebellion. You would be young Master Wingate, I take it?" Zeus nodded, surprised. The commandant's thin lips smiled. "We've heard about you, too." Callie couldn't help it; she shivered. Why would he have heard about Zeus? What on earth would he hear?

"I was not aware of that regulation. Thank you for bringing it to my attention." Mick was cool and composed.

"Only doing my job, sir. I was sure that as a loyal subject of King George, you would want to know. An Oxford man, aren't you?"

"Was," Mick said briefly. "I didn't finish my degree."

The commandant's pale, flinty gaze alighted on Callie. "Yes. We know." And what, she wondered, trembling, might he know about her?

The soldier snapped his heels together; the sound made them all jump. "Well. Sorry to disturb your dinner. I trust, Mr. Harding, you'll contact me should you witness any further breaches of the new regulation. It's important to the commonwealth, you know, to stamp out these archaic tribal traditions."

"I couldn't agree more."

"So I have your word on that?"

"Absolutely." Mick didn't hesitate, though his grandmother had gone sheet-pale.

"Very good, sir. Enjoy your stay in Ayrshire. I trust it will be uneventful." Once again, there was veiled menace in the words.

"Jennet," said Mick. She was peeking, wide-eyed, from the kitchens. "Show Commandant Henley to the door, if you please."

"Aye, Yer . . . aye, sir," she whispered, and sidled forward like a crab. "This way, sir." Their footsteps echoed on the flagstones; then Jennet's rushed back.

Mick had gone to the window. "He's got half a company of soldiers out there."

"Zeus," Callie hissed, "what have you been up to?"

"Nothing! I went to town! I bought your bloody sketchbooks."

Mick whirled on him. "And stopped in at the White Stag, did you? Hoist a few pints? Raise a few toasts to the king o'er the sea coming home? Christ, you stupid damned fool." He swept a candlestick right off the sideboard in his disgust.

"Well, how was I to know anyone knew who I was?" But Zeus was rattled, badly; Callie could tell. She squeezed his hand.

"Mick, for all they know he's just another silly schoolboy windbag," she said soothingly.

"That may have passed at Oxford, dammit, but it won't pass here! You're in the land now of Preston, of 'Bloody Clavers' and the slaughter at Glencoe. I can't have you in this house, Zeus, if doing so puts Grandmère in danger. I won't have it, I tell you."

"I can," Lady Maggie began, but he cut her off.

"Well, Zeus?"

"I was . . . indiscreet. I'm sorry." He swallowed, looking utterly miserable. "It won't happen again."

"It had bloody damned well not," Mick said with such reined-in fury that even Callie shook. Her father cleared his throat, and she glanced at him, aghast; surely he wasn't going to bring up that damned book again!

"Perhaps, under the circumstances, Harding, it would be best if we leave."

Callie's gaze flew to Mick, stricken. To her relief, he smiled, shaking his head. ''No need for that, sir. I'm sure the military is just jumpy. So long as Zeus keeps his word, and keeps his mouth shut, we'll be fine.'' Jennet tiptoed in to clear away. Mick reached for the claret and poured himself a cup, a tall one. The hoofbeats on the road to Kilmallie slowly faded and died.

28.

He was broody when he came to her that night. He stripped
off his jacket and hurled it against the wardrobe with a force
that rattled the shelves. She was a little afraid of him.

"Your brother's a damn fool."

"That he is," she said quietly, expiating.

He hurled himself now, onto the bed. She stood in the corner,
fussing at the fresh bunch of roses Jennet had put in a vase.
They still had the scent on them of the golden afternoon.

"Henley had the look of a man who enjoys making trouble."
Callie, agreeing, said nothing. He kicked off a boot. "We ought
never to have come here." She whirled on him, wounded.
"Well, what of it?" he barked. "It's God's truth. No good
will come of this."

"And nothing good has?" she asked, almost in tears.

"Oh, Christ, Cal. I didn't mean . . ."

She went and got the jacket, and threw it back at him. "If
that is how you feel, you can hie yourself to your own bedchamber." She threw the boot, too. He caught it in mid-flight, his
hands quick as a swordsman's. His grimness was awful to see.

"Stop acting like a child, why don't you?"

"I? You're the one came bursting in tossing things about!"

"Because your brother's idiocy nearly got us all clapped in prison!"

"I've apologized for that, several times! What more can I say? Would you have me cut a birch switch and give him a caning?"

"It would not do him harm."

Callie, the bubble of the lovely day burst, was bitter herself. "Henley went home. Zeus has promised discretion. And Lord knows, you'll not be giving the commandant any more cause for vexation. So what exactly are you so angry about?"

He looked beyond her, to the window giving onto the sea. "I can feel it. . . ."

"Feel what?"

"The vise tightening around me." She stared at him, taken aback. His blue eyes were a million miles distant. In the pound of the waves on the shore, she heard the faint bright rattle of a military tatoo. His head came up; his nostrils flared. Then his voice drowned out the illusion. "But I won't do it! They won't draw me in!"

"They? *Who?*"

"Your brother. Grandmère. Colin and Davey and Jessie and Walt, and all the rest of them—" He took a long, slow breath.

"I don't know what you're talking about," she whispered.

"Ach, you're part of it too, aren't you, with your Scots red hair?" His fierce expression softened as he looked at her. He patted the bed beside him. "There, lass. Come here."

She came toward him, cautious. "What is it you're afraid of?"

He reached for her, slipping her gown from her shoulder. "Blood . . . like a tide. The fire in the stone." His hand was fiery on her flesh.

Still she felt jumpy, wary. "If it is Zeus you mean, I daresay this Jacobite business will run its course one of these days. At least we have got him away from his wild university friends."

"Aye, and brought him *here,* to be steeped like a tea-leaf in the hot water of the old ways, with Grandmère dunking and dunking him in her brew—"

"Oh, Michel."

He winced. "Don't *call* me that."

"Mick. You make her sound like a witch."

"So she is! Like the one in that Hansel and Gretel story, feeding him full and then pinching his flesh: 'Is he fat enough to be a rebel yet?'" Callie started to protest again, but he forestalled her. "Oh, I know! Believe me! She did the same things with me. Thank God she only got me summers, or I might have become another of these poor simpletons crouched in the taverns, muttering about the king from o'er the sea."

At least he was smiling. She lay beside him, tucked herself into the crook of his arm. "You know your trouble. You're not used to claret."

"'In wine is truth.' I can handle the wine. It's this damned closing-in, everything coming to a vortex, that puts me on edge."

He was exaggerating. "I hardly think one brief visit from Henley constitutes a whirlpool."

"There's more to it than that." He yawned, enormously.

"Aye—all that exertion, and the lack of sleep."

"All what exertion?" Grinning, turning to her.

"The roof, and swimming—"

"And this?" He pushed his manhood up against her.

"What exertion is there in that for you? I do all the work."

"Shame on you for a liar, Calliope Chloe Wingate, lying there on your back. And who is it dresses and undresses you time and again all day long?" His hands again at her buttons, smoothing back the linen, baring her skin. He put his mouth on her nipple.

"We could just go about naked." She giggled into a sigh. "You practically do anyway, you savage, in your leathern breeches riding low."

He raised his head to kiss her, propped on his elbow. She traced with her finger the plane of his cheekbone beneath the bristling beard, the seductive line of his upper lip, the fine arch of his brow. "Do you want to paint me or make love to me?" he growled.

"Both," she answered, aching at his beauty.

"Well, then, which first?"

"Let me think on that."

Instead he tore off her dress.

So much practice had lent a sweet familiarity to what they did; she knew now the feel of his stiff manhood each time he entered her, and yet the sensation always was new. His anger had passed; he was teasing and gentle up until the drive to climax seized them. Then he pounded against her like hooves on a road, like the sea on the shore, and Callie, eyes closed, knees spread, insides burning, clung to him and screamed for fulfillment. At the instant it came, against the glow of her eyelids she saw them etched again: Michel Faurer and Madeleine atop the black horse, galloping through the waves. . . .

"Callie?" came his voice, through a haze of drowsy contentment. "What do you feel, when you cry out that way?"

Impossible to describe."What do you?" she countered.

"I . . . ecstasy."

"As good a word as any." She drew up the bedclothes, snuggling into his chest.

"Do you ever—" He stopped. She waited, patient, knowing how foreign these intimacies still were to him.

When, after several minutes, he said nothing more, she shrugged and rolled over, the curve of her back and buttocks fitting snug to his side.

"Do you ever—" he began again.

Yawning, weary: "Do I ever what?"

He laughed, kissed her hair. "Nothing. I'm sorry. Go to sleep."

She did, but with the sense he was wakeful despite his exhaustion. The last thing she heard as she drifted to sleep was one word from him:"Nonsense," in a bluff, curt tone, as though cutting off some argument he'd made with himself.

Again she woke at dawn, to lie still and watch the first light creeping over the windowsill, pricking out long drapes of dust, slanting over his feet and then up his legs like a soft yellow tide. He lay flat on his back, arms thrown above his head onto the pillows, his proud genitalia exposed and vulnerable. Callie fought back an urge to touch them, stroke his somnolent manhood: *Let him sleep, let him sleep.* He had to be overtired; what else could explain his harshness to Zeus, to her, after Henley had gone? Granted, her brother had been stupid, but he was too smart to be stupid twice; Mick needn't fear for that.

Her thoughts veered in the hush to her father. She really must think of what to say to him about all this. After all, Zeus knew; Jennet knew. If Lady Maggie didn't yet, she would guess soon enough; it was impossible to hide what she felt for Mick when he came into a room. Yet her father was not attuned to such things. And since he would not guess, she supposed she should tell him, somehow.

It would be so much easier if she could announce a betrothal. He adored Mick; he would be glad of the news. But this odd limbo, this fornication . . . he would be hard put to understand that, unless by some miracle his courtship of Laurie MacCrimmon had been similarly torrid. That was difficult to imagine, knowing her father. Still, once she'd thought Mick distant, too.

In ways he was still distant. His behavior was like his sleeping posture: manhood exposed, aye, but what went on in his head? Of that she knew tantalizingly little. Give it time, she reminded herself; it is all still so new. But she thought of the unfinished question he'd posed to her twice: *Do you ever* . . . Do I ever what? What was he asking me?

She thought, too, of his seed spurting into her, of how her womb embraced it. She knew enough biology to recognize the danger of that. It was what had, God be thanked, kept her from coupling with Harry—well, that and her odd revulsion to his touch, to his kisses. Destiny again; that wasn't meant to be. But with Mick—she tried to count how many times they'd lain together over these past two days, and ran out of fingers. If he got her with child—

Well, he would simply *have* to marry her then. And if he squirmed—God, her father would be apoplectic. She remembered the bitter battle he'd waged over a stipend for the maid his student had impregnated back at Oxford. That would look like nothing beside the war he'd fight for his own daughter's rights.

Of course, Mick hadn't any money. Perhaps that was what held him back from speaking of marriage; perhaps he felt he wasn't worthy to wed her.

Or perhaps he didn't want to. Money or no, his sense of self seemed healthy enough.

I am thinking too much, she thought restlessly, pounding down a pillow. Mick's knee, welcome weight when arching over her, was crowding her from the bed. She flopped over and saw the pile of sketchbooks Zeus had brought her stacked on the wardrobe. Mick slept with the same strange stillness he had in waking; he would prove a fine study.

Grimkin the two-hundredth-and-something was curled up on the windowseat. She nudged him off, and he hissed at her and stalked away. She sat and peeled back the cover of the sketchbook, stroked the rich, lovely, empty page with the side of her hand. Hard to believe they'd had such paper in Ayr; it was the same costly Holland rag she'd bought in Oxford. He must have paid a fortune! And the pencils were her favorite hard Cumberlands, with the blue shaft. That a stationer should carry them in that tiny village—that there should be a stationer at all! Amazing. She turned the shaft in her hand, seeking just the right grip as she eyed Mick's sleeping face. A familiar bit of engravery met her finger. She stared down at the pencil in astonishment, and saw it bore the woodburnt letter "B," from the Oxford Barrister's Shop.

He hadn't bought them here. He'd brought them to Scotland, all the way from Oxford, and carried them along everyplace since. Oh, Zeus! She felt tears in her eyes. He'd known she would not, could not give up drawing forever. And he'd had these tools with him, for her, when she realized it too.

Oh, brother of mine. Her heart swelled up with love for him at the gesture. How desperately well he knew her! He likely had sizing and canvas and tubes of oil in his trunk as well. And here, just that evening, she'd been so cross with him. What if he had made an error in judgement, blabbing in the tavern? All her life, it seemed, he'd been keeping her from making graver mistakes. She remembered, with a flush of shame, how ardently he'd argued against her betrothal to Harry. He'd been right then, too.

Who could tell how the little seeds of doubt he'd planted in her mind about Harry had taken hold there? The misgivings he'd expressed, that she'd put down at the time to jealousy or fear of losing her, might very well have been what caused her to cringe whenever Harry kissed her. It was better than fate, to have a brother like that. She would be lost without him.

She must help Mick to see that. He liked Zeus, of course, but with no siblings himself it would be hard for him to comprehend the tightness of their bond, of two motherless children and the long, dark nights when Zeus had come crying, trembling, into her bed. She must tell Mick about the pencils, and about what Zeus had said of Harry, and all the infinite minutia of their years together, the trips to foreign lands with only one another for company. She must make Mick realize that no matter what Zeus did, however foolish or feckless, she loved him with a fierce passion that could never be erased.

He might not care for that, she thought, gripping the pencil tightly. He might be envious of what she felt for her brother. Some men would be. And with the skeins of what he'd felt, did feel, for his own family so entangled, how would he understand the sort of love, pure love, nigh holy, that she and Zeus shared?

Damn, she thought, with a vague sense of foreboding. Grimkin, tail swishing, had come sashaying back to leap up in the windowseat. She pushed his paw from the page, looked again at Mick as he slept, and found she was gnawing on the still-virgin pencil. She *hated* drawing with chewed pencils.

She would just *have* to make him understand. What else could she do?

29.

A fortnight later, while measuring the west wall of Langlannoch, Professor Wingate stepped into a mole's burrow and fractured his leg. Callie, who was shearing roses in the garden just across the height of yellow sandstone, heard his faint, embarrassed cry: "I say! Is anyone there? Can anyone hear me? I believe I've done some harm to myself." It was the thirteenth of July, 1745.

"There, now, dinna I tell ye thirteen bae an unlucky number for the house o' Faurer?" Lady Maggie said darkly, when Callie and Zeus helped their limping father to the kitchens with his crumpled shin. She made him lie on a bench, and probed and twisted and frowned, while the professor, pale as Sunday bread, murmured in deprecation:

"Climbed all about the walls of Rome, I have. Stomped through Sicily and Cyprus, o'er much rougher ground than this. Went down into the catacombs without so much as a candle! And now I'm felled by a rodent."

"Actually, an insectivore, I think," Zeus murmured, watching worriedly as his father flinched at Lady Maggie's palpations.

"Whatever. I must say, I find it galling in the extreme."

"Stop talking, Father!" Callie ordered, frightened by his pallor. "Is it bad, Lady Maggie?"

"Bad eno'. But wi' a bit o' herbs 'n a splint, 'twill bae fixed. In time."

Mick had been clearing brush from around the stairs to the strand. When he came in and saw the professor laid out on the bench, the ugly twist in his shin, and his grandmother stirring some foul-smelling potion at the hearth, he insisted that a surgeon be brought. "But, Michel," Lady Maggie argued, "it bae a clean break, straight through. I ken well eno' how to splint it."

"He must have a doctor."

"I trust Lady Harding," Professor Wingate said weakly.

"Dinna *ye,* then?" Lady Maggie asked her grandson, glowering.

"Of course I do. But there's nothing wrong, is there, in having someone else's opinion?" So he rode to Kilmallie, and brought back the English army surgeon stationed there. By the time the man arrived, though, Professor Wingate was sleeping in his bed, the errant leg splinted with exquisite neatness, the pungent odor of the herbs Lady Maggie had brewed seeping through the room.

"What's that stench?" the doctor, aggravated at the lengthy ride, demanded, long nose probing the air.

"Which stench? There bae mustard-seed, heal's-all, herb Robert, tansy, sage, nettle, hyssop, 'n vervain in the poltice," Lady Maggie said crisply. " 'N in the sleepin' draught, valerian, lettuce juice, dwale, yarrow, 'n nightshade."

"Nightshade? Dwale?" The physician recoiled. "Good God, woman, they're poisons!"

"Only when ye dinna use them aright. I hae nae lost a patient yet."

"He is sleeping well," the English doctor acknowledged reluctantly. "Pulse good. Eyes normal. Still—"

"Why," Lady Maggie invited, "dinna ye hae a look at the splint?"

He examined it with great thoroughness. His eyebrows lifted. "Sound," he admitted, feeling gingerly along the bone. "Really, very . . . sound."

Lady Maggie made a noise like a snort. "Pay him, then, Michel, 'n take the gude doctor home."

Jennet, grinning, was watching from the doorway. "He hae best spend the night. There bae a storm rollin' in."

"Storm!" Zeus, silent till now, leaped for the window. "Where, Jennet? What storm?"

"Ye can see it there, on the horizon." Callie, a bit perplexed at her brother's concern, gazed toward the sea. It looked peaceable enough.

"I don't see anything," Zeus muttered.

But Callie, watching the waves and sky, now saw what the housekeeper meant: a shifting in the light, a faint but unmistakable yellow tinge to the low-lying clouds.

The doctor came and looked, too. "Seems clear to me."

Lady Maggie cleared her throat. "Jennet's folk hae a knack for predictin' the weather."

"Do they, now?" The Englishman stared at Zeus for a long moment. "Any reason, m'boy, why a storm would concern you?" Callie, steeped herself in a month of Scots drawls, found she hated his clipped speech. Zeus stared back at him, wordless.

Mick, of all people, broke the silence. "Master Wingate and I had plans to mend the pasture fence on the morrow. No doubt that's what concerns him. Isn't that so, Zeus?"

Callie watched her brother's Adam's apple rise and slowly fall. "Aye," he squeaked finally. "I should hate for the house to lose any more sheep."

Callie could hear her heart thumping. "No offense, Jennet, but you have been wrong about these things before," she quickly added. The housekeeper sputtered; it took Lady Maggie's elbow in her side to cut off her indignant reply. "I'm sure the ride to Kilmallie will be safe enough," Callie finished, praying. God, what was Zeus up to? And why must he be so transparent at it?

The doctor glanced at his patient and then back at Zeus. "Considering the dangerous herbs you've used, Missus Harding, I think it only prudent that I spend the night."

Dinner was excruciating. Callie could see Mick fuming, saw it in the furrow of his brow and the beat of his fingers on the tabletop that he could not restrain. Zeus was worse; his gaze kept straying to the high arched windows, to the gathering clouds that Jennet had predicted so accurately. Only Lady Maggie stitched the conversation together, speaking brightly, flattering the doctor with questions. The trouble was that her manner was decidedly different from the highhandedness she'd shown upstairs.

By the time the sweet came, Callie was shaking. Her imagination provided the worst possible explanations for her brother's edginess: a flock of armed Highlanders appearing on the road from Ayr; Prince Charles Edward himself knocking at the door. But the king from o'er the sea was *o'er* the sea, wasn't he? Far o'er the rising, angry sea whose distant thunder grew louder by the minute, matching the claps of thunder that beat about the house.

She and Mick even played whist after the meal, with Lady Maggie and the doctor. Zeus sat reading, or pretending to read; she noted how infrequently he turned the page, and wondered if the doctor did. Between hands, she ran upstairs to check on her father. He still slept peacefully, unaware of how his injury had brought the household to such awkwardness.

The storm gathered, grew. Lightning flashed. Rain pounded. The sea pitched and tilted, seeming about to sheer straight up the cliffs. Callie fought to keep her mind on the game, impossibly conscious of Zeus's every move. Each peal of thunder made him flinch.

Jennet, recognizing that somehow she had erred in her innocent weather-telling, plied the doctor with wine—the best port from the cellars, Portuguese sherry, French bordeaux. He had a taste for the stuff—thank God for small mercies—after months at his posting. His eyelids started to droop. At midnight, Zeus went to bed, and shortly after, the doctor declared himself finished, too.

Callie lingered, clearing glasses and ashtrays, while Mick took him to his room, hoping against hope that her lover might go straight to bed; he'd not been sparing of the claret himself. But it wasn't to be. He stomped back downstairs with an expression on his face that terrified her. "I have to go and see Father," she began.

He yanked her back by the arm, twisting it with cruel force. "What the devil's going on?" he hissed.

"I don't know what you mean!"

"Come, now, Callie! You've been preaching to me for the past two weeks about how wonderful your brother is, the strength of the love between you, all the secrets you share, stretching back twenty years. Don't tell me you've no notion why he is behaving like a scared rabbit!"

"I haven't," Callie said truthfully. "I haven't any idea!"

"By God, I've a mind to haul him out of bed and beat it out of him."

"Don't say such things!"

"Why shouldn't I? I've a bloody Englishman sleeping upstairs—"

"Who won't *be* sleeping, if you keep up this roar! Anyway, it was you, and only you, who insisted on bringing him here!"

"I was concerned for your father!" His blue eyes flashed in lightning. Wind lashed the panes; the sea was a thrashing whip. "If you are lying to me about this, so help me, I—"

"You'll what?" she demanded, edged to anger by her fear. "You'll stop sleeping with me? Cease sinning in my bed?"

"Sinning . . ." His eyes had gone dark as the skies; she felt a sudden wrenching in her heart. "That's how you think of it?"

"What am I to think? You never speak of . . ." She bit her tongue, enraged at him, herself. "Of love." She held her chin up proudly, now that she'd spoken the dreadful word.

He sank into a chair at the whist table, began to pick up the cards, his long hands, straight fingers, scrabbling over the cloth as they were wont to scramble over her breasts. "What would you have me say?"

She found she was crying, tears more bitter than gall, than his grandmother's potions. "God, forgive me. I'm sorry. I know Zeus has irked you—"

"He has done more than irk me!" The stiff cards splattered in his strong hands. "He has endangered Grandmère. He has endangered *you*—"

If she thought, if she could believe, that was the crux of his fierceness, there was hope for them yet. "Michel, I—"

"Don't *call* me that!" An anguished moan, like the wind. He laid his head on the green tablecloth, face sunk in his fists.

"Mick." She summoned up the memory of his tenderness, held it to her heart with both hands. "Mick, we know what we know. But that doctor knows nothing—"

"He bloody well suspects."

"And what if he does? I'll speak to him tomorrow, tell him Zeus was always chary of storms. It will sound in earnest. I've told you the same."

"I cannot abide . . ." He raised his head a little, so he looked right at her. "Not knowing what is happening."

Zeus's voice came softly, from the doorway. "Then I will tell you. But you must know, Mick, Cal knows nothing of this. The thought of coming between you . . ." He caught his breath. "I must be gone from here."

"No, Zeus!" Callie cried. He went on, inexorable:

"This morn, the king from o'er the sea was to sail for home."

Mick's big hands fumbled at the spilled cards. "To land—where? In my cove, that you've measured with such care?"

"No. The Outer Hebrides."

Callie's own hands shook. Mick lowered his head. "Well. Praise God for that."

"I'll have to go to meet him." Zeus's eyes were on Callie. "I shall have to leave soon."

"No, no, no!" A long-ago dinner discussion back at Oxford, with the great Dr. Tensby, flooded her mind: The Jacobites undisciplined madmen, the force of English might ready to greet an attempt . . . Her voice was nearly lost in a wild buffet of wind. Zeus looked to the high windows, rattling in their panes.

"I am sorry, Mick, for the trouble I've caused you. And, knowing you, I can't say I expect for you to understand. But this war, this cause, lies on my heart like a stone. I haven't any choice but to follow it, see it through to the end."

"They will eat you alive," Mick said evenly, tightly, in a way that made Callie's skin creep.

"That may be. But if there are enough of us, they may choke on our bones." In the cold yellow glare of lightning, Callie saw the fierceness of his eyes, the proud set of his chin, and grew still more afraid.

"If you won't think of yourself, think of your sister and father," Mick began.

"I will be thinking of them with every shot I fire, every stroke of my sword."

Mick had his hands under control once more; he squared the card deck neatly and slid it into the box, tying the ribbons with delicate neatness. Callie watched each movement. She had half a notebook filled with sketches of those hands, had rendered them again and again as though by doing so she could comprehend why his touch ignited her senses the way it did. His gaze met hers, and he shrugged a little: *See, I have done what I could. . . .*

"Then there's nothing more for it but to wish you well—and wish you gone."

"Oh, no!" Callie cried. He must not give up the argument so easily. Zeus admired him; worshipped him, nearly. If anyone could talk him out of this madness, it was Mick.

But Mick was disinclined to argue. He stood up, tall and sleek and bronze. "And the sooner the better. I am going to bed. Are you coming, Cal?"

She looked from one to the other, torn between them: her brother, her lover.

Zeus gave her a little shove. "Of course she's coming. Good night, Cal. And don't look so distressed! I won't be leaving tonight."

In her bedchamber, Mick showed the effects of the claret. He made love to her loudly, groggily, then fell straight off to sleep, leaving her to lie and listen to the screaming wind and the moaning sea.

By morning, the storm had spent its fury; under butter-thick sun, the only signs of its passing were the grass, battered down like frozen waves of green in the meadows, and a fine snow of bruised rose petals on the garden paths. Mick snored on without ceasing as Callie rose from the bed and hurried to dress. She went straight to her father's room and found Lady Maggie on a stool at his bedside. "How is he?"

"Fine, child, fine. He woke an hour or so past. Fed him broth 'n bread, I did. He said his shin war hurtin', so I gave him a bit more o' my potion. The English 'un has been by, too." Her voice oozed scorn. "I'll bae glad to have him gone fro' under my roof."

"You sat the night with Father." Callie was shamed, appalled. "It ought to have been me! I am sorry!" But she hadn't even thought of it.

"There, lass, ye had other bread to bake, dinna ye, now?" Her voice a sort of wink. So she knew. . . .

"Let me take over now," Callie hurried to say, "and you go get some rest."

"Ach, I dinna mind. Sent me back to the auld days, it did, to bae bidin' through the night wi' the wounded. If ye wuld do me a turn, ye might hie down to the kitchens 'n do wha' ye can to speed that doctor on his way."

Callie felt her father's forehead, eyed the splint, and kissed his brow. "If you're sure that's what you want.

"I bae."

So down the stairs she went, though no more eager to deal with the intruder in their midst than was the mistress of the house.

Jennet greeted her with a loud, "Mornin', mum!" and a waggle of her head toward the dining hall, her mouth grimaced. "Wha' can I fetch for ye, then? Berries? Biscuits? Porridge?"

"Just some bread and jam, Jennet, please. I've not much of an appetite this morning."

"I cannae say I blame ye," the cook muttered, with a baleful glance toward the door, "havin' to share table wi' *that.*"

That was sitting calmly, spearing forks of Jennet's hotcakes. "I'd have your cook conscripted if I could," he greeted Callie. "I haven't dined so well since my last tour of France."

"She isn't *my* cook," Callie corrected him, slipping onto the opposite bench. "My father and brother and I are only guests here. Just like you."

"Mm. Makes a nice change from Edinburgh, doesn't it? You

have a house by The Meadows, don't you? Rented from the university."

Now how, or why . . . "Fancy your knowing that. We do."

"We like to keep close tabs on troublemakers. Like your brother."

Callie poured tea, steadily. "Heaven help you, you must be awfully busy if you take notice of every gadfly like Zeus. Last year it was the plight of the American colonists he was all afire about. This year the Jacobites. Next year, who knows? More tea?"

"Please. This jam is most extraordinary." He heaped it onto his hotcakes. "But our information, Miss Wingate, says your brother's Jacobite leanings are quite long-reaching. In tight with a dangerous crowd at Oxford, he was. One or two of them are in prison now. He's fortunate he got away when he did."

In prison? Who? Callie's heart fluttered. Not sweet, shy James Cobham, she hoped, or Toby Lassiter. But she wouldn't give this bastard the satisfaction of asking. "I must say, I'm surprised you take such schoolboy nonsense so seriously. Nothing but talk and more talk, in my experience."

"Talk can be a dangerous thing. Any sort of noise can be, really. There was quite a noise down at Oxford about a painting you made, wasn't there, Miss Wingate?"

Bastard, bastard, bastard. She held her head up. "The Puritans will always be with us, I suppose. The painting wasn't meant for public display. An angry suitor's nasty trick. I do hope this nation's not reached the point where what a person does in the privacy of her own bedchamber can be turned against her. I always thought the English concept of liberty broader than that."

"Still, what one does in one's own bedchamber can be most interesting." His pinched nose quivered. "Does your father know you are Mr. Harding's paramour?"

Callie dropped her spoon with a clatter. "I beg your pardon! What business is that of *yours?*"

Jam dripped from the side of his mouth. He dabbed the crimson pulp away. "I thought not. I imagine after Oxford, he's quite chary of scandal. Makes one wonder what the dean at Edinburgh would make of the situation. Mr. Harding has been living with your family for, what, now? Two months? Three?''

From the corner of her eye, Callie saw Jennet listening just beyond the doorway to the kitchens. She had a cleaver in her hands, and a mouth puckered like she'd tasted unripe quince. ''Jennet,'' she called, ''where's my toast?'' Just let her put down that cleaver . . . She leaned toward the doctor, her voice a low whip. ''What are you driving at?''

His gray eyes were sharp and narrow, arrow-holes. ''It would be unfortunate, wouldn't it, to have it called to the dean's attention? What with your family's previous record of, shall we say, disrepute? Freethinking's all very fine in the lecture-hall, but my experience has been that universities frown on it when put into practice. I'd say the odds would be good your father would never find a post again.''

Callie wished *she* had the cleaver. ''You son of a bitch. If you do anything, anything whatsoever, to harm my father—''

''But it's well within your power to prevent that, isn't it, my dear?''

Jennet came with the toast, laid it down with a *thunk*. The doctor beamed at her. ''My good woman. Most extraordinary breakfast I've had in years. Do you think I might prevail on you for just a few more hotcakes?''

Jennet opened her pursed mouth. ''*Do* get some more hotcakes, please, Jennet,'' Callie said hurriedly. ''And a bit of bacon? And some fruit for the doctor. Some of the cherries.'' Scowling, the woman backed off. Callie leaned across the table again. ''What do you mean, 'within my power'?''

The doctor was stirring up the jam in anticipation. ''Simply this, Miss Wingate. If I were to have your assurance that Commandant Henley would be notified by you if—or should I say when—your brother departs from Langlannoch . . .'' Callie drew in her breath. ''Then you would have *our* assurance that what we know of your unorthodox dalliance with Mr. Harding would not reach the dean's ears.''

Callie's pulse was pounding; she felt it in her head, in her throat, all the way down to her toes. How did the English know about her and Mick? She thought with wild regret of the way they'd coupled in the open, on the roof, on the beach, in the fields. Had the English been spying on the house? Why not? They'd known about the judgement day. Or had this cold-hearted creature simply made a lucky guess?

It didn't really matter now. *Think, Callie, think!* She had to stay calm. "You're asking me to inform on my brother."

"I'd prefer to categorize it as acting in the Crown's best interests. You *are* a loyal subject of King George, Miss Wingate, are you not?"

"Of course I am. Mr. Harding is, too."

"Then I should think you would be eager to aid in the nation's defense."

"Oh, I am. Have no fear of that. But really, all this fuss about Zeus! Why, he's no more than a child. I simply don't see what impact one boy's wild rantings could possibly have on the nation's security."

"We spoke of the power of words. Your brother is a gifted writer. So was his friend James Cobham."

"Was?" Callie echoed, going pale.

"Well, he may be still. But he won't be penning any letters to the gazettes while he's in irons down at Newgate Gaol."

Poor carrot-headed Cobham. "What a waste," she said aloud, "of a fine young man. But if you feel Zeus is so dangerous, why don't you arrest him?"

"Commandant Henley believes your brother can be more useful while at large. Particularly if he leads us to the Young Pretender's landing-place in the event of invasion. Give us a chance, don't you know, to nip this thing in the bud."

Callie nodded thoughtfully. "Why don't you set a watch on the house?"

"We already have," the doctor said coolly. "From the moment we heard that what the locals quaintly call their 'laird' was returning. I won't say we didn't have our doubts about Mr. Harding, what with the family's history. Commandant Henley is not about to permit the spectre of some antique warrior to rise up from Langlannoch again. Fortunately for Mr. Harding, he seems to share the commandant's sentiments."

"Of course he does."

"Your brother, on the other hand. . . . Should he somehow

elude us, we would like the additional insurance of your cooperation.''

"Then you might have requested it in a more honorable fashion, don't you think?'' Damn, where was Jennet with those hotcakes? She needed time, space in which to think. "Jennet?'' she called.

The housekeeper appeared in the doorway. "I bae all out o' flour,'' she pronounced mutinously. Callie knew, and the doctor knew, too, it was a bald-faced lie.

He folded up his napkin. "Pity. But I fear I've been a glutton already. I'd best get back to Kilmallie. Miss Wingate. You may be right; perhaps we ought to have appealed to your patriotism first. May I do so now? *Will* you send Commandant Henley word if your brother leaves Langlannoch?''

So that they could trail him. So that they could, when the trail ended, kill him. *Nip this thing in the bud . . .*

The dean. The shame. Her father ruined, this time for good. Christ! She hated this Englishman with a force that was frightening.

She was taking too long. He was waiting. "Of course I will,'' she told him. "It's my duty, isn't it, to King George?'' What else could she say?

He stood, offering his hand, and she took it. "Glad to hear you say that, Miss Wingate. You're quite right. It is. I'll be back to check on your father again in a week or so. Perhaps I might stay to dinner?''

"I'm sure Lady Maggie will be honored.'' Lady Maggie wouldn't. But she'd understand.

"Are you leaving, Doctor?'' The lord of Langlannoch, beard still wet from washing, a ribbon on his queue—no leather breeches and bared chest with English in the house. Thank God, Callie thought, the bastard hadn't made his appeal to him!

"Mm, afraid I must. But I'll drop by, as I told Miss Wingate, in a few days, to look in on her father. And, Miss Wingate, you'll let me know of any new . . . developments?''

"You have my word on it. I'll see you to the door.''

They crossed the great hall, his bootheels ringing on the mosaic. "Remarkable house,'' he said, taking a last look around. "Mr. Harding is lucky it's so out of the way. So it's been spared from fighting. I hate to see the effect of modern weaponry on these old places." And that, of course, was another veiled threat. "Goodbye, Miss Wingate."

"Goodbye, Doctor. Do come again."

30.

A week later, they celebrated Zeus's eighteenth birthday, with queen pudding, crackers holding paper hats and tokens, and a bounty of gifts. The professor was doing much better by then, up and about on a pair of crutches; his present to his son was, of all things, a muffler he'd knitted. "Lady Harding has been showing me how," he explained with a pride that was touching. "While I've been confined to my bed. Remarkable process, knitting. Never gave it much thought before, though I watched your mother at it often enough. Oh, the things she would make you! Cunning little caps and cradle gowns and booties, all as neat as could be. You'd stop traffic down in the park, you would, when she took you out in them. All the mothers and nannies used to gather about—" He stopped; Zeus was staring at him over the edge of worked wool. "What? Is it that you think it a womanish hobby to have taken up?"

"No!" Zeus said quickly. "It's just that—I'm surprised."

"No utilitarian art is the realm of either sex, you know." The professor still sounded defensive. "Lady Harding tells me the men of Mick's family always did their own darning and such while they were on campaign."

"And I'm certain none did any finer work than this," his

son hastened to assure him. "Really, I'm quite overwhelmed. Thank you, Father." He wrapped it gaily over his shoulders. Only Callie knew that her brother's astonishment and gratitude were less for the scarf than for the glimpse of his life with Laurie—a glimpse unprecedented in her brother's or her memory.

"The MacCrimmons always had a knack at knittin', whether wool or a tune," Lady Maggie noted with complacence. "Yer father proved an apt pupil."

"I am going to assay a vest next, I think," declared Professor Wingate. "It's very soothing, I find. The click of the needles, the counting-out, the repetition. Just the sort of relaxation one needs after hard reading." Callie glanced at Lady Maggie, and saw her blue eyes twinkling. By God, she was a miracle-worker, if she could knit up their father's ancient guilt over his wife's death.

She looked back to Zeus, and saw him poised to pursue this matter of their mother's knitting. Best not to press Father, though. She hurried to hand him a package done up in paper and ribbons. "Here, love. This one's from me."

He felt its heft, traced its shape within the wrappings, trying to guess the contents, as he had since he was a child. "A box, a small one. Beyond that, impossible to tell." He closed his eyes and unwrapped it, opened the box, lifted out a chain and a disk of cold metal. "A watch!" he said triumphantly. "But I have got a watch."

"Not exactly a watch." She saw him open his eyes wide and turn the disk over.

"A compass." His green gaze, wide, flew toward her. "But what on earth would I need this for?"

"In case you ever get lost." It was a struggle to keep her voice offhand. "So you can find your way home. Though I'd much prefer you never have to use it."

"Oh, I doubt that I shall. Nonetheless, it's a handsome thing." He spun it on its chain, silver catching the candlelight. "So *that's* what you were doing in Ayr, that day when you wouldn't let me come along."

"Sent her to Jock's shop, I did," Lady Maggie told her grandson. "Ye ken they say he war once a pirate."

"Aye, I know. I went with her." He and Callie exchanged glances; Callie bore a trace of a blush. It had been a marvelous outing. They'd gone to market-day; he had bought her ribbons for her hair and sugared almonds, and he'd kissed her in the midst of the square, with half the town looking on. It had made a change from the arguments they'd had lately. He couldn't understand why she didn't want to make love to him anymore outdoors, in the open, and of course she didn't dare explain.

She shrugged off the sweet memory. "Mick's gift is from Jock's shop, too. There it is. The red one."

Zeus found it in the diminished pile. "A book," he posited from its weight and shape.

"What else would it be?" Mick grinned as Zeus tore off the wrapping and read from the cover:

A History of Shipwrecks Off Ayr.

"Jock wrote it himself," Mick said cheerily. "It's full of cautionary tales about the tides and rocks and shoals. Reading it would turn anyone from the notion of ever sailing off these shores."

"Would it really." Zeus's voice was dry. "I'm sure I'll find it most enlightening."

"I had hoped you would."

That left only one gift. "Fro' me," Lady Maggie said of the long, narrow package.

"Christ, but it's heavy! What is it, a meat-hook?"

"In a manner o' speakin'." Callie saw her lean forward a bit as the paper fell away. Inside was a wood and glass case, elaborately carved, and inside that a—

"Good God," her father interjected, leaning in as well. "That's damascene steel in the hilt. Early fourteenth century, or I'm an idiot."

"Close eno'," Lady Maggie assured him. "Late thirteenth, actually."

Zeus was peering at the sword-hilt in wonder. "Are those emeralds?"

"Sae they bae, sae they bae. Those twain there, they came fro' Madeleine Faurer's ear-drops, that she wore when the Scots kidnapped her fro' Durham. She had 'em put in as a weddin' gift, sae Michel would e'er hae a bit o' her wi' him, e'en

when he war fightin'. Not this Michel, o' course," she added
needlessly, waving a hand at her grandson. "The first Michel.
'N that ruby, the big one—that war a gift fro' the Bruce after
the Bannockburn. 'Twar bigger then, but Michel had it cleaved
in half, 'n used half to buy the land for Langlannoch."

Zeus was pushing the case away from him, across the table
toward Mick. "Lord! I can't take this!"

Lady Maggie seemed not to have heard him. "That sword
has been fro' Palestine to Cyprus to Jerusalem to France, 'n
back 'n forth across Scotland more times than any soul could
count. Michel had it wi' him in Spain, when he fell. 'Twar
Angus MacPherson saved their armor fro' the Moors, Michel's
'n that o' Gude Sir James Douglas. The heart o' the Bruce,
though, that they war takin' to the Holy Land—Sir William
Keith got that. It bae buried at Melrose, ye ken. Though there
bae some deny it. The Keiths bae a jealous lot."

Callie did not dare look at Mick. Professor Wingate tore his
gaze from the extraordinary weapon. "Lady Harding, this has
been in your family for four and a half centuries! You cannot
mean to simply gift it away!"

" 'N why nae? There bae none in my family will use it,"
the woman said fiercely.

Mick was laughing. Callie could scarcely believe it at first,
but he was laughing, not angry at all, but honestly amused.
"Oh, Grandmère!" He gasped for breath between guffaws.
"Do you think to goad me with my ancestor's weapon? Are
you so desperate as that?"

"The jewels alone," the professor began, and then stopped
himself. "But of course, you couldn't remove them."

"Nae, nae, not in desperate straits," their hostess agreed.
"See here." She reached to unclasp the casket, turned the
sword over. "This jasper-stone, that war a gift fro' the Bruce's
son, young David, to Michel's own son, in thanks for spiritin'
him to France after the fall o' Berwick. 'N this tourmaline, that
came fro' Robbie Stewart, when he took the throne. He 'n Rene
had been companions-in-arms, in their youth. This here—"
She tapped a yellow-green gem on one side of the quillon.
"Beryl. A gift fro' Rene's wife, one o' the Douglas girls. It
war the color o' her eyes."

It was the color of Callie's as well. She shivered in the warmth of the July night.

Zeus's face bore a singular expression, longing at war with confusion. "I am touched beyond words by your gesture, Lady Maggie. But I can't possibly accept—"

"Why not?" Mick broke in, still quite cheerful. "Why the devil not take it? God knows, just as Grandmère says, I've no use for the thing."

"But . . . but . . ."

"Out of the question," his father said crisply.

"It is awkward as hell, with all that antique stuff crowding the hilt," Mick noted. "I know. Grandmère used to make me try to swing it when I was a boy."

"We hung it in the armory, in the center just above the hearth." His grandmother's voice was dreamy. "Until Michel's father became laird, 'n wanted it melted down for a chalice, 'n the jewels sold for the church. I hid it then."

Callie felt oddly weary, dispirited, and closed her eyes—only to see the etched figures of the first Michel and his Madeleine, on the black horse, traced inside her eyelids. Quickly her eyes flew open again.

Mick had gotten to his feet. "If you want the thing, Zeus, take it. Beat the devil out of Scotland with it—if you can lift it. Raise a Stewart back to the throne." He yawned hugely. "As for me, I'm going to bed."

"I'm quite sure Zeus has no intentions of sword-fighting!" the professor said with horror.

Lady Maggie turned to him. "Bae ye, then? I should think a butcher's grandson wuld hae a fine feel for cleavin', wi' wha'e'er weapon he chose."

Zeus was shaking his head. "Such a priceless relic must stay at Langlannoch, Lady Maggie. It wouldn't be right to do elsewise."

Mick was halfway to the door. His grandmother's bitter words chased him: "To wha' point? To rust away, crumble to dust, wi' all the rest o' the place? Better it bae put to use, to the cause!"

"Now, now." Callie's father was soothing. "It won't come to fighting, Lady Harding, all this Jacobite blather. The Young

Pretender knows better enough than to force King George's hand.''

Outside, the wind whistled hollow up along the cliffs; the sea lay empty, waiting.

"Absolutely," Zeus said stoutly, adjusting his frilled paper hat. "Anyone for whist?"

31.

A week later, on a gray July morn draped with mist from the sea, Zeus disappeared. No one realized it at first. He was working on a project in his chamber, he'd told them, a surprise for everybody, and he spent more and more time there in those last days, behind closed doors. Callie would pass his room and hear the scratch of a pen, occasionally a disgusted exclamation and the crumpling of parchment, and wonder what on earth he might be up to now. He'd said no more about leaving Langlannoch; when the English doctor had made his threatened return visit, Zeus had been the gadfly Callie remembered from the old days, full of puns and witticisms, perfectly composed. The doctor had, in fact, remarked on his silliness to Callie, in a private moment with her: "If that's the face your brother's shown you all along, little wonder you never took him seriously," he told her, pulling on his gloves as she accompanied him to the door.

"Oh, it is!" she'd cried earnestly, feeling a glimmer of hope. "He's just a foolish boy, as I've said often enough. I think already his interests are shifting. You heard him at supper, teasing Lady Harding about the chair the Bruce is supposed to have sat in. Why, I'll wager in a month if you ask him about the Young Pretender, he'll say, 'The young who?' "

But the doctor only grunted, and looked at her, hard-eyed, in the glow of the door lamps. "That may be. Still, our agreement stands."

On the day Zeus disappeared, he did not come to dinner. "I saw him a few moments past," Lady Maggie announced, ladling smooth leek bisque from a porcelain tureen. "He had me send Jennet up wi' a tray. Said he war havin' a creative fit, 'n culd nae interrupt it. Looked as though he had nae changed his shirt in days."

Callie had giggled, the smooth bisque sliding over her tongue, Mick's boot caressing her calf below the table, and the prospect that afternoon, if the thick sea-mists held to cloud Henley's men's spyglasses, of making love to him out-of-doors, with the gray drizzle slicking their skins. . . . That was what they did, too, just as soon after the meal as they could. They met at the front doors, joined hands, and only made it as far as the stone bench in the garden, where they lay beneath a dripping canopy of spent roses and ripening apricots, shrouded by the fog. And when, once they had pleasured one another to the point of excess, the sun broke through high above them and turned the swirling mists to gold, they made love once more in the strange, eerie glow, their bodies still swathed in cloud although the sky was cloudless overhead.

Mick had been blithe, doing up the hooks of her gown. "Well, Miss Porcelain-skin, that was the best of both worlds. Mist to keep you from freckling, and the open air for me."

Callie felt unspeakably grateful to nature. "I must say, I don't quite understand this penchant of yours for outdoor *divertissement*. I can only put it down to a basic deficiency in the Gaelic temperament, your failure as a race to progress to rooves and featherbeds."

"Oh, come, Mistress MacCrimmon's daughter. Tell me it doesn't add an edge to your appetite to know that someone might be walking not ten feet away and never know what we are doing, hidden back here."

"Anyone who came within a hundred feet would have heard you."

"And not you?" he teased.

"Are you implying I was less than ladylike?"

"I'll state it flat-out, if you like." He kissed her, hard and swift. "And you know I loved it." Callie jerked away as she heard slow, shuffling footsteps on the stone path.

"Father!" She ran to him through the wild, tangled vines. "What are you doing out without your crutches?"

"Lady Harding gave me this to try." He waggled a cane at her. "Far more convenient, though I lose something in speed."

"But these stones are wet still from the fog! If you slip—"

"I won't, if you give me your arm." He was puffing a little from the exercise. "There's a bench back here somewhere, isn't there?"

She led him to it. Mick was already there, and dressed. "Afternoon, sir!" He helped the professor to sit, careful to keep the splint leg extended. "Good to see the sun poking through, isn't it, after such a dull day?"

"It most assuredly is. You know, I'm beginning to like the way your grandmother keeps this garden. Hardly the current fashion, of course, all this surfeit. Feels at times as though one could get lost in the shrubberies. Yet it suits the house."

"Yes, sir. I think so, too."

"Well!" Professor Wingate slapped his hands on his knees, breathing in the soft air. "What were you two up to?"

Callie shot an alarmed glance at Mick. "Just a bit of pruning," he explained, grinning back at her and flashing a knife to prove it. "After all, there's wild and there's wild. Mustn't let things get too out of bounds."

"No, no. I daresay not. Don't let me keep you from it. Get on with your work."

"Thank you, sir. Callie, would you hold that branch there? No, the one above it." For an hour he chopped and hacked, while Callie wondered whether he had any notion at all of what he was doing and the professor smiled benignly at the two of them.

It wasn't until Zeus missed supper as well that Callie felt a twinge of disquiet. Lady Maggie said again that she'd spoken with him a little while before, and that he'd asked for a tray. But Callie had been back and forth past his door half a dozen times that day, and it suddenly struck her that she hadn't heard the scratch of his pen—nor any other noise, either. She looked at Mick's grandmother, who was calmly spooning up barley-broth. The woman's pale blue gaze, utterly serene, met hers. She smiled. You suspicious thing, Callie chided herself, and returned the smile, then tried the soup. It was soothing and warm, like a mother's embrace.

After the meal, Professor Wingate challenged Mick to chess—always a losing proposition. Bright though Callie's father was, he had not the patience for the game. Mick, however, excelled at it, sitting perfectly still, as was his wont, contemplating the board, and only moving one arm at his turn, to edge a piece forward or sideways. Callie watched, and held a sketchbook and pen, but made only a few idle strokes. Tonight Mick won in twenty-six moves.

"Bah! I'll know better than to play you again," the professor said, just as he always did. "Callie, how about you? A quick game with your dear old Dad?"

But Callie was growing increasingly nervous. Zeus's rooms were just above the parlor where they played. If he didn't join them after meals, she was accustomed to hearing his footballs, the scrape of his chair—and this night she heard nothing. "In a moment, Father. I've just thought of something I must ask Zeus."

"I wuld nae gae up there, lass." Lady Maggie's voice, composed.

"Why not?" Callie demanded, hearing the edge in her own.

"Why, he bae quite busy wi' his surprise. He told me he expected it wuld bae finished tonight."

Callie thought of the mist that had wrapped the manor since riding in on the night wind at yesterday dusk. It had served to hide her and Mick in the gardens; it would have hid Zeus, too. "I'll just call to him through the door."

Lady Maggie waved her hand. "I wuld nae bae surprised if he gave ye nae answer."

Callie looked into those guileless blue eyes. *I'll wager you wouldn't,* she thought, all her disquiet rolling in on itself. She fled up the stairs and pounded on her brother's door.

Dead silence. She rattled the latch. Locked.

Soft footsteps were coming down the hallway—Lady Maggie. "I told ye he wuld gi' ye nae answer."

"Because he's not in there, is he? Where has he gone?" She tried the latch again, frantically. "Dammit, have you the key?"

More footsteps, heavy ones, and Mick behind them. "Grandmère? Callie? What is going on?"

"Ask *her.*" Callie pointed accusingly.

Instead he banged on the door. "Zeus! Are you in there?" When there was no response, he put his shoulder to the wood and shoved. The ancient hinges groaned.

"Michel, dinna break the house down!" Lady Maggie cried.

"Then give the bloody key here." She hesitated. He reared back, ready to throw himself against the door again, and she reached for the chain on her girdle:

"Here ye gae, then! Here!"

He unlocked the door, and it swung open. Callie moved through the gathering darkness toward her brother's desk. It was covered with sealed, folded letters—days' worth of correspondence. Beside her, Mick lit a candle. She stared down at the rows of names and addresses. Duncan Farquar. Zachary Fleming. Lord Delaney. James Cobham, in care of Newgate Gaol. So Zeus did know about his red-haired friend. . . . There were dozens more, names she half-remembered from Oxford, others Zeus had known in Edinburgh, and, in the center, one letter for her father and one for her.

She reached for it with trembling hands. From downstairs she could hear the professor calling, stranded by his bad leg: "Hullo? Hullo there, what's that thumping? Callie? Harding?"

"Not so much of a surprise after all," Mick muttered.

Callie cracked the seal on her letter, scanned it, and then crumpled it in her fingertips. "What does he say?" Mick asked.

"He wants me to post the letters, a couple every few days— send them with Ben or Gordie to Ayr. He's got them arranged by date. Says he suspects his mail is being intercepted. This way it will keep coming, so the English won't know he's gone."

"How very enterprising," Mick noted.

Callie whirled on Lady Maggie. "When did he go? When did he leave?"

"At dusk yestreen. Soon as the fog came in."

"That's little more than one day's start. Oh, Mick, you must go after him!"

"Must I?" He sounded bemused. "Why on earth would I? I've been urging him to leave!"

"You don't understand. The sentries won't have seen him go, not with the mist—"

"*What* sentries?"

"And if I don't tell Henley he's gone, the doctor said he'll ruin Father! He'll tell the dean at Edinburgh about you and me, how we've been living together, and Father will lose his post! The doctor said he'd never find work again!"

The professor's voice, plaintive, drifted up from the stairway: "Calliope Chloe? What is going on?"

Mick had grabbed Callie's shoulders. "What are you talking about?"

"The doctor—the Englishman. When he came, he told me they'd set spies on the house, to keep track of Zeus. That they were watching to see when he left, but that in case he escaped them, he needed me to promise I'd send word to Commandant Henley, so that they could track him to the Young Pretender. If I didn't, the doctor said, then he would tell the dean." She paused, needing breath.

Mick's voice was the bellow of an outraged bull. "*And you did not tell me?*"

"Because I knew you would be angry! Because for all I knew, you *would* send word to Henley! But I've spent all these weeks thinking, and now I know what to do. You must go after Zeus and bring him back. That way Henley's men won't kill him, and the dean won't find out about us. Zeus will be safe, and so will Father. Mick, don't you see?"

"I see that you've kept secrets from me. I see that you've lied to me—"

"Calliope? Callie?" Her father was ever more anxious.

"I'll gae to yer father then," Lady Maggie murmured, and hurried out, closing the door.

Callie reached for Mick's hand. "Oh, darling, I know it must seem confusing."

"On the contrary, it seems quite clear. Your idiot brother's gone to throw his life away on Charles Edward's pyre—"

"Lord, Mick, don't be so—"

"And you, the one soul I thought that I could trust in the world, have been finagling behind my back! Spying on my house! How *dare* you keep such news from me?"

"Because it doesn't matter! Zeus is what matters. You have got to help him. You have to go find him. I'll go on sending out the letters until you return. No one will know he's not here."

"And if Commandant Henley drops by? If the doctor calls? What will you say then?" He looked like a bull, nostrils flared, neck thick with fury. "Christ, you're as stupid as he!"

"Zeus *isn't* stupid! He's just young, and confused."

"Stop thinking of him as a baby—as your baby. He is eighteen years old. By his age, the men of my family were all heroes in battle, according to Grandmère."

"You said yourself—he'll be eaten alive!"

"And what if he is? He brought it on himself. I'm not about to risk the safety of Grandmère for his sake."

She felt the sting of tears, and blinked them away. "No. Not for his sake, Mick. For mine. For *me.*" *Because you love me.* But he didn't, did he? She could see it in his stubborn wrath, in his outrage at the knowledge she had kept from him. Oh, she'd known he would be angry, yes, but she had not expected this callousness.

He was slipping away from her on a tide of choler. She must be soft with him. She let the tears fall, unashamed. "Mick, don't you see? There's no one else to ask. Father would go, I know he would, but how can he, with his leg?" She appealed to his pride. "You can find him, love. I know you can. You used to beat him at chess. You know the way he thinks."

"Aye. And I despise it. All the advantages he has had—"

"What advantages?"

He ticked them off on his fingers, those long, blunt fingers that she loved so. "His education. All those years of travel. Exposure to the best the world has to offer—history, music, art. A family that stands by him—"

"Is *that* what's at the bottom of this?" she demanded. "Do you resent that I love him?" Was Mick jealous?

"Love him all you like! It is nothing to me."

Nothing touches him. Those first impressions she'd had of Mick Harding, Oxford student, flooded her mind. Had they been correct perceptions after all? Had she been blinded since by the way he made love to her, the fire he raised in her belly and breasts? An awful desperation clawed at her soul. "You won't go after him, will you?"

"I rather thought I'd made that plain." Standing there, so tall and handsome and smug—

"Damn you, you owe this to me!"

"Why?"

The simple question stopped her dead. "Why . . . because of what we've shared. Because of what I've let you do with me, to me!"

He clucked his tongue. "Tut, tut, Callie. You tried blackmail on me once before, as I recall, in a concert-hall at Oxford. Neither did it work then."

She clutched Zeus's letter to her breast. "By God, I'll go after him myself, then!"

"Don't be a fool. He has a whole day's start. You would never catch him."

"At least I won't have to live with myself, knowing I might have tried!"

"What about the English spies?"

"They're not concerned with me."

"And what makes you think, even if by some miracle you find him, you can talk him into coming back?"

No way to explain that to a man who'd never cared for anyone but himself. "He's my brother," she said tersely. "He will listen to me."

He stepped out of her way, with a grand gesture toward the door. "Go ahead, then. Go. Throw your own life away after his."

"At least I'll be throwing it after *something.*" Her eyes flashed pure gold. "As for you, you can crawl back to Edinburgh and hammer Homer into the freshmen, like the coward you are, and let life pass you by."

She'd stung him. She saw it by the sudden tensing of the muscles of his face, by the vein that stood out on his forehead in sharp blue relief. "I'm not going back to Edinburgh," he announced, his voice tight as a bow-string.

"You're *not?*" Her own voice a high squeak.

"No. I've finally had a response to a letter I sent Frère Descoux at the University of Paris quite some time ago. I am going to accompany him on a year's expedition. Turkey, Greece, Asia Minor. It is, you may imagine, an honor to be chosen."

She could bloody well imagine. Her teeth bared, like a cat's. "How long have you known about this?"

"The letter came a fortnight ago."

A fortnight. Fourteen days. Two weeks of a shared bed, shared baths, kisses, breakfasts, suppers, lives. . . . "And when exactly," she demanded, her wrath matching his, "did you intend to tell me?"

For the first time, his composure faltered. "I . . ."

"When I informed you I was bearing your bastard, perhaps? Was that what you were waiting for, to make your abandonment complete?"

He was staring. "Good God, Callie. You're not—"

"No, praise God, I'm not! And if I were, I'd . . . I'd . . . I'd slit open my womb and tear the bloody thing out, sooner than carry your child!"

He looked infinitely relieved; a small smile tugged at his mouth, that mouth she'd kissed so freely, had let roam over her body in reckless exploration. "You forget, Callie, I've seen you this furious before. I know you don't mean that, any more than you meant to do away with yourself at the apothecary shop."

"You—know—nothing—of—me!" Nor she of him. Christ, was that ever true. "You—you *used* me, you bastard! You knew you were going, and you went on . . . went on . . ." Sheer rage swallowed her words, her very thoughts.

"I never made you any promises," he said, very low.

Callie had moved beyond anger, into some bright blinding light of clarity, of understanding. "And that makes it all right."

He shrugged, God damn him. "It . . . makes it easier, perhaps. Look. If I am gone, disappeared overseas for a year, there's naught to make Henley's allegations stick, even if he does approach the dean. You needn't go after Zeus. No one need go after Zeus. Your brother . . . he's of age. Responsible for himself. You and your father can return to Edinburgh, get on with your lives.''

"What life do you think I would have, not knowing where he is?''

"He'll be with Charles Edward. He has made that quite clear.''

"And Charles Edward will be mowed down by the English! Everyone says so!''

"Zeus has made his own bed.''

And Mick had slept in hers. God, hadn't he any shame? "Go on, then,'' she said, seething but calm. "Pack up your dead, dry books and your dry little whisk-broom, and hie off to the ends of the earth to go digging up more dead, dry things. It's a wonder to me I ever thought you might care about the living.''

He put his hand up out of reflex to push back his long-gone glasses. "Callie. I—''

Her father, with Lady Maggie's help, had made it up the stairs. He came into the room, saw the maze of letters, and faltered; only Lady Maggie's arm held him up. "Zeus,'' he whispered hoarsely.

"Gone.'' How Callie hated confirming his fears! "It's all right, Father. It will be all right.'' She went to him, hugged him. "I know where he's gone. I'm going after him.''

"You! But how will you—''

"I'll bring him back. Never fear.'' Her eyes shot daggers at Mick, then beseeched Lady Maggie. "But I must borrow a horse.''

"The horses bae Michel's.''

"I'm sure the lord of Langlannoch won't begrudge me a horse in such exigency.'' Her gaze dared him to do it.

He took a breath. "By yourself, Callie . . . to the Hebrides . . . it's madness.''

"Will you give me the horse or no?''

"What's this about the Hebrides?'' her father questioned, befuddled.

Lady Maggie had a look on her face, contemplating her grandson, as though she'd tasted too much of her own arrow-

poison. "She will nae gae alone," she said tersely, tightly.
"All braw, true Scots will bae gaein' there, too. I wuld to God
I might. But ye may bae sure, Jennet will send Gordie 'n Ben.
They'll bae company for ye."

"Three horses,then." Callie's voice kept the dare.

"Professor Wingate." Mick appealed to him, the embodiment of reason. "Surely you don't intend to let your only
daughter trek off on such a dangerous journey."

The professor had stumped forward, was contemplating the
piles of letters. "We're to send some of these along every few
days, Calliope, is that what he's planned?"

"Aye, Father."

"Who will ride with them to Ayr, if Jennet's boys are both
gone?"

"Tomorrow bae market-day," Lady Maggie put in. "Jennet
can gae herself, 'n arrange wi' one o' the local lads to post 'em.
There bae many eno' to bae trusted—outside o' this house."

Mick threw up his hands. "You are mad. You're all mad."

Professor Wingate turned to his daughter. "And you think
you can convince him to return? He would not have gone off,
I know, if he had not believed you and me to be sufficiently
settled to endure without him."

"I agree with you, Father. But he has based that presumption
upon false facts." She stared at Mick, with her chin held high.
"I'll bring him back. Never fear."

"I suppose it would be best for you to leave under cover of
darkness. If that pesky English commandant returns, I'll say—
what shall I say?"

"Say that Zeus and I have gone back to Edinburgh, to resume
obligations. After all, we were only to stay a brief visit. You
had to remain behind because of your leg, but will rejoin us
at the first opportunity."

He nodded. "That should suffice."

Mick was scowling, unbelieving. "Christ, what a family!"

His grandmother, dark and lowering: "I only wuld ye thought
as much o' yers."

It did not take Callie long to pack; there wasn't much room
in saddlebags for hoopskirts or jewelry. Gordie and Ben were
dancing with excitement on the driveway; Jennet was sniffling

but brave. "God 'n Mary bae wi' ye, all o' ye," she whispered, returning Callie's embrace. Professor Wingate was haggard but determined.

"Mind your step, daughter. Do not put yourself in unnecessary danger."

"I won't. I love you, Father."

He kissed her cheek. "And I love you, too."

Lady Maggie came to embrace her, pale eyes a-dance in the lamp's glow. She whispered into Callie's ear, "God bae praised, he took the sword!"

Mick was nowhere in sight. Callie turned once, as they cleared the gates, to search for him, just to remind herself of her hatred. She thought she saw him in an upstairs window, a wine cup in his hand.

Part III

The Central Highlands
August, 1745

32.

From outside her tent in the camp loosely sprawled across a hill swathed in bright heather, Callie watched the archers with their longbows set, pull back, fire. The volley of arrows loosed a cloud of grouse from the brush. Typical Scots thrift, she thought, as the line of men knelt and the thin second rank— God, they had so few archers!—used their shots to fell a dozen of the birds on the wing. There was a pause while the women and children, the "gillies," as they were called, hangers-on, camp followers, beat through the heather to retrieve the birds— and the arrows. Prince Charles Edward Louis Philip Casimir Stuart could not afford to let anything go to waste.

In the old days, the days of the Bruce and the first Stewart kings, Angus MacPherson had told her, the gillies had included old or maimed men deemed incompetent to fight. Now such men swelled the corps of the soldiers. Those who limped or lacked a leg were given mounts to ride on; those too feeble to wield swords or axes were given pikes and set in the slow-moving *schiltrons*. Nothing wasted.

Callie saw the sway of one archer's long back echo perfectly the bend of his ashwood bow. Quickly she gripped her charcoal and blocked the image in on a page of her notebook. It amazed her that the dealing of death should be so lyrically graceful. Over the past few weeks she'd filled two books with such sketches—archers, swordsmen, pikemen, grenadiers, and bayonet-bearers, all training, practicing, perfecting their parts in the grand, macabre dance to come.

The archers marched, cocked, fired in the long Highland twilight. Another flurry of arrows, burst of birds, plummeting plumage. Then, again, came the children, bright-cheeked, laughing, running through knee-deep heather to retrieve the dead.

At times, the beauty of this war made her cry.

A passing soldier saw her dab her eyes with her skirt-hem. He laughed. "Homesick, lass?" Callie nodded; it was easier than trying to explain her tears. The great, hulking fellow reached to pat her shoulder in awkward sympathy. "Ach, ye 'n yer Jacky or Jamie'll bae home for Christmastide, dinna fear—'n drink yer toasts this New Year's to a Stuart king!" He gave her another quick pat, then stomped across the hill in his stout boots and plaid jalt, sword swinging at his side. Callie made sure he was out of earshot before she let loose a sob. His well-intentioned words had only pointed up a problem that bedeviled her more and more these days. Where *was* home? Oxford, which had turned her out? The ugly house in Edinburgh where she'd been so desperate and hollow? Or golden, rose-bedecked Langlannoch, where for a few brief weeks of summer she'd been happier than she'd deserved to be? No wonder Stuart's camp, with its tents and open-fire smells and lumpy pallets, seemed so warmly familiar. This was just another expedition she and Zeus were on together. For now, this *was* home.

That idiot Commandant Henley hadn't needed to trail Zeus, had he only known it. Once Callie, with Gordie and Ben, had ridden north of Strathclyde and crossed the Lennox Hills, they'd joined a steady stream of folk surging northward to the Young Pretender's landing-place. Oh, none spoke of it overtly—they were on their way, they said, to visit kin, or to find work in the tin mines, or to sail with the whalers and sealers who plied the seas. But they winked as they said so, or laughed and touched their bows or muskets or axes, and their eyes, a thousand different shades of sea-green and sky-blue and earth-brown, told another tale.

It was at Glenfinnan, within sight of their mother's home, the Isle of Skye, that she and Zeus had been reunited. She had not even recognized him as he came toward her in his uniform; he seemed to have grown half a foot taller, and sun had made his pale skin nut-brown and bleached his hair white. He had a beard, too—Zeus, who'd always scorned whiskers! It had grown in curly and thick, and surprisingly red.

It had taken little more than one glimpse of him, in his Stewart plaid and cocked bonnet and brogues, to know her mission was useless. She'd stayed on two nights, to see Gordie and Ben settled, then announced to Zeus that she was going back to Edinburgh; their father and Dorcas would be there by now. He'd astonished her by shaking his head. "Cal, I can't let you go."

"What in the world do you mean?"

"You've seen the camp. You've seen the troops. You made pictures yesterday. I saw you."

"A few sketches, folk who caught my eye—"

"Exactly. But who's to say the English didn't send you here to do just that?"

Her mouth dropped open. "Christ, Zeus! I'm your *sister!*"

"And English," he said calmly, "just like me. It's taken long enough to establish my credit amongst these men. I'll not risk what I've won—not even for your sake."

She could not believe this was Zeus, who'd crawled bawling into her bed when they were children. "How dare you try to dictate my comings and goings!"

"You left me no choice when you followed me here. You've joined a war, Cal, whether you meant to or no. You ought not to have come. I still don't know why you did."

"To try to talk you out of this . . . this madness!" She'd swept her arm at the chaos surrounding them: men striking tents in the morning haze, women dousing cookfires with water from the burn, horses milling beneath their packs, children underfoot everywhere.

He'd grinned at her, with a touch of the old Zeus. "Splendid, ain't it? Just what I imagined. I couldn't be happier."

She envied him his bliss. "Father will go mad with worry if you keep me here."

"Oh, I'll get you to Edinburgh, never fear. That's where we're headed. Anyway, if you were so bloody worried about Father, why did you leave him? Why did you leave Mick?"

"Mick's gone."

"Gone? *Where?*"

"An . . . an expedition. With that French monk he admires. Turkey, Greece, Asia Minor. He'll be gone for a year." To her, of course, he was gone for good.

Her brother had whistled low, between his teeth. "Christ, Cal. You surely can pick them." Then she'd started to cry, and he took her in his arms, arms newly laid on with muscle so that even his embrace was strange. She'd never felt so alone.

That morning they'd begun marching. Callie's horse— Mick's horse, rather—had been conscripted by apologetic Angus MacPherson, the gigantic officer with flame-red hair. "Need her for the cavalry," he'd explained. "Ye maun find a place in one o' the wagons." She rode across northwest Scotland in a crush of wives and children and chickens, her skin hopelessly freckled in a matter of days, sketchbooks clutched in her hands.

Where the devil were the English? she kept wondering, as the long line of men and baggage-trains passed Shiel Bridge, reached Invergarry, threaded the narrow pass between enemy forts at Kilchumin and Kilmallie. They could not be more than twenty miles from eager Commandant Henley, and their passage could hardly go unnoticed. What had become of his plan to "nip this thing in the bud"?

Only the day before, at breakfast, Zeus had taken note of her mounting anxiety, pitied her, and attempted to quell her fears by telling what he knew. Charles Edward had timed his invasion to take advantage of the English war with France, that had sucked the garrisons in Scotland near dry. Only some 3,000 troops were left north of the Tweed, and almost all of them were posted in the Lowlands, at Berwick, and at Edinburgh, under Sir John Cope. "That bloodsucker Henley has but a hundred fifty men at his command. I'd lay odds—and the Stuart has—he's hied them back to Edinburgh."

"How many men do we have?" He'd stared at her, grinning. "What? Do you mean you can't tell me that? I could count them if I pleased."

"No, no. It was what you said—how many men do *we* have."

Flustered, she realized she had. "I only meant . . . well, I *am* traveling with you. With them. So far as Edinburgh."

But he was still smiling. "Some twenty-five hundred." She blinked. "You asked how many men. The clan regiments of Cameron of Lochiel, Stewart of Appin, MacGregor of Glencarnock, the Macdonalds of Keppoch and Glencoe, Grant of Glenmoriston, MacDonald of Glengarry, and MacDonald of Clanranald. There are Athollmen and MacLachlans and Menzies of Shian's followers as well. More will join when we reach the Lowlands—the Duke of Perth's men, for one."

"Where are Cope and the English now?"

"Marching toward us." Callie's eyes went wide. He winked. "Never you fear, pet. Charles Edward has a trick or two up his sleeve. I'll bring him by someday to meet you, shall I? For now, I've business to attend to." She'd watched, with her heart in her throat, as he and a host of men marched eastward out of the camp. That had been yesterday morn. She hadn't seen him since, though at yesterday noon the distant bluster of guns had been heard, turning every remaining head.

She ate a solitary supper of cold oatmeal, unsweetened, and thought longingly of Jennet's perfect poached salmon. Later, in the darkness, on a pallet stretched on the heather, she twisted and turned and thought with longing of other things. But there was no profit now in remembering Mick Harding's sweet kisses, or the touch of his long, strong hands. Whatever she had meant to him, whatever he had felt as he'd held her and driven inside her, it hadn't been enough. Lady Maggie had been wrong. The pull of his blood, those centuries of proud warriors, hadn't sufficed to draw him into this fight.

He was only being sensible, she reminded herself. Just as he always had been. It was only that she'd thought, she'd hoped, what they'd shared together would have bound him to her family the way she felt bound to his.

And bound to him, too, despite the wrong he had done

her. The notion that their lives, their fates, were inseparably entwined was difficult to relinquish, though she knew now she must. Perhaps it would be easier once she got to Edinburgh, once that gray city and the gray Scottish winter beat down the memory of Langlannoch with their grim, dull force.

Or perhaps she'd sit in her room beneath the eaves with the memory of how he'd looked asleep in her bed, the summer dawn creeping over him, until it drove her to the druggist's shop again.

Frightened, she rolled over in a crush of faintly sweet dried heather, drawing up her blanket, wishing Zeus was sleeping beside her so that she might come crawling, bawling, to him.

"Did ye hear, then?"

The bright face poking through the flaps of her tent took a moment for Callie to place, groggy as she was with sleep. It was Molly MacPherson, the giant redhead's young wife.

"Hear what?" God, what a crick she had in her neck from lying on her curled arm!

"Why, we hae ta'en Kilchumin!"

"Taken—" That made Callie sit up, crick or no crick. "You mean taken the *fort?*"

"Aye, right eno'. Bain't it grand? First blude drawn, only a handful o' losses on our side, 'n the English surrendered! True, 'twar but a skeleton garrison left, but still, one maun count it a victory!"

Callie's mind had stopped listening after she heard the word "losses." "Zeus," she whispered, growing pale.

"Ach, dinna fret for him; he rode back wi' Angus, all hale 'n cocky. They bae wi' His Majesty now. I only thought ye should know."

First blood drawn. Of course she'd known it was coming, but the way Zeus kept talking about Edinburgh, somehow she'd assumed, even with the guns she had heard, it was a long way off. "Are you sure he's all right?" she asked anxiously.

"La, he'll come 'n say so his own self, soon as they hae made their report."

Callie scrambled up from her bed. She wanted to *see* him, see him *now*. Zeus in battle! It boggled her mind.

Molly put a gentle hand on her wrist. "Ye maun nae gae to him yet. He'll come when he can. P'rhaps . . . p'rhaps ye might take breakfast wi' me? To pass the time whilst we wait?"

It was the first overture any of the Scotswomen had made to her as yet. Maybe they were waiting, Callie realized, until Zeus proved himself in the fighting. She had not known, until she saw Molly's shy smile, how isolated she'd felt. "I'd like that," she said, equally shy.

The smile broadened. "Put yer clothes on, then. It bae the tent wi' the Douglas flag, three stars on white. The tall one. For Angus, ye ken."

It was a tall tent, higher by a good yard than those surrounding it, and a busy one, too, with the cookfire crackling and hens pecking dirt and laundry hung out to dry and two red-haired boys going at one another with wooden swords while Molly cracked eggs one-handed, a babe slung on her hip. "Let me do that!" Callie hastened to say, as her hostess stirred up the eggs in their skillet.

Molly laughed, gaily waving her off. "Faith, I hae nae balance any more if I hae nae a babe! This bae Libby—praise God, a girl for a change—'n them bae little Angus 'n Robbie. Angus, Robbie, bid gude day to Mistress Wingate."

They paused in buffeting each other just long enough to call out, "Gude mornin'!"

"How do you do?" Callie said, and in the same breath, "Are all of them yours?" Molly did not look any older than she.

"Sure 'n they bae. I had little Angus—he war the first— when I war scant sixteen. Patience, Libby, lamb, I'll bae wi' ye in a moment. Angus, dinna smite yer brother's head. Nah, I saw it, Robbie; 'twar but a wee blow. Dinna bae such a cry-baby, or I shall tell yer daddy. Hae ye nae bairns, then, Mistress Wingate?"

"No. I've never been married," Callie admitted, rather breathless at the woman's adeptness, juggling baby and discipline and hot pans.

"Fancy that. A pretty thing such as ye. Come on 'n get yer

eggs, then, laddies.'' The boys dropped their swords where they stood and rushed for the trenchers she spooned out for them.

"In England,'' Callie felt compelled to say in her own defense, "women tend to wed later.''

"Do they, now? Angus! Gi' yer brother back his biscuit! Here ye bae, Mistress Wingate.''

"Thank you. My—my name is Callie.'' She took the tin plate she was handed, then watched in wonder as Molly spooned her own plate full, plunked herself on the ground, opened up her bodice, and simultaneously began to nurse the baby and to eat.

"Mine bae Molly,'' she said, when she'd swallowed a mouthful.

"Aye, I know. Zeus told me so.''

The eggs were very good, spiked with some fresh-tasting greens. And there was tea, bubbling hot from a battered kettle. "Nae milk,'' Molly apologized, setting down her spoon to burp Libby. "Nae sugar, either.''

"I like it this way.''

"Ye bae Zeus's sister, then.'' Callie nodded, surprised. Molly made a vague motion with her spoon. "Some o' the women thought ye war his mistress. Ye dinna look much alike. Yer colorin' 'n all.''

Callie, blushing, could not think what to say. "He has our mother's eyes,'' she managed finally.

"She war a MacCrimmon, nae? My father's brother married a MacCrimmon. Sae we bae kinfolk, I reckon, someways.''

Kinfolk. It was an odd notion to Callie, accustomed to thinking of family in a very small way. "I suppose we are. How did you hear about the fight?''

"A rider came in early. I war hangin' the washin'.'' She laughed, grimacing at the gobbling children. "I bae always hangin' the washin', it seems!''

"So you must be. Where is your home, Molly?'' It felt strange to say the name out loud.

"We hae a croft in Lanarkshire, near Auchensaugh. Two hundred acres, mostly in cattle. *I* miss milk in my tea!''

The boys had already finished with their meal, and rushed

to reclaim their swords. "I don't mean to pry," Callie said hesitantly, "but wouldn't it have been easier for you to stay there? With the children, I mean."

"Easier?" The woman seemed surprised at the question. "It may hae been. But I culd nae hae been wi' Angus, then." Clearly that served to settle it for her. Her blue eyes, bright as periwinkles, slanted toward Callie. "Ye . . . ye make drawin's, dinna ye? I saw ye yestreen, outside yer tent, wi' yer book 'n such."

Callie nodded. "I like to draw. Yes."

"Ye bae blessed, to hae such a talent." She laughed a little. "I hae nae talents."

Callie considered the handsome, freckled boys, the contented baby lulling in Molly's lap, the tidy campsite hung with newly laundered shirts and clouts, the tasty biscuits and eggs. "You have more talents than I could ever hope for, to manage all of this!"

"Ach, this bae but woman's work," Molly said in dismissal, but she seemed pleased. "D'ye think I might see yer pictures someday?"

"They're nothing but quick little sketches, really. But—do you know, I made one of your boys, I think. Playing with their swords."

"Oh, I should like to see that."

Callie got up to fetch her sketchbook. "You may have it, if you like." It would repay the young woman's kindness, in part.

When shown the drawing of her sons, Molly sat and stared at it in wonder. "See how ye hae caught Robbie's chin, 'n Angus's wee braw fierceness!" she marveled, fingers hovering above the pencil-strokes. "Right down to their skint little knees . . . Angus, Robbie, come see."

The boys edged forward. "That bae ye, Angus!" Robbie piped, giggling and pointing.

" 'N that bae ye!" Fascinated, they stared, too.

"Dinna touch!" their mother cautioned, holding it out of their reach. She looked at Callie. "May I truly hae it?"

"Of course you may."

"Wait till I show Angus! Sae pleased he'll bae." She contem-

plated the portrait again, delighted. "But ye maun put yer name
to it for me. Ye ken, the way the painters do, down here."

"Oh, I don't think . . ." Callie tried to demur. Molly, however, insisted:

"Aye, but ye maun!"

So she scrawled her name across the bottom. It was the first
time she had ever signed a work; there'd never been any need
to. The act was, somehow, deeply satisfying. Molly nodded,
appeased. "I shall treasure this for all my days," she declared,
and then raised her head at the sound of a distant shout:
"Molly!" She smiled, nodding across the plain. "See there,
boys. Yer daddy bae come."

Those were pictures Callie would have liked to make: the
two boys tearing over the field to leap upon their father, who
laughed and hoisted them up, one on each shoulder, bearing
them easily, and the light in Angus MacPherson's eyes as he
came toward his wife and daughter, the unconscious way Molly
smoothed her hair and skirts as she rose to meet him with the
baby on her hip, and then all five of them locked in one tangled
embrace. . . . But she was distracted with staring at the man
who followed after Angus, who had dried blood smeared across
his shirt and spattered on his sun-bleached hair. "Zeus?" she
whispered.

He raised a gloved hand to her. "Hallo, pet. Is there anything
to eat?"

"What was it like?" she asked later as she crouched beside
the burn, trying to rub the brown stains from his clothes. Zeus
lay on his back with his eyes closed, his clean hair drying in
the sun.

"Horrible. Wonderful."

"Did you . . . did you kill anybody?"

"I think so."

She shivered, up to her elbows in the frigid stream. "How?"

"With my pistol."

"How close were you to him?"

"Maybe fifty paces."

"So you could see his face." She tried in vain to imagine

it: meeting someone's gaze and then pulling the trigger. "Was he young? Was he old?"

"It wasn't like that, Cal. He was the enemy."

"But he was someone's son . . . someone's father, maybe, or husband—"

"So was I." With a hint of reproach.

"Of course you are. I just—it's just difficult to think of. Remember, I used to have to squash ants for you on picnics because you were so squeamish."

"The ants had done me no wrong."

It was on the tip of Callie's tongue to say, *Neither had that man.* But she restrained herself; she knew that Zeus was still working through all this himself. It was still so new.

"Were you frightened?" That seemed a safe question.

"Surprisingly, not. There wasn't time for that. The grenadiers started picking off the sentries, and then those madmen of MacDonald of Clanranald rushed at the gates with a battering ram, and then we were in. It was all very fast—really, quite exciting."

Callie looked down at the shirt she was scrubbing. "Where is this blood from?"

"One of the Athollmen fell on me as he was hit. A musket-ball to the belly."

"Is he dead?"

"Aye."

She shivered again. "God. How horrid."

"He was extraordinarily brave about it. Said his prayers, and muttered, 'God save Prince Charlie,' and then just closed his eyes."

In the space of twenty-four hours, her brother had been shot at, had killed, had held a dying man in his arms. She could not fathom it. Such experiences ought to leave some mark beyond the blood the cold water was washing away.

But perhaps they had. "Callie," Zeus began in a new voice, measured, as though the words had been practiced, "if I should . . . if something happens to me, don't take me back to England. I should rather rest here in Scotland. Anywhere here. It doesn't matter where."

"Oh, Zeus—"

He stood up abruptly. "And you may as well stop with that shirt. It will only get soiled again. Besides, you hate laundering. I've got to pack up the tent. We'll be moving again once the wounded are seen to."

He left her by herself on the riverbank, wringing out linen and tears.

33

They camped that night just south of Dalwhinnie, in the wild, rugged heights of the Grampians. "Only another seventy or eighty miles to Edinburgh," Zeus observed, driving stakes into hard earth. "Maybe four days' march, if we went straight through. But we'll stop on the way to take Stirling and Perth." As though it were a matter of simply knocking and entering.

"What was that trouble back there as we went through the town?"

He was stretching canvas now, with quick precision. "What trouble?"

"We heard shooting."

"Oh, that. A tavern-keeper reluctant to part with his stores."

"And so you *shot* him?"

"Not I, Cal. One of the MacDonald's men." He glanced up, saw her outraged face. "The troops have got to be provisioned, pet."

"They could drink water."

"They march better on ale. Come hold this while I tie it down, would you?" She didn't budge. He sighed and clenched the rope in his teeth to make the knot. "It's a war, pet. People get killed."

"Over barrels of ale?"

"The news will spread. The next reluctant tavern-keeper will know better. It's a battle that won't have to be fought again." He gave the rope a last tug to test it. "There. Angus has a mutton leg for supper—"

"Did he shoot the butcher?"

"I didn't ask. He invited us to join him."

"I'm not hungry."

He hesitated, then finally shrugged. "Suit yourself."

Of course, as soon as he ambled off to Angus's tent she wished she'd said yes, not for the mutton but the company. Molly had been kind to her, and she liked watching the children, though she was more and more doubting the wisdom of having them along. What if Cope and the English attacked the camp— what would become of all the red-cheeked children then?

Sighing, she reached for her sketchbook. She'd started a drawing from memory of Zeus as he'd looked coming across the field to her that morning, drenched in blood and glory, sword and pistols strapped at his sides. She shut her eyes, evoking the image. If Zeus didn't live to reach Edinburgh, for their father to see the strange new man he'd become, she could at least show him this.

As she opened her eyes and began to sketch—the line of his legs, his stiff back and raised chin—she heard footsteps behind her. "If you are looking for my brother, he's with Angus MacPherson," she said without turning, not wanting to lose what little daylight remained.

"Thanks."

She drew his bonnet, and the swaggering pistols, and his hand curled on the hilt of the sword, and his short, curling beard—

"That's an exceedingly fine likeness."

Startled, she glanced up, having assumed whoever'd come for Zeus was long since gone. A young man in a blue coat and high black boots was standing, looking over her shoulder. Callie was not in the mood to chat. She grunted something noncommittal and kept working, shading in her brother's face. When the voice came again, it was from so close beside her ear that she jumped, sending her pencil-tip skittering.

"I say—"

"Look what you have made me do!" The bonnet, that she'd been so pleased with, was ruined. She grabbed for her India rubber, scowling, and began to erase the errant line.

"I do beg your pardon. I was merely going to observe that your portrait has some of the same qualities as a study of da Vinci's I once saw in Florence."

Callie stopped erasing. By what miracle had one of these uncouth soldiers ever heard of da Vinci? "Which one?" she asked suspiciously.

"It is a study for one of his Passions, I believe. It hangs in the *Biblioteca Medicea-Laurenziana,* in the third gallery on the left up the stairs."

She had been in that gallery. She even, she thought, could guess the study he meant. "The Roman guard with Christ's cloak."

"I see you know it, too."

Callie laughed, a bit embarrassed. "It's most kind of you to remark a resemblance. I must say, it escapes me."

He was kneeling beside her now, pointing. "Something in the stance, I think, and the flow of the hair into the shoulders. And of course, the expression on the face. The gambler who has won a prize."

By God, that was how Zeus had looked—as though he'd earned a trophy. Callie eyed this young man with frank curiosity. His English bore a faint undercurrent of foreign flavor. A French mercenary, perhaps? "Are you from the Continent, sir?"

"I have spent most of my life there." He was handsome, she noticed now, in a quiet way: blue eyes, straight nose, clean-shaven, with wavy brown hair that bore a tinge of Scots red. But she was suspicious of mercenaries, those men who fought without conscience for the highest bidder.

"What compels you, then, to join this war?"

He squinted up at the wide, cloud-strewn sky. "I wonder at times. Do you believe in destiny?"

Once Callie would have said yes. Now she hesitated, then shook her head. "Ah." He sounded unsurprised. "Then it would be difficult to explain." She'd let the sketchbook slide

from her lap; he picked it up. "Do you mind?" Before she
could answer, he began to page through it. "I saw the sketch
you did of the MacPherson boys. You have a real gift. I especially liked the way the youngest held his sword—that infantile
awkwardness, yes, but such passion!" Callie had been pleased
herself with the set of Robbie's hand. This unlikely fellow
showed real insight. He paused over the drawing she'd done
of the archer bending his bow. "Lovely—and archaic. The
longbow's day is finished; the musket's killed it. Pity, isn't it?
The zing of an arrow is so much more civilized than powder's
blast. And Lord knows there's more art in bending a bow than
in fingering a trigger. The way cannon are growing bigger, I
daresay the skill will be gone altogether in a century or so.
Armies will just pound one another to bits from a distance."
He sounded wistful.

"I didn't expect . . ." Callie paused; these were matters she
had not even spoken of to Zeus. But he was watching her
closely, encouraging:

"Yes?"

"The grace of it all—the real beauty. They're like dancers."
And Zeus had killed a man. "But it is awful, just the same."

"So it is."

"I really have to wonder—is it so important who rules
Britain? Is it worth men dying?" Her voice had waxed hot with
the emotion she'd been suppressing ever since she'd washed the
blood from Zeus's shirt, felt beneath her fingertips the life of
a man eddying away in the river.

The man beside her nodded slowly. "I have wondered the
same."

"Yet you came here to fight."

"Well." He shrugged blue-clad shoulders. "There's that
destiny I mentioned."

Callie looked across the hill to Angus's tent. "I never would
have dreamed that Zeus's fate would lead him to this."

"Scots blood." Her gaze, straight gold in the dying sunlight,
met his. He smiled. "My father used to tell me there's a pull
to it like the tides. I must say, I felt it—or thought I did—
when we stepped ashore."

"You came with the Young Pretender, then, from France."
That made sense of his accent.

He wagged a finger at her. " 'Pretender'—that's an English
term. I prefer 'the Young Cavalier.' " And he laughed, as
though at the absurdness of it all.

"I beg your pardon. My Scots blood doesn't seem to have
overruled my reason as yet."

The smile broadened. "And still—you are here."

"I came to fetch Zeus home. Now he won't let me leave.
He is cavalier, if you like—of my safety. He tells me General
Cope is marching toward us hell-for-leather."

Night was gathering fast. He stared up at the darkening sky.
"General Cope heard from a captured spy that we were planning
to ambush him in the Pass of Corryarrick. He's gone around
by the sea road to Inverness. We shan't encounter him."

Callie's eyes widened. "But . . . that would mean—"

"That we've a free road straight to Edinburgh. Aye. General
Cope should be more wary of relying on the enemy's word."
He grinned disarmingly.

Callie felt limp with relief. "Well, there's a blessing! Thank
you kindly for the information."

"You are kindly welcome." He straightened up, handing
her the sketchbook. "Perhaps someday you would care to do
a drawing of me."

She laughed at the suggestion, sensing that he was flirting.
"Why? Because of your surpassing good looks?"

"Naturally. Why else?"

"I am sure I don't know. I'll stick to children and foot-
soldiers, thank you. You look as though you've the means to
hire yourself a portraitist."

"Perhaps I shall. I'd best go give the good news about Cope
to your brother and Captain MacPherson. Speaking of Scots
blood, did you know MacPherson's eighteen-times-great-
grandfather fought with the Bruce at Bannockburn?"

"I didn't. But I'm not surprised. He has the carriage of a
soldier, hasn't he? Or a martyr."

"So does your brother." He made a bow to her. "Good
night, Mistress Wingate."

"Good night . . ." She didn't know his name. "Sir."

She was stretching out her pallet in the dark tent when she heard Zeus coming back across the hills, whistling. He ducked through the flaps and tossed something at her; it jingled, hitting the bedclothes. "What's that?" she asked suspiciously.

"Two sovereigns."

"And what, pray, are they for?"

"A retainer. For a portrait. Pencil will do, he said; he realizes you haven't your paints with you."

"A retainer from whom?"

"Prince Charles Edward. Oh, and he said to tell you the remark about his surpassing good looks was much appreciated." Her brother's voice rippled with laughter.

The Young Pretender—nay, the Young Cavalier. Callie flushed scarlet in the darkness, her fingers curled around the coins.

"That was a rotten trick you played me," Callie announced, glaring with mock fierceness at the man who posed before her in his curled white wig and jaunty hat, fist on the hilt of his sword.

"I was hoping you'd sketch me for no fee, like a common foot-soldier," Charles Stuart replied with equanimity.

"I don't want your money." To prove it, she fished with lead-stained fingers in her pocket, and tossed the coins at his feet.

He stooped to pick them up with lanky grace. "Then why did you consent to sketch me?"

"You've changed your left foot. Move it in closer to the other, if you please. No, not so much as that. I don't know," she finally answered his question, pencil already moving. "I suppose because, just as you said, I am here. A moment in history. Not the sort of chance someone such as me often sees."

The last of the Stuarts gazed across the rag-tag camp at his army. "We are all a part of history. What is it Shakespeare had the king speak in *Henry the Fifth?*

'He that outlives this day, and comes safe home,
    Will stand a-tiptoe when this day is named. . . .

Old men forget; yet all shall be forgot,
But he'll remember, with advantages,
What feats he did that day.' ''

Callie was frantically sketching, desperate to capture the
yearning on his young face as he recalled the fifth Henry's
victory against all odds at Agincourt. It must be just such a
miracle he hoped for in this campaign. Well, why not? Henry's
blood flowed in him, somehow, down through the long tangled
skeins that were the veins of Britain's kings. And that, perhaps,
more than the reason she'd given, was why she made this
portrait: because in gazing at him, she might be seeing the
cheekbones of Mary Stuart, or the blue eyes of Henry the
Eighth, or—who could tell?—the chin of Robert the Bruce.
God knew, he looked more the king than the dumpy German
George. She thought of telling him so, then decided against it.
Why should she encourage the enemy who'd stolen Zeus
away—who'd caused the breach between her and Mick?

Damn, now she'd thought of Mick—and all her concentration
fled, destroyed in an instant with wondering where he was,
whom he might be with, beneath the weightless blue Aegean
sky. She laid her pencil down with a sigh. Charles Edward
heard the pencil drop, and glanced toward her. "I'm sorry,"
she apologized. "That's all for this night. I have lost the light."

He shrugged, glad for the chance to move. He was a difficult
subject in that way; quiescence did not suit him. Unlike Mick
. . . "No matter. Truth to tell, I feel guilty for the indulgence,
with so much to plan. Mark it down to vanity. Mind if I look?"
She turned the sketchbook toward him. He came down from
the knoll on which she'd posed him, not nervous, exactly, but
a little bit shy. "Well! At least you haven't put on horns." He
cocked his head at the sketch. "Is that really what I look like?"

"It is to me."

"I didn't expect . . . you've made me seem rather grand."

Dammit, she liked this young man. "Well. It is rather a
grand gesture you're making, isn't it, to find your destiny?"
And that was something she had not thought about before—
how much he might be risking, when he could have been
content to go on as the toast of the Continent, everyone's choice

of most charming exile. Who hazarded more, after all—the hard-scrabble Scots crofter who saw in this contest the chance, as Shakespeare had said, to reach old age with an ageless memory, or Charles Edward, who'd left the luxury of the French court for the vicissitudes of war and the strains of command? In the end, no one would blame the foot-soldier for whatever happened. Victory was shared rejoicing, but defeat would lie on the Pretender's slim shoulders till the end of his days—unless it claimed his life.

"Yer Majesty." It was one of the sentries, trotting up to demand his attention. "The sortie fro' Stirling bae returned. Ye bade ken when it did."

"Thank you, Ranald; I'll receive them in my tent. And thank you, Miss Wingate. Perhaps we'll make a bit more progress on the morrow, if we don't reach Perth by then." He made a gallant bow and set off running, tearing off the wig as he went.

Callie watched him go with a reluctant tugging of her heart, as though the blood churning through it were fastened somehow to the heels of his high black boots.

34.

Two days later, they took Perth. On Friday, they took Stirling.
Like knocking and entering, Callie thought with amazement,
watching the delirious populace in the latter city throng the
streets, hurling hats in the air. Women blew kisses at their
conqueror; children chanted with glee for "Bonnie Prince Charlie!" And the ranks of the Young Pretender's army swelled
and swelled, like a mighty sea.

There were no English to stop them. Cope and half his
hapless troops were, for all anyone knew, still foundering about
Inverness, and what remained of King George's army was holed
up in the black hulk of Edinburgh Castle, only thirty miles off.
And with each mile marched, new recruits surged in, bringing
muskets, pistols, pitchforks, whatever weapons they had to lend
to the cause.

Zeus was in heaven. He glowed like phosphor in a beaker,
green eyes on fire. "Didn't I tell you, Callie? Didn't I say
Scotland would rally to him?"

"It's a long way from Scotland to London." Despite her
bleak words, though, it was impossible to stay aloof from the
electric excitement that ignited the faces Callie saw. She'd
filled all the sketchbooks she'd brought from Langlannoch,

pages back and front, and bought six more from a stationer in Stirling who'd raised the nascent Stuart flag outside his shop. Her fingers were in a frenzy. Nothing she had ever seen compared to the wild elation of the Jacobite soldiers; it was pure and intense as blue flame. And yet there were in it echoes of the celebrations of every civilization she had studied under her father—Greek, Trojan, Roman, Ottoman, Egyptian, Viking, Saxon. In all those sketches she had made of helmets, weapons, booty, victims, she had never glimpsed the souls of those who'd fought and died and plundered. But, Christ, she did now.

"Do you remember," she said to Zeus on the night of the eighth of September, "that Roman skeleton Father unearthed at Avebury? The one who'd run from the Saxons, throwing off treasure as he went?" Mick had unearthed it, of course, but her brother, blessedly, let that pass and nodded. "I saw him, yesterday. It was when those mad MacDonalds marched on that farmhouse. It wasn't treasure he was throwing off, but chickens. He had them stuffed in a sack on his back, and the soldiers burst into the front door of the house and he came out the back door, with chickens flying from his sack as he ran, going every which way." She shook her head, amazed at the memory of the man's panicked face.

Zeus was loading cartridges with powder and balls by the light of a lamp. "We'll reach Edinburgh within days," he noted, and glanced up again. "What will you do then?"

"What will I *do?* Rush home to Father, of course, and let him know we are safe. Can you imagine how wild he must be for news?"

"The gazettes have no doubt been covering our progress— one can only wonder with what editorial comment. I meant, Cal—what after that?"

"After that?" She stopped. "Why . . . stay on with him."

He tamped a cartridge closed. "You could stay on with us."

"Lord! Why in heaven would I?"

"Just . . . to see what's to be seen."

"Oh, I've seen quite enough, thank you."

He measured powder from his horn. "You've not yet witnessed a battle."

But she'd seen thousands of them, carved into friezes, painted on frescoes, frozen in the threads of tapestries from Amsterdam to Messina to Constantinople. She tried to imagine viewing such scenes in the flesh—the havoc, the noise, the scents of sulphur and blood and fear. "I don't think I have the stomach for that. I don't care to watch men die."

"It is the culmination of the human experience. The one certainty we all share."

"You make looking on sound a religious experience—like worshipping at Chartres."

"I imagine for artists it must be. Why else, down through the centuries, would they have chosen to depict battles again and again? Nothing so different about it each time, after all, beyond the weapons and headgear. Yet generation after generation, the world's finest talents choose to try their hands at it." He glanced at her sidelong in the lamplight. "Don't tell me yours don't ache to try."

When he spoke of it that way, of course they did. But— "No. It would not be fair to Father."

"Oh, hang Father; he's a big boy. When are you going to stop fretting about other people, Cal, and start living for yourself?"

"Be selfish, you mean." She had done that, with Mick. It had gotten her a shattered heart.

"I don't think it's selfish to pursue one's dreams. As a matter of fact, I believe it's more selfish to tie your unhappiness to others." He set the horn down to look straight at her. "I don't like thinking of you in that house, Cal, with your memories."

Of course, she'd worried about that, too. But her chin came up. "I've grown, you know, since last spring."

"And you've been hurt. Look here, Cal. I don't know all that went on between you and Mick—"

"Because it's none of your business."

"But I do know I am angry enough to kill him, were he standing here. Before I did, though, I would thank him for having started you drawing again. Perhaps, in the long run, that's the reason why your life and his collided as they did."

Memories fell upon her: white linen heaped with roses; his craven eyes as he stared at her through the bedchamber window;

his head straining back at the moment of union, teeth clenched on her name. "There was more to it than that."

"I don't see how there could be. But, Lord knows, I'm no expert on love."

"How refreshing to hear you admit to inadequacy in *something*. Do move that powder back from the lamp; I shouldn't care to be able to sketch from memory the look of your neck without your head." He laughed and did as she bade. The lamplight flickered on the new ruddy beard, his sun-toughened skin. "Do you ever think about falling in love?" she asked curiously.

"Sometimes. Lately, when I watch Angus with his children and Molly. It seems a good sort of life. Maybe, when all of this is finished, I'll follow in Father's footsteps and find a wild little island lassie to take to wife."

"A sort of noble savagess," she suggested.

"Something like that."

"Hmph. Just make sure before you wed her that she isn't secretly a doctoral candidate at Heidelberg."

"It is good to hear you laugh about him," Zeus said gently.

"I hardly know what else one can do. Except hope a wild pig gores him over there in wherever he is."

He'd finished with the cartridges; he lined them up carefully and began to count them by twos, with all the intensity he'd once reserved for discussions of Aristotelian philosophy. "You'll fall in love again someday," he mused at last, tucking them into his ammunition pouch. "How about Prince Charles Edward? He seems quite taken with you."

Callie shuddered. "No more scions of crumbled dynasties for me, thank you kindly. I can't abide the ghosts."

In mid-September, the Pretender's forces arrived within sight of the astonished populace of Scotland's capitol. No one—not even, Callie suspected in her heart, Charles Edward—had thought that they would get so far. She had finished her sketch of him, and signed it. It was very good. He sent for her in his tent on the night of the fifteenth. The little pavilion was packed with messengers and advisors. She set foot inside timidly, waiting while two Highland lairds argued violently about the best way to gain entry to the city. The prince caught her eye, smiled with raised brows, and listened, tapping a quill on his desk, while the chiefs wound on in their thick Gaelic brogues. "I'll think on what you've suggested," he broke in at last, when it was clear they were not close to stopping. "I must have a word with Miss Wingate now, though, if you'll just make way." Resentfully, glaring at Callie, the Highlanders stepped back. She threaded her way forward between the milling ranks of men, wondering what in the world this summons might be for.

"Miss Wingate. Push, I believe, is shortly coming to shove. I'm concerned about your notebooks." She blinked at him. "The sketches you have made. I have a messenger sailing tomorrow for France. I'd very much like to send the books with him, for safekeeping."

"B-but," Callie stammered.

He raised a brow again. "Yes?"

"They are only rough sketches. Half of them I never even finished!"

"They are what we have—I have—of a visual record of this campaign. I would see them preserved for posterity."

Posterity. Callie had a sudden vision of a small gallery—perhaps in the *Bibliotheca Medicea-Laurenziana*—hung with her drawings, each carefully labeled: "Member of the Duke of Perth's grenadiers, 1745." "Foot-soldier under Cameron of Lochiel, 1745." The notion took her breath away. "Of course, if Your Majesty wants them . . ."

"Thank you; His Majesty does." He seemed bemused by something. "Am I no longer 'the Pretender' to you, then, Miss Wingate?" Lord, what had she called him? *Your Majesty.* It had just slipped from her tongue. Embarrassed, she started to speak, but he waved her silent, with a grin. "You'll be compensated for the sketches, of course, at some point in the future. Though it could be the far-distant future. Right at the moment, my resources are a bit tied up. I trust you understand."

"Certainly, sire." Sire! There, she'd done it again!

"Very good. Monsieur Beauvais, would you kindly accompany Miss Wingate to her tent and take charge of the notebooks? Oh, and Miss Wingate—do have your pencils sharp on the

morrow. I trust we'll see a bit of a battle. I would very much
appreciate your recording it.''

The eyes of the men, haggard yet raw with zeal, followed
her from the tent.

The next morning, a company of dragoons under the banner
of Colonel Gardiner rode out from Edinburgh Castle. Charles
Edward's men, Zeus among them, cut them to ribbons alongside
Coltbrig Hill before noon. The rejoicing was ferocious; even
on the walls of the old city, the Stuart flag appeared. Angus
MacPherson had to show for it all a single-wound on the left
side of his neck. Callie, watching Molly calmly dress it, shivered
to see how close the redheaded giant had come to death. ''Don't
you worry for him?'' she whispered to Molly when Angus was
out of hearing.

''Sure 'n I do. But his family bae lucky in war. He'll live
to ripe old age, just as his father 'n his father's father did.''
The blond Scotswoman looked at her appraisingly. ''I saw ye
wi' yer sketchbook, up on the hill. Wha' did ye make o' it,
then—yer first battle?''

Callie paused, trying to think what to say. It had been what
she'd imagined, feared, and yet had been something more: a
breathtaking spectacle, a riot of movement and color—horses
charging, plaids flying, pennants streaming, the flash of bayo-
net-steel, and the slow puffs of smoke from the guns rising in
the clear air. She had longed to be far away, on a hillside in
Athens—and she had longed for her paints. She'd seen a musket-ball strike a horse in the head and spatter red gore in an
arc like a rainbow. She'd seen men running over the backs of
their fallen comrades, who'd raised mute, impuissant hands.
She'd drawn the small, tidy pile the Jacobites made of their
dead in the long, trampled grass. *Nothing wasted?* she thought
sourly.

''I wish,'' she said finally, ''there were some other means
of resolving these things.''

Molly laughed outright, cradling her daughter to her breast.
''Wha' other could there bae? Ye hae seen little Angus 'n
Robbie. Gi' a boy a stick, 'n he will make it a sword or a
musket. Oh, it lies deep in 'em, it does, the wantin' for war.''

Callie thought of Mick. ''Not in all men.''

That made Molly purse her pretty lips. "In all true Scotsmen. Ye cannae winnow it out o' 'em wi' any sieve." And her tone was proud. "Why d'ye think the young prince chose Scotland to start in? He ken well eno', dinna he, o' wha' stuff we bae made?" Then her face softened as she looked down at Libby. "Still. I do think, sometimes, we women hae the worst o' it, to bae sittin' 'n waitin'. Mayhaps, by the time she bae grown, the warrin' will bae done."

Zeus was unscathed in the fighting. "A skirmish," he told Callie, by way of dismissal. "There will be no true battle until Cope catches up to us—or we reach England. But by then, you'll be gone." He paged through the sketches she'd made, then glanced up at her in surprise. "Not what I expected."

"What do you mean?"

"Well . . ." He traced with a finger the tilt of a dead Scotsman's bonnet. "You've caught the glory of it. I didn't think you would."

"Despite all my best intentions, I find it hard not to be impressed by the willingness with which men rush to die. Why *do* the Highlanders scream that way when they charge?"

"Who knows? Perhaps because if they didn't, they'd cry."

The Highland Charge was the prince's most formidable weapon. Bred by centuries of internecine warfare in the secret glens and hidden passes of the Gael's wild homeland, it required no drills, mandated no practice, demanded only the barest form of discipline. The Highlanders assembled with their best fighters to the front, four deep, armed with their antique muskets and Spanish pistols and flintlocks, as well as broadswords and dirks. Behind this ranking massed the remainder of a clan's troops, youths and old men and occasionally, Callie had heard, women, who might carry nothing but axes or pitchforks for defense. The whole unit marched toward the enemy; when the front line came within musket-range, it let loose a volley, then immediately flung down its firearms and surged forward, screaming with a noise like a banshee, swords and daggers drawn. Callie had seen the charge in action that morning for the first time, and had assayed to sketch it. The result, which Zeus was contemplating now, was like nothing else she had ever drawn: a churning tangle of hats and legs and weaponry and open, yowling mouths. "Remarkable," he commented, with another side-long glance at his sister. "It rather reminds me of an early Greek frieze: the sense of motion, the faces."

"I am pleased with it. I'll try it in oils, I think, once I am home."

"Make the canvas big—huge."

"Yes. I thought so, too."

He set the sketchbook down and began methodically to clean his musket. "Donald Cameron has some sort of ruse afoot to get his men through the Canongate—don't mention that to anyone, though. You could be home with Father by tomorrow night."

Tomorrow. To sleep in a bed again. To have a bath! It seemed impossible. "Will you come with me, to see him?"

"I am a soldier, Cal. My comings and goings are not of my own dictation." He paused in the careful polishing. "I doubt I would anyway. He must be dreadfully disappointed in me."

"I will tell him he has no cause to be."

He looked up at her quickly. "Do you mean that, Cal?"

"God, yes. I still think this war is madness. But it is one hell of a grand adventure. If I were a man, I daresay I would go on with you."

He leaned toward her, urgent, appealing. "Do. Do come with us. Stick it out a while longer. I know, I can feel in my bones, that we are on the verge of a great victory. You can be there to record it, seal it in men's memories forever after. It's a chance for immortality."

But Callie shook her head. "I don't really care about that. Father needs me. And besides, I don't want to be anywhere about when you die. I couldn't stand that, honestly."

He came and put his arm around her. They sat that way until the first light of dawn, talking in hushed voices, laughing, remembering, celebrating the bond between them, their past, their abiding love.

35.

Clerk Street, the evening of the 17th of September. Students rushing by in a haze of hot debate: were they being invaded, or saved? A fine view from St. Leonard's of the Jacobite troops amassed in Holyrood Park. Donald Cameron's ruse had worked—Bonnie Prince Charlie was within the city walls.

And so was Callie, thin and freckled and bedraggled, her pack slung over her shoulder. No one took the least notice of her as she made her way along thoroughfares she only vaguely recalled, as if she'd seen them in a dream. Then Chalmers Street, and the blunt gray outline and inelegant windows of . . . home. She paused on the cobblestones, waiting to see if she felt any rush of warmth—felt anything at all. She didn't.

She climbed the steps and let the door-knocker fall.

The woman who answered was a stranger. Disconcerted, Callie stepped back, checked the house number again. The woman was smiling, waiting: "Aye? Can I help ye?"

"Is this . . . Professor Wingate's house?"

"Aye, right eno'." She was Scottish, this woman, red-haired, tall and fine-boned. Who the devil was she?

"Is he at home?" Callie peered beyond the woman's skirts, half expecting not to recognize the furnishings. But no, there was the hall credence cluttered with artifacts, the hat tree, the umbrella stand. . . .

"The professor bae at table," the woman noted, still pleasant. For the first time, Callie heard the vague murmur of voices, laughter, clinking cutlery. A dinner party? "Can I tell him who bae callin'?"

"I'm his daughter." Callie thrust her pack at the open-mouthed woman and pushed past her to the dining room.

The double doors were open. There were candles on the table, and the best damask cloth, without a single wrinkle. It was still the first course. A dozen young men turned to gape at her—her tangled hair, her patched, worn clothes, the very unladylike freckles. At the head of the table, Professor Wingate rose, beaming, to his feet. "How absolutely delightful!" he declared, coming to embrace Callie. "Here is my daughter Calliope, just in time to join us. This year's crop, my dear." He waved a hand toward the students. "What do you think?"

It took some minutes to convince her father that she was not just then appropriately attired to join his little party. The students stared at her, awestruck, as she explained: "I've been a month on the march, Father, all the way from Glenfinnan. I haven't—" She noticed the gaping students, lowered her voice. "I haven't had a proper bath in all that time."

"You found Zeus, then." She nodded. "I knew that you would. How is he?"

What, she wondered, if she'd had to tell him Zeus was dead? "He is well." More than well. "We'll talk about it later. Just now, I really must freshen up. Do forgive the interruption," she told the gawking students, with her best once-upon-a-time-betrothed-to-an-earl's-son smile.

The professor was already moving back to his place at the table. "Certainly, certainly. Perhaps you'll join us for coffee?"

Callie fought down an urge to break into hysterical laughter. "Do you know, Father, that Charles Edward's troops are camped not half a mile away?"

He smiled benignly. "That's what we were just discussing. Do hurry back, my dear, and shed some light on this remarkable turn of events. Meanwhile, gentlemen, eat up, or the roast will get cold.''

Out in the corridor, the Scottish woman hurried toward her, apologetic: "Beggin' yer pardon, Miss Wingate, but I had no idea—"

"Where is Dorcas?" Callie asked in confusion.

"Ye mean the housekeeper afore me. She would not come back fro' England, the professor told me. Said she feared for a war.''

Canny old Dorcas. "Who hired you, then?"

"Why, the professor, mum. Came to the agency 'n interviewed ten candidates. Glad I was of it, too, when he chose me. Ach, he's a charmin' soul, yer daddy.'' And she smiled.

My daddy. Interviewing housekeepers. Giving dinner parties for the students. Getting on just fine.

"If ye'd like a bath, mum, I can bring up water. . . .''

"Thanks very much, ah—"

"Elspeth, mum. Elspeth Connall.''

"Elspeth. But you've clearly got your hands full. I'll see to my own bath.'' Callie headed for the stair, then turned back. "What wine is that you've served with the oysters?"

"Why, a Château Filhot. Second growth.'' She winked. "I dinna think they'll notice.''

Callie fought down laughter again. "No, most likely not,'' she agreed.

Soak, rub, scrub. The water in the tub was a horrendous brown by the time Callie finished. Combing out her hair seemed to take hours. While it dried, she opened drawers, peered into the wardrobe. Her own clothes looked strange. Hard to believe she'd only been four months away. She touched her blouses, skirts, looked up at the box that held her wedding gown. Harry, Oxford, all of it, a million lifetimes ago. She went to the window, stared down into the garden. Someone had been planting. In the dusk, a line of spirea and saxifrage along the back wall bobbed heavy heads.

There came a knock at her door. It was Elspeth Connall, in a crisp apron. "The gentlemen have left, mum, all but yer father. I thought ye'd like to know.''

"Thank you, Elspeth. I'll come down. I—I like what you have done in the garden."

"Well, mum," she replied with a pleased smile. "Beggin' yer pardon, but I did think it looked a mite bleak."

Her father was in the drawing room, with his pipe and a glass of brandy. "How is your leg?" Callie asked, perching on the sofa.

"Coming right along. I scarcely ever think of it."

"You seem to have found yourself a treasure in Elspeth."

"Mm." He nodded, sucking the pipe. "She's more cheerful than Dorcas ever was, that's for sure. She made a most extraordinary sauce for the lamb. Not a speck of dill in it. There's some left, no doubt. She could bring you a plate—"

"I'm not—not especially hungry."

"All the gazettes say the Pretender's army is starving. I'd hoped, of course, that was an exaggeration. Though you do look thin."

"We had enough to eat. Oatmeal, mostly. Could have stood some honey on the stuff. Father—" He glanced up at her. "Were you worried about me?"

"Of course I was! But there didn't seem much that I could do about it. I knew you were with Zeus. I trusted you to look after one another. You always have."

She remembered her promise to her brother. "You should see him, Father. He's changed, utterly changed. I hardly recognized him. He must be nearly as tall as you now. Shot up all at once. He has a beard, too, and muscles! Our Zeus—can you believe it?" And he has killed men. But she left that unsaid.

"Odd, isn't it, what life brings us to? My children, on the march with an army. This Pretender . . . have you met him?"

"Oh, aye. Zeus and he have grown close. He's remarkably cultured. I . . . I sketched him. At his request. We had several long conversations about da Vinci, and Florence. You would approve of him, I think."

Professor Wingate knocked out his pipe. "I can scarcely say I approve of what he's done. Put the whole nation in a dither—and it's all for naught, in the end, you know. You heard Dr. Tensby. He hasn't got a chance."

"No one ever thought he would make it so far as Edinburgh."
Callie realized, surprised, that she was defending the Pretender.

"Only because General Cope made a wrong turn on his way
to Inverness. I must say, I continue to be appalled at your
brother's lack of common sense."

"But if you saw him, Father . . ." She was quiet a moment,
trying to put into words what she had felt when she saw Zeus
coming across the plain after the battle for Kilchumin, drenched
in blood and glory. "I think, for him, the end result doesn't
matter. It is the process, the becoming, that has involved him.
It really is quite . . . grand. When we took Stirling—" He
looked up sharply. "Force of habit. When *they* took Stirling.
The celebration in the streets, the excitement of the faces—I
made sketches. Hundreds of sketches. But the prince has sent
them off to France, for safekeeping."

Her father leaned down slowly to light a match from the
fire. "You've been moving in illustrious circles, Calliope. I
trust it hasn't gone to your head." He drew in smoke and
loosed a wreath of it toward the ceiling.

Her chin came up. "I was proud he wanted them. I won't
deny that. But I came home to you."

Elspeth hurried in, drying her hands on her apron. "Just had
to finish the washin'-up. Can I bring ye anythin', mum? A bite
to eat? Wine 'n cheese?"

"Wine and cheese would be lovely. Thank you."

Professor Wingate was fingering his pipe-bowl. "They've
given me two new courses, you know. No more Homer for
freshmen. I've got one young man who seems quite promising—my new assistant. Reminds me a bit of Mick Harding.
Extraordinarily well-read in the ancients. I think you'll enjoy
meeting him. I've invited him on Tuesday, for tea. And I'm
to present a lecture to the faculty next month. 'Birth of the
Gods' again. If you've time, I've a few sketches I could use.
I need a copy of that Damocles in my study. Much enlarged,
of course."

Damocles, who'd been seated at a banquet beneath a naked
sword suspended by a single hair. Ten thousand years dead, if
he'd ever even been alive. "Father," Callie said. "There are
five thousand enemy soldiers camped within sight of your bed-

chamber window. It's entirely possible classes may be suspended, in light of that fact.''

His pipe had gone out. He was trying to relight it, and his hands were shaking. ''If the Pretender is so cultured as you profess, I trust he will not interfere with the educational process.''

''This is war, Father! It may inconvenience you a bit, but it is!''

He seemed not to have heard her. ''By the by, there's a performance of *The Frogs* on Wednesday next by the university players. They're quite good, actually, although the accents take some getting used to. Perhaps you'd like to come? You used to be quite fond of Aristophanes.''

Callie sighed. Elspeth had come in with a tray, and set it down beside her. ''I dinna kken white or red,'' the housekeeper said with chagrin, ''so I brought 'em both.''

Callie poured herself a tall glass of red. She suddenly felt a great wash of pity for her father. All around him, history was being made, and he seemed oblivious to it. The prospect of a lifetime of dull sketches of dead Greeks loomed up before her. The wine on her tongue tasted of summer, of sunlight filling grapes full to bursting, before fading to must. ''Father,'' she began again.

He bustled up from his chair. ''Speaking of Mick Harding—'' Had they been? ''I've had a letter from him. It's somewhere here on the mantel.'' He searched for it among a neat pile of papers. ''Ah, yes. Here it is. Perhaps you'd care to read it?''

''I don't think so.'' She gulped more wine.

''He wrote it from Paris. Really, a most peculiar missive. I couldn't make hide nor hair of it. He seems . . . apologetic. I don't know why he should be. Do you?''

She looked up at him. He was extending the letter. She took it from him between two fingers, the way she might handle a dead mouse. How did one alter a lifetime's worth of pretending, set the course true again? Perhaps it was best done bluntly. ''I can't imagine—unless it is because he was my lover at Langlannoch, before he proved himself a cad.'' Four months ago, she never could have spoken those words. But she longed somehow to jolt him into the present, into immediacy.

His hand went up to push at his spectacles. "Ah. I see. I
... was he your first? I do beg your pardon; that is none of
my business." Past his spectacles; he was rubbing his eyes.

"Father." Callie was astonished. "Are you—crying?"

"Just a bit of smoke." He took a long breath, still rubbing.
"Though I must admit, it is a bit of a shock to discover that
one's children are strangers. Zeus run off to be a soldier ...
and now this."

Callie looked down at her hands with the crumpled letter.
"He was my first, aye, as you put it." She owed him that.
Christ, she owed him everything. Didn't she?

"Might I inquire ... why him?"

The way he'd scrambled over the roof, breeches slung low
across slim hips. The nights she'd struggled to capture his
manhood in paint. The sight of him coming out of the sea, with
his long hair sleeked back. "Why Laurie MacCrimmon?"

Her father actually blushed. "As banal as that," he murmured, and then caught himself. "I mean, of course, as simple.
There is much to be said, I suppose, for animal attraction."

The spirits of Michel Faurer and Madeleine, etched within
her eyelids. But it hadn't been fate, had it? Just the itch of the
flesh, as her father said. "I imagined it ... something more."

"We all do. You were fortunate, daughter."

Something in his voice threw up her guard. "How do you
mean?"

"Well. No repercussions." He busied himself with his pipe.

"Is that what I was?" She heard her own voice rise in pain.
"A bloody repercussion?"

"Of course not! I only meant—oftimes there are."

"Like an unexpected child, who forces unexpected
choices?" In her heart, close-guarded convictions were shattering. Of course. Why else would the up-and-coming Oxford
scholar have wed an illiterate piper's offspring?

Her father's back was rigid. "Dammit, Calliope. I did the
right thing by her."

"But did you love her? Did you ever love her?"

"How in God's name did we get onto this subject?" He
cleared his pipe with such force that charred tobacco scattered.

"Oh, damn," Callie whispered. "Oh, damn, damn, damn!"

Her mother's piquant face—so much like her own. The Gaelic cradle-songs. The sweet, blessed laughter. The shelter of white arms, the vaguest memory of a white breast tugged at amongst Scots-red hair . . .

Her father, helpless, spread his hands. "We had so little in common. . . ."

"You bloody fraud," she hissed at him. "All your grand talk of equality, of leavening by education—"

"But one must start with something," he argued back at her, "some common ground! Some realization of man's past, his wrenching pull toward civilization. A knowledge of the *lack,* at least!"

She thought of Molly MacPherson's tentative comment: *I hae nae talents . . .* "She'd have been better off if you'd left her on Skye," she told him bitterly.

"Do you think I don't know that? Do you think it does not haunt me?" Tears were streaming down his face. "But what about you? Could I leave you there to be drowned in ignorance—in the sort of bull-headed blindness that leads to this madness?" He made a gesture toward the darkened window, toward the troops that had raised their tents in Holyrood Park. "I only wanted . . . what was best for you."

She was curiously unmoved by his tears. "Does Zeus know?" she demanded. He hung his head. "Well, does he?"

"He found a copy of the marriage certificate, several years ago. He saw the date. He can add. I . . . I've burned it since. But, Calliope, you must believe me—you were worth it. You *are* worth it."

"Worth the sacrifice you made, you mean, in wedding her?" He flushed again. "Oh, Father. It is nearly subject matter for Sophocles, wouldn't you say? All your efforts—your *sacrifice*—and here is Zeus, run off with his blood-relation heretics." She had a mad impulse to approximate for him the chilling Highland Charge scream.

"The irony has struck me, more than once," he said heavily. "Thank God I still have you."

Elspeth was at the door, hesitant. "If there'll be nothin' more, sir—"

"No more, my dear. Thank you for your efforts this evening.

That sauce for the lamb was quite extraordinary, as I was telling my daughter.''

"Yes, sir. Thank ye, sir. Good night. 'N goodnight, miss.''

Her footsteps faded. Professor Wingate rubbed his forehead absently. "I don't know what more to say to you, Calliope. I did my duty by your mother. I trust she was not . . . miserable. She loved you very much. You and Zeus gave her great joy. As you have given me. It is good to have you home again.''

Home—the mysterious ambition. This house wasn't home, she knew—but she knew also that she needed time to think, to digest. *He's grown old,* she thought. *He has an old man's regrets. He could have lied to me about this.*

She stood up and kissed his papery cheek. "Thank you, Father.''

"I'm not at all certain what you have to thank me for.'' He yawned, and tried to hide it. "Forgive me. It's been a taxing day. Company for dinner and a meeting with the dean this morning that went on for hours.'' Callie thought of how she'd risen at dawn, washed up in frigid water, eaten cold oatmeal, helped Zeus strike the tent, ridden in the jolting wagon, set the tent up again and then made her way here—and *his* day had been taxing! Well, it was all a matter of what one was accustomed to, she supposed.

He'd taken off his glasses. "What I've told you must have come as quite a shock to you, I imagine.'' *There* was an understatement. "But I do trust, Calliope, that it won't impel you to do anything . . . rash.''

"Such as what?'' she asked curiously.

"I hardly know. But chasing after Zeus as you did—well, that's hardly the sort of behavior I had come to expect from you. I can see now it must have been Mick Harding's influence on you. Under the circumstances, I'm glad he went off on his expedition. Despite all that's gone on, there's no reason why you shouldn't pick up the pieces of your life, find a nice young man to marry. This new assistant of mine—'' He went on talking. Callie wondered which of the goggle-eyed students he had in mind for her now. Her father's voice turned fretful: "Though, under the circumstances, I wouldn't mention any more about this unfortunate interlude with the Pretender's army, if I were you. Not the sort of thing that's done, is it, by proper young ladies?" The shouts of celebration. Blood on Zeus's shirt. Her hundreds of sketches, consigned just like that to oblivion.

The sleeves of the gown she'd put on hung loose against her toned, hardened body. Her old clothes did not fit her any more. How could her old life?

"I thought," she said with a touch of desperation, "that we could talk, Father. About where I've been, what I've done." About how I have changed. . . .

He yawned again. "I scarcely think that's necessary. After all, it's all in the past. And it *has* been a most taxing day. I'll see you at breakfast, my dear. Elspeth makes the most astonishing crumpets. Light as heaven. Good night, my dear. It *is* good to have you home."

When he'd kissed her and gone, she sat back down on the sofa. Mick's letter was still crumpled in her hand. She went to smooth it out. How apologetic had he been? In what way? She then reconsidered, pitching it onto the fire. The paper yellowed, crumpled, curled, edges darkening. She saw his strong, slanted handwriting shrivel and disappear into a sheet of ash that imploded onto the logs.

From beyond the window she heard young men's voices raised in heated debate: was the soul rational, or merely sentient? Why would angels *care* to dance upon the head of a pin? Her gown bunched at her shoulders most uncomfortably.

She poured herself another glass of wine—and stared at the fire till it burned down to cinders. Her father had been right: it *was* very odd, what life brought one to.

36.

Zeus was putting on his plaid in the thin light of dawn. Despite all these months of practice, it was still awkward for him, this wrapping and twisting and pleating. He missed Callie's hands. Fumbling with the length of wool, he stared at the city, in the direction of their father's house. Perhaps, if he'd told her about Laurie . . . but that wouldn't have been fair. Someday the old man would tell her—likely on his deathbed, where she'd have no alternative but forgiveness. The professor always had known how to work an audience.

Cope's troops were back in Lothian, brought by ship from Aberdeen to Dunbar. Charles Edward's men were this day to march toward them. The next day, or the day after, the two armies would meet. It would be the first real test of Jacobite strength against King George's forces.

He wished his sister could be there.

He'd truly thought he'd won her over—well, not he, exactly, but the panoply of war, the pipes and drums and flags and bonnets, the rippling agitation, the horror and the joy. He knew she'd felt it, could see it in the sketches she'd produced so prodigiously, wearing her pencils to stubs. If there was one thing his flirtation with the Jacobites, begun so innocently, had taught him, it was that human beings had callings. His, amazingly, was to this: tents crawled from at daybreak, mingled oatmeal and water and blood, his pistols and broadsword—Michel Faurer's broadsword. And hers, he'd believed, had been to chronicle it all.

Well, he ought to have known better, after she'd come *that* close to wedding Dreary Harry. It was different for daughters, no doubt. Sons were expected to rebel. But girls—women—bore the guilt and the burden of dutifulness. Poor soul, he thought wistfully, poor Callie, condemned to such a small sort of life.

He'd hoped, after it began with Mick, that she'd find the strength to reject all the stultifying expectations. It had demanded great courage for her to take a lover, even one so acceptable to their father as Mick. And the way she had *shone* during those weeks at Langlannoch! He'd always thought her beautiful, of course, but she had been transcendent then, incandescent, radiant. It hurt his heart to remember her happiness, the way she'd glowed from the heart out, like a curtained candle, like the moon in clouds.

But she'd picked the wrong man. God, so had Maggie—pinned her dreams to a grandson who ran from this conflict like a frightened hare. Callie's disappointment in Mick would no doubt be assuaged by the comforts of whatever fellow she next turned to. But Maggie's wretched, dashed expectations would endure for all time.

"Need a hand wi' that, then?"

Zeus started, realizing he'd been standing outside the tent-flap, half naked, for some minutes now. Angus MacPherson grinned, striding up to him, taking the cloth in his hammy fists. "Gaiin' clammy, bae ye, at the prospect o' Cope 'n his thousands?"

Zeus shook his head, letting the Scotsman wrap him. "Just . . . thinking."

Angus clucked his tongue. "There bae a fair rue for a soldier, havin' thoughts in his head. As I tell my boys, ye maun ne'er gae thinkin'! Nae regrets, nae contemplation. The Scot wha' e'er starts in thinkin' bae a dead man, sure."

"I am only half Scottish."

Angus paused with the plaid bunched over Zeus's shoulder. "Nae, lad. Ye bae Scots, through 'n through. Strong blude we hae; a bit o' muddlin' cannae staunch it." He raised his red head. "Hark, there. D'ye hear the pipers? Bae it nae the sweetest sound ye e'er hae known?"

And sure enough, inside the wool cocoon, Zeus's heart was racing. "The sweetest sound," he agreed, and turned his back on Edinburgh, on his sister, on the still-empty lecture halls of the university.

The women bade their men farewell in the half-light. These strong Scottish women—no one dared tell them their place in life; they seized it, feet solidly set, and dug in to stay. Strange that the lack of civilization should mean for them increased freedom. Well, who defined civilization, anyway? How long had it been since he had read a book, and yet when had he ever felt so wise? You could read about the fall of Troy from now till doomsday, but if you'd never stood outside the enemy's walls with your weapon drawn, how would you understand?

Lily-handed Helen. The face that launched a thousand ships. One of Angus's cousins, a Douglas, had a daughter named Helen. She had hair like fire. She'd brought him ale once when he'd supped with her father. Her hands had been cool and white. She was young yet—no more, he guessed, than fifteen. That was all right, though; the war was still a long way from over. By the time it was—

Angus poked him, nearly topping him over. "Thinkin' again?" he demanded with a scowl.

"Your cousin Cormac's girl Helen—is she promised to anyone, Angus?"

The scowl faded to a wide, slow smile. "I'll make some inquiries. Now gae hie yerself off to yer regiment."

Zeus would march with the Duke of Perth's men. He searched the park for his commander's pennant, saw it fluttering atop Dunsapie Hill. He started toward it, enjoying the rub of the plaid as he walked, the flap of his kilt, the swing of his powder-horn and the heft of his musket. Mighty Zeus, off to war. He hummed the call of the pipes.

"Zeus!" Someone was calling him above the clatter of men

girding for warfare. "Zeus!" He turned and saw her running toward him up the hill, burdened by a bulging pack.

"Callie?"

She dropped the pack and kept on coming, faster. "Afraid— that I would miss you," she gasped out, stopping then, a little distance away.

Why that expression on her face? "Has something happened to Father?"

"Something has happened to me." She was still catching her breath. "Oh, Zeus. Why didn't you tell me about her— about Laurie?"

So the old man had confessed. How? Why? "It wasn't my place."

"Perhaps not—but it would have lent some perspective." She looked him up and down, in his plaids and bonnet. Then she started to laugh. "No wonder she used to sing of Tam O'Shanter, snatched away by fairies. You're the changeling child, all right, come home again."

"And . . . you?"

She glanced back at her pack. "I guess I'm home as well."

"Callie. I'm so glad."

The tattoo of the drums was summoning him. "You have got to go," she told him, nodding toward the ranks of his comrades.

"I want to hear about it—"

"There will be time later." Maybe so, maybe not. She was running along beside him as he climbed the hill. "I'll try to catch a ride in a provisions wagon to the battlefield."

"What's in your pack there?"

"Sketchbooks. I knew I'd never find a shop open, so I brought my old ones. As many as would fit. I'll just rub off the pictures in them as I go along."

Rome, Athens, Florence, Venice, Byzantium. Man's history, wiped out as they marched toward London. Zeus grinned, enjoying the image. And she, of course, knew what he was grinning about, and smiled too.

They'd reached the regiment. The men were already moving. Zeus fell into place, into step, to muttered jests and jeers:

"Wha' the hell kept ye, then, mate?" "Thinkin' better of it, war ye?"

"Soldiers never think," he told them archly.

"Ach, listen t' the Oxford boy!"

His sister couldn't run any farther. He glanced back and saw her waving, calling: "Take care, Zeus!"

"You do, too!"

Sun broke through clouds all along the road toward Dunbar, making shifting shafts of light and shadow on the long ranks of warriors. Cameron's piper was keening *"Coghiegh nha-Shie"*—"War of Peace." The breeze was stiff, off the Firth of Forth; it whipped the men's kilts at their knees. Zeus looked back one last time, his heart full to bursting. She was standing all alone at the berm, smiling after him.

Charles Edward's army sighted the enemy on the twentieth of September. Cope had dug in just north of the village of Tranent, facing south, protected by a long stretch of marsh and ditch before him, the town of Preston and the Forth behind him, and the walled enclosure of Seton House on his left flank. The Jacobite commanders sent down men to test the marsh. Impassable, they reported. Charles Edward weighed his options. There was high ground in the narrow pass between Seton House and Cope's forces; they could swing wide by night, 'round the marsh, to claim it.

Cameron of Lochiel pointed out, justly, that such a move left Cope an open road back to Edinburgh if he chose to decline battle. Charles Edward's blue eyes glinted. "He missed us in the north," he noted. "No English officer hoping to keep his command would dare let us escape again."

The Jacobites kept marching. The night was moonless. As the sun rose over Preston, Cope's troops were greeted by the sight and sound of 1,400 Highlanders swooping down on them at full charge. Cope's artillerymen got off a single round before disintegrating. Cope ordered Gordon's elite dragoons to flank the Highland columns to his left. The Highlanders were still screaming. The dragoons ran up on their own artillery guard in full flight. Cope's bewildered infantry managed one disjointed volley. The Highlanders kept coming.

The entire Hanoverian army turned and ran.

That was Prestonpans. It was over in minutes—so quickly, in fact, that the Highland reserve never caught up to the battle. They made up for the lack in the pursuit which followed, hounding Cope's soldiers all along the strand. Hundreds of the young, green Hanoverians died; eighty officers and a thousand foot-men were captured. Charles Edward's casualties: less than fifty in all.

Callie, rumbling at the rear of the Jacobite wagon-train, missed the fighting, but was in time to record the aftermath of victory. It had a different quality from the heady merrymaking that had followed Edinburgh and Perth and Stirling; it was at once more grim and somehow more sacred, as though every man present knew a force beyond that of arms had been at work here. She got close enough to Charles Edward to sketch him as he viewed the prisoners.

Zeus chuckled when he saw the picture. "Lord, Cal. Why not just paint a bloody halo on his head?"

"What are you talking about?"

"You've made him look just like Jesus!"

"No one knows what Jesus looked like," she said in derision, snatching back the portrait.

But the solemn figure in the sketch did have a sort of holiness to it.

37.

England again—a coal-scarred English city rising in the distance. Callie, keeping her wrists loose to counteract the jolting of the wagon, made a quick, deft outline of its smokestacks and spires. "Wha' town bae this, then?" asked Molly, who sat squashed against her with Libby dozing on her shoulder. Molly expected Callie to recognize every landmark they'd passed since coming over the border just south of Kelso; after all, Callie was English, wasn't she?

"Lord, I don't know." Callie tried to picture a map of her native land. "Leeds? Sheffield?"

"Manchester," the wagon-drover threw back at them above the clatter of hooves. "My sister's brother came here t' work at the cotton mills. We visited 'em once."

"Manchester!" Callie doubted it; that was all the way on the west coast of England. Why would Charles Edward be marching south by such a roundabout route?

Molly noted her perplexed expression. "Wha' bae it, dearie?"

"Nothing. Nothing at all."

But Molly was married to a MacPherson. She gazed up at the sky. "I see by the sun these two days past we hae been marchin' sou'westward. I should think we wuld hae turned east, toward London, by now.''

"I'm sure the prince knows what he's doing," Callie assured her. "After all, it's been going swimmingly so far." And it was. The border stronghold of Carlisle had capitulated to the Jacobites after a mere week's siege; since the victory at Prestonpans two months past, Charles Edward's army had encountered little in the way of organized resistance.

Molly brushed a few flakes of snow from the baby's cheeks. "I reckon sae. . . ." She did not sound convinced.

"What is it? What do you know?" Molly, tied to half the commanders in the camp, it seemed, by blood or marriage, found out things sometimes that Callie had no way of learning.

Molly hesitated, looking to see if anyone else in the wagon was listening, then leaned her blond head close. "Some o' the Highlanders bae gettin' restless," she whispered. "A whole batch o' MacDonalds—nae the Clanranald men, but the Glengarry—hae already gone home."

"No!" Callie could not believe it. The wild, fierce Highlanders, who'd won Prestonpans with their lungs as much as with their guns, deserting?

Molly shrugged, shifting her sleeping daughter. "Ye maun ken—they bae a long way fro' home. 'N some o' the clans—well, I will nae say they bae undisciplined, but I will say this: they bae unaccustomed to a campaign such as this, days spent marchin' 'n marchin', 'n nae plunderin' by the prince's orders, since he will nae hae the populace turned against him. There bae clans see little purpose in fightin' if they cannae take booty."

The wet snow sent a chill down Callie's back. "But what about restoring the Stuarts to the throne?"

Molly's blue eyes were shrewd. "Ye hae seen the Highlands, luv, 'n the way folk live there. Truth to tell, who wears the crown in Windsor Castle cannae make mickle difference to 'em. They march for pride, 'n for the pleasure o' warrin'. Take that fro' 'em, 'n who can ken how long they'll stay?"

Charles Edward's reception by the residents of Manchester— the citizens threw open the gates, and thronged the streets to cheer him—pushed this disconcerting conversation from

Callie's mind. She remembered it a few days later, however, when the Jacobite forces had finally turned eastward on their march. The snow-speckled fields of Derbyshire evoked the landscape around Oxford; for the first time, she thought with a hint of nostalgia about the years she'd spent there. "Do you think we'll see Oxford again?" she asked her brother as he warmed water for tea in the early winter dusk.

"I very much doubt it." His voice was abrupt.

Callie stared at his straight back in the twilight. "Is something amiss?"

"There's something very amiss." He paused, ducking the tea-ball into the pot. "The Highlanders are deserting."

"Molly mentioned that to me. But look at all those Manchester men who came out to join us!"

"One hundred forty-three," Zeus said succinctly. "And not a one among them seasoned as a soldier. Unemployed riffraff, that's what they are. The scum of the city. One of them admitted to the duke that they were fully prepared to turn out for whichever army got to Manchester first."

Callie took the hot tin cup she was handed. "Well, you were not a seasoned soldier, either, when you started this campaign."

"No. But I believed in the cause, at least." He sighed, blowing on his tea to cool it. "It's the same with the Highlanders, dammit. There just isn't enough zeal anymore to hold them."

Callie looked out over the camp, which still seemed reassuringly huge. "Come now, Zeus. How many really have left?"

"Stuart reckons a thousand." She gasped, and nearly spilled her tea. A thousand—out of six thousand they'd set forth with from Edinburgh? A sixth of the troops?

"Good Lord, Zeus. I hadn't any idea."

"And the further we get from their homes, the more will be going."

"What are we to do?"

That made him smile. It still amused him, she knew, to hear her side with the rebels. "I suppose Charles Edward has two choices. He can press on for London, losing men like flies all along the way . . ."

"Or?" Callie asked, when he did not finish.

"Or he can turn back. Retreat."

"Retreat?" Callie thought with despair of all the long days of marching. "You mean . . . go back to Scotland?"

"He may have to. You cannot fight a war without soldiers. And there's been some disconcerting news. The Duke of Cumberland's been brought back from the Continent."

William Augustus, the Duke of Cumberland—the second son of George of England. He was only twenty-four, but he'd been soldiering since the age of thirteen, and had gained for himself a redoubtable reputation in campaigns in Germany and Flanders. "The martial boy," the English called him, with great pride. Back in Edinburgh, Zeus had told her, the gazettes had been clamoring for months for Cumberland's appointment to quell the Jacobite rebels. He was the one hero whom everyone in England seemed to feel could do the job.

"Are you afraid of him?" she asked curiously.

"A jolly sight more than I ever was of Cope. That makes two English armies now that will be hounding us, his and General Wade's."

"How far are we from London?"

"From Derby, it's a ten-day march."

Ten days. Christ, they were so close, had come so far. Callie ventured one last question. "What do you think Charles Edward will do?"

The tea was cool by now. Zeus sipped his morosely. "I don't know. I'm not even certain, if he asked my advice, what I'd propose to him."

The next morning, in the wagon, Callie paged backward through her sketchbooks. There had been a change, she saw now, in the faces she'd drawn over the past week, subtle but distinct: the fire had gone out of them. Whether it was the vanishing Highlanders, the strain of this mid-winter march, or just the distance from Scotland, from home, the soldiers looked weary, and the women and children who remained with them anxious and bleak.

Ten days' march to London. What would Charles Edward choose?

He reached Derby, and paused there for the space of two days.

His approach was scaring London senseless. Already there had been a vast commercial panic in the City—runs on banks, bottoms dropping out of markets, shipping and trading disrupted entirely. Lord George Murray, the most seasoned of Charles Edward's commanders, noted that the prince had managed to wreak havoc on the English capital from a distance; why risk moving closer, especially since Cumberland and his army were at Stafford, less than thirty miles off? Callie sat and sketched the faces of the Jacobite leaders while they tallied the size of the enemy troops they were likely to encounter. Between Cumberland, Wade, and the forces Londoners would muster, they reckoned thirty thousand.

On the sixth of December, looking pale and grim, Charles Edward gave the order to turn back.

Knowing they were headed home at last spurred his army onward. Despite high-drifting snow, by mid-December they had covered more than a hundred miles, and were nearing Penrith, only a day's march from the safety of Carlisle. It was in the tiny village of Clifton, just south of Penrith, that the Duke of Cumberland caught up to them.

The first attacks were by mounted dragoons, who swooped down on the Highland cavalry in the lanes outside the village. While the horse-soldiers skirmished, Cumberland sent three regiments marching across Clifton Moor to attack the Jacobite rearguard. It was dusk; Callie and Molly, just ahead of the rearguard in the wagons, saw the advance and heard blasting musket-fire. "Angus bae back there," Molly whispered as they huddled low together, arms around Libby and the boys. After the initial gunshots came the clash of hand-to-hand fighting—and the Highlanders' blood-curdling screaming. Then, gradually, the sounds grew more distant.

"Which way are they going?" Callie demanded, raising her head to scan the darkness.

"Back across the moor," Molly declared with satisfaction. "Beat them off, we hae." Then she screamed as a hand groped toward her over the side of the wagon.

"Molly, luv." Her husband's voice, weak and strained. "Molly. I bae hit."

"Oh, Jesus 'n Mary." Molly thrust Libby at Callie and leaped from the wagon. "Where, Angus? Where?"

"My leg. My left leg."

"Daddy, bae ye hurt?" Little Angus demanded, leaning forward to see him. Libby had started crying. Callie tried to soothe her, hugging her close, and above her wails heard Molly's intake of breath:

"God in heaven, Angus. How got ye here on this?"

"How d'ye think? I crawled."

"I need light. Drover, gi' the lantern here."

"I dare nae light it, mum, nae wi' the enemy sae close!"

"Damn yer black hide, gi' me the lantern!" He hesitated, then swung it toward her. Callie heard her rustle in her skirts for her flint. "Callie. Keep the bairns back."

"Angus. Robbie. Come over here, pets, to the other side. Your mummy needs to look after Daddy." She could grasp Robbie by the collar, but with the burden of the baby, little Angus was beyond her reach. The scratch of flint, the sizzle of the wick, and then a soft glow of flame that illuminated Molly's pale face, and that of her son, still hanging over the edge of the wagon—

"Daddy, where bae yer foot? Daddy, yer foot bae gone!"

"Well," Molly said with grim humor, coming out of her tent to where Callie was wringing bloodied rags in water, "he *will* live a gude long time now, wi' his soldierin' done for this campaign."

Callie rubbed tear-streaked cheeks on her sleeve. She'd never in her life seen anything like that raw stump, so fresh and new and red. "Molly, I'm so very sorry." Inadequate words, to the wife of valiant, crippled Angus.

She just shrugged, huddled in her shawl. "It could hae been his heart . . . or his head."

"What will you do now?"

"Ride as close to home as we may. Keep an eye out for the gangrene."

Callie tried to imagine how she'd have felt if it had been Zeus who'd come crawling through the dark to that wagon, with his foot blown off. Thank God he'd been far to the front, with the Duke of Perth's troops. But oh, poor Molly! "If there's anything I can do, anything at all—"

The Scotswoman touched her shoulder, comforting *her,* Callie realized with wonder. "Keep doin' wha' ye bae doin', Callie luv. Make yer pictures, for the whole world t' see." Inside the tent, Libby was whimpering. "Damn. I thought I had her down." Then the small, pitiful sounds broke off. "P'raps I hae."

"You must rest, too."

Molly paced a little, back and forth on the snow-covered ground. "I dinna feel like restin'. I feel . . . ach, I dinna ken, exactly. All at odds wi' myself. Ye start a thing, 'n it seems sae grand at the startin'. Then it winds on 'n on, 'n ye weary o' it, yet ye maun keep gaein', for if ye dinna, where war the sense o' startin' it at all?" It was, Callie thought, a fair summation of Charles Edward's campaign.

She remembered her words to her father on the night she'd left Edinburgh. "Perhaps the sense is . . . in the doing," she told Molly softly. "Not in the winning, but in trying. In proving . . . that it was worth being tried."

Molly shrugged again. "That wuld seem t' bae the way o' the Scots." Then, finally, she seemed to crumple, and started crying. Callie put her arms around her and held her tight as she keened and mourned on the cold, wind-swept field.

38.

Angus's foot was not given in vain. The Jacobite resistance at Clifton proved too much for Cumberland and his men. Exhausted by their forced marches, the weather, the prospect of more wretched, hilly terrain up ahead, they halted their pursuit. Charles Edward and his tattered invasion force limped back across the Scottish border on the twentieth of December, untroubled by the enemy. Then they marched on to Perth, to renew from there the fledgling sieges the prince had begun on the castles at Stirling and Edinburgh.

Molly and her family left the army in Lanarkshire. Angus had ridden north in the back of the wagon, wrestling with his boys, talking quietly with Libby. The jolting ride must have been agony, but Callie never once heard him complain. Molly declared herself satisfied with his progress. There was no sign of infection; the stump healed up cleanly. As a parting gift, Callie gave her friend a sketch she'd made of her husband with the baby sleeping on his chest.

"I'll miss you," she told Molly, tears starting.

"Come 'n see us. We will nae bae gaein' anywhere, nae for a few months at least. Unless, o' course, ye bae headin' back to England." Her blue gaze was sly.

"Live amongst the enemy?" Molly said in mock horror. "How could I ever again?"

Angus rumbled a laugh. He was standing, though on crutches. "Ye see, Molly, luv? We hae made a conquest after all, o' Callie 'n her brother." He and Zeus embraced. It was a little awkward on Zeus's part, but not at all on Angus's.

"The whole army will miss you," Zeus told his comrade-in-arms.

"If ye hole up in Perth till springtime, I may yet join ye there. Granted, the MacPhersons ne'er hae been known for their horsemanship. Still, I might learn t' bae a fair cavalry-man."

"By springtime, I'll bae ready t' fight," little Angus said stoutly. "Will I nae, Daddy?"

Callie met Molly's gaze above the children's red heads. Molly's chin was held high. Her husband ruffled his son's curls. "This springtime," he said easily, "or the next, or the next."

"There's the sort of family," Zeus murmured, his voice wistful as he watched them set off across the barren Lanarkshire hills, "that I wish ours could be."

Callie dried her tears, aware of a sudden emptiness inside her. Lord, she *would* miss Molly and the children, and brave, strong Angus. "Start a new one of your own," she suggested. "How is Helen Douglas?"

Her brother flashed a grin. "Still too young to wed, her father tells me. What about you? Any soldiers caught your eye? Cluny MacPherson said Sunday last that he admires your art."

"Cluny MacPherson wouldn't know a Michelangelo from a hacksaw."

"That's the trouble, Cal. You intimidate them, these poor Scots. Never fear, though. There are supposed to be reinforcements at Perth. A thousand Irishmen. They're reputed as artistic."

"As madmen, you mean. No, Zeus. I fear you were right in what you said last year at Edinburgh. I am doomed to be an old maid, and you to support me."

"At least I know a trade now." He patted his pistols and the jeweled hilt of Michel Faurer's sword. "We shall never want—so long as Scotland stays at war."

There were reinforcements at Perth—the promised Irishmen, fresh from battle on the Continent, and, surprisingly, a few clan regiments, late-comers newly raised under the flag of Lord Strathallan. The Jacobites dug in for a Christmas of sorts, spirits replenished. The mighty Duke of Cumberland had been recalled to London, to supervise the capital's defense in case of French invasion. General Wade had been relieved of his command of the Hanoverian troops in Scotland, replaced by Lieutenant-General Henry Hawley. Common gossip held that Hawley was George of England's bastard son, and that this connection was the sole reason for his preference. Whether that was true or not, the Scots would far rather face him in battle than Cumberland.

Perth was only some forty miles north of Edinburgh. "Would you like to go home to visit Father," Zeus inquired of Callie, "for the holidays? I could arrange an escort." He'd been made a lieutenant himself, more, he jested, from sheer longevity than from worth.

That dark, gray house; Professor Wingate's new crop of students; the vaunted teaching assistant; Elspeth running the place, and her father's list of sketches to be made, by now no doubt grown long . . . "Not for the crown of Britain," Callie told him, quite seriously.

So she was at Perth on Christmas Eve, quartered in a lodging-house with a dozen soldiers, when Zeus burst into her room. "Cal. Come quickly."

"What for?" she demanded, irritated at the interruption. She'd just bathed, and was combing out her hair.

"Put on your cloak and come see."

"I'll catch a bloody chill!" But he was thrusting the cloak at her, wrapping it 'round her shoulders. "Zeus! I've got a cup of decent Rhenish poured. It is snowing outside. There's a fire in the hearth, and my hair is damp. Nothing outside the sight of Hawley surrendering could drag me away."

"This is better than Hawley surrendering," he promised, with his green eyes aglow.

"Just tell me what it is."

But he would not stop pulling. Finally, in frustration, she threw her comb aside and followed. He cajoled her down the stairs and out the door, across the square toward the inn where

Charles Edward was headquartered. The night was bitter cold. There were pipes on the air.

"So," she said, coming to a stop at the sight of soldiers lining the street. "More clan regiments. Reinforcements." But Zeus was grasping her hand, yanking her through the lines of men. The faces they turned toward her were oddly familiar. At the sight of one, a handsome young fellow with a claymore stuck in his belt that was fastened with a thistle buckle, a name rose to her lips: "Walt . . . Walter Coady."

He tipped his bonnet to her, grinning. "At long last, mum."

Zeus tugged her over the threshold of the inn just in time to see their leader, a tall man with a black queue, bend to lay a sword at Charles Edward's feet.

"Michel Douglas Harding, laird of Langlannoch," the tall man rumbled, straightening slowly to his full height, "come to fight for the cause, milord."

He looked dreadful, Callie thought, sitting nervously across the room from him. He looked weary and haggard, and he had a cold that made his eyes blear and turned his nose red. And yet, in spite of that, he looked splendid in his kilt and plaid and bonnet. The pattern of the cloth was one she'd seen often at Langlannoch, on chair covers and such—bands of black and gold against a forest-green ground. She'd never realized it was his family's plaid.

He was drinking Rhenish, and eating stewed rabbit and bread with the rote methodicalness she'd marked in him so often at table. Zeus was doing the talking, recounting for him breathlessly all that had happened in the campaign so far. He was listening, and asking an occasional question that revealed he already knew a great deal about Charles Edward's aborted English invasion. He scarcely seemed aware of her presence. She began to wonder what she was doing there.

Zeus had made the invitation. "Callie's got a room to herself," he'd told Mick once the formalities of his regiment's registration were accomplished. "We can talk there. Eat, too. You look like you're half-starved."

"We made the march from Ayr in three days."

Zeus had whistled. "Christ! You must have been flying. Come along, then. The food is decent, too."

And here they were, the three of them, in front of the fire. When they'd entered, Callie had to fight back an instinctive impulse to straighten up the place—hide her hanging laundry, dispose of the bath and its water, make up the bed she'd spent much of the past few days in. Merely having a bed again was such a luxury. But so what if the place was a mess? Let him see how she'd been living while he'd been drenched in Mediterranean sunsets. And this shabby house was one hell of a lot better than life on the march had been.

Zeus seemed more than prepared to let bygones be bygones. But Callie found she was furious with this man, so angry that she could feel herself shake. How dare he waltz in now with his troops, now that the hard work was finished, now that it seemed in all likelihood far too late for them to make any difference? Where had he been when they'd trudged down to Kelso, when Angus lost his foot at Clifton, when they'd nearly been cornered at Derby? Back then, another two hundred soldiers could have tipped the balance, convinced the prince to go on to London. Where was the bloody sense in turning out for an already-lost cause?

Zeus had brought his tale 'round to their retreat upon Perth. He paused for breath and to gulp down wine. "But you haven't said a word about where you've been all this time, Mick. How was Frère Descoux to work for? What is new in Greece?"

"We never made it to Greece. All the ships in France were put on call in case of an invasion of England. I spent the past six months stuck in Paris, at the university."

Callie couldn't help herself. "I trust it was cozy."

He raised his heavy head to her at last. "I imagine it was paradise, compared to what you've been through."

That took the wind out of her sails. He turned back to Zeus. "I couldn't even get home again from France. Had to ship aboard a freighter to Ireland, and from there I hired a sloop to come across the North Sea. Had a hell of a time convincing a fisherman there would be jewels to pay him at the end of the trip."

Lady Maggie's jewels. Zeus read Callie's thoughts. "And how is Grandmère? Delighted beyond words, I imagine."

"She has got what she wanted."

"So she has." Zeus went to pour more wine. The bottle was empty. "Damn. I'll go and fetch another."

"No!" Callie cried, rising to her feet. "I'll do it!" She did not for the world want to be left alone with Mick Harding.

But Mick had pushed himself from his chair. "Please. Allow me."

The door had no sooner closed behind him than Zeus turned on her, outraged. "What is the matter with you? You might at least act glad to see him!"

"Why the devil should I?"

"Because—because he's here! He's seen the light at last."

"Johnny-come-lately," Callie muttered bitterly.

"But it's a bloody miracle that he has come at all! And called out all those men—"

"Who'd have gladly come six months ago, if he had bade them."

"Well, he bade them now! I swear, I don't understand what you have to be cross with him about!"

"You weren't there!" she shot at him, her fists clenched. "You did not hear me ask him—hear me *beg* him—to go after you! You don't know how I pleaded, how I lowered myself—" She broke off, because her brother was nodding his blond head thoughtfully.

"I see. You wanted it to be for you. You resent that he found other reasons—"

"I don't give a damn about his bloody reasons!"

"Then why are you angry?"

"You stupid fool, because it's too late now! Because the war is lost!"

He stared at her. "If you believe that, why are you still here?"

"I gave my word to Charles Edward. I'll see it through to the finish."

"But this *is* the finish. You just said so. The war is lost."

"You know what I mean." She was exasperated. "I'll stick it out until he surrenders. It won't be very long now."

Her brother got up, strode to the door, and flung it open. ''I think it would be better if you went now. And I'm sure the prince would agree. There are nay-sayers enough on the English side.''

''Zeus, do keep your voice down.''

''Why should I? Are you afraid somebody else might learn you've written off the cause? You needn't worry, you know. Everyone's noticed already. Ever since Manchester, the pictures you've drawn have shown just what you're saying—that you've given up, that the fight is done.''

''I draw what I see,'' Callie snapped in fury.

''No. You're an artist, Cal. You draw what you feel. And you've felt this campaign was hopeless for a long time now.''

Despite her wrath, she paused. He wasn't right about that. He couldn't be. ''If that were so, why wouldn't the pictures have changed after Clifton? We won at Clifton.''

''And your best friend's husband had his foot blown off. That was when your work *truly* turned bleak.''

She flopped onto her chair. ''Oh, what difference does it make? They're *my* sketches. *My* business. Nobody else sees them.''

Mick appeared in the doorway, a pitcher in his hands. ''You are quite wrong there.''

Zeus darted toward him, with an expression on his face that Callie could have sworn was alarm. ''What's that in the pitcher, then, Mick?''

''Cider. The troops have sucked the cellar dry.''

''Oh, well, I like cider just fine—so long as it's good and strong.'' He poured a cup. His hand was trembling as he gulped the drink down. ''And, praise God, this is! Here, Callie, let me fill you up. I think you'll like this. Reminds me a bit of the stuff we used to have at Oxford. In touch with anyone from the old gang at Oxford, are you, Mick? I heard Tom Gregory was in France. Perhaps you might have seen him?''

Callie was staring at Mick, who looked disconcerted. ''What do you mean, I am wrong?''

''Come sit back down, Mick,'' her brother said hurriedly, ''and tell us all about Frère Descoux.''

''*What do you mean, I am wrong?*''

Mick's blue eyes, seared with disbelief, searched Zeus's anxious face. "You mean—she doesn't know?"

"Know *what?*" Callie screeched, with a rising sense of betrayal.

"Oh, Zeus." Mick's voice was leaden. "That really is unfair. I can't believe you haven't told her. What were you afraid of?"

Zeus seemed to hesitate, on the edge of a precipice. But his sister's bewildered outrage tipped him over. "After Oxford, after that, you ask what I was afraid of? What the hell do you *think* I was afraid of? That she wouldn't agree! That she'd start pondering whether it was proper—whether Father would think it proper. That knowing would affect the sketches. That the notion of all Europe looking over her shoulder would freeze her hands up again, just the way the incident at Oxford did!"

Mick nodded his head in slow acknowledgement. "Perhaps so. But then . . . why did you invite me back to your rooms?"

"Because I feared it would seem odd if I didn't." Zeus took a deep breath. "Because I hoped the two of you would send me off and tumble into bed. I thought I'd have the chance to talk to you privately tomorrow."

Callie could not catch her own breath; her heart was pounding so quickly that she feared its bursting. *All Europe?* "Zeus!" The name came out desperate. "Zeus, what are you talking about?"

He would not meet her eyes. "Oh, Callie. Oh, damn. Oh, dammit all to hell."

So it was Mick, finally, who told her. "Your sketches have been reproduced in all the gazettes on the Continent, Callie. France, Italy, Germany, the Netherlands. They've all watched this war through your eyes."

"No," she whispered. "No!" And then she lunged for her brother, went straight for his head, pummeling him the way she had when they were children. "God damn you, no! How bloody *dare* you! How dare you pull such a trick on me?"

Mick had to pull her off him forcibly. The touch of his hands on her arms, her shoulders, made her go rigid for a moment. Then, "Let go of me," she spat, clawing at him.

"Calm down, Callie. Callie! What's done is done. There's no help for it now."

"Oh yes there is! I can strip the flesh from his face!"

"I was only thinking of you!" Zeus protested, ducking, moving behind his chair.

"You rotten liar, you were thinking of yourself! You and Charles Edward—you *used* me!"

"And so what if we did? You are famous, Cal! Ask him!" He pointed to Mick. "No matter what happens in Scotland, to Charles Edward, you will always be famous! It's immortality, just as you've longed for. Only not in some little gallery in Florence—" How the devil had he known about that? Of course. Charles Edward. "But everywhere, every place where people care about freedom and justice and what is right." And then his grand pose deflated. "I *should* have told you, Cal. I wanted to tell you. But I was too afraid. I didn't want you to stop drawing again."

Her muscles went slack. Mick's grip on her loosened. "Because you needed me," she ground out.

"Because I love you. Because I am proud of you—proud of your talent and your courage. Because you're all I have and I need you—" He swallowed a sob. "I need you to be strong."

His mournful little-boy look wasn't enough to win her over, not after this deception. "Get out," she spat. "Get out of here. Out of my sight."

"Callie, please. I—"

"No more!" She'd raised her fist to him. "I don't want to hear any more! You say I'm all you have. Well, you were all that I had. Now I haven't even that. I cannot bear to look at you."

He hesitated for a moment, searching her gold-green eyes. But what he saw wasn't encouraging. "I really am sorry, Cal," he whispered. Then, craven, he slinked out the door.

Callie drank her cider, quickly. It *was* strong. Mick's voice broke into her choler. "You went a bit hard on him, don't you think?"

"You can bloody well shut up. And you can get out, too."

He started for the door, realized he'd left the pitcher of cider, and came back for it. "He's right about your being famous, you know. You were a celebrity at the University of Paris. The students toasted you in the inns. 'Brave Callie Wingate,' they called you. Your name was on everyone's tongue.''

''And did you boast of where your tongue had been on me?''

Despite the wrath in her voice, he met her gold gaze evenly. ''No. I . . . worried for you. I even found myself praying.'' The notion clearly still amazed him. ''Praying. Me. After all these years.''

''I'm honored to have been the means to your reconversion.'' The sarcasm dripped from her tongue like acid.

''Drop the charade, Mick. For all I know, the two of you arranged it this way.''

He blinked, dumbfounded. ''Arranged it? How?''

''You know! Zeus disappearing while you—while you diddled with me in the gardens, and then your refusing to go after him, goading me into going—so that he could make me his tool. His propaganda artist—''

Now he looked merely angry. ''That's beneath you, even to suggest it. I refused to go because you'd lied to me, kept secrets from me. Betrayed me.'' He glanced at Zeus's empty cup. ''Perhaps now you know what I felt.''

''I've never known what you felt!'' she cried at him. ''I've known what you thought, what you believed, what you'd read, what you'd learned. But never what you felt. Because *you* never told me! Because you kept all that closed up inside you, locked without a key. So don't you dare chastise me now for not understanding.''

His gaze, midnight blue in the candlelight, dropped to the floor. ''I suppose I deserve that. No. I know that I do. Very well. Shall I tell you now how I felt about you?''

Beyond the closed door came the swearing of soldiers barging up the hall to their beds, bumping into walls, tripping over the floorboards. Callie smiled a little at the sounds, welcome and familiar. ''You needn't bother. It is too late.''

''I don't care. I'll say it anyway.'' His eyes rose to meet hers. ''I was terrified of you. Even when I held you in my arms, kissed you, made love to you, you terrified me. You were like nothing I had ever encountered before. I'd never wanted anything the way I wanted you. I wanted to—to subsume you, swallow you whole, hold you within me forever. And wanted just as much—or maybe even more—to drive you away.'' He shrugged his plaid-wound shoulders. ''Perhaps you can't know. But after my . . . after my mother died, it was as though the world went black. I thought she loved me. I *knew* that she loved me. But I wasn't enough. Or else—she'd never loved me as I trusted she did. You want to know what I felt?'' His knuckles on the handle of the pitcher were white. ''I hated her. For killing herself. For abandoning me as she did. For not loving me the way I loved her. And I knew that in the end, hatred was all love led to.''

''You were only a child,'' Callie said scathingly.

''Aye—a bereft, bewildered child, left to muddle it all out with a father who'd turned his dead wife into Christ, and a grandmother mired in the ghosts of the past. I read my books, and I went to my lessons, and I did lock my heart away, God damn it. Who the hell wouldn't? At least it kept me safe. Or so I thought, until I walked into your father's house at Oxford, with its cluttered tables and walls and its mishmash of artifacts and its smell of varnish and supper—all history, you see, but all *made* history, discovered history, dug-up pasts of other people's lives instead of the overwhelming burden of one's own ancestors. I thought, this is a home. I want to live like this, someday.'' He drew a breath, glanced at the pitcher, poured his cup full and drank. ''Then Zeus. I didn't even remember Zeus from Langlannoch; I'd never seen him. I'd only had eyes for you. You'd been like the wild, bright birds the Atlantic wind sometimes blew into Grandmère's garden—accidents of nature, never to be repeated. And now here you were, in this unfamiliar place that felt like home.''

Callie felt the need to move. She stood up, tested the drawers she'd washed and strung on a line across the fireplace. They were dry. She began to take them down and fold them, with her back to him. He went on talking, as though the flow of words, now they'd started, could not be staunched.

''And then later, at Langlannoch again, when you were mine. . . .'' That word still held a world of wonder. ''God, Callie. What can I say? That I loved you? You must know that I did.''

Her own voice, surprisingly, was calm. "It would not have hurt to be told."

"I came that close to saying it a thousand times. But I felt . . . you know how the Hebrews would not speak the name of God, had code words for it instead, lest saying it would some-how make Him less holy? That was what the word 'love' had become for me." He paused. "I'm sorry. I did love you."

Callie made neat creases in a petticoat with the side of her hand. "Then why wouldn't you go after Zeus when I asked you to?"

"Because I thought—I felt—love shouldn't make such demands. Demands against clear reason. Against all hope, all odds. Dammit, it was just the sort of thing Grandmère was always nattering at me to do! 'Pick up the sword, Michel! Reclaim the family glory!' I'm not that sort of man! I'm not a warrior. I'm not a hero. I'm the sort of fellow who likes sitting by myself in a room, reading Virgil." He stopped, reconsidered. "Or sitting in a room with you, doing anything at all."

"Yet you are here at Perth now."

"For one reason only. Do you want to know what it is?"

She was not at all sure that she did, and so she said nothing. But she heard his footsteps as he moved closer behind her. She hurried to put the piled laundry atop the dresser, to put distance between them. Then she turned back to him. Though the room was cold, sweat had sprung up on his brow. He was holding his regimental bonnet in his hands; those strong, blunt-fingered hands.

"I haunted the coffeehouses in Paris, Callie, picking up gazettes, searching for your drawings. I went to all the foreign quarters, to the places where the students from Italy and Germany drank, so I could see their newspapers, too. It was like holding a little piece of you from far away, to see those sketches and your signature. I felt awed. And ashamed. The picture you made after Prestonpans, of the Scottish dead—I cried when I saw that. Your art did for me what two decades of Grandmère's bullying could not do. I saw . . . my history. My family's history. I saw destiny."

"Zeus had no right to deceive me about those sketches," Callie said angrily. "To use my art that way—"

"But, Callie, all art is used! What was Michelangelo doing when he painted the Sistine Chapel? Seeking to convince the masses of his vision of God. What are the windows at the cathedral at Rouens meant to do, or the friezes of the Parthenon? Or, for that matter, the mosaics in any Roman household—what do they cry out? 'My master is rich. My master can afford me.' How about the sketches you made for your father's lectures? They were all intended to persuade, to convince his students that his theories were right."

"That was different." Her pursed mouth was stubborn. "Michelangelo knew what he was getting into with those ceilings. I knew what Father wanted of me."

"You gave him more than what he wanted, just as Michelangelo gave Pope Julius. You could not help but do so, because of what you are. Have you ever stopped to wonder how much of your father's reputation was due you instead?"

"That's nonsense. Those were only copies, replicas. Any competent draftsman—"

"That's absurd, Callie. Listen to me. I've seen the effect your work has on people."

"Well, I should like to have been aware that it was being used to that effect! You said yourself that Zeus did wrong."

"I did. And yet I cannot help but be grateful to him. Those sketches did more than keep alive your memory for me. They . . . haunted me. And then, when they stopped—"

"When did they stop?" she broke in, surprised.

"When Charles Edward got so far south as Manchester."

She nodded, understanding. When, Zeus had told her, the fire had gone out of them. When she'd begun to doubt the cause.

"That's when I knew you were dead."

She stared. "When you knew I was *what?*"

"Dead. You had to be. What other reason could there be for the Pretender's agents to end such an eminently successful propaganda campaign? The whole Continent agreed with me. All of Europe mourned. Whatever one's political persuasion, one couldn't help but be moved by brave Calliope Wingate, who had given her all for Charles Edward's cause."

"So you . . . you never expected you would find me here."

"Not in the flesh, no. But in the spirit. I fought like the devil to get back to Scotland, just to share in the escapade that had taken your life."

"Did you believe in it? Had your opinion of the odds changed?"

"Quite the contrary. I was more sure than ever it was hopeless. That didn't make any difference. I was overwhelmed by the desire to kill as many of the bastards who had killed you as I possibly could. Really, my emotions were quite feral."

"It must have been a dreadful disappointment to you, then, to find me alive."

He smiled at her, and at that moment was impossibly handsome. "Quite. Now I find myself burning to kill them just for the false agony they put me through." He came toward her, stretching out his hand. "Oh, Callie. Do you want to know what I felt when I saw you standing there by Zeus tonight? A rush of longing and love—and what Doubting Thomas felt when he touched the Lord's wound. A knowledge that God lives."

She evaded his reach, grasping for her cup to put more space between them. "Well. It must be a very moving experience for you, all this new-found religion. I trust it will stand you in good stead in the battles to come."

"To hell with that, Callie. What about you and me?"

"There isn't any you and me, Mick. Not anymore. All of that is over."

His beautiful eyes went wide. "Callie. What do you mean?"

"I've had some epiphanies of my own since we have been apart. Not the least of which occurred in this room tonight, with Zeus. On the whole, I must say I agree with your pre-resurrection view of love. Most unreliable. Who needs it?"

He nodded slowly. "There is someone else. You have found someone else."

"Aren't you listening to me? I have found *myself*. I've learned to stop living for my father—oh, you really must get Zeus to tell you about him. You had ten years with your mother. I had twenty with Father. Twice the potential there for betrayal and abandonment. And now Zeus! I tell you, a soul would have to be mad to believe in love nowadays."

"Callie. I love you." His face strained with yearning.

"You ought to have caught me in my youth, then. Before I watched men die. Before I saw women made new widows, and children left without fathers. Before I learned what you knew long ago—it is best to keep one's heart locked up tight."

"You don't mean that!" He was aghast. "Christ, I've chased your soul, your shadow, across oceans and time! I came here to die for you, Callie. You can't do this to me!"

"I can do as I please." There was a great wash of release in saying those words. "I can do as I please! You said yourself—I've a grand reputation in Europe. Whatever happens to Charles Edward, my future's assured. I'm immortal. I'm a deity. I, Calliope Wingate. What in God's name do I need you for?"

"For . . . for comfort. For love!" He took a breath. "For children. Our children. So that we can face whatever is to come together, hand in hand, side by side."

There was exquisite pleasure in turning him down. "I am sorry, Mick. But I'm just beginning to enjoy living my life alone."

When he left her, his head bowed with the futility of further argument, the light gone out of his eyes, she surprised herself by not crying. Where had this strength that surged through her come from? When had she grown up so completely, so totally? It had been a long, slow time coming, she realized, and won at hard cost. Defections, disappointments, and betrayals, all adding up to one ineludible conclusion: The human condition was to be alone. Try as you might to share another's thoughts or hopes or dreams, secure as you might be in another's love or trust or understanding, it was all self-delusion. You could never know another person, because the soul was an absolutely solitary thing.

Oddly enough, she didn't find this prospect bleak. On the contrary, it was liberating, empowering, razing as it did all the crippling, constricting apparatus of social responsibility. She owed nothing to her father, to Zeus, even to poor Mick, who had chased her chimera all the way to Charles Edward's camp. Their happiness or unhappiness wasn't her concern, because she hadn't the means ultimately to affect it.

We make our own happiness.

When in her life had she been most happy? When she was drawing or painting for her own purposes—solitary and selfish. When she was reading, listening to music, watching a play— all individual intellectual pursuits. At Langlannoch, with Mick, though that had hardly been solitary. Yet perhaps it had. What she'd felt at the moment of sexual climax was more intensely private than any other emotion. Hell, the language hadn't even words adequate to describe it; it couldn't be conveyed.

And who was to say the sensations would not be every bit as intense with any Tom, Dick, or Harry? Well, not Harry, maybe. But her experience in such matters was far, far too limited to enable her to judge. I shall have to keep an eye out for prospective lovers, she thought with bemusement. Enlarge my perspective. Everything *was* a matter of perspective, wasn't it?

In the meantime, she would remind herself that loneliness was nothing to be afraid of. It was the way one entered the world, the way one made her way through it, and ultimately, sooner or later, the way one must leave.

39.

Zeus approached his sister cautiously as she stood by her easel, sketching an artillery officer directing the positioning of a half-dozen heavy guns newly arrived from France against Stirling Castle's sturdy walls. "Good morning, Cal."

"Good morning, Zeus."

He watched for a moment as she outlined the blunt barrels of the cannon. "The prince has been quite pleased with this last batch of sketches you've done," he mentioned. "Says, in fact, that he's got you to thank for these new guns."

"Tell him you're welcome for me."

He grinned, a little nervous still. "I shall."

She set her charcoal down. "What do *you* think of them?"

"I? Oh, I, well . . . you have certainly been prolific. Never knew you to churn drawings out more quickly."

"Churn?" Her upper lip curled. "I detect in that verb the hint of disdain. Perhaps you feel that in my prolificacy, there's been some lapse in quality."

"No, no. Not at all. Though I have remarked a certain calculation in the posings. That scene you set up of Charles Edward receiving those guns, backed by the cheering soldiers—"

"If you want propaganda, you must have propaganda," Callie said evenly. "Tableaux. Stage settings. Vistas."

"Perhaps so." He didn't sound convinced. "But I miss the more intimate sketches you used to make."

"What, like this?" She paged back in the sketchbook to a drawing of a woman crouched over a small, plain coffin, while behind her a man hacked at the hard ground with a pick-axe.

"Good God, Cal. What's that?" He stared at the image, transfixed.

"One of the prostitutes in town. She got herself with child by one of the soldiers. Gave birth last week. The baby died. She couldn't find a priest willing to baptize it, on account of her profession. So of course it can't be buried in hallowed ground. She's paid the farmer there six shillings to dig a hole for her on his croft. She says it's quite a pretty spot in summer—down by Cambuskenneth Abbey. She brings her clients there sometimes."

He cringed, holding his hands over his ears. "Don't tell me any more. I can't stand the sadness on her face."

"Yes. Rather odd, that. One would think a baby would prove a hindrance in her circumstances. But she was quite overcome with grief." Callie paged forward to the sketch of the cannons again. "Still. Not quite the thing to send off to Paris to garner donations. Now that I'm aware of how my work is being utilized, I'm keeping some of it out of the prince's hands. I should hate for this to show up in the French coffeehouses as, say, an illustration of a woman burying her child, who was murdered by the evil Hanoverian soldiers after they'd raped her and pillaged the household."

Zeus looked pained. "Christ, Cal. You know Charles Edward. He wouldn't do that."

"His soldiers once killed a pub-keeper over a barrel of ale."

"There have been atrocities on both sides. There always are, in a war."

"Precisely. No need to over-inflate truth." She picked her charcoal up.

"You are angry with me still." He sounded miserable.

"No, Zeus. I'm not. Really. I just prefer knowledge to ignorance. Having some measure of control. It's all this damned not knowing, being in the dark—with Father about Laurie, with you about the sketches. Now that I know, I've taken charge of my life.''

"That's sort of what I came to talk to you about, Callie.''

She sketched in the jaunty feather on the captain's bonnet. "This isn't a mere social visit?''

"Not exactly. It's about Mick.''

"Ah. How is our fledgling rebel faring?''

"He frightens me, Cal. He frightens everyone around him. He is out of control.''

"Mick? Out of control? Rather hard to imagine. How so?''

"He keeps volunteering to the prince for the most outlandish missions.''

"Such as what?''

"Oh—he says Lady Maggie told him of a family legend that there are tunnels in the walls of the castles at Edinburgh and Stirling. He wants permission to search for them and lead a handpicked group of men inside the walls.''

"Mm. Sounds farfetched, I'll agree. But there might be something to it. What does Charles Edward say?''

"That it would be suicide. The walls are lined with musketeers. What did you say to him, Cal, that night when he came, to make him act this way?''

Callie held up her charcoal. Judging perspective. "Just what I said to you now. That I have taken charge. That there is no room in my new life for him. Is he—an adequate soldier?''

"He was born to soldier. You should see him practice with his axe. It is terrifying.''

"Mm. Interesting. Makes one wonder whether there might truly be something in the blood, doesn't it?'' She squinted at the cannon. "Perhaps I ought to make a sketch of him for Lady Maggie.''

"You had best do it fast,'' her brother told her glumly. "As soon as there's a battle, he's going to be dead.''

"I thought you said he was born to soldier.''

"Well, that's what soldiers do, isn't it? They die in bloody wars.''

Her green gaze slanted toward him. "Zeus. You sound so vexed. What is it to you if Mick Harding dies?''

"I should think the question is, what is it to you? You were his lover once. You loved him once." She started to speak. "Oh, don't you dare deny it! I saw you with him at Langlannoch. I saw what it did to you, how it transformed you."

Sighing, she set the charcoal down. "Yes, well. I've been transformed again. And you've only yourself to thank for it, for dragging me along with the army in the first place. You ought to have let me go on home to Edinburgh."

"By God, I wish I had. At least I'd know that you had some heart left in you."

"What's that supposed to mean?"

"Don't you see, Cal? You've become just like these sketches—cold and calculated."

"Yet Charles Edward is pleased with my sketches."

"Because they serve his purpose!"

"And it serves my purposes to be this way! I have plans, Zeus. I can use this war as well as it can use me. Once it's over, I am heading for Paris. I'll have a studio there, and I'll paint anything I damn well want to. I'll paint nudes. Nude men, nude women, nude dwarves—any unclothed creature I please. And there won't be anyone to say me nay—not you, not Father, not Mick or any man."

He stared at her. "You never mentioned this before."

"I've only just found myself with the liberty to think about the future. What's the matter? You were always urging me to break free, in the old days."

"Break free, yes, but not so violently."

She looked him up and down in his soldier's uniform. "Your break's been violent enough."

"I suppose it has. Well. I hope you'll be happy."

"I'm quite certain I'll be. Now, if you'll excuse me, I have work to do." She started on the shadows underneath the cannon wheels. Zeus didn't move. Annoyed by his presence, she turned on him. "What? What is it? What do you want of me?"

"Do you think you might at least talk to him?"

"Oh, Zeus. There isn't any point—"

"And where's the bloody point in him throwing his life away for nothing? If you could just give him something, some bit of hope to cling to—"

"Lie to him, do you mean?"

"Of course not. But for God's sake, Cal. This new dream of yours . . . this studio in Paris. It wouldn't have been possible without him. He started you drawing again."

She pondered that for a moment. "I suppose one might conclude I owe him something for that. Very well. I'll talk to him. But I won't give him false hope, Zeus. No more deceptions. I've already been a party to too many."

"Do it fast, Cal. Hawley's troops will be marching out from Edinburgh any day now to confront us."

"Is tonight soon enough?" she asked wryly. He nodded, satisfied at last. "Then will you please go away?" He did. She stared at her sketch for a moment, then rubbed out the wheels' shadow; already the light that cast them had changed, forcing her to begin again.

Mick hesitated on the threshold, before the open door. He wanted to prolong this moment while she sat bowed over her sketchbook by the fireplace, still unaware of him. The flames played over her curling hair, caught back carelessly in a pile at the nape of her neck that left her shoulders bared against the rich umber of her gown. She'd never looked more beautiful to him. And yet he knew that if he moved, even breathed, the spell would be broken; she would turn, and there would be only coldness, or, worse, pity in her eyes. He stood as long as he could, watching her ply the pencil with her usual singular concentration. Then he must have sighed, or shifted his weight, and she raised her gaze.

Not pity, at least, but curiosity—the same cerebral interest she might have shown for a giraffe or a tiger in her doorway. He cleared his throat, realizing it needed it. "You sent for me?"

"Hallo, Mick. So I did. How kind of you to come." *I would have come through hellfire. . . .* "Won't you sit down?" She indicated the chair across from hers with a hand graceful and white as a lily. Mick felt his heart start to splinter. He ought not to have come; it was beyond human strength to look at her and know he'd never have her again. Well, damn. If she was distant now, that was his own fault, for having let her slip so far away. He'd always known, since that first golden afternoon when she and Zeus had invaded the garden at Langlannoch, that she was too grand, too splendid for the likes of him. Wasn't that finally what had driven him across the sea to Frère Descoux—knowledge of his own unworthiness?

She nodded toward the table at his elbow. "There is claret there. I remember you like claret."

"I've . . . stopped drinking." The taste of wine was inexorably linked for him with the taste of her mouth opening beneath his. He sat, awkward in his kilt, arranging the folds, fussy as a schoolgirl. His bare knees above the plaid stockings stuck out like great bony moons. He tugged the chill wool down futilely. He thought desperately for something to say. "I'm surprised you have it, though. My men tell me drink is hard to come by."

"Charles Edward and I have an arrangement. I explained wine fuels the creative process."

"Does it?"

"Sometimes." Her smile was oblique. "How are your men?"

"Restless. They long for battle. A siege is hardly to their liking, after waiting so long to join the war."

"According to Zeus, they'll be satisfied in their longing soon enough." *And I,* Mick thought in despair, *will I never be satisfied in my longing?* "Zeus is worried about you."

And you—are you? "I don't see why he should be."

She set aside the sketchbook and picked up her wine glass. He saw her tongue flick to test its edge—an unconscious gesture that made him tremble. Her eyes met his above the rim. "He feels you're suicidal," she said bluntly. "Over me."

Mick fumbled for the decanter. "Perhaps I will try some wine."

She leaned toward him as he poured it out. "Mick. You must understand. What has happened to me really has very little to do with you. It's the culmination of a lifetime of events. Charles Edward has spoken to me of his belief in destiny. I don't share that belief. I think that what we are, what we become, is the inevitable summation of what has gone before in our lives. If we are here, now, both of us, separate, you and I, that is because we had no other choice. Our upbringing impelled us this way.''

He surprised himself by finding strength to argue. ''How is that different from destiny?''

She laughed, a sound like water rippling over smooth stones. ''It is more logical, certainly, than thinking we are bound by fate, or by the stars.''

He swallowed some of the wine. It burned going down, tart to bitterness. ''And have we force to change?''

''Absolutely!'' She leaned toward him. The motion made white mounds of her breasts above the earth-brown bodice. He could feel their weight in his fingers, and the bright rosettes of her nipples hardening to his touch. ''We have, and we must! To give in to circumstance is every bit as cowardly as surrendering to what men call fate. If you are languishing for me, Mick Harding, you must stop it. You must stop it now.''

''And how would you suggest I do so?'' he asked heavily.

''You must take a lover.'' His head jerked up involuntarily. ''Had you lovers in Paris? Oh, I dearly hope so.'' His expression must have betrayed him, for she clucked her tongue. ''Don't you see, Mick? We were each other's first. You must move beyond that. You must realize that half—nay, nine-tenths—of the sanctity you hold me in is circumstantial.''

''Is that . . . what you have done?''

He held his breath while she paused to sip wine. The notion of sharing her, of any other man touching her, penetrating her, was physically painful. He felt his scrotum wither, felt his manhood, that had been at awkward attention ever since he'd entered the room, fade to flaccidity. ''Yes,'' she admitted finally. ''Yes. I have. Because it was the only way.''

''Who?'' He ached to draw his sword, cut the bastard's head off. ''Who? Is it Charles Edward?''

''Mick, it doesn't matter.''

''Don't you bloody tell me what does or does not matter!''

She smiled again. ''You are angry. Good. Go on. Be angry with me. Hate me. Despise me.''

''I do! I do hate you!'' Satisfied, she settled back in her chair. He wanted to wipe that smile off her face with his fist, or with the hard, taut manhood she'd once kissed so eagerly. "But that won't stop me loving you."

"Paradox," she said brightly, like a debating coach tallying points.

Bewildered, he shook his head. "Is this a game to you?"

"On the contrary, it's deadly serious. Mick, think it through! To love again, you must be free of me, as I am free of you."

"I don't want to be free," he muttered in abject despair. "I only want . . . you. No one else." And then his outrage mounted into a moan so raw that it was animal: "How could you take another lover, after what we shared?"

He thought he'd disconcerted her; she rose from her seat, put her back to him, and moved toward the dresser in the corner of the room. But she came back with a tray. "Cheese and biscuits?" she asked, extending them to him. "It's a very nice Cheshire. Those mad MacDonalds seized it straight out of Hawley's wagon-train on a raid."

He knocked the tray from her hand with a blow that made her back up hurriedly. "Damn your biscuits and cheese."

"Oh, really, Mick." But there was fear in her eyes. He was unreasonably glad to have put it there. He rose to his feet, and she moved further away.

"I'm free to die for you," he announced, "if I bloody well please." Then he strode toward the door.

"God, Mick!" she cried at his back. "I can't believe this is you! You used to be such a reasonable man!"

He whirled to face her. "There is reason in me still. Without you, I've no cause to go on living. Therefore, why shouldn't I die? Take that knowledge to your other lovers, Callie. Live with it as I have lived with your cruelty. Take it to your grave. But I hope—God, how I hope!—you will live with it a long, long time."

"I'm not to blame!" she raged at him, her fists clenched. "Not for what you feel, not for what you do!"

"Go on telling yourself that," he said in fury, "every night, where you now speak prayers."

"I don't speak prayers," she told him after a moment. "I haven't since I was a tiny child. You know I don't believe in God."

"Strangely enough, I have come to. No other force in the universe could have devised a torture so exquisite as the torture of life without you has turned out to be."

"My, my, Mick. Who would ever have dreamed you had it in you to be so overdramatic? And to think I once imagined you a cold fish."

He could have killed her for mocking him. He truly could have. Instead he left her, went back to the chill comfort of his own bed, and lay awake for hours, dreaming of the sweet release of a musket-ball shattering his chest.

40.

Lieutenant-General Henry Hawley left the shelter of Edinburgh Castle with eight thousand men on the thirteenth of January. The sky was overcast, but the air oddly warm, with a breeze from the south. Charles Edward, who'd had nearly three weeks to plot his chosen position, left a thousand Highlanders behind to sustain the siege of Stirling Castle and marched the remainder of his troops, some five thousand strong, out to Plean Muir. Hawley came to rest three days later near Falkirk, across the River Carron. Advised by his scouts of the strong enemy position—at the top of a ridge of moorland, about a mile from his camp, that threatened to provide an ideal downhill run for a Highland charge—Hawley sent a decoy force, commanded by Lord Drummond, marching straight up the main road to Falkirk. Charles Edward refused to be deceived. He maintained his forces at the top of the ridge, playing a waiting game.

Callie liked the ridge. It gave a broad vista of the countryside that would surely be the scene of battle, yet was steep enough that she could set up an easel and be reasonably sure no English soldiers, not even the dreaded cavalry, would reach the top. She spent the evening of the sixteenth of January sketching soldiers honing weapons by the light of campfires, and went to bed with the music of pipes dancing in her head.

Dawn brought an onslaught of rain. Zeus fretted over sodden gunpowder as he dressed for battle. He had the hang of his plaid by now. Callie kissed him goodbye with curious detachment, concerned with whom she might coerce into holding an umbrella over her easel while she worked. One of Angus Mac-Pherson's cousins, an elderly fellow who'd lost one arm at Prestonpans, eventually volunteered the other to do the job. As she set up her sketchbook, she saw Lord George Murray's Highlanders ascending the ridge from the west. Hawley countered by dispatching three choice regiments of dragoons toward the eastern face.

Callie, contemplating angles, perspective, saw the dark-green bonnets of Mick's Ayrshiremen ranged behind Murray's troops. It was not a desirable position, coming second after the advance, for if Hawley's dragoons had absorbed any lesson from Prestonpans, it ought to have been to break the Highland Charge by firing while the wild Scots were still at enough distance to allow for reloading. But the damp gunpowder, she thought, rubbing rain from her brow, should keep Walter Coady and the rest safe. It looked to be the sort of battle Charles Edward seemed to long for, in which modern accoutrements such as guns and artillery would play less a part than good old-fashioned swords and pikes. She made a few desultory strokes with her pencil—charcoal would have melted away in that weather— just so the MacPherson cousin wouldn't think his arm was being wasted. But really, there wouldn't be much to draw until the armies engaged.

Drums were sounding. Soggy pipes were wheezing. Callie sighed; she could see clearly from that vantage point that Hawley hadn't even got his infantry arrayed.

It was with some astonishment, then, that she watched his three regiments of dragoons charge.

She started blocking in moving enemy bodies, wondering idly how long they'd manage to wait before giving fire. Surely these idiots had learned by now that every second between range gained and volley delayed meant certain trouble. God, this blasted rain! She squinted at the lines of red and plaid; she could not make out expressions or faces. "We've got to move closer," she told MacPherson.

"Suits me," he told her, and hoisted the easel up under his arm.

They hadn't gotten more than a few feet when the Highlanders fired their guns. You poor damned fools, Callie thought of the English, as what looked to be a hundred of their mounted dragoons went down in the sluicing mud. Caterwauling Gaelic screams rent the sky as the Highlanders threw down their useless muskets and charged. Callie blinked as she saw the Ayrshiremen's dark bonnets fly right through the thicket of Murray's men. They *were* eager for battle, she thought; Mick hadn't lied about that. And the stupid, stupid English, less than ten yards away, were trying to reload.

She turned to search for Zeus's regiment. They were far to the right, assigned to guard that flank. She turned back. The dragoons—what was left of them—were already in retreat, crashing back into their own infantry. God, what a mess war could be! Still, the quick repulse of Hawley's choicest men would make a lovely sketch. She worked feverishly for several minutes, trying to capture the chaos.

"Jesu," the MacPherson cousin murmured, twisting so that rain splattered past the umbrella onto her paper. "Wuld ye look at that?"

"The sketchbook's getting wet," she snapped. "Do you mind not gawking?"

He paid her no attention. "They bae out o' their minds," he marveled, and Callie, drawn against her will by the wonder on his ancient face, looked down the ridge past the body-littered point of first encounter to where a small wedge of dark-green bonnets was plunging straight into the heart of Hawley's still-intact right flank.

Mick was at the front of that mire. She scanned the little block of green against red, searching for him—could she even tell him, at this distance? But she could; he'd led the charge, was a good five yards ahead of any of his Ayrshiremen, and he had lost his bonnet; she could see his black queue whipping back and forth as he ran. There's an image to send Lady Maggie, she thought, and quickly ripped to a fresh page of her sketchbook. But when she looked back down at the battlefield, he was gone from her sight.

"Madmen," the MacPherson muttered in complete admiration.

Callie's pencil had fallen from her hand. "Their leader," she whispered, staring at the block of green. "What's become of him?"

"Ach, he bae gone down."

"Gone *down?*" She contemplated the rain-soaked scene laid out before her. "What do you mean, gone down?"

"I saw an axe catch his head. Just as well. He wuld hae caught hell anyway, fro' the prince. He dinna care for such lack o' discipline."

The chill rain seemed suddenly to have seeped into Callie's heart. *He saw an axe catch his head.* That head that had lay upon her breast. The thick black hair she'd caught her hands in as he knelt above her, matted with red blood. Those gentian-blue eyes dark with passion, gone blank for all time. God, he couldn't be dead! "Mick!" she screamed, and caught up her skirts. "Oh, Mick, I was wrong!"

Destiny. As she ran down the ridge, her heart pounding, she saw through the blinding rain the image of Michel Faurer, the first Michel Faurer, atop his black horse, far in the distance, and felt her own body awkward with bulk, as though she bore a child in her belly, weighting her down. But that was absurd. We make our own choices, she reminded herself. We are creatures of our own becoming. The past has no hold—

Then why was she running to Mick now?

"Lass, stop! Lass, ye'll bae killed!" MacPherson, appalled, at her back.

Her eyes were green as bottle-glass. Her own hair was black, flying.

She was bound in love to Michel Faurer, bound for all time.

"Michel!" She was in the thick now of the carnage, plunging past bloodied knights, muddied horses. "Oh, God, Michel. Live. At least live until I tell you I love you." The battlefield was a morass of dead men and rain. She ran toward the beckoning backs of the green-bonneted soldiers he had led from Langlannoch, led on what he'd called an escapade. But there was nothing childish, nothing glib about the prayer she whispered as she ran; it was brief and direct: "God, let him be alive. Please, dear God, let him be living still."

So many dead men. And the dying . . . hands reaching toward her; grasping, imploring: "Ha'e mercy . . ."

And the deafening roar of the guns. Someone, somewhere, had managed to reload.

"Michel!"

The musket-ball stopped her in mid-stride.

Fire at her breast, searing, blazing. Legs crumpling, weak rags. Her hands pawing wet earth, the fingers clenched like claws. The taste of mud in her mouth, and a slow seeping like rain, only from within. The lowering sky swirling, turned black. And utter, raw despair, because she had not reached him, had not told him that fate was real, inescapable, and his was tied to hers. . . .

Time for one last prayer. "Oh, God. Forgive me." Mick, you forgive me, too. Lips too weak to move. A sudden flash of memory—the rock at Avebury. Heat clenched tight within, and the soft snow swirling. First kiss. Branded forever.

And that was the end.

Part IV

41.

Something lay beneath her heavy head, soft as satin. An odor hung on the air of dead things—dust, mold, decay—overlaid with the faint sweetness of roses. But they smelled long dead, too. Callie lay in utter darkness. She could see nothing, hear nothing—except her faint, quiet heartbeat. Could she taste? Callie ran her tongue against her teeth, and there was death in her mouth, too—a taste like blood and earth and musty wine. *Last rites.* The notion flitted through her mind like a dusky moth, settled, and made her struggle to move in her dark cocoon of silk and roses. Great God in heaven. She'd been buried alive.

She opened her mouth, tried to scream, engulfed in utter panic—and then flinched as flesh, gentle, with the clean scent of soap, descended on her face. "Soothe, soothe," a voice whispered close at hand—a voice half-familiar, like a dream, unexpected, tantalizing. Whose voice? "Soothe, mum. Dinna fear. Ye maun rest, now. All will bae well."

Callie licked her dry lips. "Who . . . who are you?"

"Why, it bae Jennet, mum."

Jennet. She tried to place the name, but couldn't. What was the matter with her brain? It seemed so sluggish, thick. Jennet who? She tried again. "Where am I?"

"Ach, at Langlannoch, luv. Where else wuld ye bae?"

Langlannoch. The word seeped into her dull, clouded mind like opium, numbing her terror and confusion. At Langlannoch. No evil could befall her here. She'd come home to Langlannoch, to the warm sun and roses. Home to Michel . . .

She let her head sink back against the satin, succumbing to the sweet lure of sleep.

When she woke again, she felt more steady, though her temples ached with a low, steady pounding. It was night; there was still nothing to see. "Jennet?" she whispered, the name an odd, dry little croak. "Jennet, are you there?"

"Here, mum." She heard a rustle of skirts, and then the hand, clean and soothing, stroking her cheek. "Thirsty?"

Callie nodded as well as she could. Her head still felt swathed in bunting. A cup touched her lips. Lovely, cool, fresh water. She drank thirstily until Jennet pulled the cup away with a caution:

"Nae too much, then, pet. Ye maun take things slow."

The darkness was becoming annoying. "Light a candle, Jennet, please."

There was a little silence. "I hae best fetch Lady Maggie," the housekeeper said then, skirts swishing, moving away.

"Don't leave me here alone!" Callie cried in fright. "For God's sake, light a candle!"

"I'll bae but a moment. Dinna thrash sae; ye'll loose the bandages." Footsteps padded off; a door opened, then closed. Bandages? Callie thought, and felt her torso with one limp hand. Her stomach, her breast—a wad of padding there, held tight with linen. No wonder she'd thought she was swaddled.

There were more footsteps, two sets, and then Mick's grandmother's voice, brisk as sea air: "Sae, then! Come back to us, hae ye?" Another hand on her cheek, moving up to her forehead. But Callie could not feel it there. "Nae fever still," Lady Maggie murmured with approval. "Out o' the woods, Jennet, wuld ye nae say?"

"Aye, mum. Except for—"

"Quite. Well, Calliope Chloe. Ye gave us the devil's own scare. Wha' can ye remember, pet, o' wha' happened?"

Callie searched her mind, found only a muddle of confused images—Zeus in his bright bonnet, a stamping of horses, rain drenching down, a one-armed man with an umbrella held high. "Remember about what?" she asked, dazed.

"About the battle, dear. At Falkirk."

Falkirk. The ridge. Cope's dragoons ascending, Murray sloshing to meet them, and a wedge of dark bonnets pressing through the lines, surging toward the enemy. Angus's cousin, chiding but admiring: *Madmen.* Mick with an axe in his head. She caught her breath in a sob.

"There, now," Lady Maggie said quickly, holding tight to her hand. "Ne'er ye mind. Ye had a mite o' metal in yer chest, but we dug it out for ye, dinna we, Jennet? Healin' up nice 'n clean, it bae. But ye maun keep yerself still 'n quiet, 'n nae move about, sae the skin can stitch. If there bae anythin' ye need, just ask o' me or Jennet."

"I should like a candle," Callie said. "I should like to see."

Lady Maggie's hand, still holding hers, lifted it to her forehead. Callie felt the taut linen beneath her fingertips, touched it questioningly, realized it covered her eyes. "What's this?" she whispered.

Lady Maggie's voice, still brisk and matter-of-fact: "Ye war standin' sae close to the musket, pet. The gun maun hae misfired. That bae wha' saved yer life. The ball exploded in the barrel. But the powder-blast—it burned yer eyes. Sae we hae bandaged them up, too. We maun gi' them a fair chance to heal afore we let in the light."

Powder-blind. The notion would have ripped open her heart, if Mick's death hadn't already done so. She turned her head away from them, these loving, gentle women. What more was there to say?

Time passed—how much time Callie had no way of knowing, bereaved as she was of the cycles of day and night. Jennet or her mistress came now and again, to feed her sips of broth and tonic or to put a fresh bandage on her chest. But the bonds of cloth across her eyes were never removed. Sometimes Grimkin nuzzled at her hand, or curled up by her feet and purred, a small, comforting sound. Other than that, Callie was alone.

Once, when Lady Maggie was with her, Callie heard her draw the curtains back, and felt heat against her cheek. "Sunlight," she murmured, touching the warmth.

"Aye, sae it bae. A fair, bright winter morn. How could ye tell it, though?"

"I could feel it. Here."

"Ach." There was disappointment in the syllable.

"When will you take these bandages off?"

"Any day. Any day."

She didn't sound convincing. "I know about powder-blindness," Callie offered. "I know it can be permanent."

The Scotswoman swallowed something like a sob. "Well. We maun hope for the best."

"I don't care," Callie said. And she didn't, not now that Mick was dead. What was there to see in a world bereft of him, anyway?

"Ye needs maun care," Lady Maggie told her fiercely.

No sense arguing. The potions they gave her eased the ache in her flesh and bone, but never that in her heart. Callie went back to sleep.

Later that day or night, she woke to an unfamiliar sound— a soft, low snoring. "Jennet?" she said, reaching for the chair beside her bed.

The sound broke off. The housekeeper got up, her footsteps sounding heavy and weary. She opened the door, and came back in a bit with a bowl of cool water. She dabbed it on Callie's throat and chest, held the cup for her to drink. "Thank you," Callie whispered. Jennet said nothing. But she laid her hand on Callie's knee, just out of reach.

Morning again. Lady Maggie drawing the curtains, and the rush of warmth on Callie's skin. She felt more like herself than she had—less thick-headed, less drowsy. When Lady Maggie held the potion to her lips, Callie shook her head. "I don't want it."

"Ye maun take it, pet, for the pain."

"I want to feel the pain." She put her hands up to her bandaged eyes. "How came I here?"

"Soldiers brought ye."

"How did they know to bring me here?"

A small pause. "They war Michel's men."

Sorrow swamped Callie's heart. She wanted to tell Lady Maggie that she shared her grief, but could not find the words. "Did—did we win, then, at Falkirk?"

"Aye. We won." Lady Maggie spoke with great satisfaction.

But to Callie, it was little comfort. She caught her fingertips in Grimkin's soft fur and lay quiet, seeing only into her heart.

Later, when the warmth of the sun had fled, Jennet was there with broth, and spooned it up in silence. Callie ate the same way, guarding her emotions. It would not do to give in to despair in front of these brave women, who'd lost much more than she had. She remembered the cold, harsh words she'd spoken to Mick that last night in Stirling, when he'd come to her rooms, and would have given her eyes ten times over to have them back again, unsaid.

But life didn't give such second chances. She began to tremble, and grasped for Jennet's hand, desperate for human contact. "Jennet—"

The spoon clattered to the floor. Jennet's fingers were long and calloused and blunt-tipped. And big ... Callie didn't remember them being so big. "Jennet?" she whispered.

"Callie." His voice. A ghost's voice.

"You're dead," she told him, clinging to his hand. "You caught an axe to the head."

"No tougher spot on a Harding than the head. You should know that by now." He bent down a little and held her fingers to the bandage at the nape of his neck. "Almost as good as new. See?" Then he caught his breath, realizing what he'd said. "Oh, God, Callie. Your eyes . . ."

"I don't care." She moved her hand to his face, still not believing he was there. Memory drew his features as she traced them—the strong planes of his cheeks, the wide mouth, sharp chin. All intact. All in place. "Christ! I don't care! How long have you been here?"

"All the time. All along. Here with you. In this room." She

remembered then his quality of stillness, how long he could go without moving. A rush of wonder filled her. ''I brought you back from Falkirk.''

''But your grandmother said—soldiers. She never said it was you!''

''I asked her not to tell. I didn't know . . . I was not sure you would want to—'' See me, he'd almost said, but had stopped himself this time. ''To have me here. After what you said at Stirling. . . .''

''But I thought you were dead!''

''I did not imagine that would grieve you unduly,'' he said with some hint in the words of the stiff Oxford scholar.

Second chance. Answered prayers. Callie drew in a long, deep breath that filled her heart with redemption. ''I was so stupid, Michel!''

''Don't call me—oh, hell. I suppose you may as well. Yes. You certainly were. What in God's name could have possessed you, to run out on the field like that in the midst of a battle?''

She could not stop touching him—his hair, his face, his shirt, his strong arms. ''You. I was possessed by you. I'd been wrong, and I had to tell you so before you died. I had to tell you I love you.''

''You damned near got yourself killed!''

''If you were dead, I did not want to live.''

She felt him shiver beneath his fingertips. ''Callie. Don't say such things.''

''You said that, once, to me. I was so cruel to you—''

''It doesn't matter.'' The air between them stirred. She felt his mouth brush hers. ''What does it matter now?''

But she felt compelled to apologize, explain. ''I felt so . . . I was just so angry! At Zeus, at Father, at you.''

''I know, Callie. Do you think I don't, with my temper? If I hadn't been so furious with you about that damned Commandant Henley spying on the house, none of this would have—'' He stopped; she'd started to giggle. ''What? What is it?''

''I was just thinking of that threat he made—to tell the dean about you and me. And how I thought that would be the most dreadful thing that ever could happen.''

He laughed, too. "A war does lend a certain perspective, doesn't it?"

"I wouldn't care now if Henley had it published in every gazette in the world. I'm proud that you and I——"

"I know." He moved the chair closer to the bed, so that he could put his arm around her, hold her to his heart. "Does that hurt you?"

"Nothing hurts me anymore, now that you are here." She nestled back against him. "Is it morning or nighttime?"

"Night. Can't you hear the owl in the garden?"

She could and listened more closely. "How long is it since you brought me home?"

"Home. God, I love to hear you say that." He kissed her hair. "Three days." They sat in silence, listening to the owl's mournful hoot. Then he brushed her cheek with his hand. "Callie. I've got to go back."

"Why? To get the bastard who shot me?"

"Nay. I already killed him." He spoke as a soldier, matter-of-factly. "Because my men are there. Because I got them into this. I've got to see it finished."

Born to soldier. Callie nodded against his broad chest. She'd long since forfeited any right to argue. "When?" she whispered.

"I'll stay through the night."

So little time. "Come into the bed with me," she begged him. "Hold me."

"You need to rest."

"I will, if you are beside me."

He hesitated, then moved her gently back onto the pillows. She heard him grunt, bending over to pull off his boots. Then, "Shoo, Grimkin," he said, and the cat sprang off the coverlet at her feet. The mattress shifted as he settled in by her side. Slowly, carefully, she rolled over to face him, felt with her fingers for his mouth in the darkness. He cupped her palm, kissed it. There were tears beneath her touch. "Mick. Don't cry."

"I'm sorry. Oh, God, Cal. Your eyes."

"Has your grandmother said what she thinks? About my seeing again?"

"She is certain you will!" But he'd said it too quickly.

"Liar. Tell me the truth."

He took a breath. "Fifty-fifty. But likely never the way you once did."

"Well! That *is* honest." She mused on it, realized that it frightened her less than she ever would have believed. "Do *you* mind?"

"Only for your sake."

She probed the bandage tentatively. "You saw them. Are they—deformed?"

"They look exactly the same. Like the ocean. Like beryl. The most beautiful eyes in the world." His voice caught in a sob. She reached toward him, found his hair, tugged his head against her linen-wound breast and held him as he cried.

"Mick. Stop that."

"I am sorry. I'm trying."

"Stop it," she murmured into his ear, "and make love to me."

He drew back. "Callie. I can't."

A wretched thought struck her. "Is it ... what I said at Stirling? About taking a lover? Mick, I swear on my heart that was a lie, only a bitter lie. There's been no one but you. There only ever could be you."

"Hush, goose. It isn't that. I thought that mattered, once. But when I saw you lying there on the field, saw your blood—Christ! I wouldn't have cared if you'd slept with every soldier in the damned army, if you just didn't die!" She heard him draw in breath. "And then the surgeon said ... he had so many men to care for. I don't blame him. But if there was a chance, any chance, for your sight to be saved ... I thought of Grandmère. And Charles Edward let me come. That's another reason, Callie, why I must go back."

"He only wants me to draw him pictures again."

She'd meant it as a jest. But she felt the shudder that shook him. "I see," she said, and she did. "There's little chance of that."

"God, I would give my life—"

"Hush, Mick, hush!"

"It was because of me!"

"It was because I love you! Because I had wronged you. Oh, Mick. Don't think of what we've lost. Think of what we've been given! A second chance. The chance to make things right. There must be a God, for see how we've been blessed!"

"My dear, brave Callie."

"Make love to me. Please."

He laughed uncertainly, holding her close. "You're wrapped up like a . . . like a mummy, love! I'd hurt you. I wouldn't know where to begin."

"Go and fetch the *Kama Sutra,*" she told him. "I seem to recall it had any number of suggestions. Unless . . ." Her hand crept downward to his breeches. "Unless I simply don't attract you this way." But his manhood made a gratifying bulge against her palm. She let her fingers tighten on it through the cloth, heard a groan escape him.

"Callie. Have mercy."

"Make love to me, Michel. I need it—" In her darkness she saw him marching, heard the pipes and the drums. "In case there may be worse to come." *In case I never hold you again.*

He put his hands to either side of her face and kissed her, long and gentle and sweet. His tongue touched her lips, parted them, pushed inside her. He tasted clean as sunlight. Callie sighed happily. From beyond his back came the sound of the door opening, and Lady Maggie's gasp:

"Michel! Really! I dinna think—"

He raised his mouth just long enough to say, "Go away, Grandmère."

After a moment, the door closed again.

He laughed, and hiked Callie's nightdress up above her waist.

It was odd not to see him as he touched her. She used her hands as her eyes, running them over his face, down his throat to his shoulders. "Take off your clothes," she whispered. "Nay. I'll take them off you." He lay still while she untied his breeches, her fingers pulling at the unseen knot. It was hard work.

"Let me help you," he offered.

"I can do it." And she did, finally, though the effort left her panting.

"Callie. This isn't wise."

"I don't want to be wise! Damn wisdom!" She relented. "You can deal with your shirt and hose."

"I don't want to hurt you," he whispered again.

"Not having you is hurting me." She grasped his manhood, drew it to her thighs. "Not having you *here* . . ."

"Oh, God," he groaned, swelling at her touch. She felt his blood surge beneath her fingers, and was consumed by such a flood of gratefulness that she scarcely could abide it. To be with him, holding him again—she did not deserve this mercy. And yet, mercy is never deserved, she realized. It is a gift freely given, in spite of our unworthiness.

He had his mouth to her mouth, arching over her, exquisitely careful not to lay his weight on her. She felt the tip of his queue brush against her bare shoulder, and in her blindness the sensation was more arousing than his kiss at her breast would have been. Soft brush of hair, soft sweep of softness . . . and between her thighs, his manhood, upright, rock-hard. Warmth burned within it.

"Mick," she started to say.

"I know," he astonished her by whispering. "Avebury. Fire in the stones. In the bone. Why do you think I kissed you there? Because I had no choice. It was my destiny." The word he'd once been so afraid of, spoken with such ease. Callie lay back, felt the smooth, broad head as it pierced her, drove inside her, and felt the joining worth any loss, any loss at all.

"Am I hurting you?"

"God, no!" He was giving her new life.

He thrust deeper. "Now?" For answer she clung to him, parted her legs, pulled him tighter. "Callie. Callie—"

"Yes, Mick. Yes. Don't you dare stop!"

"Callie, I cannot hold back!"

She didn't want him to. Her flesh was aflame, hot rivers of fire flowing, bathing him in the blaze, and only he could quench her, satisfy her, bring the rush of white heat that would be her release. She moved against him, beneath him, drew him so close that she felt their beings, their very souls would melt together in the wild inferno. He was a great unseen mass of flame, and their love was the fuel.

"Callie!" he cried, thrusting straight to her heart. "Callie. Callie . . . oh!" A rush of incandescence, their skin stretched raw, glowing, and in her womb the most amazing explosion, so bright that it would blind dead eyes.

Black figures flickering against the luminescence. Michel Faurer on his black horse, and his bride's black hair.

When she could speak again, she had to tell him. "Michel. When you make love to me, I see—"

"Him."

"Who is he? Who am I? Who are we?"

He shook his head against her hair. "Callie. Love. I don't know."

"Do you see her, too?"

He hesitated. "Yes."

"And the *horse?*"

"Aye. The horse, too," he admitted after a moment.

"Michel. What does it *mean?*"

He fell back on the pillows. "The transmigration of souls, I suppose. Metempsychosis—that's what Plato called it."

Callie knew her Plato. " 'The wheel of birth,' " she whispered, " 'revolves inexorably.' I don't believe in such stuff."

"No," he assured her. "Nor do I."

"But, still. They are there."

"Perhaps they are our guardian angels." He leaned over to kiss her mouth.

"I don't believe in angels either. Lord, I have just come to believe in God!"

He twined her hair in his fingers. "I never studied much theology. Not current theology, I mean. Only ancient things. But Plato did hold there was a finite number of souls in the universe. Perhaps theirs are ours. Perhaps a love so great as theirs can never die."

"Mick. That's twaddle."

"Aye. I know. Still, it's a pleasant notion to hold, isn't it, when I must go away?"

"I would much rather hold you."

He pulled her close to his heart. "Do you hate me for leaving?"

"No. I rather feel as though you must. And that's disquieting, too. It isn't like me to be so selfless."

"Of course it is. Look at the lengths you were willing to go to for Zeus."

"Oh, well, Zeus. That's different. He's a part of me."

"And I . . . am I part of you, too?"

She felt for his mouth, found it, kissed it. "You are the best part of me. You have been my salvation."

"As you have been mine." He returned the kiss. "When I come back again, will you marry me?"

"You know that I will."

Grimkin leapt up to join them. "Damned cat," Mick muttered, kicking it from his legs.

"Don't be so harsh. He may have been here to see them. You know what they say about cats' lives. Is that it, Grimkin? Do you recognize your first master and mistress?" The cat meowed loudly, in what sounded astonishingly like feline consent. After a moment, Callie laughed, and then Mick did, too. "Lord, this house is filled with ghosts."

"I used to be afraid of them," Mick said softly.

"When you were little, you mean."

"Oh, no. When I was grown."

"And . . . now?"

He sighed, stretched out beside her. "Now I feel like Sisyphus. All that time spent shoving at unnecessary stones—I suppose I knew all along in my heart that the past would reclaim me. I wonder what would have happened if I'd listened to Grandmère, joined the rebels at age ten or twelve."

"You never would have come to Oxford. You never would have met me. Except, perhaps, that first time, when Zeus and I invaded your garden."

"And I'd have chopped off your heads at the first hint of your English accents."

"You'd have been my noble savage. The man in my painting. I used to dream about you, you know. Saw you lying on furskins down below, on the mosaic floor. Imagined you with your wife, and a passel of children. Lord, I wonder what's become of that painting."

"Ten shillings says the dean's wife has it hanging in her boudoir."

She laughed again, holding tight to his hand. It still seemed such a miracle to have him, live and breathing, lying at her side. "Lady Maggie says Falkirk ended well. But you were there, you know that. Did you see Zeus?"

"Aye. His regiment never even engaged. We made mince-meat of the English before ever it could."

"Angus's cousin said Charles Edward would be angry with you," she remembered.

"Oh, he was. He docked us a month's pay for contradicting orders to remain at Murray's rear guard. But since none of us has seen tuppence since we came to Perth, what difference could that make?"

"What do you think of him?"

"God, I feel for the poor bastard. Talk about a rotten destiny. Imagine being the last hope of the Stuarts."

"Worse, even, than being last of the Faurers?"

"A thousand times worse. All I risk disappointing is Grandmère—and the ghosts."

"Zeus told me you were born to soldier."

He paused. "It's rather frightening to discover I am infinitely suited to an occupation I have always despised."

"Well. Grandmère always said that it was in your blood. Is it at all . . . gratifying?"

"Oh, that's most terrifying of all. It is very much so." He stopped again. "Not one's axe hitting flesh. That is not at all pleasant. But the part beforehand, the moments when you stand at ready with the pipes in your head and the drums in your heart, and the scent of victory tickling your nose—that is impossibly seductive." He turned his head to kiss her. "Nearly so much as you. I have seen—" And he stopped.

"What?"

"Ach, it is nonsense for me to speak of this to you."

"Of what?"

He went on slowly, searching for words. "It is almost . . . as though there is a change in the light. A different way of seeing the world. A bond to the earth, to the grass and the heather. One can almost watch them growing, hear their roots reaching, grasping. Twigs spring out at you. Bugs seem ten times their size.''

"Perhaps . . . the knowledge that your blood could soon be watering them.'' The notion made her shiver.

"Aye, that. But more. The realization that things meet. That things would meet anyway, eventually. But that you've chosen to face it, confront it, even chase it—that you are being bold and brave. That you've become a man.''

"What about the cause?'' she whispered.

"I don't know that the cause matters. It's more like some tribal duty, some rite of passage, entry into the priesthood. It makes me think of all the ridiculous customs and secret ceremonies one must undergo at Oxford. Do you know what they are? Substitutes—weak, cabalistic, scholarly replacements for the grasp of your weapon in your fist, the enemy in sight, and your whole self rigid with anticipation.''

Callie remembered what Molly MacPherson had said: *Gi' a boy a stick, 'n he will turn it to a sword or pike . . .*, "I'm not at all certain how it makes me feel about the future of the human race—that you, of all men, should succumb to such seduction.''

"Oh, don't think I haven't thought about that. But really, it would be presumptuous of us, wouldn't it, to imagine that simply because we know the world is round and one can't fall off the edge, we are more civilized than the ancient Egyptians or Greeks? The human spirit doesn't change. It will still ache for conquest even if we someday learn all the secrets of the universe. There will only be other worlds to conquer then.''

"We are doomed,'' she murmured.

"We are destined, rather. To be what we are. A cruel, marvelous machine.'' His fingers wound through her hair. "And yet so infinitely fragile. So much grandeur wrapped in a thin strut of bone and blood and flesh.''

"It's a wonder we have the nerve to go on procreating.''

She felt him smile against her. "Oh, there's no wonder in that. Not anymore. Not to me.'' He slid his hand to her breast, felt the bandage there, and winced. "Though you may feel differently at the moment.''

"Oddly enough, I don't. It's like the story of Pandora's box, isn't it? Nothing left in it but hope."

"And yet hope is enough. Oh, they were wise, those Greeks." He kissed her, full on the mouth, and she felt his loins press against her. "Willing to risk the future of mankind again?"

"As many times as you can stand it."

"Don't dare me. I'm newly susceptible to dares."

They made love again, more slowly, the desperate edge gone from their passion, replaced by wistfulness and deep cherishing. And Callie thought, *Love is hope. This is what hope is.* At the moment of climax, the black figures etched against bright light danced a marvelous dance. . . .

Sleepy, spent, she curled against him. He held her as a farm-wife holds eggs, delicate and firm. The night spun out its cloak, laid it gently across them. Grimkin purred, gold eyes wide, at the foot of their bed.

42.

Spring was creeping into Lady Maggie's garden, twisting bindweed, unraveling fritillary, forcing up thick fuzzy stalks of elecampane. Callie knelt and scrabbled with her fingers for the small, swirled blooms of dog-violets, traced their smooth, fleshy leaves, could almost feel the mottling there. Something smelled like heaven. She sat back on her heels and raised her nose to the chilly wind, then stood and followed the scent, hands held well out in front lest she blunder into a tree or wall. There it was—at the foot of the stone bench. Jonquils. She lay flat on her belly and buried her face in them, drinking in the sweet fragrance, picturing in her mind the pure yellow of their honeyed bells.

"Wha' in God's name—why, ye'll catch yer death o' chill!" Jennet's indignant cry brought Callie's head up. " 'N after all the trouble 'n work we had to save ye in the first place—talk about ungratefulness!"

"It isn't cold. There is warmth in the earth now. Feel it," Callie invited the housekeeper, beckoning.

"Crawlin' about on all fours like some wild creature—wha' bae I to do wi' ye, then?" Jennet hauled her upward by her elbows, dusting off the front of Callie's skirts with brisk hands.

Then she plunked her down on the bench. "Sit. Here. Until I come 'n fetch ye for dinner."

"Yes, Jennet," Callie murmured contritely. "I will. I am sorry." She folded her hands in her lap and sat, counting slowly to a hundred—more than enough time for Jennet to reach the front doors. Then she stood up, feeling her way along the bench to the apricot tree—

"I said sit!" Jennet bellowed from not ten yards away.

"Cheater," Callie muttered.

"I'll tie ye to the thing if I maun."

"You wouldn't dare."

"Dinna try me, lassie."

"Oh, very well." Gracelessly, Callie dropped back onto the bench, and nearly fell off the edge, having misjudged the distance.

Jennet clucked her tongue, rushing up to steady her. "I should think ye wuld hae learned by now to bae more chary! Hurt, bae ye?"

"Not a bit. And I do wish you'd stop treating me as though I'm made of glass."

"Glass breaks," the housekeeper said darkly, " 'n sae will ye, if ye blunder about sae." Her broad hand brushed a hank of curls from the bandage that still masked Callie's eyes. "Gae slow, pet. Dinna ye ken how cross His Lairdship will bae wi' me if he comes back to find ye all bruised 'n battered? Look here; ye hae torn a hole in yer stockin'."

"Where?" Jennet guided her hand to it. Callie felt the small rip in the cloth, could discern every loose thread. Like her sense of smell, that of her touch was sharpening, filling the void left by her useless eyes. "I can darn it, if you'll thread the needle."

"Ach, child, dinna trouble yerself." She had regret in her voice, for having spoken so sharply.

"Jennet, I have to learn."

"Nay, ye dinna, pet, for ye'll always hae me. Now do sit quiet, bae a lamb, or my soup will hae curdled. Promise?"

Something, suddenly, had made Callie quite dizzy. She sat, gripping the seat of the bench with both hands. "I promise."

She felt Jennet move closer, lay a hand on her forehead. "I had best take ye in, pet. Ye bae gone over all pale—"

"I am fine. Go and see to your soup!" Damn, there came the dizzyness again. She breathed in, conquered it, smiled. "I am perfectly fine."

"Well . . ."

Callie shoved at her. "Go!"

Muttering a final dire warning on the consequences of disobedience, the housekeeper went. Callie counted once more to a hundred, but this time when she reached it only bent forward to put her head between her knees.

She was assaying too much, too quickly; she knew that. But it was only within the past week that the weather had warmed enough for Lady Maggie to give in to her pleadings and allow her out into the gardens. And after long weeks of winter spent stuck in her room, this freedom was intoxicating.

Still, she had to pace herself, find a balance that would let her build her strength but not strain it. These bouts of dizzyness were signal enough to her to mind her step.

She must be strong when Mick returned, surprise him with what she had accomplished. She put a hand to her bosom, felt the letter tucked there, and drew it out, smoothed it on her lap, fingers running over the unseen words she knew by heart. A rider had come with it just last Sunday, on his way through to Carlisle. Lady Maggie had given him a ruby ring for his trouble in making the detour, just to ensure other messengers would be willing to do the same.

It had been their first word from Mick in more than six weeks, since the morning he had left Langlannoch to return to the campaign, and it was full of news good and bad. After Hawley's ignominious defeat at Falkirk, the Duke of Cumberland had been recalled to lead the Hanoverian forces—that was the bad news. Kilmallie, retaken by the English during Charles Edward's march southward, had now been retaken by the Scots. That was the good. There were well-wishes for Callie from the prince and, Mick wrote, "all your entire army of admirers." And a postscript: Angus MacPherson had rejoined the troops at Perth, just in time for their march northward to Inverness.

"Inverness!" Jennet, listening, had exclaimed. "Why, that bae halfway to John o' Groat's'. Plannin' to fall back till the sea bae lappin' at their ankles, bae they?"

Lady Maggie was calm. "The Highlands hae always been the source o' Stuart strength. It makes sense for Prince Charlie to gae there to regroup, now that Cumberland bae recalled."

But the news had given Callie pause, too. Ten days from London they'd been, once upon a time, and now nearly back to the beginning again. "Is that—all he writes?" she asked. It was lovely to have heard from him, of course, but somehow she'd expected . . . more.

A smile crept into Lady Maggie's voice. "Nay. There bae another page, addressed to ye."

Callie's heartbeat quickened. "Oh! Read it, please!"

She heard the snap of the seal as it broke, then a pause and a sigh. "What?" Callie asked eagerly.

"He writes . . . he prays ye will bae readin' it wi' yer own eyes."

"But I can't. Yours will have to do."

Lady Maggie cleared her throat, then cleared it again. " 'My dearest love,' " she began. " 'I thought of you last night as I lay on my pallet, as I think of you every night, and my entire being ached to be holding you, kissing your white breasts, tasting your sweet mouth, thrusting deep inside you and hearing you cry out my name.' "

"Oh," Callie said as she paused, and felt her throat redden. "I beg your pardon. If you'd rather not—"

"Nae, nae, lass! I simply dinna ken the boy had it in him." His grandmother had laughed. "Michel, Michel. Will wonders ne'er cease? Well! Where war I? 'Deep inside you—' "

"After that," Callie told her, flushing even more.

"But I like that part. Dinna ye?"

"Lady Maggie!"

"Ach, forgive me, pet. I dinna mean to make a jest o' it. Here, then. 'The nights stretch long without you. I remember you as sunlight and roses, and the thought of you melts the snow beneath my feet.' "

"He bae a fair poet, bain't he?" Jennet broke in with breathless admiration.

"Sae he bae. 'We may yet conquer England'—that bae him again, pet—'but no force, not even death, should it come, can ever conquer my love for you. Tell that rascal Grimkin I am

counting the hours till I can displace him.' '' Callie laughed
shakily, her hands curled in tight fists. '' 'Spring will soon be
there. Have a care not to freckle in untoward places. You are
in my heart always, as I know I am in yours. You were right.
We have been blessed. Here's a kiss for each eye—oh, I trust
they are healing!—and one for you, well, you know where.
There is talk of sending some of us home for spring planting.
Dust off the *Kama Sutra*—' ''

"The wha'?" Jennet echoed, perplexed.

Lady Maggie had chuckled. '' 'And take down your hair. I
want to lose myself in it. Warn the ghosts I am coming. Watch
for me. I am aching for your sweet love.' And then he signs
it—'Always, Michel.' ''

She'd folded up the letter again, and pressed it into Callie's
hands. The three women sat for a moment in silence. Then
Jennet let out a sigh. "Ach. These Faurer men—"

"Puts me quite in mind o' my Douglas," Lady Maggie said
dreamily. "I hae a letter he wrote me after Sheriffmuir, back
in '15, that—well. That bae neither here nor there. Anyone for
a spot o' wine?"

Engulfed in her memories, Callie had not heard Jennet's
footsteps approaching in the garden. "There, now! There bae
a gude lass, to stay put as I tell ye! Come on, now, I'll take
ye in for yer supper."

Callie, tucking the letter back into her bosom, felt her gorge
suddenly rise. She leaned forward, retching. Jennet gasped.
"Christ in heaven! Dinna I tell ye ye war doin' too much?"

Callie wiped her sour mouth with her kerchief. "I'm sorry,"
she whispered. "Please, don't tell Lady Maggie."

"But I needs maun tell her, if ye bae ill!"

"I'm not ill. It is just what you said—I exerted myself too
much."

"Here, now, dinna step in it. Gi' me yer hand. Ach, pet.
Ye'll hae to change yer dress."

"I'm sorry," Callie said again. "I'll wash it. I'll change
myself, and then I'll wash it. I know you've so much to do—"

"La, I dinna care about the laundry, lass! Just come along
inside. I'll fetch ye somewha' clean to put on, 'n then ye can
hae some nice hot sorrel sou—" She never finished the word

before Callie vomited again, miserably, ashamedly. "God in heaven, child! Wha' bae the matter wi' ye?"

"I don't know. Just don't tell Lady Maggie!"

She heard the housekeeper sputter in frustration. "If ye bae ill, ye little fool, she can heal ye!"

But Callie was afraid, desperately afraid. The blindness had done something dreadful to her body—put it out of balance, thrown it out of kilter. Why else would the mere mention of food, any food, make her stomach wrench? It had been weeks since she'd enjoyed a meal; even the scent of cooking was nauseating. That was why she'd begged so relentlessly to be allowed outside. If Lady Maggie knew of it, she'd confine her to her rooms; Callie was certain of that. And the aromas of bread, roasting meat, Jennet's impeccable stews, would waft up the stairs.

Just thinking about it made her queasy again. She clutched Jennet's elbow. "I'll be better tomorrow. I swear it." If willing it could make her so, she would be. "Just say I was tired. Bring something up to my room." Where she could toss it out the window, or feed it to Grimkin.

"But, pet. Nice hot sorrel sou—"

Callie pitched forward abruptly. If there'd been anything more in her belly, she'd have lost it. Jennet listened to the retching, clucking her tongue. Callie wiped her mouth again. "Please, Jennet. One more day."

But at breakfast the next morning—scent of bacon, odor of biscuits—Callie vomited right at the table. Lady Maggie, seated across from her, called for Jennet to clear up the mess. Then she said softly, "How long has this been goin' on?"

Jennet, washrag slapping the wood, ignored Callie's imprecating grasp at her wrist. "Long eno', that bae wha' I say. Nigh on a month, that I ken."

"Ye hae been nauseous?"

Callie hung her head, hands twisted in her lap.

"Smell o' food makes ye wretched?"

"It is just not seeing!" Callie exclaimed. "It's affected my appetite. Nothing so strange in that, really."

"Ye cried out when I changed the bandage on yer breasts this mornin'. Why? Bae they sore?"

"The water on your cloth was cold," Callie mumbled. She was not about to admit to that discomfort, too. Her nipples ached constantly; she'd put that down to the bandage. Why shouldn't they hurt, bound up in linen all the time?

To her chagrin, Mick's grandmother laughed. "La, pet! Why in God's name wuld ye hide such news fro' me?"

"Because you've worked so hard to make me well again! Because . . . because what's wrong with me must be something awful." It had to be, didn't it? "Something even you cannot cure."

"Ach, ye bae right in that." Her voice was very grave.

"You know what it is, then?"

"Well eno', I suspect."

"Is it . . . fatal?"

At her side, Jennet had begun to chuckle. Outraged, Callie clawed at her blindly. "How dare you laugh?"

"Oh, pet, forgi' me! But I ought to hae known. . . ."

"Not fatal, Jennet, wuld ye say?"

"Nae, nae. But true eno', ye cannae cure it."

"Not that I wuld care to," Lady Maggie said with complacence.

Callie stood up, palms flat on the table. "Damn you both, what is wrong with me?"

"Either a boy," Mick's grandmother told her, "or else a girl."

Callie sat back down, breathless. "Either a *what?*"

Jennet bent to kiss her. "Faith, luv. Ye bae bearin' a bairn."

"Bearing a . . . you mean, having a *baby?*" Callie had started trembling.

"Another laird o' Langlannoch," Lady Maggie noted with approval. " 'N to think I tried to chide Michel when I saw him at the makin'! Praise God he sent me packin'."

Callie's hands crept downward to her belly. "A *baby* . . ."

"La, how I suffered fro' the retchin' wi' my Rene!"

" 'N I wi' Ben," Jennet put in knowingly. "Nae a twinge did I hae wi' Gordie. But, ooh, that Ben! Had to do the washin'-up wi' a handkerchief o'er my nose—d'ye recall that, m'lady?"

"Oh, aye, aye, sae I do. I remember that I wrote my mother askin' her advice. 'Fennel tea,' she writes back. Sae I brewed up a whole vat o' the stuff, took a taste, 'n straight off brought it back up again! I dinna hae the soreness in the breasts, though.''

"Faith, but I did! Gordie war not e'en weaned yet, ye ken, when the retchin' started. 'N his father, God rest his soul, why, he said to me—"

"When?" Callie interrupted.

At her side, Jennet paused. "Let me think, now. Gordie war scarce two, 'n he bae eighteen now, sae it wuld hae been—"

"No, no, I mean me!"

"Oh! Well!" Jennet calculated. "Seven weeks since the master bae gone—"

"The last week in January," Lady Maggie put in. "Sae. The end o' October, or the start o' November. Nine months in all. Surely, child, ye ken that." She sounded faintly accusing.

"Of course I do. It's just—" Her mind was in complete muddle. A baby! It was the last thing in the world she'd expected—yet she ought to have known. She drew a breath. "I must send word to Mick."

Lady Maggie's voice was cautious: "If ye think that bae wise . . ."

Callie's head came up. "You don't . . . think he'll be pleased?"

"Ach, I daresay the lad will bae ecstatic. Still—"

"What?"

"Well. I war only thinkin' . . . wha' such news wuld mean to a soldier. He bae a soldier now, ye ken."

That pierced Callie's fog. She nodded in slow understanding. "It might take the edge from him."

"The edge," said Jennet wisely, "bae wha' keeps 'em alive."

Callie thought of Angus and Molly and their offspring. "Some men deal with war and families. Some have their children along—"

"Some men bae nae Michel," his grandmother noted. "If ye could hae seen him, Callie, when he brought ye here—nigh sick to death he war wi' worry. Tears rollin' down his cheeks— he dinna cry sae when his own mother passed on."

"You think I ought not to tell him."

"Ach, that bae yer own decision to make. Dinna listen to me, child. Hear in yer heart."

To keep such news a secret. Not to share the joy that was surging through her, filling her to bursting—impossible! And yet, she thought of the encampments, the nights that passed so slowly, the way he'd spoken, with such delicate wonder, of the moments before battle, and the grass growing up through the earth. . . . His newfound courage was a tenuous thing.

"If he comes home for the planting," she began, and the two older women spoke in quick chorus:

"Oh, aye! If he comes here—"

"If he should visit—"

It was not until that moment that she realized how unlikely they believed such a visit to be. "He only wrote that to encourage me," she whispered.

There was a long silence. "Ach, lass," Lady Maggie said finally. "If ye made one stitch for every day the women o' this house hae waited for their men to come home fro' battle, ye wuld hae a tapestry that reached to the moon."

Callie's palms were clammy. Still, "I can wait," she said proudly.

Lady Maggie's long fingers caressed hers from across the table. "We'll wait together," she said.

43.

Callie had entirely too much time for thinking. Try as she would to find something to do with her hands, the range of choices was appallingly small. She could card wool—painstakingly, fingers crawling through the rough, oily masses of fluff. She tried to learn to spin, Jennet's patient, gentle voice in her ear—"Steady, luv. Keep it steady wi' the wheel. Tease the wool out slow. Feel it—there! Nae. Well, hae another gae." She could sew on hooks and buttons—if Lady Maggie or Jennet did the needles, and marked the places first with their own stitches. Really, little point in that; they might have sewn the stuff on themselves in half the time. She could clean beans, shell peas, knead bread, though this last always ended with a mess in the kitchen for Jennet. She assayed knitting, lost count of the rows. She felt stupid and useless and always, always, sick to her stomach. Knowing the source of her nausea hadn't eliminated that.

Sometimes she broke down crying. "How will I ever look after a baby, when I can't even slice fruit?"

Lady Maggie would hold her and soothe her. "Ye'll ne'er bae alone, pet. Ye'll always hae me 'n Jennet to help ye, 'n Michel, too."

"Who knows if he is even alive still?" she wailed once in frustration.

"Bite yer tongue, lass. Ye ken that he bae." But the end of March came and went with no further word from him. April ran riot with the gardens. Easter. Death and rebirth. God who loved the world so much that he gave his son . . .

Callie found herself thinking, too much, about her own father. Odd to imagine she herself was living proof of the passion she'd always assumed he lacked. All their lives, she and Zeus had shunted their parents into boxes: Laurie was raw emotion, William Wingate logic and reason. Each was neatly packaged and tied. But twenty-odd years ago, on the Isle of Skye, something had come unwrapped. A young man who'd spent his life reaching up had tumbled down, down in the heather, into a net of Scots-red hair and small white arms.

And Laurie, she pondered, sitting on the garden bench beneath the apricot tree—what could Laurie have been thinking? Even two decades past, her father could never have been the embodiment of any girl's dreams, so tall and thin and gangly, spectacles perched on his nose, his face buried in books. Unless—and here she caught her breath, had to grasp the bench for mooring—Laurie's dreams had been too big for Skye, for the shepherds and crofters who would have been her suitors. Plunked in their midst, her nondescript father must have seemed as outlandish and exotic as—well, as Mick had first appeared to her bestriding this garden wall. What if the impetus had been Laurie's? It took two to tumble. A shaft of guilt pierced her. Life was far too complex to be reduced to boxes. Perspective shifted with the light, with the tide, with the angle of seeing. Nothing once viewed would ever again look exactly the same.

"Hush!" Lady Maggie's whisper at her ear made her jump. "Harken! D'ye hear it?" Callie cocked her head, listened. Birdsong rang out in the air, high and thrilling and sweet, a wild trill of melody and grace-notes. "A nightingale," Lady Maggie murmured with awe. "Only knew it to come sae far north once before in my life. Ach, hark to the pretty thing!" They listened in silence. "He'll bae off southward by mornin'," Lady Maggie said sadly, "for he'll find nae mate here." Almost as though he'd heard her, the bird poured out a crescendo of heart-stopping beauty, then paused. The whole garden seemed to hold its breath, waiting. Lady Maggie sighed. "He bae flown away. Still, 'twar a blessin', war it nae, to hear him? Chances such as that dinna come often in life." A lesson, Callie thought, I surely ought to have learned by now. "I hae best get back to my weedin'. Unless bae there anythin' ye need o' me, pet?"

"Lady Maggie. I'd like to . . . could you write out a letter for me? To my father?"

Mick's grandmother bent to kiss her cheek. "Ach, I war hopin' ye wuld find yer way to writin' him, pet."

It was a difficult letter to compose at first. So much news to tell, so many months apart. Callie scarcely knew where to begin. Lady Maggie waited patiently with pen and paper. Finally Callie dictated:

Dear Father,
When last we spoke, it was of repercussions. Now it seems I'm to have a repercussion of my own, late October next. Congratulations, Grandpapa! Mick is the father—and, yes, he does intend to do his duty by me. I am only now starting to have some glimmer of all that entails. Forgive me for having left you so abruptly, and for my self-righteous anger. I only hope I'll prove half so splendid a parent as you have been to me.

After that, it went more easily.

Two mornings later, Callie woke, opened her eyes beneath their mask of gauze, and saw Grimkin leap to her side—well, saw his shade, really, the bulk of him, shadow against lighter shadow. Still, it had been so long since her eyes had registered anything at all, she sat up screaming for Lady Maggie, tearing at the bandage. "Wha'? Wha' on earth, child, bae—"

"I saw Grimkin! I saw him!"

She heard Lady Maggie mumbling in enraptured Gaelic, then in English: "God 'n Mary bae praised!"

She could not get the bandage undone. "But *how* could I see, with this still on me?"

Lady Maggie pulled Callie's frantic fingers from the gauze. "Faith, lass. Feel. It bae as sheer as veil. Ye can see straight through it. 'Twar only for show, that ye might gae on hopin'. But the healin' had to come fro' inside." She untied it gently. Callie looked about her in wonder: faint spire of bedpost, fainter hulk of wardrobe, Grimkin a purring splash of darkness against pale linen sheets.

"Oh, God," she whispered in wonder. So much less than once, aye, but so very much more than nothingness! To see Mick again, even as a shadow! To be able to look upon her baby's face . . .

"Ye maun keep out o' bright sun," Lady Maggie cautioned. "Dinna strain yer sight. Dinna try too hard. Gi' it time."

She could make out the blob of lilacs on the bedstand, see movement in the doorway, white apron, dark dress. "Jennet!" she cried. "Jennet, Jennet, I *see* you!"

"As I live 'n breathe! D'ye, now? Praise bae!"

No more leisure for self-pity now, not with this new world of half-light to explore. Features on a face she still could not make out, but she could discern contrast, detect motion, find her way across a room without smashing into anything. On sunny days she flitted through the halls and chambers of Langlannoch, watching the miraculous interplay of light and dark around her; when it was overcast, she walked through the gardens and saw the wind stir the leaves. Firelight entranced her. Fog was more marvelous than books had ever been. White-capped waves on the sea were an ever-shifting tapestry. April was heady with promise—until the night Gordie came home.

He came in through the kitchen doors, making Jennet screech in surprise: "Gordie! Bae that ye, Gordie?" Lady Maggie came running; Callie went more slowly, picking her way through the candlelit hall. Jennet hung, teary, on her wraith-thin son. "God bae praised, God bae praised—but where bae yer brother?"

"Oh, Muther." Callie had never heard a voice so weary. "Muther. I bae sae sorry—"

"Ben," the housekeeper whispered, swaying. "My baby. My Ben—"

Gordie helped her to a bench, knelt before her. "I wuld to God it had been me. But he war brave, Muther. La, he war sae

brave! Ne'er one word o' complaint had he all these long
months—yet ye ken how frail he bae. He war. Oh, Muther,
Muther, he war stronger than me. . . .' '

Callie could see Jennet's body rocking back and forth against
the light from the hearth. "Tell me how," the woman keened,
as Lady Maggie came to her side.

" 'Twar a battle, Muther. A big one. On Drummossie Muir,
near Inverness. Agin the Duke o' Cumberland. Half of us had
gone out lookin' for food. Night came on. The call came for
marchin'. It seemed awry to me, wi' sae few men. But still,
we marched. Ach, we war sae hungry, Muther. Hungry 'n tired.
There war nae food to bae had in all the land around—nae
bread, nae ale, nae neeps e'en, much less meat. We marched
'n marched through the night, 'n then they turned us 'round,
'n we marched back to the camp again—why, I dinna ken. Sae
tired we war! 'N nae sooner to bed than they waked us: Time
to bae marchin'! Off we went. By noon, we saw 'em—oceans
'n oceans o' 'em lined up agin us. It looked to bae a million
men."

He took a breath. "We brought our guns up. It war rainin'.
Everythin' war in a muddle. We had the M'Donalds, Muther,
on the left line! When every soul in Scotland ken it bae their
privilege since the time o' the Bruce to lead the charge on the
right!"

Lady Maggie was wagging her head: "MacDonalds on the
left—faith, that bae madness."

"Sae it war. Oh, Muther, if ye culd hae seen their guns!
They maun hae lugged every cannon in England up to the
Highlands! 'N us wi' twelve pieces, 'n half those old 'n skent.
Then the sky grew darker, 'n we fired the cannon, they war
far off still, mayhaps five hundred yards. They fired back—
such a roar, such a flashin'! 'N our lads just dropped down in
waves. Dropped in waves, they did, right where they stood.
La, 'twar a dreadful sight."

"What of the Highland charge?" Callie murmured.

Gordie's gaunt face whipped toward her. "There war nae
order to charge! Ready we war, 'n waitin', waitin', prayin' we
wuld hear the signal. But the guns just kept poundin', 'n more
lads fell down, till the bludy bastards had nae more balls. Then

they loaded wi' grapeshot, 'n it came flyin' toward us—God, Muther! Mowed down like the grain we war, 'n still nae order to charge!''

"Where war Bonnie Prince Charlie?" his mother demanded.

Gordie shrugged his shoulders. "Nae one culd ken. To the rear, I reckon, wranglin' wi' those generals o' his. Then, finally, *finally,* we got the signal, 'n we charged. But oh, we war thin by then, Muther. 'N the guns tore the cry fro' our mouths. But we went. Aye, we went. Ben war still wi' me then."

Lady Maggie pressed a cup of ale into his hand. He downed it in one swallow and went on, talking raggedly, almost incoherently. "Clan Chattan in the lead. Stewarts, Camerons, Athollmen 'n us to the right. The cannon just sliced up the center. They came bangin' in agin us, 'n we pushed into Wolfe's Regiment. Hand-to-hand we war, agin all their best—Barrel's men, Munro's. Somehow, we pushed through. 'N for wha'? There behind 'em war another five thousand men, 'n us wi'out our muskets. Trapped between their first 'n second lines, we war."

Callie had closed her eyes. Her months with the army let her see it all too clearly. With enough troops, enough time, with Cumberland to lead them, the English had at long last learned to outwait the charge. Tears streamed down her face as she imagined the terror of those boys and men, caught in the midst of the enemy.

"Ben went down then," Gordie whispered. "Just to my side he war. A musket-ball to his head."

Jennet was quietly sobbing. Lady Maggie's voice cut through her moans like a lash. "Where war the bludy MacDonalds?"

"They wuld nae charge, mum. They war that angry at bein' set to the left."

"Oh, oh, oh!" Mick's grandmother pounded her fists on the table. "The vaunty, prideful fools!"

"I think our second line held," Gordie went on. "I think retreat war sounded. But where, God, where war we to retreat *to?* They'd blasted down the walls o' Culloden Park. Their cavalry came through 'em. They war ringed all about us. Oh, Muther. Such a baleful day. I pray to heaven I ne'er see its like again."

His mother heaved a great sigh. " 'N why, then, bae ye come back here? Why bae ye nae at yer prince's side, fightin' to avenge yer poor brother's death?"

Gordie straightened up slowly. "I wuld bae, as God bae my witness. But the prince dismissed us. Sent us home. The war bae finished, Muther. It bae all o'er 'n done."

"Sent ye home?" Lady Maggie's voice held disbelief and something more: the crumbling of a vision held for a lifetime. "Sent ye *home?*"

"Aye, mum. He said—" Gordie swallowed. "He said he war sorry. Ach, wha' more culd he say?"

Callie saw Jennet's head turn toward her. "Gordie. Wha' o' His Lairdship?"

"Faith, Muther. Who can tell? I had my hands full. I culd nae e'en stay by Ben's body. They wuld nae stop houndin' us, wuld nae stop shootin'. Cumberland—the devil take his soul; he bae a bludy butcher." He, too, glanced at Callie, then at Lady Maggie. "He may yet find his way. The roads—"

"When was the battle?" Callie summoned courage to ask.

"The sixteenth, mum. God rue the day."

Two weeks past. "And . . . my brother?"

"God help me, mum, I cannae say."

But his voice, that awful, weary voice, said it all. Callie's hands curled on her belly. Mick and Zeus. They would not have walked away from such a fight.

The newfound light around her convulsed on itself, seemed to shatter and spin. In her mind's eye she saw the man on the black horse riding, frantically riding, charging at the ranks of a vast sea of enemy. . . .

And then she saw nothing. "Jesu, m'lady, catch her!" Jennet's frightened voice cried out, but from a great distance.

Oh, Mick. Oh, my poor love.

44.

Langlannoch wa a house of mourning: curtains drawn, spoken whispers, visitors from the village bearing blossoms and sorrow in their arms. No one had been untouched by the tragedy of Drummossie Muir. Davey and Liam were dead. Walter Coady was dead, his pretty Jessie left a widow. Jock MacKenzie, dead. Day by day, in the unraveling beauty of springtime, stragglers trudged home, reported what they knew. They all came to Langlannoch. They all made their condolences to Jennet, and to Lady Maggie. They each told their story, halting, apologetic, almost, to be still among the living. So much pain, so much grief. Callie could hardly bear to hear any more. And yet she sensed that the telling was vital to these men, these unlucky survivors of the death of Scotland's dream. So she listened, fingers clenching knitting needles that scarcely ever moved, while they spun out their tales.

His Lairdship had led the charge into Munro's battalion. His Lairdship had been a whirlwind, dealing death to all around him. His Lairdship had told jests, shored up spirits, when they found themselves pinned between the English lines. His Lairdship had hacked a score of men to pieces. His Lairdship, it seemed, had done everything that day but survive.

Callie couldn't sleep nights. She was tortured by memories, regrets. What if ... what if ... And all of it useless. Mick had made his own choices; he always had. What was, was.

Jessie Coady came to call. She sat in the dining hall, sniffling. She'd brought the baby with her—he was a baby no more, though. He was now a rambunctious toddler, climbing up all the chairs. "To think he'll ne'er remember his daddy—oh, m'lady! Wha' bae I to do?"

"Make him remember," Lady Maggie told her fiercely. "Keep the memory alive."

Crofts, shops, herds, left with no men to tend them. A dozen widows just in Ayr. And all over Scotland, it would be the same. Callie thought her heart would break with the woe.

She still held out some hope for Zeus. Perth's men had been in the rearguard; everyone agreed on that. But for Mick, trapped at the heart of the carnage—

Lady Maggie was so strong, though. She had to be.

"Ye look tired," the Scotswoman observed gently, on an evening in May when the day's visitors had left them. " 'N ye had nae much appetite at supper. Hae ye need o' a sleepin' draught?"

Callie raised her chin up. "I don't think so. No."

She was starting to show. Jennet had let her waists out for her. The last laird of Langlannoch swelled her belly. "Lady Maggie. What if it is a girl?"

"It still will bae a Faurer."

"Even though we were not wed?"

"Blud bae blud." With rich anticipation, Lady Maggie continued. "Think, lass, how lucky we bae."

Perhaps it seemed that way, if viewed through the smoky glass of long centuries. Callie, though, felt numbed, lost, frightened by a brutal world. With Mick gone, she'd lost her sense of belonging here. There would be no more dark figures dancing at the moment of climax. She contemplated going back to Edinburgh, to her father, to the safety of lecture halls and supper parties. But destiny had rooted her to Langlannoch, like the apricot tree.

The stream of survivors tailed off, finally ended. Somehow, life went on. Jennet cooked and cleaned. Gordie, mostly silent, mended hedges, sheared sheep. Lady Maggie sewed, proposed names: Anne? Perhaps Catriona?

There was no question at all, of course, which to choose for a boy.

In early June, when they'd all grown used to quiet, Gordie came running in from the fields with his scythe in his hand. "Men comin'," he gasped. "On the southward road."

Mick's grandmother set her sewing down. "How many?"

"Four—five, maybe."

"Mounted?"

"Nay. Near crawlin'."

Callie refused to give in to false hope. Lady Maggie called for Jennet from the kitchens: "Can ye feed another half-dozen mouths?"

"I can feed wha'e'er I maun feed."

"Gae out 'n greet 'em, Gordie," Lady Maggie directed. "If they bae Scots, see they stop for a meal."

Callie went up the back stair, to watch from a window. *Watch for me,* he'd said. Her eyes, still too weak to see from a distance, strained to pierce it anyway. Nearly two months now. It just couldn't be.

She saw the splotch of Gordie as he ran through the gates, searched the stretch of road, dust-light between summer's lush greenery. The patch of darkness that was Gordie met another dark patch, bigger, shifting, up the road. Then a bit of it broke off, came tearing toward the house at a pace that seemed impossible.

Her heart stopped. She wound out the casement.

"Callie!" the dark patch was screaming.

It was Zeus's voice.

They had a royal feast that night, with the last of the bordeaux and brandy brought up from the cellar. For they had a royal visitor: Prince Charles Edward, the last of the Stuarts, had come to dine. "There was to have been a ship for us at Troon," Zeus explained, "but Cumberland's men beat us to it. Lying in wait there, they were. A dairymaid tipped us off. We caught a ride on a fishing sloop that left us outside Girvan. And I thought, since we were so close—''

''He means, on account o' we had nae place else to gae,'' Cluny MacPherson, yet another of Angus's cousins, put in, laughing.

''Well, that too,'' Zeus concurred. ''And I had told them, Jennet, all about your jam.''

Lady Maggie set the prince in the chair Robert the Bruce once sat in, but that didn't keep her from demanding of him. ''Well? Wha' went wrong, then?''

''I also promised them,'' Zeus said gently, ''that you wouldn't badger.''

''Let her be, Zeus,'' Charles Edward murmured. ''She has the right to ask.'' Callie wished that she could make out his face. His voice held the same bleak futility that Gordie's had when he came home from the battle. And why not? Two months on the run he had been, with a price set by the English at 30,000 pounds stirling on his head. It was a tribute to what the Scots thought of him that no one had turned him in. ''What went wrong where, Lady Margaret?''

''Ach. Ye tell me.''

Callie saw him shift in the chair.

''Well,'' said Charles Edward. ''I suppose I'd have to hark back to my grandfather James, and his stubborn affection for the Church of Rome. Or perhaps to great-great-grandfather James, who would not be contented with the crown of Scotland, but let himself be saddled with England's as well.''

''Oh, hell,'' said Zeus. ''Why not trace it back all the way to the beginning? 'When Adam delved and Eve span,' were they Jacobites or Whigs?''

''In my day,'' Lady Maggie said darkly, ''there wuld hae been nae surrender.''

'' 'He that fights and runs away,' '' the prince quoted vaguely, '' 'lives to fight another day.' Forgive me, Lady Margaret. I know you are disappointed in me. I am disappointed in myself.''

''Ye maun hae men, clans, yet, that wuld fight for ye!''

The prince leaned toward her. ''I am killing this country. You opened your arms to me, and what have I done in return?

Bled you of your fathers and husbands and sons, scorched your fields, razed your houses—''

'' 'N wha' for, if ye leave us now?'' Lady Maggie cried in bitter rage.

"What was it ever for? For my right to be king? Or for the right of my people to live in peace, sleep without fear, have bread to feed their children? So help me, that were better served had I stayed in France.''

"God—chose—ye.'' Lady Maggie stabbed a finger at him. "God made ye Stuart!''

Callie thought she saw the shadow of a smile on the prince's face. "He made me what I am. He birthed me in the Age of Reason. So who's to say, dear, dear lady, that he didn't make me for this—to lay an end to it all?''

His hostess was disgusted. "Ach, nae laird o' this house wuld e'er hae left the fight unfinished.''

"The men of this house,'' the prince said quietly, politely, "were better men than I.''

There was a hard silence. Then Lady Maggie, softened. "La, lad. I dinna mean—''

"I did.''

"Callie.'' Zeus said brightly, rubbing her shoulder. "We're going to France, you know. Eventually. You can come with us, set up that studio you wanted. Now that your eyes are getting better—''

Cluny MacPherson broke in, clucking his tongue. "Bae ye daft, Zeus? Who can ken when we'll find a ship to take us there? It culd be months yet o' runnin' 'n hidin'.''

"Callie can outrun you still, Cluny, you overgrown lug. What about it, pet? You and I together. Another adventure.'' His arm curled around her. He smelled of the road, of sweat and dust and worn leather and freedom.

She swallowed, hard. "I can't.''

"If it's your eyes, Cal, I'll be your eyes.'' He would, too. She knew that.

"It bain't her eyes, ye bludy fool,'' snorted the blunt Cameron of Lochiel, who was running with them. "Look at the lass!''

"What? I *am* looking at her. She looks lovely.'' Cluny Mac-

Pherson was chuckling quietly into his wine cup. "What, then? What is it? Callie?"

She hadn't planned to tell him, not with what lay before him. He would need that edge. But, neither was it fair not to, now the older men had guessed. "I am going to have a child."

"A *child*." She might have said an alligator, from his tone. "You? *Whose* child? Oh, Christ, Cal! Is it . . . can it be Mick's?" She nodded, head down, shy at that table full of men. "I'll be damned."

"Lady Margaret." For the first time, Charles Edward's voice lost its weariness. "Permit me to offer my sincerest felicitations. Langlannoch lives on." Then he got up, came around the table, and kissed Callie's cheek. "I grieve for your loss," he whispered, "and rejoice in your gain."

"Thank you."

"I'll be damned. I'll be damned," Zeus was still muttering in amazement. "You weren't even speaking to the man the last I knew of it!"

"Who needs words?" Cluny mumbled into his cup, shoulders shaking. Lochiel elbowed him.

"When, then?" Zeus demanded.

Callie blushed. "That's surely none of your business!"

"No, I mean—when will it be born?"

"Oh! The end of October." A silence came over the room again. She could almost hear their minds, though, counting back.

"Falkirk," the prince said softly. "Our last victory. There's something fitting in that."

" 'Twar ye gave him leave to bring her here," Lady Maggie mentioned.

"Oh, I'll take full credit, absolutely. Just, please God, don't name it after me."

"Ye bear a fine name," Lady Maggie told him. "Dinna ye e'er bae ashamed o' that."

"There's a German philosopher, Lunt or Bunt or something," Zeus noted, "who theorizes our names provide our destiny."

Cluny MacPherson laughed outright. "Wha' can it mean, then, that ye cannae remember his?" The laughter faded to fondness. "Ye see, though, Mistress Wingate, why we maun hae yer brother wi' us. How else wuld uncouth savages such as Cameron 'n I bae exposed to such things? I reckon by the time we reach Paris, we'll bae ready to stand for our doctorates at the university."

"If they gave doctors' hats for heart," Charles Edward said, "every Scot would have his." Then he rose again from the Bruce's chair. "Speaking of reaching Paris, though, we'd best be on our way."

"I'd hoped ye'd stay the night," Lady Maggie cried with regret. "We hae room 'n to spare—"

"Pay her no mind," Zeus advised the prince. "She only wants to be able to add it to the family lore that Bonnie Prince Charlie slept here."

"Cheeky laddie," she chided, slapping his hand. " 'N wha' if I do? Ye all o' ye bae fair done in. Spend the night. Gordie can ride up to Ayr 'n send a boat back for ye, that can take ye o'er to Kintyre. There bae MacDonalds there—" Callie sensed a collective wince. " 'N MacLeans 'n Duarts," Lady Maggie added hastily, then could not help but pose the question: "Why, pray tell, did ye set those mad MacDonalds on the left?"

"I thought—God help me—to teach them a lesson in martial discipline. Instead they taught me one, in Highland pride."

"They wuld nae hae changed the outcome," Lochiel growled.

"No. Nothing would have," the prince agreed. "But lives might have been saved." He sighed, straight from his heart. "Christ. The awful waste—"

"Those wha' live hae their stories to tell," said the old MacPherson chief. " 'N babes yet unborn to tell 'em to." He wore defeat like his plaid, at home with all its intricacies. Little wonder. He'd worn it all his days.

Callie was suddenly unbearably proud that such blood ran in her veins, would run in that of her child. "How is your cousin Angus?" she asked him.

"Well eno', for a lame man. We bided wi' him for a night, some time back."

"Ye maun do the same here," Lady Maggie said firmly. "Ye'll bae safe eno'. There hae been nae English about. Jennet!

Jennet, gae 'n call Gordie down." He'd been posted up in the tower to keep watch, just the same.

But before Jennet could move, they heard mad footsteps tumbling down the stair to the kitchens. "Soldiers," Gordie gasped out, clinging to the lintel.

Charles Edward was on his feet in an instant. "Coming which way?"

"The road fro' Kilmallie."

"Kilmallie?" Cluny echoed, perplexed. "How culd they ken we war here?"

In her mind Callie pictured the hard, ugly face of Commandant Henley. He could not have kept watch on the house all this time—could he? Or was it just since Drummassie? Had he sensed somehow the prince would wind up here?

"That scarcely matters. We must fly. Lady Margaret, you must come with us." The prince's voice, commanding.

"I'll nae leave Langlannoch."

"Christ, woman! If they know we've been here—"

"I dinna care. I'll nae gae."

"There's no use arguing it," Zeus interrupted Charles Edward's sputter. "She *won't* go. We must, though. And you, Callie."

"Aye, lass." Lady Maggie caught her under the arms, raised her up from her chair.

Cluny was easing upright, too. "Hold on, hold on. How many soldiers, laddie?"

"I wuld guess half a company. Mayhaps fifty men," Gordie announced from the doorway.

"Fifty—Jesus!" Charles Edward exclaimed.

"I hae a skiff," Gordie put in. "There bae but little moon. I can sail ye o'er to Kintyre, if need bae."

His mother had come in from the kitchens. "Ach, Gordie. That wee boat—sae far as Kintyre—"

"It is better than nothing," Zeus noted. "How many of us?" Callie wondered if he even remembered the book Mick had given him for his birthday: *A History of Shipwrecks Off the Coast of Ayr.*

Gordie calculated. "The sea bae calm eno'. Five, I'd say. 'N me."

"Come on, Callie." Zeus grabbed her hand. "We're going."

"No, Zeus. I must stay."

"Don't be absurd, Cal! Think of the baby!"

"I *am* thinking of the baby. The English won't harm three helpless women. I'll be safe." She drew in breath. "And I want the baby born here."

Lochiel was shoving the prince toward the kitchens. "There bae nae bludy time to argue it, Zeus. If she wuld stay, she bae stayin'."

"But—but—" Callie's brother stammered.

She shrugged off Lady Maggie's arms to kiss him. "Go! Write to me from France."

"Callie, how can I leave you?"

She turned to Lochiel. "Go on, then. Go without him."

"No!" Zeus cried.

"I bludy will, laddie, if ye dinna come now." He and Cluny and the prince were halfway to the back door.

"Dammit, Callie!" Zeus said in anguish. "What if they kill you?"

"What if they kill *him?*" She nodded toward Charles Edward.

"I'll send her upstairs," Lady Maggie promised him. Her hand had found Callie's and squeezed it. "They will nae e'en ken she bae here."

Still he hesitated, searching his sister's face. "And you'll go? Do as she says? You swear it?"

The sound of hoofbeats was audible now, at least to Callie. "On our mother's soul. Now, for God's sake, go!"

One last time he leaned toward her, kissed her. His fingers grazed the slight bulge in her belly. "Don't name it Persues, either," he whispered. "If you knew how I love you—"

"I do, Zeus. I do."

The back door closed behind them. Lady Maggie began reaching for plates "We maun clear away. Leave but one place, Jennet. Callie, hie yerself up those stairs."

"Leave two places, Jennet." The housekeeper, trenchers piled to her ears, swore in fearful frustration.

"One place!" Mick's grandmother ordered, twisting Callie's

arm with ferocious force. "Ye swore on the soul o' yer mother!"

"Laurie would understand."

Lady Maggie leaned in so close that Callie saw her eyes glint. "Ye get yerself up those stairs, or sae help me God, I'll send those soldiers out to the strand after Bonnie Prince Charlie 'n yer brother."

"You never would."

"Dinna ye try me!"

Well. It *was* the heir to Langlannoch Lady Maggie was protecting, Callie thought as she went up the stairs, hearing Jennet dumping trenchers into the sink.

After feeling her way about in the darkness for so long, the lack of light was no hindrance to her. She went first to her bedroom, scanning the sea beyond the walls, hoping by some miracle she might catch sight of Gordie's sail. But even the slight quarter-moon was in shadow. All the better for them, she thought, and crossed the hall to Zeus's room. Its casements gave out on the road to Kilmallie. She couldn't see the troops, but she surely could hear them. Not far off, she realized, and then, heart pounding, heard the creak of the gates.

She darted back to the top of the kitchen stairs. Water frantically pouring, dishes and silverware clinking, then the slam of the cabinets—and Jennet's whispered prayers. There came a thumping on the front doors. She ran toward the graceful but treacherous twin staircases leading off the Great Hall, and hid herself in the shadows. A bright flare of light appeared on the wall—Lady Maggie, lighting a torch there. More thumping. Mick's grandmother's slow, even steps . . .

She never made it to the doors. They burst open. Damning her faint vision, Callie peered around the corner-post. An English voice yelled out—not, praise God, Henley's: "Where the devil are they?"

And Lady Maggie's voice raised. Gaelic spewed from her mouth, the words unintelligible but the outrage clear. Callie listened with her heart in her throat.

The subterfuge gave the soldiers pause. Lady Maggie rattled on, indignant, a whirlwind of vituperation. Callie wondered what in hell she was saying.

So did the English. Someone cleared his throat. "Is there an interpreter?"

"To hell with the interpreter!" another man decreed. "Search the bloody house!"

Callie shrank back into her shadow. She heard a clatter of bootheels rushing toward the closer staircase. Lady Maggie cryed out what was, in any language, a warning.

And then a loud crash as the old wood gave way.

Thuds and moans. Muttered curses. One clear comment: "Christ, the bloody place is falling to pieces!" The English regrouped after a moment's pause. "There must be a back stair!"

Another rush of boots, into the dining hall. Another pause for contemplation: "Look here, sir. Only the one place set."

And the man who'd commanded the search, yet again: "With eight bloody pots of jam?"

Lady Maggie, then, her tone more measured, invitational. One more brief pause. "Well, sir. It's very good jam."

"Get up those bloody stairs!"

Callie felt her way along the corridor, knowing where she was going. The upper story, then the door to the tower, hidden behind the tapestry. From there to the roof—she tried hard not to think of the height. Perhaps the moon would have widened. In her womb, she felt a faint flutter, like wings. The unaccustomed sensation made her catch her breath.

God. What a time to realize, to truly feel, that the child within her was alive.

Yet she had the sense as she ran that she was no more than shadow, invisible spirit, and that the house around her was filled with such spirits, folding weightless, welcoming arms to shelter Langlannoch's heir. The floor beneath her feet never creaked; ancient doors swung open soundlessly on rusted hinges. When she gained the topmost hallway, she stopped to listen. Far below, she could still hear Lady Maggie spitting indignation at the soldiers. There were other sounds as well: the clash of breaking crockery, sword-blades slashing cloth, axes hacking at wood. God. They were gutting the place.

More clattering boots, close beneath her. Callie flitted down the hallway, searching for the tapestry. Gordie had left the tower door ajar. She slipped inside, flapped out the heavy hanging, and pulled the handle closed just as the English reached the upper corridor.

She heard them rush past the tapestry, bursting into rooms, kicking open doors, overturning beds and wardrobes. Was there a bar to this portal? In utter darkness, she felt with her hands. The metal fittings, aye, but if there was a plank about, she couldn't find it. No matter. They'd never even realize the door was there.

Up the narrow, twisting staircase, climbing toward the sky, palms flat on the walls for balance. Her heart was still beating fast, but she felt oddly calm, protected, in the sanctuary of the tower. Through her mind there flashed the image of the house as she and Zeus had first seen it, minarets spiring into the clouds against a backdrop of gentian-blue sea.

How many times, Callie wondered, did Mick and I climb these stairs to the rooftop to make love? She could almost feel his hand clasping hers, hear his laughter ripple in anticipation. God, she'd loved his laugh. For a moment she stopped, let it ring in her ears, echoing off the stones. Something struck her. *He* was one of the ghosts now, one of the sheltering spirits. He'd make certain no harm came to his own.

The little door to the parapet loomed before her. She pushed it open, then closed it at her back silently. Here there was a bar. She shoved it into place, felt the close grain of strong, ancient oak beneath her fingertips. Then she straightened on the narrow walkway. The moon had come out from the clouds. The night wind swirled up from the water, teasing her face and hair with salt softness. Again she stared out over the waves, thought she saw a patch of white against the wine-dark ocean. Gordie's sail—but it might have been the moon on a bird's wings, or a splash of foam atop a swell.

She started forward toward the flat stretch of roof where she and Mick had shared such pleasures. . . . *What do you feel when you make love to me?*

"What do you?"

"Ecstasy . . ."

God, she could almost see him there, rising to meet her in the moonlight, tall and dark. She smelled the scent on the sea-wind of sweat and leather. The apparition was so real that she caught her breath. Michel . . .

Shadow on shadow. Sheltering spirit, with its arms out-stretched—

Sweat and leather, yes, but—her nose curled at a whiff of something alien. Pipe-smoke. And beyond his shade, more shades ranged on the rooftop, stretching out in a sinister line.

"Mistress Wingate. Not, alas, the bird for whom we were hoping. But well-caught, nonetheless. We took the ladder up." She knew that clipped English voice. It was Henley, damn him. His hand caught her arm in a grip like the grave. "Now. Suppose you show us the proper way down. And, Mistress Wingate. Do mind your step."

45.

Callie and the soldiers made a slow, grim descent to the kitchens. Men were everywhere on the way, tearing apart the house. Jennet sat in tears at her table, surrounded by strangers and smashed jam-pots. Lady Maggie still poured forth a torrent of Gaelic that, when she saw Callie with Henley behind her, cut off in mid-stream.

"Mrs. Harding." At her back, Callie felt the commandant make a bow. "How very nice to see you again. Now, suppose you tell us where the Pretender is."

There was a moment's pause.

Henley caught Callie's arm and twisted it behind her, so sharply that she fell to her knees.

"I dinna ken nae Pretender!" Lady Maggie cried.

"I beg your pardon. Bonnie Prince Charlie, then." Slowly, Henley reached down and pulled Callie up from the floor by her hair. She could not quite conquer her cry of pain.

A matching cry ripped from Lady Maggie. "Ach, dinna hurt the poor lass! Can ye nae see she bae blind?"

Henley's long, ugly nose swam toward her. "Is she? Really?"

Callie fought not to focus. "From a powder-blast at Falkirk," she told him, but flatly, not asking his pity.

"Sir." A soldier leaned forward, whispering. Henley's pock-marks dripped off, disappeared into a shadowy whole as he stepped back to survey her.

"I do believe you're right, Lieutenant Cochran. Mistress Wingate! Are you with child?"

Jennet's sobs escalated. Callie hesitated, then nodded. What would denial gain her? She heard the slap of Henley's hands as he rubbed them together in delight. "Blind and bearing! What an absolutely splendid state of affairs! You won't even have to close your eyes when I let my soldiers have their way with you, nor fret about the consequences. Lucky, lucky girl!"

"Oh, ye bludy bastard," Lady Maggie spat.

He turned on her. "Of course, it's in your power to prevent that. Tell me where to find the Pretender." Lady Maggie said nothing. Henley shrugged, then bent to whisper to Callie: "I feel it is my duty to warn you. They have been a long time without women. Some of them may prove ... rough." His finger trailed down her throat to her breast. Callie shuddered. Lady Maggie screamed at him in Gaelic, curses old as the stones.

"Sir," a soldier blurted, crisp-voiced, saluting. "We've been through the house from top to bottom. I'll stake my commission he's not here."

"But he *was* here. Where was he going?" More silence. Henley's cold finger hooked into the top of Callie's bodice. "One or two," he murmured to her, "I much regret, have the French pox. Do you know what that does to a baby? Causes it to be born blind." Laughter rippled in his voice. "Suppose we let them have first go at you, shall we?"

Callie didn't move. His finger was hard at her breasts. But she saw, or sensed, Lady Maggie capitulating. "They bae gone to—"

"No!" Callie screamed at her.

"They bae gone to Kintyre! O'er the sea to Kintyre!"

"Damn you! It's a lie, a bloody lie," Callie shrieked at Henley. He struck her, hard, making her stumble, shocking her silent.

"But ye maun nae hurt her!" Lady Maggie cried out. "Ye maun nae hurt Michel's babe!"

Henley had wrenched Callie to her feet. "Michel's babe," he said, with something in his tone that made her bowels curdle. "Is that the father, then? Mr. Harding? Is it another laird to Langlannoch you're bearing? Dear, dear, dear. We simply mustn't have that."

Lady Maggie flew at him, clawed at him. "I told ye wha' ye wanted! Let her gae, let her gae!" A swarm of soldiers held her back. Henley was shaking his head, his ugly pocked nose bobbing.

"King George's men make no deals with criminals. You've harbored a traitor here. The penalty for that is death."

At the outermost edge of Callie's field of vision, a dark shade flitted past the open door that led to the yards. Another ghost. She'd be among them soon. Henley turned, still gripping her arm. "Lieutenant Cochran. Take your squad up the road to Ayr. Commandeer a vessel. Set out for Kintyre."

The shape that was Cochran paused. "Sir. The girl. I really don't think—"

"I really don't think," Henley cut him off abruptly, "what I do with the girl is any of your concern."

"No, sir. No. Still, our orders state—"

"Our orders state that we are to deal with enemies of the crown as we see fit."

"But, sir. A pregnant woman—"

"Do you want to spend the rest of your life, Cochran, mired in the hellhole of Scotland? By Christ, I'd murder every damned boy-child in the country if I could! I'd out-Herod Herod! Now get going, or I'll shoot you, too, as a traitor!"

Still Cochran hesitated. Henley let go Callie's arm, pulled a pistol and cocked it. "As you wish, Cochran." Horrified, she clenched her eyes shut.

It came in a rush: the thunder of powder igniting; the sharp scent of sulphur, so near she could taste it; the thud of flesh against the floor.

Lady Maggie grabbed her—pushing her, imploring her: "Run, dearie! Run!"

She blundered forward, straight into Cochran. Then whose body had fallen?

Suddenly, there was another burst of fire. Soldiers were

screaming. Lady Maggie yelled, "Jennet! Move yer carcass! Run!" They burst through the door, then into a blast of fresh air. A black shade in the darkness—

"Grandmère. Down to the strand. There are horses. Go! I'll cover you from the wall."

"Michel?" Callie whispered.

He took that moment to kiss her. Then his musket blasted again, shattering the window panes. "Go!" he shouted. "Go on!"

Jennet ran on one side, grasping her, tugging her along. Lady Maggie ran on the other.

From inside the house, a cacophony of utter disorder. The steady slide of cartridge into the breechlock. Another deafening blast—

"Come on, come on," Lady Maggie urged her, dragging her over the dew-wet grass.

"But it's fifty men to one! He'll be murdered!"

"Can ye help him now? Can Jennet? Can I? Come on, lass! Ye maun run!"

Callie ran, blindly, out to the wall, slipping, skidding, sliding, with the two women close at her sides. They reached the steps hewn from the rock, Jennet in front of her, Lady Maggie behind. "Gae, gae, gae!" Lady Maggie kept urging. The stairs were slick with spray; all Callie could see was the thin moon in the sky, and out to sea, the white birds soaring. She heard the frightened whinnies of horses. "How many are there?" she gasped out as her boots struck sand.

"Three," Lady Maggie told her, pushing her up into a saddle.

"Laird in heaven," Jennet was mumbling, "if ye culd ken how many years since I hae been atop a horse—"

" 'Twill come back to ye, dinna fear." But Lady Maggie had to push her up, too, huffing and puffing, before scrambling into the saddle behind Callie. She whipped the reins, screamed out something in Gaelic, and the horses shot off.

Callie glanced back through a tangle of hair. "Where's the other horse, then?"

"I lied to ye, pet. There war only two."

"But what about Mick?" she wailed.

Lady Maggie had an arm around her belly, tight like iron. "Michel can fend for himself. If it truly war Michel."

"You saw him, though," Callie called above the wind. "He kissed me! He had a damned bloody gun!" No ghost could feign that.

"Stranger things hae happened at Langlannoch," Lady Maggie said stubbornly. "Hold the pommel tight."

Down the strand they thundered, gunfire blaring in the distance. Callie's heart was pounding like the sea against rock. It *was* Mick. It had to have been. He was alive still—so long as the guns went on shooting.

One more blast. Another. Another—

She was counting the seconds. Five. Ten. Twenty. Nothing.

"Oh, God," she whispered.

Lady Maggie's grip was a vise. "Hold to the pommel!" she screamed in Callie's ear.

But Callie didn't want to hold on. It was too cruel a trick of fate, to have him brought back to life again only for this. She had rather he'd been naught but spirit in the first place.

His mouth, though, against hers, had been too warm for a dead man.

Lady Maggie yanked the horse's head to the right. "Cliff," she called briefly to Jennet. "We maun gae up to the road."

Callie's ears rang at the skitter of shifting shells beneath hooves. Her head snapped back with an ascent so steep that it threw her against Lady Maggie's breast. *She was willing to betray Scotland,* Callie thought, *for the life of this babe.* Such intensity was frightening. She wished suddenly, uselessly, that she'd never seen Langlannoch, never felt the heavy weight of its pull on the blood. *Christ, let this be a girl. Better yet, let it die.* As Charles Edward had said: Lay an end to it all. There was no place in the world, in the hard, modern world, for devotion so raw.

There was a solid thud of gravel underfoot. They had gained the road. "We'll make for Ayr," Lady Maggie decided, digging in her heels. "There bae folk eno' to hide us there, till the English move on. 'N we maun clear the docks. Nae ships to take the bastards to Kintyre."

They rode on in silence, except for the clatter of hooves. Then Jennet gave a cry. "Someone bae followin'!"

Callie had heard it, too—afar-off rattle, faint. Lady Maggie whipped the reins. "Gae on, gae on!"

And then a sound that made her yank the bridle with such force that the poor horse screamed—the thick, black belch of cannon. "Wha' in God's name—" The air in Callie's ears shuddered. "Jesu in heaven!" Lady Maggie cried out. "Lan-glannoch! The house!"

She whipped the horse around to the south. "M'lady," Jennet called after her. "M'lady, ye cannae gae back!"

"They bae blastin' Langlannoch!" Sorrow deeper than bone, stronger than death. "Oh. Oh, dear God. The towers—"

Hoofbeats coming closer. Lady Maggie's wordless sobs. A great crumpling noise in the distance.

Callie felt the child in her womb quiver with woe.

Another cannon-burst. Another. Jennet was riding after them, pleading, screeching. "M'lady! Come back!"

And someone was galloping toward them. Black shape, black shifting mass. Michel Faurer, on his black horse—

"Grandmère! For God's sake, where are you going?"

"To Langlannoch! Where in hell d'ye think?"

A long arm grabbed the reins, spinning them back around. "But it's only a house!"

"How dare ye say such a thing?"

"It is only a bloody house!"

Warring hands on the reins brought both mounts to a halt. "It bae Langlannoch!" Lady Maggie said, in the sudden silence.

The scent of leather and sweat, sweeter than roses, rose in the air. His Callie felt fingertips against cheek. "Let them batter it down into dust, so long as you are safe."

A long pause, long as a lifetime. Callie kissed the palm of his powder-stained hand. Lady Maggie looked at them in the faint moonlight. Then she shrugged. "Ach. I suppose ye bae right, Michel."

"Callie. Come over here." He lifted her up into his arms, straight out of the saddle.

"Is it truly you?" she whispered, held to his heart.

"Truly me." A kiss from him, mortal, real.

"What took you so long?" she asked him.

"I was trailing bloody Charles Edward over half of Scotland. One step behind him, one step ahead of the English. Guarding his back. It seemed . . . the proper thing to do."

"You might have sent me word you were alive."

"There wasn't time to. And who would I have sent? The country is bereft of men."

She felt his arms curl around her, felt his hands on her belly, gentle with wonder. "Had I known of this," he murmured, "I would have."

One last cannon-blast. Jennet wheeled toward them, impatient. "Yer Lairdship. We maun get on to Ayr!"

"So we must." He rode with his mouth against her throat, drinking in her scent.

She had ten thousand questions to ask him. Where to begin? "How did you get away?"

"I drove off their horses—all but these three." Those dozens of horses. . . . "If they hadn't been making such a commotion wrecking the place, they'd have heard me. The bloody fools. So eager were they for plunder, they hadn't even left a watch in the yards."

The mention of plunder stirred Lady Maggie's regrets. "They'll hae the tapestries," she whimpered. "They'll hae the Bruce's chair! The bed Michel 'n Madeleine slept in—"

She was cut off by another bluster of cannon-fire. Mick raised his voice above it. "Be reasonable, Grandmère. You sheltered the prince there. I killed their commandant. How could we ever go back?"

"Still . . ." Callie could feel the sad weight of the memories of an old woman, the last keeper of the flame that had been Langlannoch. "There maun hae been a way—culd ye nae hae blown up the cannon?"

"It took me long enough to get rid of the horses! Do you think I was about to let that bully Henley have his filthy paws on Callie one second more than was necessary?" His hands, clenched on the reins, slipped down to brush her breasts, as though his touch could ease the horror she'd felt. Callie leaned against him, reveling in his touch—the press of his thighs on hers, the wild drum of his heart.

Lady Maggie let out a snort of disgust and spurred her horse onward, putting space between her and this thoughtless ingrate grandson. Callie heard Mick's laughter at her ear. God, that sweet laughter he had always been so sparing of, that she'd never thought to relish again except in tortured memory.

"I'd gone up to the rooftops," she twisted to tell him. "I thought I'd be safe there."

His black queue swept her throat. "I know. I saw you there, against the moon. It was the first sight that greeted me as I topped the crest of the hill. I feared you were a ghost."

"I thought Henley was your ghost."

Mick paused. "Are you still blind, as Grandmère told him?"

His shade in the doorway. His hands now before her, strong blunt fingers pale in the moonlight. The mane of the horse streaming back, and the long dust-bright road . . . "I can see all I need to see. All I want to see."

He ducked his head to hers, his voice low. "I watched as Henley and his men met you up there. I thought . . . if this house cannot shelter her, if those ghosts cannot keep her safe—Grandmère was right. I might have blown up the cannon, or rolled it off the bloody cliffs. I think . . . I think I left it there purposely."

She caught her breath. "Oh, Lord. Mick. Don't ever tell her that."

The wind rushed by overhead, drawing in its wake wisps of cloud, like disfranchised spirits. Will they follow us wherever we go? Callie wondered. Which, in the end, held more heat: stones or blood? History wasn't something you could shrug off like a greatcoat. Michel Faurer himself had once been a stranger in this land, all he had of his past borne in his heart and his head. Yet when he'd staked his claim at Langlannoch, it had been that past he harked back to—the Templars in the Holy Land, minarets and mosaics and apricot trees. Would another Langlannoch rise up someday, in some place as incongruous as this?

One last cannonade, but in the past, in the distance. As the far-off thunder subsided, Callie saw that Lady Maggie had reined in ahead, lying in wait for them, for a final round.

"Naught left but dust now," she shouted in fury. "I hope to God ye bae satisfied, Michel Douglas Harding!"

His mouth at Callie's throat. A kiss like a promise—"I *am* satisfied, Grandmére. And so should you be. Answer truly: which part of the legend did you, in your deepest heart, know I would never live up to?"

All was silent.

"Well, Grandmère?"

The answer, grudging, slow, straight from the pages of the monks' chronicles at Iona: "One o' the great luvs o' our time."

He grunted, his arms fast around Callie and their child. "So. He built it for his true love. And I let it fall for mine."

Epilogue

From The Edinburgh Weekly Journal, *June 23, 1748*

University Tattle

Professor William Wingate, recently named dean of the newly created College of Antiquities and Anthropological Studies, has just returned from the Continent—Paris, to be exact, where he was honored guest at the opening of a retrospective showing in the University Gallery of the works of his daughter, the well-known artist Calliope Harding. Included in the showing was the masterpiece that has caused such a furor in artistic circles abroad, the huge oil painting entitled, *The Highland Charge*. Critics of the work claim its broad swaths of striking color and lack of clear cohesion are the result of Mrs. Harding's failed eyesight, damaged in a gunpowder blast at the battle of Falkirk. But the *enfants terribles* of the Paris art world have embraced this bold new direction, claiming it frees the artist from the constraints of merely reproducing flat reality(!). Asked to comment on his daughter's vision, Dr. Wingate told us, "Oh, I can't make head nor tail of the painting. But there's nothing wrong with Callie's eyes."

Also present at the opening ceremony was Mrs. Harding's husband, Professor Michel Douglas Harding, who served briefly on the faculty of our own university several years past; he is now a distinguished lecturer in the Classics Department at the Sorbonne. Dr. Harding's grandmother, Mrs. Margaret Harding, attended the gala in the company of the couple's two young sons, Michel and Rene.

Rounding out the family aspect of the affair was Dr. Wingate's son, Persues, with his new bride, the renowned beauty Lady Constanza di Fiorti, granddaughter of the late Giovan Gastone, Grand Duke of Tuscany. Lieutenant Wingate and his bride are recently returned from a wedding trip to the Americas. His father reports that Lieutenant Wingate has accepted a commission in the army of his wife's uncle, King Louis of France.

Among the many luminaries attending the opening was Prince Charles Edward Stuart, whose patronage of Mrs. Harding first brought her work international renown. He remains (happily, we trust) in residence at the French court.

Our congratulations to Dr. Wingate on his daughter's *grand succés*.